EXCISE

Book Two of the
ETHER COLLAPSE Series
Written by RYAN DEBRUYN

MOUNTAINDALE
PRESS

TABLE OF CONTENTS

Acknowledgments

To have written and published one book is a dream. To have an opportunity to publish a second is more than I could have imagined.

Thank you to Mountaindale Press – you believed in me and have created a family of people that help each other grow.

Thank you to everyone who has read book one, your support made book two possible and your input helped it become something greater!

RECAP

Rockland and his group have managed to rescue just over eight thousand individuals from Ottawa and Corsair's devious regime. Rocky originally travelled to Ottawa to find his family but now puts that goal on hold. After killing Corsair and eradicating the evil regime inside the militia, the group now must make a cross country trek back to the safety Algonquin Valley offers.

Rejoin Rocky, Sela, Azoth, Jason, and Joe as they struggle to keep the eight thousand under leveled survivors of the first two Ether waves safe.

Character Sheet of Rockland Barkclay at the end of Book 1

Rockland Barkclay Level 21
> **Class: Apprentice-Dark(Azrael) Revenant,**
> **Level 1 Strategist**

Leadership Class:
Class Skills: Dark Blade, Dark Mend, Dark Cloak, Shadow Clone
> **Health Points = 230/230 Points**
> **Dark Ether Pool = 190/190 Points**

You have 7 stat points and 2 skill points to distribute.
> **Stamina – 23 (Strength of Body +5)**
> **Strength – 29 (Strength of Arms +5)(Strength of Arms +10)**
> **Agility – 37 (Speed of Arms +5)**
> **Dexterity – 30**
> **Intelligence – 19**
> **Wisdom – 27**
> **Charisma – 29**
> **Luck – 7**

Weak Skills

      Non-Class Combat Skills: Combatant – 19, Ether Channels – 13, Ether Manipulation – 11, Stealth – 24, Swordsmanship – 24

      Common Skills: Barter – 5 , Camouflage – 7, Endurance – 20, Perception – 21, Tracker – 12, Trance Meditation – 15

      Profession Skills: Actor – 5, Butcher – 17, Cook – 2, Herbalist – 14 , Miner – 1, Skinner – 17, Trader – 5

Moderate Skills

      Non-Class Combat Skills:

      Common Skills: Analyze – 2, Sneak – 5

      Profession Skills:

PROLOGUE

The second wave of Ether had been a massive discharge, undoubtedly as ample as the first. The wave had thundered with the pent-up, first-tier energy, frying her exposed dendrites and forcing her to initially recoil. When that same energy had combined with the returned steady tide of local Ether, it had far surpassed her expectations. Even she was unable to overcome the eons of slumber that had degraded her infrastructure designed to cope with such influxes.

Her slowly frying dendrites continued to curl around herself protectively as the crashing wave dumped more and more wild, chaotic energy on to her surface. Eventually, the energy had filled every crevasse around her until she was forced to seclude herself behind her mental walls from fear of it sweeping her away.

After days hidden away, the non-intelligent lifeforms and fauna creeping along her surface had finally filtered enough of the virulent Ether that she could come out of her protective state and begin surveying the damage. Gaia felt her soil settle comfortably when her sensitive dendrites discovered almost all evolved wildlife, including her golems, withstood the tidal storm of energy. Stretching her mind away from her recent respite showed her that, in fact, all of her flora and fauna had undergone massive evolutions, increasing their life energy and filtering effectiveness drastically.

A moment later, the planet quested far deeper, feeling the magma in her heart spin faster.

Where were her champions? What had happened to them?

A momentary rumble could be heard across the planet as her search failed to find massive collections of her champions, quieting only when Gaia's dendrites told her they were still alive.

The champions remained seemingly unchanged, evidently because their sapience had prevented the energy from acting according to its will.

Gaia scrutinized the imbalance between the powerful creatures and her chosen champions. Her Essence recovery was already accounting for an almost eighty percent loss of the humans since she had first awoken. The surface shuddered briefly when Gaia recalled the process of creating the creatures so many millennia ago. To call it uncomfortable was an understatement. The act of splitting her Essence and sharing it with the creations remained utterly terrifying. If she didn't remedy this soon, she may be forced to create champions again to protect her surface from her brothers and sisters.

Immediately, Gaia searched for areas where her humans could survive and grow. Using the Atlantean Net, she accessed any conquered Territories but felt her burning-hot volcanic blood grow cool when she uncovered a scant few conquered Territories listed in the twenty-one rotations since the Atlantean Net began monitoring. Imprinting the locations on her body, she hunted out the first alphabetically, this 'Algonquin Valley', and noticed a small group of citizens starting to build lodging and organize themselves.

As she calculated distances from other pockets of survivors, something in the area made the ancient god feel brackish, and her consciousness seemed to tremble before she locked down her defenses. What had tried to attack her just now?

The people of the Territory didn't have the combined power amongst them to register on the shields she had in place. With her defenses tight, she investigated the area in search of the culprit of her foreboding. As she delved around the Territory, widening her senses, she felt something strange to the northeast of Algonquin Valley.

Gaia usually could sense everything on her surface, but an entire area in that direction had become a void. She focused on the region only to feel the area resist her influence and try to attack her again. It was like a kitten clawing at a full-grown hound, but it still worried her, as everyone knows that kittens turn into vicious, unruly alley cats if they aren't dealt with.

The energy signature felt familiar to her. It was weak, yes, but it seemed like a sibling or some other being that tickled the edges of her mind. In desperation, she swept the area in all directions, and immediately southeast, she found a group of humans headed directly towards the Territory.

The group wasn't large and seemed to be in a quandary. She was glad to see a group progressing towards safety, if plodding. To Gaia, it looked like a group of four exhausted champions, and some strange quadruped was their only real protection. Oddly, the beast and the man on its back vibrated with strange resonance to Gaia's senses, but even this group of four was weakening. To her, it appeared that this group should have failed long ago, the wildlife's far superior levels shattering them and their entire caravan. Gaia was bewildered that these people had survived, which made her dendrites inspect the situation more closely.

A part of her categorized every member of the larger group effectively before it arrived at the smaller group of four and the pet creature. Another member of the four was unique, having been gifted the druid class by her own hand. Gaia hadn't specifically watched the tiny druid. She couldn't be present for all of these minutiae on her surface. No, the Atlantean Net had notified her of a problem, and the woman's resurrection had been her solution to it. The choice had been simple and concise. In fact, she had a small backlog of similar decisions currently, but before she got to those, it was time to solve this uneasy imbalance or tether it.

CHAPTER ONE

"This is Selaphelia Ardensai. A group of distant creatures is amassing on the east side of the column. Over." Sela's voice came through over the earpiece radio Rocky currently wore.

Rockland Barkclay was currently flying around the column, scouting for dangers. He first patted Azoth on his shoulders and through a very weary mental voice asked, "Can you fly to the east side of the column, big guy?"

Azoth turned his lion head, making an unnatural bird-like angle with his neck, and mentally responded, "Rocky need sleep. Azoth scout, Rocky sleep," as he banked to the east.

They had learned early on that having Azoth scouting or relaying communications was a bad plan. Not only was he directionally challenged but he was also extremely incompetent at counting. His first mistake had been in relaying Sela's precise instructions about a herd of elk. Azoth had led the way to the northwest side of the column, and the herd had passed on the southwest. Luckily, the mistake wasn't critical, and they managed to bag a few for food.

Especially when you consider how tough the other monsters seem to be on this hell march.

His second failure had occurred when he was in the crow's nest, meaning scouting from the sky. He had relayed and amassed a large portion of the army to tackle, "Tenzy panthers. Attacking from rear." It had turned out to be three panthers attacking from the side and had cost a few people their lives. It was at that point that he had been relegated to become the vehicle for Rocky to scout.

As they approached the east, massive creatures began to take shape. They were dusky brown, mutated lizards marching in single file. At first, Rocky thought one had arms but realized a moment later that it sported a massive tree trunk protruding from a gaping wound in its side. On Azoth, he circled the group, noting marks of combat on all of them, and he quickly dove and centered on one to Analyze.

Land Lizard
Master-Dirt Devil
Level 29
Heavily Injured
Moderate Analyze failed to provide additional information.

These creatures were extremely strong. Normally, he would have left them, hoping they would go in another direction, but with their injuries, this was free food the caravan couldn't afford to pass up.

He clicked on his radio, then yelled, trying to talk over the whistling wind, "They're heavily injured but Master Class Level 29. I suggest we finish them off."

"This is Ground Shark. You forgot your moniker, Eagle Eye, and to say over. Over," Joe chimed in, making Rocky roll his eyes. He hated radio etiquette. It made him feel like he was back in elementary school playing with walkie-talkies.

I walkie and I talkie! Look at me; I can walkie talkie...

His brain was a little fried due to lack of sleep and a seven-day march through lands infested with scarily strong monsters. The trip to Ottawa hadn't been nearly as dangerous as this; plus, he hadn't had so many people to look out for.

His debuffs alone told the story.

De-Buffs

Sleep-Deprived
- **Until you get a full night of sleep, you will find it harder to think and stay awake.**

- Effects -25% Intelligence, -25% Stamina –
  Effects doubled due to use of Alchemy Potions.
- Lasts until you get a full night's sleep and go 24
  hours without a potion.

Skunk Shower
- You have been sprayed by an evolved monster,
  Peppy Le Skunk.
- Effects -50% Charisma.
- Lasts until treated.

Dance of the Dreamless
- You have not slept for more than eight hours
  throughout a week.
- Effects +125% chance to hallucinate.
- Lasts until you get a full night's sleep.

Unclean x7
- You have not bathed or showered in over a
  week.
- Effects -25% Wisdom, -15% Charisma.
- +50% Chance of catching Disease.
- Lasts until showered or bathed.

Weakened Body
- Your body has been pushed beyond its current
  limits.
- -50% Recovery of Ether and Health.

Toxic Blood
- You have high PH levels in your blood due to
  high use of Alchemy Potions.
- -50% Effectiveness of future potions.

- **Lasts 24 hours, will renew and increase every time a potion is used.**

The hallucinations were sometimes relatively simple things that didn't affect his day in the least. He waved to the flying cartoon squirrel beside him as it started and flew off into the distance, probably realizing he wasn't his namesake moose friend, then blinked it away. Other times, the illusions had cost people's lives, and Rocky hadn't even had the mental capacity to comprehend those tragedies yet. The group of eight thousand souls that started this trip had been reduced to just under five thousand, and he felt his heart stutter as his brain took that distasteful path.

Sela luckily interrupted, "Selaphelia Ardensai here. We are low on food and need a restock. Any view of what injured them? Over."

He looked down at the massive lizards that were twenty feet wide and at least forty feet long and nodded. One of those things could feed everyone, probably.

Then he scanned the horizons in both directions, looking out for anything big enough to have done this. Sela was absolutely right, and this level of damage implied a stronger foe nearby. He clicked his radio. "Eagle Eye. There is nothing close enough to see. I think this is our best chance to restock food. Everything else over the last few days has been nearly impossible to take down. People might starve soon." He let go of his radio button, then remembered and clicked it again. "Over!"

He glanced down and saw the three members of his group standing ready while riding on top of the nearest tank. The tanks were each covered in huddled survivors who were either sleeping in their scheduled shifts or desperately stealing a brief reprieve from walking. They were probably discussing the danger level of attacking the foe, and so he waited for their decision.

Gritting his teeth at the reminder of the people depending on them, Rocky commanded Azoth to fly around behind the lizards to cut off the most direct path of retreat and waited for the group's decision.

Sela clicked back on. "Selaphelia Ardensai here. We have to risk it. Over." He ordered Azoth to attack the largest and least injured one.

As the massive, truck-sized Chimera folded his wings and dove, over the radio Rocky stated, "Give 'em hell!"

The lizards gained size quickly as they descended, and Rocky reassessed them. The alpha was probably seventy-five feet long and also happened to be the one Azoth was targeting. The others were closer to fifty feet long but were as tall as a three-story building.

He only had a moment to reconsider before Azoth back-winged furiously, and Rocky felt the g-force of the sudden deceleration try to press his body into the straining back of the Chimera. With his increased Strength, Rocky easily maintained his posture and even untied the ropes holding him in place. Once the momentum of the dive stopped with a jarring impact on the alpha lizard, Rocky leaped off of the Chimera's back towards the trailing lizard with the tree protruding from its side.

These creatures were seriously heavy hitters and may have even compared to the boss monsters in Ottawa. While they had been forced to fight a few Master level creatures on the trip so far, all they had been able to manage was a single kill, only injuring the others enough to make them retreat. This was also the first time Master class creatures were in a group.

Rocky felt in his bones that this fight would have been a death sentence for his party in any other situation. His nerves ratcheted up a few degrees, thinking about something hurting these enormous beasts. If they weren't near death, one would be quite capable of wiping out the entire caravan alone.

He summoned his Shadow Clone mid-leap and saw it use Stealth, while simultaneously the head and neck of the impaled lizard catapulted diagonally up at Rocky's flying form. In desperation, he cast his Dark Cloak and curled into a ball. Luckily, his clone was summoned above his position, as the head missed it and only glanced off his butt. It turned his curled-up flight into an untold number of careening, airborne somersaults. Even injured, these creatures weren't going to be easy prey.

As he spun, he felt his cloak turn into a bit of a sail and arrest his circular momentum. It helped enough that his crash landing was a bit easier to turn into a roll. He heard a shocked mental sound from Azoth as he went to right himself and saw the Chimera get half bucked, half pulled off of the three-legged alpha lizard as it took off at a blistering sprint away from the group after severing its own tail as a defense mechanism. The acceleration of the massive beast forced Azoth's wings fully open, and the wind caught them, turning him into a paraglider which ripped his claws through the tough skin and forced him up into the air.

The other two injured creatures saw the alpha flee and literally dropped their tails entirely off their bodies and opened up their throttles following after the largest lizard. The one who had attacked Rocky with its head attempted to whip around to follow, but the tree limb skewered into the ground and brought the creature up short.

The jarring motion was enough of a delay that the rest of the group adjusted their original targets to the final remaining creature. It was gargantuan, and once it was fixed between the hammer and anvil, its eyes went wild. Its lizard brain now clearly in fight mode; it went on the offensive and would have chomped Rocky in two if not for a hastily erected shield by Zippo.

Rocky saw the air in front of him crack like a pane of glass and knew the young man had just saved his life. A single, massive vine with a circumference as wide as he was shot out of the ground and wrapped around a leg of the creature.

That would be Sela's newest skill.

A plasma bolt of what looked to be red hot magma claimed a bulbous eye, bringing forth a wailing, dinosaur-esque roar as Joe engaged one of his shooting skills. Zippo flung a few Fireballs once he conjured them, ensuring he stayed away from the side Sela was constricting with her vines.

Rocky smiled seeing the group's easy flow in a dire situation. His Shadow Clone flashed into the beast's side and sunk his two daggers into the creature's other eye, disabling that orb as well. It was his turn now, as the creature reared back from the mounting damage, exposing its throat to him like a pig to slaughter. He used five charges of Dark Blade to ensure the beast would die, then released them horizontally.

The skill distorted the air between the five long, black claws as they flew towards the exposed throat, and the group held their breath. The blades screeched on the white scales of the exposed neck, but thankfully, the softer underside scales relinquished the fight quickly. The blades sank through, nearly severing the whole head in a spray of lime-green blood.

He felt a moment of jubilation before he was sobered by the distant sight of the other three tailless lizards escaping. Azoth was above them, and so Rocky mentally called him. While that fight had seemed somewhat easy, he had nearly died. If it hadn't been for Zippo…

Not to mention the fact that they were all injured before we even engaged, and we only killed one.

Sela walked up beside him and exclaimed, "Well, this one and the three tails will be enough food to feed everyone for a few days." Rocky froze, remembering the last time he had looked at Sela and hallucinated a rather embarrassing moment.

He coughed to cover his embarrassment and looked at the lizards without looking at Sela. "Yeah—umm— the food is going to be great. Better get back in the air. I will leave skinning and butchering to you!"

He jumped on Azoth's back and told him to take off. Azoth wasn't happy, though. Whenever they were forced to leave a meal behind, Rocky would hear about it, and this time was no different.

"That perfectly succulent, crispy piece. Zippo cook especially for Azoth. Azoth just takes one bite. *Pleeeassse.*"

Please was his newest word, and he used it far too frequently in an attempt to get his way, playing on Sela's and his softer nature. However, Rocky couldn't let the beast go eat his fill. If he did that, then there would be no one on the lookout for other danger. Sela would butcher the tails and lizard before storing it in Rocky's bag of holding for the massive Chimera to eat when she took her shift as the lookout.

Sela, as a druid, could transform between different animal forms, one of which was a massive raven. This was helpful as it gave Azoth a break for a few hours every day, which the Chimera used to eat and then sleep atop a moving tank. The reason Sela wasn't often up in the air scouting was that she lacked any way of communicating effectively in bird form.

Currently, her best option was to screech and circle the area of danger, but that left the group rather uninformed of the opponents' strength, numbers, and overall threat level. Frequently, she would come and land with them and transform into a human to give the details, but that meant that she might use as many as three transformations in one fight. Considering that she had a maximum of four per day before she was stuck in the form she inhabited until midnight, that was a huge problem. The other option of relaying information through Azoth had been dismissed due to his numerous errors in translating.

That was precisely what Rocky reminded Azoth of as he tied himself into the saddle on the pet's back, "You will get to eat in a few hours, buddy. Sela will take over soon!"

He managed a half-circle of the caravan before the landscape blurred beneath him. He blinked rapidly and shook his head to clear his eyes. This roused him for another minute before weights dragged his eyelids down. He felt his head droop, and his chin hit his chest.

His eyes flashed back open, and the fuzzy landscape came back into view. He just needed to close his eyes and allow his body to rehydrate them so he could see properly, just for a moment. With that iota of permission, his heavy eyelids locked down, and his brain hit the snooze, which allowed his mind to replay one of his worst days since the Apocalypse.

***

"My name is Zippo! Not Jason or Jay. Only my parents called me Jay, and they're dead!" Zippo raged at Rocky. "Stop treating me like a child or your younger brother!" His shouts were punctuated by the fire flaring up, producing waves of intense heat.

After his pronouncement, he stormed away from the fire, finally allowing it to begin burning languidly again. Rocky felt his skin slick with sweat, and as a cooling breeze blew over him, he felt goosebumps rise and his body shiver. To distract himself, he looked into the diminished pyre, noticing that the wood was nearly entirely consumed, so he threw on a few fresh logs as he considered Jason's—no—Zippo's position. Sela and Frankie also remained silent for long moments, emotions vibrating inside of all of them as they each thought over the young man's words.

"I think he wants his name to be different because it somehow disassociates him from the losses he has suffered," Frankie contemplated into the poignant hush after a solemn pause.

Before the emotional explosion, Rocky, Sela, Zippo, and Frankie had been sitting around the fire eating and talking about the arduous first day of the journey. Rocky couldn't deny they had been lucky. They had managed to kill three elephantine-sized monsters that had attacked the caravan. The three kills were a boon for the survivors' food supply. However, the seven other attacks they had barely repelled were the real problem. That thirty percent success statistics kept him apprehensive, but he pulled his mind back to the topic at hand and glanced at the man who had spoken.

Frankie Cocozza, the well-dressed, efficient military man, was one of the survivors from the militia group, and Joe had promoted his rank as soon as they began the hike earlier that day. Unfortunately, Joe's promotions weren't system-recognized and didn't impart stat points like Rocky's would be able to when they got back to the Territory.

Regardless, when they returned, he would consult Joe about who to promote, but in the unofficial military hierarchy, Frankie was now in charge of the troops' therapy and mental management. While it seemed like a hasty promotion to Rocky, Frank's class was that of a psychologist after all, so it made logical sense.

Rocky pursed his lips, considering Frankie's opinion on Zippo, but remained silent. He knew that Zippo preferred not to be called Jay. On that first day after saving Jason, Alex, and Oliver, he had accidentally upset the young man in the same way. He wished he had a good excuse for the slip-up, but he could only blame his social awkwardness. He operated under an athlete's assumption, which dictated shortened names gave a level of comradery. That closeness was often superficial and fleeting, but in that moment, you were brothers fighting for the same cause. Maybe he could shorten Zippo to Zip, but that sounded derogatory or condescending—like Dip.

With her mouth full of meat, Sela was next to break the silence as she shrugged, "He is still a kid. He will grow out of it… probably."

Frankie rolled his eyes while throwing both hands into the air, showing he strongly disagreed with Sela's rather casual dismissal of the problem.

Rocky scratched his messy beard and gracelessly chose to return to the subject before Zippo's outburst, "Sela, Zippo still did have a point in the conversation we were having before." Rocky coughed inelegantly. "Why does the system naming convention seem to not specify breeds of creatures we fight? Like it might name a Wolf a Dire Wolf. However, snakes that evolved from a rattlesnake are still just a Terror Snake—"

Happy for an excuse to talk about something less emotionally charged, Sela, who was currently between bites, cut him off with a gesture of her meat on a stick, "As I was saying," she glanced after Zippo, clearly indicating why she had stopped, "its name was Dread Snake, and in a way, it does mean something; you just don't know how to interpret the name." She paused for a moment and turned her spit, looking at the uncooked center of the red meat before deciding to place it back over the fire for more cooking. "For the most part, Dread signifies that the creature has venom or some other effect that isn't obvious to you. If the effect is particularly deadly, it will be termed Dread by the system."

Rocky raised an eyebrow in surprise. "Well that's pretty important to know, Sela! Also explains the Dread Chimera for Azoth. However, Azoth is something we would have called a Manticore, which is a type of Chimera, true, but one of the more dangerous breeds."

Sela continued to turn her meat over the blazing campfire. "What does the system care about the specific genus? It is of the species Chimera, and it has a deadly poison. Those two things are classified." She looked at Frankie and Rocky and pointed at herself and then them in turn. "Humans gave these creatures names because they needed to know more and wanted the creatures defined. You have told me about this rattlesnake, for example. It seems that a smart person would have heard about a rattlesnake, and if they were out to catch it, they would approach it a certain way based off of its most common way of reacting to attack. Most others would avoid it because it was considered deadly."

She paused again and shrugged, seeming to come to the end of her descriptions. Frankie picked up, stroking his chin, "I see. So, we gave it a name to help us better convey information about it to others?" Sela nodded and turned her spitted meat in the fire. Frankie speculated further to himself, "The system doesn't classify things into the names humans have chosen but, instead, names that fit into categories selected a very long time ago."

Frankie continued to talk to himself and even pulled out a little journal, seemingly scrawling his ideas. Rocky wanted to ask Sela more questions before she started eating again. He looked quickly at his own meat over the fire and turned it again before opening his mouth to voice his next query.

He was brought up short by the earth shaking him around like dice in Yahtzee. A moment later, he was picking himself off of the ground as he spat blood from his bit tongue. "What in the feline diarrhea just happened?"

Frank gave him a surprised look, but Sela answered quickly, sounding amused despite the seriousness of the situation, "Probably just another tremor, more localized this time. We've had them every day since the second wave hit four days ago."

This was news to Rocky, who tilted his head and asked, "We have?" Joe, Zippo, and a group of ten other people ran towards his campfire as he looked over the sprawling camp and saw other people picking themselves up off the ground.

As he got to his feet, he saw that their meat had ended up in the fire. He picked them both out and set the spits back up as he waited for the group of people to make it to them.

Joe arrived first, and after asking if everyone was ok, he gave a brief report that the people in the caravan were a little shaken, but no one was severely injured. Rocky responded, "Thank Darkwing Duck!"

Zippo shook his head in clear confusion. "Who's Darkwing Duck?"

Rocky's head jerked back, conveying his surprise at the sudden change in topic. "Huh? Darkwing Duck was a character from the Looney Toons. Why are you bringing him up?" Rocky asked, his voice slow and confused.

Everyone looked at each other and then at Sela, who had begun silently convulsing in what seemed to be laughter. She was doubled over and waving her hand helplessly at everyone. Rocky, who still didn't understand why Zippo had brought up Darkwing Duck, asked slowly, "Why did Zippo just bring up Darkwing Duck? Am I missing something?"

Frankie seemed to gather the situation the fastest. "Actually, you brought it up, Rocky, but by the way you reacted, you don't recall doing so. Are you feeling okay?"

"No, I said, 'Thank Chocolate Fudgesickles'!" Rocky spat, and Sela's laughter grew more audible. Rocky thought back on what he had just uttered. "Not Fudgesickles, Wagyu… What the Pidgeotto!" He was starting to realize that something was drastically wrong with the way he was speaking.

By that point, Sela was rolling on the ground, which had attracted the attention of everyone for a good distance. Sela was the oddity, as everyone else around was tilting their heads or clenching fists. It was clear that his ancestral companion knew exactly what was happening and was the only one, by the confused looks on everyone else's face.

It was Frankie again who summed up the situation in a hypothetical sort of way, "It seems that this new system is changing what we say or what others hear." As he spoke, he fiddled with a red bracelet on his wrist. Bracelet might have been the wrong word; from what Rocky could see, it looked like a glowing string.

"Wait, are you telling me that the system isn't allowing me to swear?" Rocky sputtered. Sela's laughter only grew, and he growled at her in anger.

This is fluting great! Damn it! It does it in my head too? I don't even notice it unless I pay attention.

After realizing it could change his internal thoughts as well, he was well past the point of speaking; all he could think of was that this system had access to his thoughts or somehow could distort what he was saying in some other way. What if it was manipulating all of them in ways they couldn't see?

He felt his heart pounding against his ribs, and the looks on everyone's faces mirrored a horror that was only growing in magnitude. The currents of fear pulsed out from each person who stood around the campfire and began moving throughout the camp.

Like a sharp knife cutting warm butter, Sela's voice snapped everyone's attention to her, "Calm down! In my entire life, I never saw evidence that Gaia or the Atlantian Net was able to control people …" Her face betrayed what little confidence she had managed to instill into those words.

Surprisingly, the others in the group seemed to calm down at her words, but Rocky, who knew Sela well, saw the small shimmer of fear in her eyes. Perhaps she was just more used to living with the system, so this was an old, uncomfortable companion to her, like an annoying cousin.

Rocky shook his head, the motion clearly conveying his sentiment that it wasn't functioning as intended, but he did see the need to placate the situation. Sela forced a smile and returned to a tone of amusement as she teased, "None of you turned off the filter in your interface, so it has been stopping you from swearing since the first trickle of Ether returned."

At Rocky's violently audible growl, she shrugged. "It is in the interface preferences menu."

He quickly opened his windows and navigated to interfaces preferences.

The filter cannot be removed at this time. You have attempted to curse multiple times through the filter. In addition, you have been reported for poor language on forty-seven occasions. If you go without being reported for swearing for one year and seven days, the block will be able to be removed.

Shame on you!

He heard muttered exclamations around the fire, and a few people let out a surprised laugh obviously receiving a similar message. Rocky shook his head, not at all sure how to feel about the situation. What else was he missing in his settings? He and Sela needed to have a very long conversation soon!

The need to diffuse the situation took precedence. So, he tried to lighten the mood and asked everyone listening, "How long did each of you get? And how many times did you get reported?"

Sela's face flushed bright red, and she tried to nonchalantly sit down without drawing attention to her clear attempts at trying not to laugh again. Rocky felt his jaw clench, and he stood up before he thought about it. "What the Oompa-Loompa did you steeling do, Sela!" Rocky shouted.

Everyone broke into laughter along with Sela, who had tears rolling down her cheeks. She held up two fingers and between gasps choked out, "That's—two—more!"

Oh, we are going to be having a discussion about all of this!

The butt of the joke, Rocky, didn't feel like it was very funny, but since screaming at the top of his lungs wouldn't do anything, he forced a smile on to his face. His blood was still pumping in his ears, and the black smoke of his Dark Cloak, triggered by his emotions, curled around his fists. He took a deep breath trying to calm himself. It wasn't like swearing was necessary, not like that was the only way he could convey emotion.

Or is it?

The ground shook again much harder than before, and Rocky was rattled around like clothes in a dryer. The massive quakes succeeded in removing the spotlight off of him but continued for much longer this time. Suddenly, the noises of casual fear and discomfort turned to screams of terror around him. He intensified his fight to gain control of his body as the earth itself shook the thoughts from his head.

He managed to brace himself on all fours and raise his head with a jerky neck to see the massive, segmented body of the worm that broke the crust of the earth in the middle of the camp.

***

His recollected nightmare was interrupted painfully as the ropes tying him into Azoth's saddle tightened. The implementation of the ropes had clearly been good foresight by Sela, and the nearness of a deadly fall pumped adrenaline into his system.

That dream soured his mouth as he righted himself in the saddle. First, that moment was when he had broken his oath to keep everyone in the caravan alive. Second, the possibly more serious implications of the system manipulating his inner thoughts, speech patterns, and possibly more. Then finally, the fact that he was supposed to be keeping watch from up in the sky flying on Azoth's back, but he was failing at that too.

"See monsters?" Azoth mentally mumbled to Rocky. Azoth, who normally had boundless energy, was flagging after the most recent fight.

He didn't answer as those horrible memories of the first night looped in his mind, causing his mouth to twist. His self-promise of keeping everyone alive was destroyed in a single moment. The worm hadn't even attacked them, just surfaced and returned back into the earth a few kilometers away.

His brain wanted to highlight all his failures, and despite trying to focus on scouting, Rocky was so tired that he quickly fell prey to his traitorous neural network.

CHAPTER TWO

The trip back to the Territory had been maddeningly glacial. At first, Rocky had thought it was because of the speed of some of the survivors, but he quickly realized that it wasn't the under-leveled humans causing the pace to tarry. The turtle crawl was due to the frequency of monster attacks.

He looked down and spotted one of the rather large, mass-produced, Ether-powered tanks. The sum of those three hundred futuristic laser tanks and the accompanying six hundred energy weapons the military had purchased had proven nearly useless. It had taken the entire battalion firing on one target to finally bring it down, and unfortunately, the energy weapons had a recharge time of approximately three days, which meant they needed to be used sparingly. At least they still functioned as vehicles after they'd spent their load.

The upside to the more powerful monsters was that they were usually of a larger size as well. This meant that the caravan was fed, but the downside was the constant need for the strongest fighters to remain awake. That meant Sela, Zippo, Joe, and Rocky were pulling triple duty.

They all were using the Elixir of Shortened Sleep abundantly—the Alchemicy Potion Rocky had purchased at the Aretrean Bazaar let one hour of sleep substitute for eight. Of course, this was before the Toxic Blood started stacking.

Now, at a rough guess, the caravan of survivors numbered around five thousand. Of the eight thousand they started with, this number might seem fantastic, especially when compared to the quest goal of a measly eight hundred. However, Rocky had vowed to try to make it back with everyone.

In retrospect, a very small number of the deaths were stupid hunters who had been the providers for small groups of survivors back in Ottawa. The 'experience' of fighting those monsters in groups of fifty or more in that first week no longer lent itself to the evolved and more powerful beasts that had been a side effect of the second Ether Wave. He shook his head, remembering trying desperately to dissuade some of the more stubborn groups that were no longer with them.

His nightmarish flashback was so recent, he could vividly remember where the vast majority of the losses could be laid. They could all be laid at his feet and had happened on that first night. That monstrous worm had literally burrowed out from under the encampment, and in a single moment, an entire section, sleeping thousands of survivors, had fallen into a cavernous burrow. Since then, the group camped more spread out and with as much tree cover as they could manage because it appeared roots impeded underground creatures.

They had spent nearly half a day looking for any and all survivors of the worm 'attack'. In the end, the worm's death toll accounted for nearly two thousand five hundred lives.

Stop counting every casualty, and scout.

For the rest of his shift, he'd seen nothing but distant monsters. All of them seemed to be injured, and none of them seemed willing to venture in and attack the caravan in their current states. Never did he catch a glimpse of what was causing the damage. His nerves were so frayed because it seemed like the creatures doing this must be following the caravan based on all the injured monsters they were finding. Was it like a territorial T-Rex?

If this creature or creatures attacks the caravan, I don't think we can stop it... The military isn't strong enough, despite their numbers...

He circled over the group and saw his military commander Joe talking with a group of his militiamen. Joe was in charge of the Ottawa Militia group that had formed under particularly false pretenses. The group had been much larger, but due to the deranged Corsair's plots, Joe now led a pruned group of near on nine hundred men and women who had chosen to try to protect *all* of the survivors in Ottawa after the initial wave.

For the hundredth time, Rocky considered if Corsair had someone under him capable of manipulating people into doing the horrible deeds that had been committed by a select few. He still hadn't been able to confirm if there had been someone or not. But considering it again now made his stomach tie itself in knots. Something inside of him felt that the real mastermind behind everything might still be out there.

That was most likely because he was now in charge of everyone's safety. Taking on that role wasn't his usual style, but foisted into it as he was, he took it very seriously. To him, that meant looking at every situation from angles others wouldn't consider.

Those thoughts circled in his head until he landed to trade places with Sela. As Azoth touched down, he grumpily asked her again without really looking at her, "Explain to me again why we couldn't have just bought a codpiece transport from the shop to speed this up?"

I really need to pick a word to use as a swear word. These random changes are making me sound ridiculous. Also increasing my filter time if Sela is reporting me still.

Sela coughed to hide what sounded like laughter, but when he looked at her, she just looked tired and blessedly— uncompromised. Sela cut off his train of thoughts by responding tiredly, "Rocky, people in a shop aren't going to sell you good military transport ship technology. If anything, it would have been old, rusty sell-off from a planetary military that had been stripped of everything. Even the engines would have been replaced with obsolete tech before a sale. If you want to be flying around in a tremendous rust bucket after seeing and hiding from the massive creatures that are flying around up there, you are dumber than I thought."

Rocky scowled, but Sela had shifted and taken to the skies before he could respond. Honestly, he knew he was only cranky from lack of sleep, and he agreed that a rust tub was not the answer to their current problems, but these damn injured monsters were making his skin crawl.

He swallowed a lump in his throat before telling Azoth to go eat and sleep lightly. He pulled an Elixir of Shortened Sleep from his pocket and swirled the murky, sandy-colored liquid around. Could he afford to sleep for one hour?

He sure hoped so because he desperately needed it. He swigged back the foul concoction and quickly climbed up and laid down on the nearest tank.

***

Sela had been up there for the last few hours, and they hadn't seen another attack. Rocky could see the top of a line of trees in the distance that he hoped demarcated the start of the old boundary to Algonquin Park. His Territory didn't take up the whole area inside the old boundary, but if those trees were the park, they were getting close.

If Sela could stay aloft until they reached that tree cover, though, they could make camp, and everyone could sleep. If that was even possible.

He glanced over and saw Azoth still curled up on top of a tank that seemed to groan under his massive form. The Chimera, who appeared to be a strange combination of lion, eagle, lizard, goat, and scorpion, was curled in on itself in such a cat-like posture that Rocky felt himself smile.

He looked around and had to admit that being amongst the remaining survivors was disconcerting. It wasn't anything overt, but he felt like he could feel their eyes on him, maybe judging him for the losses. Or maybe it was the skunk odor...

The feeling of discomfort intensified jarringly. In front of him, at the edge of the forest, he spotted the yellow eyes of a massive, silver wolf with sun glistened metal fur glaring at him from the spot where shadows met the light.

All of his hair stood on end, and his blood both sped up through his veins and sent a shiver over his limbs. He could still remember the massive fight that had broken out between Azoth's mother and the wolf that he could see in the distance.

The fight wasn't something he could have matched now and certainly not then. If the two sides of the conflict hadn't fought to a near-perfect draw, he wouldn't have gotten his Territory. He took a steadying breath and tilted his head as his heart continued to pound nervously. He was pretty sure this was a hallucination of Steel, the alpha of the wolf pack that had fought Skandranon, Azoth's mother, but…

He glanced around and spotted a soldier beside him. "Just to be sure, there isn't a massive metal wolf over there, right?" he asked in a nervous voice.

The man's eyes widened in alarm, and his head jolted in the direction that Rocky indicated. A moment later, the man's eyes narrowed slightly, and he pursed his lips. "Sir, I don't see any wolves, metal or otherwise, in the direction you indicate."

The soldier whose name patch read Barnes turned his gaze back to Rocky and gave him a look that clearly questioned his sanity. This had become relatively commonplace over the last few days of hallucinations, so he just smiled sheepishly and shrugged. Then he turned his attention back to the enormous silver wolf, remembering having to stab it through its eye to put it out of its misery.

Knowing what he knew now, it was entirely possible that the alpha wolf would have made a full recovery. The advent of Ether had also brought a massive boost to healing for humans. While he hadn't seen this same recovery rate in monsters— usually because he didn't let them live long enough—he had witnessed its regenerative properties in his pet, Azoth.

During the fight to overthrow Corsair, Azoth had gone wing to mechanical booster against a juiced-up Mechano-Lord. While Azoth had eventually won the battle with a bit of help from Rocky, he'd been left badly burned and nearly featherless. Within half a day, the massive creature had recovered enough to fight again.

Rocky assumed that there was some sort of mathematical algorithm that could be applied to the healing effects Ether imposed and made a mental note to ask Sela during his interrogation—umm—questioning of the woman. As the group passed by the hallucination of Steel, the great wolf bent its front legs and placed its head on the ground, almost seeming to bow to Rocky.

He's kind of cute when he isn't attempting to tear out throats.

Unsure what to do, Rocky nodded his head once in the hallucination's direction, and the entire thing puffed into smoke.

Sela cawed once as she landed beside him and transformed back into her human form. The bird call made Rocky look at her, and her face made him want to run away. Her mouth was pressed into a line, and her eyebrows were drawn together so closely that they nearly touched. It would appear that she didn't have good news.

"I think there is a storm brewing, Rocky!" she began in a near shout before realizing others were around and blushingly lowering her voice. She finished much more circumspectly, "I think it is an Ether Storm."

Rocky looked at her, waiting for more, and he could see her frustration rise at his blank look. So, before she could start up again, he merely stated, "And?"

Sela's face turned red, and she looked up to the sky for a moment as if praying for patience. Then she looked back down at him. "An Ether Storm is hard to explain, considering I have never actually seen one and only heard of them in legends." With that simple statement, she pointed at dark blue thunderhead cloud forming far off in the distance. "Ether Storm!" she emphasized rather needlessly.

The direction she pointed made Rocky groan and remember the nuclear meltdown that they witnessed from afar on their trip to Ottawa. The massive, paranormal thunderclouds were forming above the site of what used to be Chalk River. He couldn't be sure, but it seemed like the ground under the clouds was off somehow.

It was only for a second, but the trees seemed to be warped, and the grass appeared to be black in color. From this distance, that could just be shade from the clouds. Remembering his hallucinations, he slowly asked, "Is the ground—"

His slow speech wasn't satisfactory to Sela as she cut him off, "Black, yes, the ground in that direction is festering and black. The storm, Rocky!"

Rocky tore his gaze from the area, and his mouth formed a hard line as he asked, "Okay. I can see that those clouds don't look natural. Want to try to remember what you've heard about Ether Storms, then?"

Sela ground her teeth. "It was honestly a legend, and the gist of it was to not be caught out in one." She was nearly growling, and Rocky figured it was time to start being a bit less abrasive; they were both tired. She continued, forcibly relaxing her jaw, "It was almost like a bedtime story to scare children. Or maybe it was to suggest not running away from the safety of their Territorial town before they were strong enough?"

That was quite possibly the most confusing description Rocky had ever heard. He was going to ask for more, but a flash of blue lightning made them both look in the direction of the mounting thunderclouds. A moment later, a massive boom echoed over the group, and everyone stopped in place to join the two looking at the ominous, multihued thunderclouds.

Instead of asking for more information, Rocky looked to Sela wide-eyed and asked, "What's closest for cover?"

Sometime after her rebirth, Sela had gained a sense of the land around herself. Rocky had discovered this fact when she unerringly was able to direct the survivor group to good cover for the night. Her range was getting better too—now at a few kilometers of distance—and she could often tell if a cave or forest would be large enough to house all or most of the group.

Sela blinked once before her nostrils flared, and she closed her eyes tight in concentration. A moment later, they flashed open, and she nodded. "There is a cave at the very edge of my senses! The Territory is still half a day through forest terrain." Then she pointed towards the storm. "The cave is in that direction."

Captain Crunch!

Rocky fingered his button on his ear's radio to allow him to communicate and declared in an overly loud voice, "Joe, we need to move. Now!" Then he let go of the button and spoke to Sela alone, "Is it big enough for everyone?"

Sela nodded, but then pressed her mouth into a firm line so hard her lips turned white. "But like all caves that size, there is something already inside."

"Of course there is," was Rocky's response under his breath as the survivor group came slowly back out of their frozen state and turned into a disturbed ants' nest. The only other cave they had found to house the whole group of five thousand survivors plus had housed a rather large and dangerous rock slime. They had only beat the thing by repeating tactics that Rocky and the boys had used and luring it to water. Otherwise, large caves like that weren't exactly common natural formations.

The survivors were well on their way to becoming an angry beehive when Joe and Zippo sprinted over.

Rocky pointed at Zippo. "You are coming with Sela and me to clear out a cave. Joe, I need you to get the entire group to move in that direction. Fast!" Rocky pointed towards the storm.

Joe, who had real military experience, didn't even blink. "How much time do I have?"

Rocky continued, pointing directly at the ever-expanding storm wall, "Want to race?"

CHAPTER THREE

Zippo rode on top of Azoth, and Rocky strangely rode on top of Sela in cat form. While Azoth could carry both Zippo and Rocky, he would already be slower than Sela on the ground. Since the group needed speed to get to the cave and clear it before the survivors arrived, they had chosen to distribute the load. They had also opted for Azoth to remain grounded in case the storm had typhoon-level wind fronts leading it. As expected, Azoth was already lagging behind the much more agile cat form of Sela.

Since Rocky didn't have to do any work, he absent-mindedly checked his status page.

Rockland Barkclay Level 21
> **Class: Apprentice-Dark (Azrael) Revenant**
> **Level 1 Strategist**

Leadership Class:

Class Skills: Dark Blade, Dark Mend, Soul Blade, Dark Cloak, Shadow Clone
> **Health Points = 190/190 Points (-70) (Sleep Deprived)**
> **Dark Ether Pool = 150/150 Points (-50) (Sleep Deprived)**

You have 0 stat points and 0 skill points to distribute.
> **Stamina – 19 (+3) (-7) (Strength of Body +5)**
> **Strength – 29 (Strength of Arms +5) (Strength of Arms +10)**
> **Agility – 37 (Speed of Arms +5)**
> **Dexterity – 30**
> **Intelligence – 15 (+1) (-5) (Sleep Deprived)**
> **Wisdom – 20 (-7) (Unclean)**
> **Charisma – 10 (-19) (Unclean + Skunk Shower)**
> **Luck – 10 (+3)**

Weak Skills

> **Non-Class Combat Skills: Combatant –
> 22 (+3), Ether Channels – 13,
> Ether Manipulation – 11, Stealth –
> 26 (+2), Swordsmanship – 26 (+2)**
> **Common Skills: Barter – 5, Camouflage –
> 7, Endurance – 22 (+2), Perception
> – 24 (+3), Tracker – 16 (+4),
> Trance Meditation – 15**
> **Profession Skills: Actor – 5, Butcher – 19
> (+2), Cook – 2, Herbalist – 19 (+5),
> Miner – 1, Skinner – 20 (+3),
> Trader – 5**

Moderate Skills

> **Non-Class Combat Skills**
> **Common Skills: Analyze – 10 (+8), Sneak
> – 12 (+7)**
> **Profession Skills**

He'd become extremely used to having a status sheet, but he could still remember that first morning—afternoon—waking up, his body changed, and finding this thing. Back then he hadn't had much basis to go on but had made some logical guesses as to where he was strong and weak. Now, however, he'd talked with the military officers, and they had conducted a tally to see where most people's baseline stats had been. From the Ottawa survivors, the average was eight across the board in stats, except for luck, which started significantly lower in almost all the individuals. Those numbers could be flawed, but they seemed accurate, considering he'd been above that mark in some and below in others.

Looking at the screen now, he was disappointed he hadn't leveled in a while. The lack of levels was particularly discouraging when he remembered the massive fight in Ottawa because surviving it had felt like a prodigious victory. Then again, he hadn't fought anyone, just outsmarted them. He really hadn't even left Stealth until Corsair was on death's door.

He'd killed Corsair and gotten the Etherience notification, but since he had really only provided the final blow, he hadn't gotten much Etherience. All and all, he'd been left with just over one million Etherience to level 22 when he left Ottawa. That number was minuscule, though, when put into context; level 22 to 23 needed over twenty-six million Etherience in totality.

The current monsters that they'd been fighting were far too powerful for him alone, and sometimes, even with help from his friends, the monsters escaped. This meant that he was always splitting Etherience over his group of five and occasionally with the entire military. The trek back had further highlighted a future problem for survivors. They needed a safe place to level and live. Sela assured him that the Territory was just that.

Fingers crossed! I would like to be able to plan my stat allocations a bit more instead of being forced to assign them like those seven I had saved up in Ottawa.

The difficulty of achieving a new level was making his mind reel. The daunting task of becoming a Journeyman was huge. Then he was forced to consider trying to catch up to Master class monsters that were only getting stronger.

With an exasperated sigh, he opened his nearly full Etherience bar to check its exact progress.

174,231 Etherience to reach level 22.

Each level doubled the amount of Etherience needed, and Rocky remembered a conversation with Sela; she'd told him this is what people of old had referred to as 'the grind'. She had somehow insinuated that it happened at every class rank and that often, people would take years to complete it at higher ranks.

Knowing she had been a Master class before she died, Rocky's eyes had widened, and he had asked her how long it had taken her. She pursed her lips and looked away into the distance before responding very quietly, "My guild helped."

Often, it was easy to forget that Sela had lost everyone she ever knew or cared about from her previous life. She just seemed so strong and assured, like nothing could hurt her. Rocky often thought of her as a rock, and it was sobering when moments like that one came around, and he saw a glimpse of her fragility.

The wind from the storm nearly knocked him off of Sela's back and did successfully jar him out of his distracted thoughts. While the storm was still about fifty kilometers or more distant, it was growing in intensity and power. It was definitely a good call to have kept Azoth on the ground.

Sela didn't veer in her course, and Rocky scanned the landscape to try to make out something that looked like a cave. All he could see in the direction they were headed was a large hill, but since he trusted Sela implicitly, he assumed the cave must be on the back end of it. This was why when his vision suddenly seemed to turn black, he accidentally pulled Sela's fur in panic.

Sela yowled in complaint and slowly came to a stop. Rocky looked backward and saw Azoth and Zippo pass through a monstrous passage behind him. It must have been a gaping hole in the ground about twenty feet in diameter. Rocky blinked rapidly as he climbed off Sela's back and walked to the cave entrance.

Looking back the way they had come, Rocky realized how he had missed this massive cave in the earth. Like a crater, the edges of the hole had risen, and on every side, the grass was tall and unbent, obscuring it from view.

He needed to mark the area for Joe. So, Rocky pulled out one of the lamp posts that was in his bag of holding. These lamp posts were previously used by a samurai golem in Pembroke, and he had been planning to melt them down, but right now, they were the only thing he could think of that would be long enough to be seen above the four-to-five-foot-high grass.

His muscles strained under the weight of the post, but thanks to his high strength stat, it wasn't an impossible task to lift it above his head. Twisting with all of his rather impressive power, he then drove the light post about three feet into the soft ground. After making sure it would stand up for a few moments, Rocky dog paddled dirt from around the pole, grass and all, on to the side of the cylindrical metal. Sela, Jason, and Azoth joined in, the latter a bit too exuberantly, causing dirt to spray in all directions. It was the work of a few minutes, but once they had enough dirt around the pole, they began to pack it down around its base. After the quick shod foundation, about six feet of the twenty-five-foot pole was covered.

Once complete, he clicked his radio button. "Joe, I have marked the cave entrance with a lamp post—shoot, Eagle Eye here. Over?"

A quick response of, "Affirmative," was all he received in response, which added to his abundant confusion about radio etiquette.

Turning back towards the cave, he walked in again. It wasn't nearly as pitch black inside as his adjusting eyes had initially protested. In fact, it was rather bright with the massive open hole at the top. The cave descended at a fifteen-degree angle for approximately one hundred feet before Rocky lost the ability to see further because the land either began flattening out or ascending.

"Want a light source now or later, Rock?" Zippo asked in his mock-business-like tone, which was all kinds of wrong from a fifteen-year-old. Zippo could now conjure a Fireball and have it hover above himself to provide something akin to a miniature sun's worth of light.

"Might as well do it now to get our eyes accustomed to the light source as we descend. Sela, is the creature still inside?" Rocky responded, realizing that they probably only had a fifteen-minute window at most before the survivors arrived or the storm overtook them.

An orangish light cast back the darkness even farther, and Sela raised both of her cat brows and shrugged, indicating that she couldn't tell anymore. Rocky's eyebrows shot nearer to his hairline, and he swallowed visibly.

Great! Time to explore the cave cautiously while being quick... Seems contradictory.

"Alright. Let's storm this place!" Rocky quipped while smirking, which caused Sela to growl, Zippo to shake his head, and Azoth to look around to figure out what had changed the mood.

Sighing to himself, he led the way down to the bottom of the minor slope with the others following behind. To further his disappointment, Azoth mentally sent, "What funny?" after the flopping pun.

Rocky looked at his pet and mentally sent, "The others don't have a sense of humor." Azoth tilted his head, looking confused, then looked over in Sela's direction.

A moment later, Azoth chuffed loudly, and Rocky glared back at Sela, who wore a cat smile across her rather pleased looking face. He felt his cheeks go red, and he turned back around, trying to pretend he wasn't curious about what she had told Azoth to make his pet laugh at him.

Once they reached the bottom of the decline, Rocky realized he had been right, and the ground now had a bit of an incline going back up into darkness. Once Zippo closed the gap with Rocky, the slope up resolved itself out of the pitch. The slope ascended quickly in comparison with the downslope before leveling out and turning a corner.

Rocky led the way again up the incline and stopped just before the corner. Zippo sent the light source floating around the bend first without prompting, and Rocky waited for a slow count of two before he peeked his head around. There in front of him was a massive, hollowed-out chamber of stone. Something about it made Rocky even more hesitant to enter. Part of him was screaming that this was a perfect space to safely ride out the storm for everyone, but something about the cavern felt wrong.

Is this a hallucination? Also, with all our stats diminished, can we even beat whatever lurks within?

The tiny sun hovered before the room widened out fully, which effectively damped its light. He turned to Zippo and asked, "How far away can you control that Fireball?"

Zippo formed his mouth into a line and closed his eyes. The Fireball moved another five feet forward before it stopped. Zippo started to sweat but stated through his clenched teeth, "About that far right now."

He was definitely improving with his spells, but it seemed like he was still somewhat limited. Rocky knew he had been trying to practice moving his firewall up into the air and cast it on spaces he wanted it to be. Unfortunately, this trip hadn't given the group much time.

As soon as the Fireball crossed the doorway, a loud bang sounded from behind them, and semi-familiar words appeared on a blue box in front of Rocky which caused him to clench his teeth.

Welcome to the Arena Dungeon.

You have entered in a group of four; challenges will be scaled to match. Harder and harder waves will be sent against your group until you face the Arena Champion.
Good Luck.

Level: Unknown.
Age: 22 days
Best time: N/A
Clears: 0

As soon as he mentally cleared that notification, a counter popped up in his upper left corner, counting down sixty seconds. If this wasn't the worst time to find a Dungeon, Rocky would eat his socks, and he had been wearing them since they started this hell hike. Quickly glancing back the way they had come, he saw a solid piece of stone blocked their way out. If the survivors made it down to the bottom of that entrance and were stuck there during a storm…

Well, there would have been water pooling down there if a drain didn't exist. So perhaps…

Regardless, a storm might overwhelm the drainage capacity. The problem didn't bear thinking about. They would just have to crush every wave as fast as they possibly could and pray it would be enough. Another problem came to the forefront of his mind quickly after he resolved that decision. What if the Dungeon reset and then five or so thousand people came in?

With some effort, he managed to push down the feeling that accompanied that thought. It was still a slowly mounting stress on the back of his mind, unfortunately, but nothing could be done now.

Maybe I can talk to this core as well? Talk about stuck between a Dungeon and a storm wall!

"We are staying here to use this door as a funnel and a line of sight portal in case the enemies have any ranged amongst them. Get ready!" Rocky spat out and pulled his sword out of its scabbard as the clock passed the thirty-second mark. Even though the scabbard wasn't particularly necessary anymore, he found that having a liquid sword crawl on his body could get a little uncomfortable at times.

Wind began to swirl in the cavern, and Rocky's eyebrows rose steeply because he didn't feel any movement in the air in the space he was occupying. "Is anyone else seeing this?" he asked.

"The crawling walls?" Zippo asked back.

"See nothing but cavern?" Azoth responded, and Sela pointed a paw in a specific direction behind the swirling winds that Rocky now saw.

Oh, what a perfect time for hallucinations.

"The walls aren't *crawling*; there isn't a massive *tornado* inside the chamber, and whatever Sela is *pointing* at isn't there. We are *hallucinating!* Azoth, you'll have to lead the attack against any *real* enemies you see! Got it?"

"Af-form-ativ-ey," Azoth mentally sent, accompanied by his massive, nodding lion's head. He moved to take up the entire doorway, his bulky, sixteen-wheeler-sized body cutting off anyone else's view of the room.

Rocky wanted to tell him to move over or at least step back so the group could also see, but trying to get exactly what you wanted from Azoth was like pulling teeth; they just didn't have the time. So, instead, he just sent out a silent prayer that Azoth would respond the right way to whatever threat materialized in front of him.

As soon as the counter reached zero, Azoth's back lizard legs flexed then dug furrows into the ground as he bounded through the opening with puppy-like exuberance.

Here we go. Drunken hell. Why is the massive Chimera the only one of us not hallucinating?

Rocky rushed after his pet into what looked to him to be a massive, spiraling tornado. Typically, he would have played this a bit more cautiously and tried to set up some sort of strategy to defeat each wave. However, with their time crunch and debuffs, this was probably the best scenario to see everyone outside safe. Not to mention Azoth didn't do subtlety…

Once Rocky passed through the fictitious storm, he could see blue light materializing creatures in front of him. He assumed they were forming in the center of the chamber, and the group rushed towards the swirling, blue patterns. Sela bounded by him quickly, catching Azoth before turning invisible on his right side.

Rocky veered his run left and also engaged Stealth and Dark Cloak simultaneously. Once Dark Cloak activated, he felt his vision increase drastically, and the shadows around the room gave up their secrets just as Zippo's Fireball raced by in the space he had just occupied.

Four snarling, Doberman-sized rats formed in the swirling light just as the Fireball exploded in their midst. Rats this size would be terrifying to fight, and Rocky knew that they would be terrors for the group if the group didn't manage to crush them quickly. It had been a lucky break that he hadn't expected. The creatures needed to form, and that gave them the advantage of surprise.

The Fireball was unfortunately mistimed and splashed on to the space, flaring up and receding to leave still-forming, rat-shaped blue light. He heard Zippo make a noise of disgust behind him, but then the creatures seemed to pop into existence and fall to the ground.

He managed to Analyze one of the creatures as it landed.

Member of The Ratpack
Splinter
Level 11
Apprentice-Ninja

Azoth's jaws chomped down on the head of one of the rats a moment after it formed, and his clawed, feline paw knocked another one careening into the air with a squeak. Rocky diverted to follow the airborne enemy, not wanting to let it recover and get behind anyone. Another screech signaled Sela landing on the back of another and severing its spinal column with her Sabertooth canines.

A quick glance back as he continued to follow the flying rat told Rocky only one of the original four creatures remained alive in the center of the Arena. Azoth and Sela were already splitting up to circle the poor thing. He turned back to his target as it landed with a thud. He winced in pain as he listened to a few loud crunches of what must have been either shifting or breaking ribs, but a moment later, he had buried his sword through the rat's chest before it could even regain its feet.

A new countdown timer appeared in Rocky's vision as he turned away from the corpse of the rat to see Azoth toss his head to the side to dislodge the final member of the rat pack from his teeth. The creature flopped to the ground, and before his eyes, the corpse slowly sunk into the ground. He quickly glanced behind him to see the same phenomenon occurring to the other creatures there. It was disappointing they wouldn't be able to butcher the creatures for meat, but the thought of eating rat did make Rocky shudder a little. Western culture standards still slightly affected him even though this wasn't at all the same Earth from the pre-Ether crash era.

The group gathered back up as the timer counted down from the sixty seconds again. Rocky clenched his teeth, realizing that the countdown timer might be the most significant problem for the group's objective. He forced his jaw to unclench and sighed before voicing his concern, "Honestly, this timer might be the bottleneck if all the fights are going to be that easy."

Hell mode initialized.

All waves prior to the Champion will be released
simultaneously.
Remaining waves: 14
Good luck!

I need to learn to keep my big mouth shut.

The group glared at him, except for Azoth, who jumped up and down in place as his excitement got the better of him. Rocky pointed in all four cardinal directions before saying, "Each one of us takes a side. Don't let any creature by you, don't hold back, and don't downward dogging die!"

Damn it all!

Zippo summoned two Fireballs—one into each of his hands—Sela turned invisible, and Rocky triggered his Stealth again, still wrapped in his Dark Cloak skill. The group had fought a lot of battles together over the last week, and each member trusted the others implicitly. For Azoth, Sela, and himself, he felt that they would each die before they let a monster through. For Zippo, it might only be his intense desire to continue to get stronger; the young man was tough to read during a quick glance due to the perpetual snarl on his face. Rocky felt like this type of comradery could only be forged in the heat and blood of combat.

Rocky felt his body calm slightly as the clock finished its last few seconds.

3...2...1...

At zero, blue light lined the chamber. The group stood at the center of a maelstrom of indigo, forming creatures hell-bent on their destruction. Rocky rushed towards the nearest forming group and arrived to see a Volvo-sized turtle pop into existence just as Dark Tidings removed its head before it could retreat into its massive shell. Spinning off and somewhat over the collapsing shell, Rocky saw his next target and cast Analyze.

Member of the Primate Gang
King Louie
Level 17
Apprentice-Chest Basher

The creature was with three other primates, and each one was banging fists the size of car tires against their chests. Rocky triggered Stealth again and lunged towards King Louie in a fencer's thrust. The sharp end of his Soul Blade pierced the chest and came out the back of King Louie as a surprised look passed over his face. The other three stopped hammering and hooted questioningly at the now silent King as he tumbled backward off the blade. Rocky didn't let them question long as he spun into their midst, slashing his sword high to decapitate one of the creatures. He raised his foot and powerfully kicked another one that seemed to be the fastest to react to his initial attack.

The kick spiraled the beast on to its back, and the last remaining primate swung a fist at the deeper shadows that contained Rocky. As the fist neared him, he felt Dark Cloak push on it slightly, and he ducked below the encroaching haymaker while simultaneously casting Shadow Clone. A second, near-identical Rocky popped up behind the fist and jumped at the off-balance creature, puncturing its hide with two identical black daggers.

Rocky allowed his momentum to carry him towards the downed gorilla he kicked, which was struggling back to its feet. Before it gained them, Rocky's Soul Blade punctured its chest, making the final primate gang member collapse lifelessly. In the moment of respite, Rocky saw that the last two groups of enemies on his side were already formed and charging his way.

He glanced at his Ether bar and saw that he had approximately eighty-five of his original one hundred forty remaining. He hated doing it, but he grabbed an Ether Draught and chugged its content. It would only be half as effective due to his current debuffs. However, he couldn't hold back. Rocky charged his Dark Blade ability with two stacks, loading fifty Ether points into the blade before he slashed horizontally along the ground at chest height. He had become used to the way that his Dark Blade acted during the Ottawa battles and the ensuing week of the hell march. So, Rocky had left the perfect space for the two segregated, black energy blades that shot out of his weapon to stretch from a foot above the ground to a maximum of six feet in the air.

There were two primary energy blades which were separated by about five feet. In between each of the black slashes, static energy coalesced and dissipated continuously. As the edges sped towards the final four staggered groups, Rocky watched, hoping that none of the creatures would survive one of his most offensive and powerful abilities. A moment later, something akin to meat going through a grinder played out in front of him before the summoned ability buried and gouged into the rounded wall.

Having gotten used to fighting powerful Master class enemies, Rocky just felt his stomach pang once at the grisly sight. Usually, this ability did some pretty hefty damage in the way of gashes and cuts, but this was something else entirely. Clamping down on his stomach's single moment of disgust, Rocky turned to see who might need help and saw that everyone else in the group was finishing off their enemies with as much ease as Rocky had.

A few short breaths later, a new counter popped up in the corner, accompanied by a message.

Congratulations! You have earned the right to challenge the Champion.
Monstar
Level 22

Journeyman-Spinner
Good luck.

Rocky gulped at the class name.

Please don't be a spider. Please don't be a spider…

He just kept repeating the words over and over in his head as the clock counted down to zero.

CHAPTER FOUR

Rocky spun in a fast circle, trying to see the indigo light that signaled the forming of a monster. A roar from Sela made him turn towards her feline form. She was looking up at the ceiling, and Rocky felt his heart fall. He glanced up.

On the roof was an unmistakable indigo forming spider web with a massive ball of light, creating something in the middle.

Damn it! How do we even attack it up there!?

He looked at Zippo first, for obvious reasons, "Think you can burn the Spider or the web? Maybe force it to come down?"

Straight faced, Zippo shrugged and formed two massive Fireballs, one in each hand. Then he just glanced up and waited to see his target. Again, his quiet demeanor created a pang deep in Rocky, but there was no time to try to talk to him now.

Rocky glanced at his Dark Ether bar and saw it climbing slowly, inching back towards eighty points. He groaned and chugged back another Ether Draught. He watched a stack join his current debuff. Then he watched another one join the rest.

Drunk 1
- **You have drunk too much alcohol over a set period, and your body is slightly inebriated. If you consume more alcohol, this effect will worsen.**
    - **-1 Intelligence**
    - **-1 Agility**
    - **-1 Dexterity**

Lasts 1 hour. Renews if more alcohol is consumed.

Damnit, I forgot these potions have an alcoholic base.

Considering he had been imbibing them every day, he assumed he'd just crossed some threshold because of the speed at which he had just consumed an additional two. Regardless, his Ether bar began climbing faster, and he readied his Dark Blade ability.

Azoth roared as the massive Spider formed and fell the short distance on to its now physical web. Rocky mentally sent, "Stay on the ground. Attack it once we get it to come down here. If you go up there alone, you will probably get caught in its web."

Azoth, of course, took off, and Rocky swore inwardly. Zippo launched his first Fireball at the web right under the Spider, but the hot air balloon-size Spider just moved on the web and then used its legs to excise the burning portion.

Rocky mentally screamed at Azoth, "Get back down here, right now!"

Azoth's response, which he must have sent to both Sela and himself based on her growl, was petulant, "No, you forgot the magic word!"

"Please!" he shouted but saw Azoth increase his wing beats instead of coming down.

Rocky could feel his heart speed up as an internal timer began beating out desperately. Azoth was in trouble. They needed to hurry. So, Rocky commanded, "Target the edges of its web, Zippo." He also sent a single-charge Dark Blade at one of the edges of the web and quickly charged a second. Zippo flung his spell, and a large portion of the network began to burn and curl away from the fire that now coated the wall.

The Spider let out an eerie wail as the web dropped a few feet because two of the supporting edges had just come away. Rocky sent his second Dark Blade skill at a third edge of the web and saw Zippo forming two more Fireballs. As soon as his ability severed the third connection to the wall, the web swung down towards the group. It pivoted on its remaining attachment and unfortunately acted like a fly swatter.

Azoth, who was under the web, got struck from the sky by the sticky, crisscrossing strands. The momentum of the swinging Spider silk carried him into the wall, which cracked under the combined weight of the Chimera and the Spider.

A glance at his own Dark Ether, which showed him he was nearly dry. Luckily, Zippo flung one of his two new Fireballs at the top of the now vertical web. As the final strands began to burn, the Spider seemed to vibrate with delight as Azoth began fighting against the sticky webbing, which started to tangle him up more.

Rocky took off at a sprint and was happy to see Sela's tail already in front of him by a good fifty meters. As they closed in on the trapped Chimera, the Spider moved with jerky quickness and was suddenly attempting to bite Azoth. They had a bit of luck on their side, as Azoth's scorpion tail, somehow untrapped, lashed out, which barely held back the many-eyed arachnid. The Spider ducked and dodged a few desperate strikes before it dug two of its front legs into the shoulders of the giant Chimera.

Azoth yowled in pain and anger, and his tail began lashing furiously at the two offending appendages. Unfortunately, the tail had now also become entangled, thanks to all the thrashing. This allowed the Spider to dart in with its fangs, biting into Azoth's neck just as Sela arrived. She jumped on to the Spider's back and sank her massive canines and claws into the bloated abdomen of the creature.

As Rocky approached, the final strand on the ceiling released and dropped the three fighters from the roof into a massive pile on the ground, and a dust cloud formed at the area of impact. Azoth's health bar was a sickly yellow in Rocky's interface, and he felt his heart clench as he saw Sela's bar drop from full to half in an instant.

He cried out and leaped into the cloud, hoping he wouldn't be too late for either of his closest friends. With his enhanced vision, he made out webbing in bundles everywhere and cut his way through, hoping to get a line of sight on Sela to cast Dark Mend. A few steps later, he saw what had done so much damage to his ancestral companion. The Spider was lying on its back with all eight legs above its body, rolling back and forth and attempting to flip on to its dagger-like feet. Each time the Spider rolled, it careened over a desperately clawing and furious black Sabretooth tiger.

Rocky didn't hesitate; he cast a double dose of Dark Mend on his companion and felt his head go light as he nearly bottomed out what was left of his Ether reserves. Then he closed the last distance with the creature who had just managed to flip over. Rocky swung and took off two of the eight legs simultaneously. Ichor liberally sprayed in every direction from the stumps, and he waded through it as the Spider backpedaled away.

It tried to snap its fangs at him, attempting to keep him at a distance, as it retreated towards the wall. Rocky leaped towards the leg that it was using to support the retreating attack and struck, removing a third leg and unbalancing the creature further. Unfortunately, the roll he used to stand back up allowed the Spider to create more distance. He pulled a gravity grenade from his bag of holding, knowing it was the least damaging if his friends got caught in the crossfire. He needed to end this fight before it got up on the wall, or this fight might go on too long to save the survivors who may already be outside.

He ran forward in a short burst, depressed the pin, and threw the oblong-shaped grenade directly towards the creature's gaping mouth. The creature was already nearly at the wall in its desperate retreat when his throw sank home.

Nothing but net!

The arachnid continued up the wall as he ran to Sela and poured a Health Potion into her fanged mouth.

As feline Sela swallowed, the Spider screeched angrily at them from the safety of the roof.

Be careful what you eat!

Then the Spider's abdomen crunched in on itself with a wet pop. The chittering outrage and revenge turned into a short-lived squeak as the creature died instantly from the sudden internal blender. Rocky felt himself slowly rise into the air and realized that this was going to hurt when he came back down. He saw Sela and Azoth follow him up a moment later, and as he turned, he found Zippo also airborne.

As if in slow motion, the Spider continued to shrink in on itself in fits and bursts, spraying ichor that would get caught in its own gravity before, suddenly, all that remained was a ball of Spider parts the size of a beach ball. The group floated forty feet off the ground, rotating in lazy circles for about thirty seconds.

During that time, a notification popped up, and Rocky read it.

Congratulations! You have completed the "Arena Dungeon."

> **Bonus:**
>> **For the first completion of the Dungeon, your group has been awarded 180,000 personal Etherience per party member.**

The Dungeon has been classified as a Level 18 zone.

51,923,149 Etherience remaining until level 23.

Rocky had a single moment to realize he had leveled, then the ball and the group plummeted out of the air.

Each person hit the ground hard, but Zippo and Azoth hit the hardest. Sela, being a cat, landed on her feet with ease. Rocky, due to his high Dexterity, Agility, and Strength, landed on his feet and turned any momentum left into a roll, which took a good third of his health and cracked some bones, but he otherwise remained uninjured. Zippo screamed out in abhorrent pain, and Azoth didn't make a sound despite dropping to a quarter of his massive health pool.

Unsure who to attend to first, Rocky was saved from choosing as Sela transformed back into a human and ran to Zippo. Rocky went to Azoth, whose health bar still flashed a sickly yellow, and used Analyze on the still form of the massive Chimera.

Azoth
Apprentice Dread-Chimera
Level 21
Paralyzed
Health Points 204/965

When Rocky walked around and looked into Azoth's eyes, he saw them move to meet his. Then Azoth mentally sent, "Azoth, listen next time. Azoth, sorry. Rocky help Azoth?" Not sure what he could do, he shouldered the beast and pushed with all his might. He barely managed to turn the massive Chimera on to his side, so gave up on getting him upside down. Once Azoth was on his side, Rocky pulled out a Health Potion and poured it into the Chimera's open mouth, attempting to turn the beast's head and force gravity to take the elixir down its throat.

"The only thing to do now is wait for Paralyze to elapse, I'm afraid," he mentally told the birdbrain who breathed out a defeated, cat-like huff.

"Rocky! Going to need an elixir and some possible healing over here," Sela called over, and he bit his lip and ran over to check on Zippo.

Zippo had broken both femurs and had coated the ground nearby liberally in vomit. His already pale complexion was very green. Looking at the boy, Rocky immediately took out the two remaining Health Potions and handed them to Sela. Then he whispered, "I am going to have to pull the bones back into alignment, buddy. This is probably going to hurt—"

Zippo luckily passed out as Rocky pulled the first bone back into a semblance of the shape it was intended to have. It was a good thing he had conked out too because the second bone that Rocky was forced to move around had broken the skin. After both legs were straightened, Sela poured the two Health Potions down Zippo's throat. Rocky checked his Ether pool and cast a Dark Mend on the boy to help speed the recovery on both legs.

Just as they finished up with him, a voice called out, "As victors in the arena, I must inform you of the danger that is outside! There is a large group of humans coming to attack. I can let you out the back way and hold them inside if you would like. Would you like to use the back exit? Honor to the Gladiator!"

Rocky groaned and looked around, hoping to find an object that he could speak to. Unfortunately, there wasn't a prominent area that would house the Dungeon core. So Rocky appealed to the air, "There is an Ether Storm about to hit outside. That large group is with us, and we need this place for refuge. Our group was sent to clear the cave. Can you please let them in?"

There was an extended period of silence before the same emotionless voice quoted, "Gladiators, under Atlantian Law Special Allowances twenty-one dash one-zero-zero subrule one A, asylum will be granted to groups in dire need. Your group will be given refuge here due to the bravery of the initial combatants." As the Dungeon spoke, Rocky heard grinding of what must have been the massive stone door that had fallen and closed his group in. A moment later, screaming could be heard as people rushed into the cavern.

By the sounds of the wind down the tunnel, the storm had already arrived, and it was a close thing for the survivors. The tail end of the survivors looked really bad, with clothes and skin-stained blue. Anywhere the blue liquid touched skin, it seemed to sink into the person, and the area instantly bruised. Those individuals began to shake as Rocky screamed out, "If you have any of it on your clothing, take it off now! Anyone who didn't get any of the rain on them, move away from the others."

Once everyone was through the entrance, the Dungeon resealed the door with a grating sound. As the door closed, Rocky heard Joe shout into a held radio, "Hunker down, button up the hatch, and don't stick your head out until we come for you." He paused for a moment. "Swap out the air in the morning using the turret. Who knows how long this will last? Whatever you do, don't let any get on you."

After the initial confusion and fear, Rocky was looking at a group of about a thousand shaking individuals who were staring back with eyes filled with fear. He queried the remaining group if anyone had spare clothes or blankets for the afflicted, and soon, the thousand or so sickly individuals were huddled together as Rocky, Joe, and Sela deliberated.

"I Analyzed one of them, and it doesn't seem like anything is wrong." Rocky's words were punctuated with another individual falling over unconscious, so he amended, "At least nothing that I can figure out."

Joe looked over at the huddled and scared group and then back at the two others. "Honestly, the door opened just after the storm hit." He looked back at the door they entered through. "I was about to order people to head back and try to make it into the tanks."

He took a long breath and let it out before completely breaking down, "That would have probably killed everyone, though. What about the soldiers in the tanks? I don't even know if they're waterproof. I should be out there with them. I left no one in charge."

Rocky placed a hand on his shoulder, which steadied the man. He breathed in and out for a long moment before his military calm took control again, and he addressed Sela and Rocky, "We lost a hundred or so out in the tunnel. If they got hit by too much of the 'rain', they just went into instant convulsions. I was forced to abandon those who fell because the 'rain' was too copious."

Then his eyes softened, and his voice changed to entreaty, "Please guys, we can't lose any more–" His head snapped to Sela, and his look took on hope, " Sela?"

With Joe's pleading eyes on her, Sela was forced to shrug, as she was just as lost as the rest of them. "I honestly have no idea what is wrong. It seems like the Ether rain is attacking their bodies. Since any healing Rocky offered is Ether-based, it isn't helping. We are all out of Health Potions, and trying to bleed out the 'rain' seems like a bad idea. I think we have to wait and see what happens. None of them claim to have any debuffs that would help us understand what the 'rain' is doing."

Joe swore again and stalked off to gather reports from others. Rocky looked at Sela and wearily whispered, "Get some rest. With that outer door closed and the storm outside, we can't do anything right now. Let's at least take the break this will offer us. I'll keep an eye on the sick and check on Zippo."

Then I'll probably find a nice comfortable stone...

Sela smiled wearily, probably guessing his internal thoughts, before moving off to join the rest of the survivors and continue organizing everyone. Rocky glanced again at the survivors and then over to a semi-lucid Zippo. Rocky moved over to the young man and cast another double stack of Dark Mend.

Instantly, his face unclenched a little as the numbing properties of Rocky's spell removed some of the pain. He looked up and muttered, "Thanks, Rock."

Rocky lowered himself to the ground and smiled. Seeing the boy hurt broke something in him. Maybe that was why he chose to try to talk to him about the distance he was creating around himself. As soon as he opened his mouth, he was unsure what to say. So, he mumbled out, "Listen… Zip. I don't know if I'm the best person to be having this discussion, but I think you need to hear it all the same."

"No one really knows what you're going through. Not even me, who also lost Alex and Oliver. Loss is unique to every person, and each of us handles it in our own way. All I can tell you is that closing yourself off to others your age isn't going to help you."

Rocky clenched his jaw at the conversation and realized that this was probably another reason he had been avoiding having this particular discussion. He recognized his own coping method for the death of two young men, who were part of his adopted family. Rocky was also in denial about his own family, and talking about it was forcing him to confront that as well. He felt a lump in his throat and swallowed; maybe this was good for both of them.

Rocky continued, "It was my fault. I should have sent you all back as soon as we heard the gunshots. I shouldn't have asked you and Oliver to go secure the school. If I would have left you all behind, we could be making this trip together." Rocky reached up and brushed an errant tear from his cheek and looked over at Zippo.

What he saw was a young man fast asleep. As soon as Rocky had removed the pain that was keeping him awake, the exhaustion from the last few days had hit him like a sack of bricks. Rocky felt the tears flow from his cheeks freely now that he didn't have to hide them anymore. His body convulsed angrily as he held back the sobs that wanted to accompany them. Just because no one could see him cry right now didn't mean that if he began bawling uncontrollably, they wouldn't hear it.

Guess I'll count that as a practice run.

His thought lightened the mood enough that he was able to wipe his face and stand up. He first went to go look over the healthy survivors. Walking by the large group of huddled and scared people who were mostly all asleep was somewhat disturbing. The whole cave was silent other than the collective inhales and exhales of a large group of humans, but every sleeping form twitched and moved in the deep throes of nightmares.

It's strange that this Dungeon hasn't spoken again since everyone came inside. Wonder why that is…

He continued his trek around the cave and smiled when he saw Sela fast asleep amongst a group of women. A few moments later, a group of perhaps fifteen militiamen stood to attention and saluted him. He awkwardly nodded back, hoping to allow them to sit back down, which they tiredly did as he continued his slow circuit of the cavern.

As he finished his initial circuit and returned to being back near the wounded, he immediately tilted his head and gazed at the group. Something was definitely off with the group. All movement had ceased, even the tremors that had been plaguing each individual. For a moment, he breathed a sigh of relief. Then the noise of his breath caused his skin to break out in a cold sweat. The group wasn't breathing!

Garth Fekind
Level 6
Apprentice Time-Warp
Irradiated-Ether Mutation

Moderate Analyze failed to provide additional information.

Rocky blinked rapidly, trying to understand what he had just read. That's when vibrant blue eyes snapped open, and one of the survivors shot herkie jerkily up to a sitting position with a feral expression and howled.

Crowded hells…

CHAPTER FIVE

After the first unbreathing, blue-eyed, corrupted survivor sat up, it was like watching prairie dogs as more eyes and heads sprang into sitting positions. Rocky took a deep breath, and like a scene from a horror movie, the noise of that made all of the eyes triangulate on his position. He gulped. He made a quick decision and felt himself frown; unfortunately, he had to warn everyone, and he had to do it now!

So, he steeled his resolve and shouted at the top of his lungs, "Wakethecluckup! Hurrythe– Gwahh!" As he screamed, the horde of at least a thousand undead survivors sprang to their feet and began closing the ten-foot gap in a slow, plodding mob. The good news was that they were moving slowly, and it didn't look like they had any intelligence behind those inhuman, blue, swirling eyes.

The bad news came a moment later as they all opened their mouths in unison and screeched into the semi illuminated Arena. The rounded roof and walls reverberated the sound around the room, and Rocky fell to his knees as a debuff floated to join his laundry list of others.

Remorseful Cadence
- **You have been forced to feel the emotions attached to the death of loved ones. This call affects one living human for every newly risen undead in the horde. Current affected in Raid party 1125. Lasts until the one linked with your call has met their final death.**
    +50% more powerful emotional response
    -3 Strength
    -2 Stamina
    -3 Wisdom

-3 Charisma

Rocky felt the same loss and dark depression he had when his father had died. Then he felt a surge of cold anger begin to rise up from deep in his gut. Something inside of him bellowed with every emotion he could ever remember feeling.

You cannot force me to feel this again!

Then what he called his inner demon came fully awake with its anger amplified. Rocky stood up slowly and drew his sword as smoke poured off his shoulders. He reached up, touched his ear, and felt his nano under armor cover the lower half of his face. He kissed the flat of his Soul Sword, currently in the shape of a katana, to his forehead in respect for the fallen survivors and shot forward.

He took the head off the leading creature with his first strike and then was forced to backpedal as hands shot into the forming Dark Cloak questing for his flesh. He grimaced and pulled a throwing dagger from the bandolier slung around his waist. He let fly and struck a Zombie uselessly in the shoulder. He grimaced and reminded himself that he needed to practice with the ranged weapons.

That was when the military formed up behind him, and around one hundred laser rifles took aim. Rocky glanced back and noticed that most of the remaining army was on the ground, rolled into fetal positions and crying. The group hesitated for a split second, not wanting to shoot the images of people they had known and protected a few hours ago. The moment of hesitation stretched on.

Rocky screamed at them to fire, but only a few tensed trigger fingers, the laser bolts tearing through undead flesh but not killing enough of them. The horde continued to plod forward, and Rocky felt his anger surge hotter as he continued to scream and fought desperately to keep the crowd back from the militia.

Sela, in human form, joined him a moment later, and they still weren't able to make any headway, as they were forced to strike and retreat or be overwhelmed. Azoth's roar sounded from across the cavern, but the Chimera wasn't fully unparalyzed as was evidenced by only his front feet working to try to drag his massive, two-ton carcass into battle. Sela and Rocky continued to scream at the militiamen who let off occasional gunfire. However, the majority held their fire right up until the first creature reached the line and bit savagely into the man's bracing arm that held his rifle.

The man screamed, and then all hell broke loose. In amongst the healthy survivors, undead began to rise. Some of the initial group had been too scared to admit they had the strange bruising patterns of the spattered rain. They didn't wish to be quarantined away from their loved ones. Now they bit savagely into those same loved ones' flesh.

Joe finally overcame his own debuff as his men and his charges began dying, and he shouted out, "Kill them, damnit! Fire now, you maggots!" That was when the military started unloading into the plodding horde, and the waking, healthy survivors scattered or attacked the corrupt members in their midst.

Once the military attacked in earnest, the unarmoured and low leveled horde of undead didn't stand a chance. Unfortunately, the hesitation had already cost them. They weren't dead yet, but they were now showing the same symptoms as the original group of the infected survivors had been. Rocky swore and looked at his arm, where he could see blood welling from a bite mark through the Nanoweave under armor.

He quickly glanced at his debuff bar, and an eyebrow raised unbiddenly. He didn't have any debuffs?

Is this how all of those survivors died? Not sure what was even happening. Not able to see it coming…

He felt frustrated tears well up in his eyes at this world. Not for his impending death but for the deaths of all these innocents that were at his feet. Suddenly, he heard Sela scream his name, and he turned to see a group of at least two hundred Zombies digging at an area on the floor.

He walked over, and the military joined him. They stood poised, pointing their weapons at the undead. The undead didn't even respond to their presence and just continued to dig into the floor with bleeding and broken hands. They dug with a ferocity that Rocky found unnerving, mouths curled in a rictus snarl and drool dripping down their chins.

"Gladiator! Stop them before they reach and corrupt my core... please!" a familiar voice echoed through the chamber. It was almost unrecognizable as it was filled with desperation and fear. Before it had been professional and announcer-like in its word choice.

Rocky jumped at the sound, then shook his head and told the military to open fire. He wouldn't allow the undead to destroy the Dungeon that was playing host to the remaining survivors—even if he wasn't long for this world. A moment later, the cavern had two hundred more corpses adorning its rock tiled floor.

Rocky shook his head sadly at the needless death and told the nearest group of militiamen to strip. Sela and Rocky inspected the fifty individuals and confirmed only one had been bitten. After that, Rocky piped up, "I have also been bitten. Everyone who has not been marked, go and inspect others. Have them form lines and make sure no one tries to hide their injuries. I am not yet showing symptoms. So, don't assume that people will show symptoms if they are infected."

As everyone began to leave, he felt a small hope rise in his chest; his head still downcast, he asked, "Sela, this isn't an illusion is it?"

Since there was no response, he looked up. Sela's eyes were wet, her lips twisted and quivering. Rocky quickly changed the subject, fighting the forming lump in his throat, fiercely holding back his own tears, "Sela, you go see to the women in the group. Try to keep them separate and private as they might be a little self-conscious of having their bodies inspected. As you clear more ladies, have them help." Then he turned to look at others, not able to look at her sadness and stay strong. To the group, as a whole, he stated flatly, "Have the infected sent to me."

As the group left, he sat down with the other infected militiaman. Sela stood staring at him for a time before she too dropped her head and moved off. Rocky turned to the other member of the 'cool kids' club' and smiled wanly. "Looks like we get to wait." Rocky Analyzed the man to at least find out his name.

Joshua Kent
Level 9
Apprentice Deadshot
Health Points 55/100

Joshua opened his mouth, and his voice was trembling, "How can you be so calm about this… sir? I mean, do you not see the debuff that is slowly counting down? It's ambiguous and doesn't say we'll die at the end of it, but evidence suggests…" He gestured at the nearby corpses that were sinking into the ground.

Rocky froze and double-checked his debuffs. No, he still didn't have one. "*Joshua*, I need you to tell me *exactly* what that debuff says."

"*Okay*, can't you just *read* yours? But yeah—sure, whatever. Irradiated Ether Bite. You have been infected with corrupted Ether by an infected bite that is attempting to change your body. This terrible Ether has latched on to your Ether pool and needs to be cleansed. Otherwise, it will succeed. Time is short."

Rocky shook his head and tried to understand what that could mean.

Maybe it was because his Ether pool was practically empty and so this foreign Ether hadn't had anything to grab on to? Worth a shot...

"Do you have any skills or spells that use Ether, Joshua?" Rocky asked, staring at the young man pointedly. The man nodded slowly, clearly unsure where this was going. Rocky couldn't figure out why the others hadn't had this debuff.

Maybe this is a debuff for people bitten, and there isn't a debuff for the people who got hit by the rain?

He crossed his fingers and continued hopefully, "Whatever that skill or spell is, could you cast it repeatedly until you drain yourself of all of your Ether pool?"

Joshua nodded a little more vigorously, starting to see where Rocky was going. He stood up and picked up his rifle beside him and aimed it at a wall away from everyone else in the cavern. Then he fired off round after round, empowering his skill into each shot. One talent was obvious to Rocky as each shot stuck the same spot on the wall, which was at least one hundred feet in distance. The second skill of the man wasn't as evident, however, so he asked, "What skills do you have?"

"Deadly Accuracy and Armor Punch. The second is not doing much against that wall over there, but I assure you lasers don't normally dig furrows into solid stone." He continued firing, and a moment later, Rocky's eyebrows rose when each shot began missing the spot on the wall and just leaving scorch marks where they did strike.

"That's odd," Joshua looked at his weapon like it was at fault, "I have fifteen Ether in my pool according to my character sheet, but I can't imbue it into a shot. And I only have ten shots left with this rifle." Rocky blinked and then motioned Joshua to come to sit with him again.

So, either it was because my Ether pool was already empty or something else was at play here...

He couldn't go back in time and empty Joshua's Ether pool. So, Rocky started thinking about anything that could have cleansed his Ether pool. That's when he remembered what had happened after the second wave of Ether had struck earth. Rocky had meditated and learned a skill called Ether Manipulation. He tilted his head as other afflicted survivors began coming over to sit with the two, all of them with fear on their faces and a resigned cast to their eyes.

Not on my watch!

Rocky put up a single finger toward Joshua in the clear 'give me a moment' gesture and then closed his eyes, diving into himself like he had during that second Ether crash. He had forgotten to do any sort of meditative exercises over the hell march, and it showed as his inner channels were sloppy and unkempt. Luckily, they were still circulating his Dark Ether pool. His skin started sweating when he found the foreign Ether attempting to cling to any Ether that was present in his body. While it hadn't succeeded yet, if it had been left their long enough, it would have.

In his mind's eye, he stopped circulating his Ether and allowed the corrupted parts to latch on to his shifting pool. Then with a vindictive smile, he gathered up his entire Ether pool that remained, forced it out of his body, and dumped it into the ambient Ether around him. He instantly got a massive headache, but when he exited his Meditation, he saw two notices in front of him.

Irradiated Ether Bite
- **You have been infected with corrupted Ether by an infected bite that is attempting to change your body. This terrible Ether has latched on to**

**your Ether pool and needs to be cleansed.
Otherwise, it will succeed. Time is short.**

—

**You have successfully cleansed Irradiated Ether Bite.
Congratulations! You have learned a new skill.**

Ether-Cleanse
- **Ether Cleanse is a spell that can purge
  corrupted Ether or Ether-based poisons from
  your system. This spell is only castable on
  yourself and utilizes a portion of your Ether to
  isolate and remove the corruption.**
    **Weak - Each level decreases the amount
    of personal Ether needed for each
    cleanse.**

Current rank: Weak Ether-Cleanse Level 1.

That was good news and bad news for him. First, he now
knew how to save everyone who was already sitting around him
and anyone who joined them every few minutes. However, he
was under a time constraint. Rocky looked over to the hole in the
ground where the infected undead had been digging and
queried, "Dungeon, can you please create a stage for me?"

The Dungeon responded haughtily, "My name is
Maximus. I don't respond to Dungeon."

Rocky blinked rapidly and sucked in a breath, waiting
for more. When it didn't come, he shook his head.

Okay. Moody much!

"Maximus, could you please create a stage for me? I
need everyone to be able to see me." Rocky was rewarded with
the sound of shifting stone, and then suddenly, he was flung into
the air as the ground under him became a perfect, round pillar
and pistoned him up.

He came down on his stomach, and all his held breath was forced out of him. He gingerly got to his feet and dusted himself off, muttering about, "ungrateful Dungeons," under his breath. Then he climbed on to the raised, round dais in front of the shocked and confused but slowly growing crowd of forty infected.

He coughed into his hand to cover some of his embarrassment at what just happened. "Alright, everyone! Anyone who is currently doing nothing, I would like you all to gather around. I am going to try to teach you a skill that will make what just happened treatable. For anyone infected currently, I need you to pay extra attention and learn this now. We are going to start with Meditation."

He sat down in a meditative posture and began explaining as best he could what the Samurai Training Scroll had taught him. He kept a calm and slow cadence to his speech, pulling from yoga and meditation videos he had listened to during his basketball career. He sat there for about half an hour until the very last of the infected raised a sweating hand joyously proclaiming that they had learned the Meditation skill.

Then he raised a hand and told them they were only halfway there and continued teaching them to sense their own Ether and how to begin circulating it through their bodies. It was frustrating work, mostly because of the unknown timer that hung over all of their heads. The first infected turned quickly, and Rocky had to surmise that it was because the rain was concentrated when compared to the bite.

As soon as people learned the skill, they were able to dump out their Ether. Rocky, who had since been hobbling around and helping each person individually with the exercises, tried desperately to explain the process over and over again, his mind in a fog. Unfortunately, time ran out for ten people, and when he saw them slump out of the meditative posture, he knew.

With frustrated tears in his eyes, he decapitated each of the fallen so they couldn't rise to attack their loved ones.

As soon as the last newly dead Zombie's head hit the floor, Rocky fell to the ground like a stringless puppet and was asleep halfway to the floor.

CHAPTER SIX

Rocky awoke after his first full eight hours of sleep in almost a week and wanted to roll over and go back to sleep. This was the first time in weeks he didn't have to worry about the next monster attack or how to stay awake and scout. However, he had one of those headaches that spoke of oversleeping, and he knew he wouldn't get back to bed. So, he stretched audibly and sat up.

A wolf skin blanket slipped off of his form, and he smiled, knowing he hadn't had the cognitive process to pull it out the previous night. Sela must have come by and tucked him in. He quite literally was a few feet from his makeshift, pedestal stage. He must have passed out instantly upon completing the Meditation and Ether Manipulation training session.

He glanced up at his debuff bar and sighed with relief. Most of the debuffs had dropped off, and a few others had lost some stacks.

Debuffs

Skunk Shower
- **You have been sprayed by an evolved monster, Peppy Le Skunk.**
- **Effects -50% Charisma.**
- **Lasts until treated.**

Unclean x9
- **You have not bathed or showered in over a week.**
- **Effects -30% Wisdom, -25% Charisma.**
- **+60% Chance of catching Disease.**
- **Lasts until showered or bathed.**

Weakened Body
- **Your body has been pushed beyond its current limits.**
- **-25% Recovery of Ether and Health.**

Toxic Blood
- **You have high PH levels in your blood due to high use of Alchemy Potions.**
- **-50% Effectiveness of Future Potions.**
- **Lasts 24 hours, will renew and increase every time a potion is used.**

He had gained stacks of Unclean, which made him nervous, as the chance of disease had further increased, but in that same vein, he hadn't really been given an opportunity to jump into a safe lake to bathe either. His Weakened Body had recovered slightly, and if he could go today without imbibing a potion, he would be free of toxic blood. The Skunk Shower probably required an Alchemy Potion to cleanse.

His Charisma stat being hampered by seventy-five percent wasn't great and explained a lot of the strange looks he got. However, because of his Leadership class, his Charisma was far higher than it would have been anyway, so he took the reduction in stride.

He considered getting up and making breakfast, but before that, he should probably check his notifications. A quick thought brought up all the windows he'd skipped and minimized yesterday. He clicked recap to condense them.

For killing 1 Reptilian Creature: Level Master 25: Your group has been awarded 523,031 Etherience.

For killing 4 Mammalian Creatures: Level Journeyman 35-49: Your group has been awarded 322,200 Etherience.

For clearing an Arena Dungeon: Waves 1-15: Your group has been awarded 1,243,343 Etherience.

Your personal Etherience amounts to: 479,882 Etherience

For killing 1,043 Ether Warped Sapients: Level Apprentice 4-9: Your raid has been awarded 32,324,643 Etherience.

Your personal Etherience amounts to: 113,412.

    51,809,737 Etherience remaining until level 23.

—

Congratulations! You have reached level 22! You have been awarded 1 Stat point and 1 Skill point.

    51,809,737 Etherience remaining until level 23.

—

Congratulations! Your Soul Blade "Dark Tidings" has consumed enough souls to gain a level!

Dark Tidings – Soul Blade

    Level 6

        150/150 Ether Pool

    The Strength of Arms VI

+12 Strength as long as the Blade has Ether from its pool to draw on. Unlock higher levels of your Soul Blade for more.

The Strength of Body VI
+6 Stamina as long as the Blade has Ether from its pool to draw on. Unlock higher levels of your Soul Blade for more.

* Dark Tidings refuses to absorb any more Golem Essence. Find it a new source of sustenance. *

* Dark Tidings has found its favorite sustenance. Sapient Essence will count double. *
—

Congratulations! You have learned a new skill! Teaching
- You have attempted to teach others and gained a skill for teaching. A good teacher forces a student to learn, a great teacher grows with them.

   Weak – Each level increases the chance to impart the desired information to others.

Current rank Weak-Teacher Level 1

The first two Etherience gain summaries were from before the Dungeon, and he ran his tongue over his teeth. He'd managed to climb to level 22, which was good news and probably had done so before the bonus for the Dungeon completion.

He sobered from his momentary elation when he reached the final summary. Over a thousand people had died, and the system had just equated it to Etherience gains. The last notification mentioned that the Etherience had been split between the raid, and by his small portion, he assumed that everyone in the Dungeon had been somehow included.

Looking around the room, he realized that many of the remaining survivors looked slightly healthier, and he Analyzed a few just to check his hypothesis. The fact that they were all level 10 and above now confirmed it.

The first few kills had been shared between Sela, Zippo, Joe, Azoth, and himself. The rewards for killing Dungeon monsters and the Dungeon bonus had only been the four, not including Joe, but based off of the drastic increase in the remaining survivor's levels, it would appear that the system had included everyone in the raid.

The Etherience being shared was similar to bailing water manually on the Titanic after it hit that iceberg, but it was something. The chocolate icing on top of the turd cake, so to speak. Rocky felt instant guilt at the thought that this was probably a better starting point for his Territory.

Maybe it's better to just hike the last leg and get into the Territory before eating breakfast? I mean, we have to be really close, and it would be much safer– Wait, what if that storm hit the valley?

He felt cold sweat break out all over his skin, and he shot to his feet, panic written across his face. Sela, who was nearby and was also just waking up, jumped. She stared at him with wide eyes, and after a moment of him standing stock-still, she asked, "What is it, Rockland?"

"That storm must have hit the Territory. What if we go back and all the people are–" Rocky's throat closed at the horror of his realization.

Despite his panic, Sela yawned aggressively, smiled, and answered amusedly, "You are forgetting what I told you; Territories have Ether regulation in place, and the outer limits of the Territory would have warded off anything like that storm." She stretched languidly before continuing in a serious tone,

"However, those limits will erode in time if storms of that magnitude continue to strike."

Rocky felt his shoulder drop away from his ears, and he sighed deeply as the fog of sleep cleared from his mind. He'd spent a grand total of perhaps a day in his Territory. He knew the Territory was one of his strongest assets because owning Algonquin Valley increased his stats gained per level from two to four. It also gave him the ability to promote its inhabitants to military ranks, which made their stats acquired per level rise from two to three. In essence, his Territory was going to make everyone in it stronger and safer by leagues.

He looked around again at the remaining survivors and grew gloomy, remembering his further failure to maintain his oath of the previous night.

It wasn't like he would have been able to figure out that his Ether Manipulation skill had the potential it did without events playing out as they had, but that didn't stop him from mourning the loss of so much life. He decided to start the day by trying to teach anyone who didn't acquire the skill yesterday. Not only did this skill make it possible to cleanse the corruption from the Irradiated Ether, but it also increased the Ether gains per fight as well as lowered the personal Ether cost of skills. In summary, it was a great addition to anyone who was living in his Territory.

When he voiced his intention and asked for the military to gather everyone up and inform them of the session, Sela stood up and gave him a funny look. Then with shock and a little respect in her voice, she added, "I want you to *know* that in my *day*, you would be considered an *idiot* for sharing such a valuable *skill* and *ability*. This *one* skill would have set you apart from *everyone* in time, and you are just *giving* it away?"

Rocky took a deep breath, but Sela forestalled him with a raised finger; her eyes grew distant as she continued sadly, "I am not criticizing you! Truthfully, having this skill when I was alive would have probably saved my life."

She paused to look up at the ceiling, and her voice grew angry, "Considering that many people within my guild were mighty, I doubt no one had discovered this *skill*. I can *honestly* say that I am conflicted because if that is true, my family let me die!"

Her head snapped down, and her eyes, filled with hurt, bored into Rocky. She continued after a moment, her voice filled with more emotion than Rocky could discern, "But I can't help but think about ways to protect its secret from enemies…"

Rocky tilted his head, having not considered that this skill would be something that would make his enemies stronger if they learned it. Truthfully, he didn't think he had any enemies. Right now, he was operating under the modus operandi of saving anyone he could and preventing the deaths of humans as a species. However, his most recent trip to Ottawa and Corsair's evil spoke volumes about his innocent thoughts.

He opened his mouth, "How could you even *protect* something knowledge-based?"

Sela shook her head and forced a knowing smile. Her voice smoothed as she responded, "We should make forming a guild top priority. Then make this skill proprietary to the guild. If you do that, then anyone who leaves the organization would lose access to the skill and would be unable to teach it as well. Maybe have a chat with everyone this morning about the importance of not sharing it to bridge the gap?"

From Sela's smile, Rocky could tell that she already had the last little speech planned before they had even started the conversation. He shook his head at her artful mastery of teaching in a way that allowed him to believe it had been him reaching a conclusion. In truth, she had reached the conclusion the previous day, and she knew Rocky was stubborn and had rightfully worried that telling him to be careful who he shared this with would make him obstinate. While he'd lost much of his naivety, he still operated on the belief that humans were one group, and they were all in this together.

After his speech and subsequent practice in Meditation, Ether Channels, and Ether Manipulation, Rocky walked to the entrance that everyone had entered through. The Dungeon had raised the door after the storm ended, but that didn't mean that they could leave this way. A slowly draining pool of steaming, fluorescent blue water resided at the bottom of the entryway, and Rocky didn't think swimming through Irradiated Ether would be safe, no matter how many people had learned the new skills.

Some people had still failed in the second session, and Rocky was beginning to see a correlation between people with a low Intelligence stat and failure to be able to sense the Ether inside or outside of themselves. They had all been able to learn Meditation, but a good thirty percent hadn't been able to pick up the Ether Channels and Ether Manipulation skill yet.

Rocky assumed the group could wait out the evaporation and slow drain of the storm waters, but he also remembered the Dungeon mentioning a backdoor. So, he walked over to the repaired hole in the floor and asked, "Hey, Max, any chance you can open up the back door and let us leave?"

"I can… but since you owe me so much, I have a favor to ask you, Gladiator," a bodiless voice spoke from everywhere in the cavern, which made all the survivors jump and look around. Rocky just recoiled and tilted his head, wondering where the Dungeon was going with this.

"You see… all of that corrupted Ether you brought in here, and the corrupted water in the entrance is slowly seeping into my constructed body. Now, I know how to cleanse my Ether already like you have shown everyone else. The problem is that I cleanse the Ether and the Irradiated Ether just seeps back into my body. This has also removed my ability to gather all of my Ether and move to a new location. So… I am hoping you can take my core and move me to a new area unaffected by that Ether Storm?"

Rocky easily heard the desperation in the Dungeon's voice and inwardly smiled. Perhaps Maximus' predicament was his fault, but that didn't mean he couldn't use it to his advantage. Currently, Rocky was assuming that the nuclear meltdown in Chalk River was causing the Irradiated Ether as well as the storms. While he had no idea how he was going to stop it, he did know that he had to. First, his Territory was far too close to the site, and secondly, he had a quest because of Sela's unique class!

Red Quest
    Party Quest - Druid
        Contain the Destruction
A location near your Territory has suffered an enormously destructive force which has warped the Ether. The outcome of this tragedy is yet unknown. Gaia wishes for you to examine or contain the potential threat this may pose.
    Rewards:
        Etherience
        Crystallized Ether
        Greater Territorial Perk

He looked over the quest again as he deliberated. The Dungeon interrupted him with a very helpful reminder, "Also, Gladiator, are you going to loot Monstar or are you just going to force me to look at his mutilated body until the elapsed time runs out and I can reabsorb him?" Rocky grimaced, having wholly forgotten the loot in the ensuing chaos.

I guess it was a little hectic after the win… The survivors rushed the court, so to speak!

His greed menagerie perked up excitedly as he walked over to the beach ball crushed corpse of the Spider. Wondering what type of loot the corpse held, Rocky touched it and mentally thought, "Loot." A moment later, he was holding a silk robe of some kind and a gnarled staff. He used Analyze on them.

Spider Silk Robe of the Arachnid
- **This robe was created from the silk webbing of Monstar the Spider, Arena Dungeon Stage 15 Boss Monster.**
  - **Quality: Great**
  - **Stats: Unknown**

——

Staff of the Arachnid Eye
- **This staff uses an Eye of Monstar the Spider, Arena Dungeon Stage 15 Boss Monster, as its focus, with a carved staff of Elder Wood as its Ether pool component.**
  - **Quality: Great**
  - **Stats: Unknown**

Once he read the names of both, he noticed that the staff had a round Spider eye clutched in a wooden carving of eight Spider legs. The robe was subtler, but it had a webbed pattern either woven or embossed on to it. They both made his skin crawl, but that didn't mean he wouldn't be getting them unlocked at the shop. If they were good items, perhaps Zippo could use them or some other caster in the Territory. Rocky stored them in his bag of holding.

Standing back up, Rocky dusted himself off and looked around the chamber, finding Azoth exploring the cave and many others looking at his group curiously. They could all hear one side of the conversation, but not his, so curiosity was natural.

"Don't get used to that level of loot, Combatant. You were the first to clear my Dungeon, so I had to give you the good stuff," Maximus the Dungeon huffily interrupted his thoughts as Rocky walked back in the direction of where his core was.

Boy, this guy sure is temperamental. It's like he doesn't trust us at all.

"Listen, Max, I can help you out, no problem, but the only safe place in the area is my Territory…" Rocky left the end of his sentence floating, hoping that the Dungeon would take the bait.

Maximus was silent for a moment but then answered in a very monotone voice, "Are you suggesting placing me as one of your four Cardinal Dungeons?" The way he said the last bit made Rocky raise an eyebrow as he realized Maximus had just used "Cardinal Dungeon" as a proper name.

What the hell does that even mean?

Sela had begun walking over to him and so had Zippo and Joe. They had been hearing one side of the conversation this whole time, but the last thing the Dungeon had uttered must have perked up all of their ears.

Sela was, of course, the first to speak, and it wasn't to Rocky that she directed her question but the Dungeon, "Listen, Dungeon, what is the meaning of 'Cardinal Dungeon', and what are you proposing?" Sela's voice was very stern, and Rocky's eyebrows shot up into his hairline.

Sela had killed numerous Dungeons in her past life and, for some reason, had an inherent mistrust of the constructs. Rocky hadn't had the time to ask her about it, but he could tell by her tone that she hadn't gotten over that particular aversion and probably wouldn't anytime soon.

"As I have told Rockland Barkclay, my name is Maximus, and I will be addressed as such," Maximus responded glibly, and Sela's face turned a deep shade of red. Her jaw muscles hardened–

Before it got out of hand, Rocky interrupted, "Maximus, I understand that calling you Dungeon must be considered rude as there are many of you. However, I need you to understand that the lady you are taunting is one of my closest companions." He paused for a moment before adding under his breath, "She is also extremely dangerous."

Sela smiled wickedly, and her eyes softened slightly at Rocky's words. Rocky wasn't much of a mediator, but he knew which side he would lean to if this 'Cardinal Dungeon' nonsense wasn't above board. The sound of shifting stone suddenly sounded, and Sela was encased in a cage of hardened brick.

Turns out it can hear pretty well... Honestly, LFD was so much more open and pleasant than this pompous hoplite!

Rocky's face went ashen, and he groaned. He turned the groan into an exasperated tone, "I think we have gotten off track here, Max. Just answer her questions and let her out. Otherwise, I don't think I will even consider whatever it is that you are proposing with this cardinal nonsense."

The glare Sela gave him through the bars she was now attempting to break apart with her hands could have melted metal. Her teeth were bared preternaturally, and her face would have made a thundercloud jealous.

After a long pause, the rock cage receded slowly, which caused Sela to let go of the bars. Rocky looked at her pointedly to try to rein her in.

Max answered, despite the staring contest, "Stupid humans, I am young and know very little of this world, but I do know that every Territory can make an alliance with up to four Dungeons. These Dungeons are called Cardinal Dungeons as they are placed in the North, South, East, and West of a Territory. It is a mutual agreement between leaders and the Dungeons. That is all I know from the readings I have access to."

Sela closed her mouth with a click and then obstinately asked, "Why have I never heard of these Dungeons then? If every Territory can have them, why have I never seen them?" She looked at Rocky with an expression so torn he could literally feel raw emotion radiating from her. What the full range of that emotion consisted of was hard to determine, but he could see the hurt in her eyes.

"I don't have answers to that question, angry woman. All I can tell you is that the documents I have access to claim that it is of great mutual benefit to both Dungeons and leaders. It implies that all Dungeons should strive to become one of these Cardinal Dungeons."

Joe and Zippo had been standing together, looking out of their depth through most of the conversation. Now though, Joe looked at Rocky and Sela before adding imploringly, "This could be really good for the Territory, don't you think?"

Rocky just raised a hand to forestall any further discussion and motioned for everyone to gather in a circle to talk. Looking over his shoulder at the hole, he apologized, "Sorry, Max, we are just going to discuss this really quick. Would you mind giving us a little privacy?"

"I'm kind of aware of everything that happens inside these walls, Gladiator, but I will try to be… elsewhere for a time."

Rocky addressed his next question to Sela, "What is your issue with Dungeons, Sela?"

Sela clenched her jaw and looked away before answering with heat in her voice, "I lost a lot of young recruits to Dungeons. Friends, family, and even lovers." She looked back to him. "Rocky, I get that this isn't the same world, but it was gospel when I lived that Dungeons were evil invaders of Gaia. None of the Dungeons spoke to us, for example…"

Sela drew in a deep, exasperated breath. "No one would ever consider letting one live. There were rumors that farming them for Etherience made them stronger. If this mutual pact existed, I can't understand why the leaders of my time were in a perpetual war with the Dungeons."

Licking her incisors, she added, "Every time I entered a Dungeon, I knew it was life or death. The Dungeon knew it was life or death. I just can't believe that the leaders…"

Rocky was taken aback at the vehemence in her voice. It was clear she was angry not only at the Dungeon they stood within but with the memory of the people she knew. Either they had lied to her all those years ago, or something was drastically different in this new world.

"Sela, do you not want to get to the bottom of this? Why would this Dungeon lie to us? If it is lying, we would just destroy it once it sets up in our Territory. I truly think that having Dungeons in Algonquin Valley will only benefit everyone inside. I mean, if handled right, it should be a safe training area for everyone, including the Non-Power Classes you mentioned."

Sela waved her hand at Rocky, telling him that she didn't want to answer the questions or that she didn't have good answers to the questions. Rocky looked to the remaining two. "What do you two think?"

They both glanced at Sela with concern and then at Rocky. Zippo shrugged like a typical teenager looking longingly at Azoth playing in the back of the cavern. Joe, who was very much interested in the outcome, mused, "I think I agree with Rocky," a look from Sela made him hastily add, "but let's see what this process would entail before we commit to anything?"

Rocky shrugged and called out to the Dungeon. For the next half hour, the group listened and asked questions of Maximus. Sela brooded the entire process but kept her animosity in check because that was what Rocky wanted. She had asked a few questions of her own and had even used the Dungeon's name, which he also appreciated.

It turned out there was a contract of sorts between the Cardinal Dungeons and the Leader of a Territory. In the contract, the leader could specify terms, and the Dungeon would be forced to follow them. The Dungeon had standard terms that must be upheld, as well. The Dungeon shied away from a great many questions, which made Rocky skeptical, but because of the implied benefit, it didn't stop him from being interested.

At the end of the conversation, they had reached a point of wait and see. The group was going to bring the core to Algonquin Valley with them, and they would decide whether to form this agreement after they saw the terms of the contract. Otherwise, Rocky agreed to fly the Dungeon core far enough away from the meltdown.

I wonder what has become of LFD if this Dungeon is in such dire straits…

CHAPTER SEVEN

After the agreement was reached, the Dungeon, as its last act inside of its former body, opened the back passageway, and Rocky collected the strange, opalescent stone that rose to the surface in front of him. It was very beautiful but also raw and uncut. It reminded him of a baseball-sized piece of salt with its smoky interior and rough, cloudy edges. However, it glowed a vibrant indigo-blue that he was forced to look away from.

Rocky had placed it in his backpack and had worn it for the remainder of the trip to Algonquin Valley. He wasn't wanting to put such a unique and precious, possibly living thing in his bag of holding, not trusting that the space would keep it alive or that it wouldn't react poorly with the construct. The passageway exited a good kilometer away from where they came in, and Joe sent a team to collect the tanks and the soldiers inside them who had been left by the main entrance. Luckily, with the tops closed, the tanks were watertight, and while the soldiers were a little shaken up by the ferocity and sounds they'd heard, they hadn't lost any.

The group left the Dungeon just before noon, Rocky estimated. They had decided to have a quick breakfast while still in the safety of the walls of the Dungeon, and now with everyone fully rested, no one complained. He glanced back at the group of survivors and reconsidered their silence. While he met many individual's eyes, more often than not, those eyes were unfocused and unseeing. Each individual was reliving the night before, and he wondered how many were numb to it like he felt?

He faced front and then craned his neck up into the sky to try to see Sela's raven form through the interspersed canopy of trees. It was getting a bit too dense to make out her or Azoth up there, and he considered calling them back. He dismissed the thought shortly thereafter, knowing that at least one of them was able to make that decision for herself. Rocky bit his inner cheek;

they'd already been walking for a few hours and were extremely close to the edge of Algonquin Valley, but he was unsure exactly how far.

Something in the distance caught his eye, and he held back a curse, thinking it was movement. Squinting and tilting his head, he became surer nothing was there, but something was definitely strange. Tongue tracing his incisor, he tilted his head to glance at the tree he was walking under and then quickly looked forward about two hundred meters. Next, he tried looking for what trick of the light or shadow was causing the trees in the distance to look brighter and more vivid.

Unable to discover it from this distance, he continued to lead the group forward. About halfway to the destination, Sela and Azoth crashed through the canopy, one of them gracefully landing beside him. The other shook the ground with his uncoordinated, bulky frame.

Sela changed back to her human form, and although he had seen it many times, he watched with fascination. Her feathers receded, and large raven wings suddenly began to take on the shape of human arms. Since her raven form was quite close in size to her human one, she didn't enlarge or shrink noticeably, but within a few heartbeats, her eyes and beak had changed to become the beautiful and familiar face of Sela. Rocky was entirely unsure what happened to her armor and clothes during the transformation, but every time she returned to human, she had them on.

Are you disappointed with that?

Luckily, as soon as she had a human mouth again, she interrupted his thoughts with a statement, "Those greener trees up ahead denote the boundary."

Rocky's eyes widened, and his head snapped forward, then he hesitantly queried, "Why are they greener, though? What has happened to these trees?" He motioned to the trees nearest them.

Sela looked at the tree he had indicated. "Two reasons I can think of. First, Algonquin Valley benefits from certain bonuses that will aid growth of fauna and resources. Secondly, I think the Ether Storms have been raging in this area for a while now. So, the lackluster appearance of these trees may indicate that they are struggling to continually cleanse themselves of the corrupted Ether."

His jaw clenched, and he nodded solemnly, recalling the Red Quest to investigate the area that was most likely responsible for this. Perhaps leaving it for later all those weeks ago was a bad idea. A quick look back allowed him to dismiss that errant thought as they resumed walking. He'd saved all these people, even if they weren't his family.

Sela pushed his mind off the depressing thoughts a moment later, "I only have two charges for shape-shifting for the day." At his raised eyebrow, she smiled. "I stopped in at Algonquin Gorge and told them we would be there around dinner time. I also dropped off a good portion of the meat we had collected into the Territorial Inventory. I believe they will try to prepare an impromptu feast and celebration, if I read the mood right."

Rocky felt his shoulders creep up his neck. Speaking for himself, having a party seemed like a horrible idea.

What would they celebrate? All the death? His failures?

But Sela's smiling face made him pause. Sela noticed his change in mood and shook her head. "In war and life, you must always find something to celebrate. If you fail to see the positives that surround you, your soul will wither and blacken, until one day, the whole world is *against* you."

Rocky blinked. "Where did that come from?"

"My father used to tell me that when I was in a poor mood," she somberly added and looked up through the canopy towards the sun. "I think it applies to our current situation.

There are going to be a lot of unhappy people in the days to come."

She slowly lowered her head and came to a stop right at the dividing line between the healthy trees and the rest of the forest. She brought a hand up and wiped a sparkling tear from her cheek and continued, "You have brought them to an unbuilt and unmanned Territory. If you think our struggles are over, I think you will be very disappointed. But that doesn't mean we can't celebrate the accomplishment!"

Rocky felt his chest tighten around a lump in his throat. He couldn't even imagine what she was going through. He was about to reach out to… squeeze her shoulder, hug her, something, but people walking by them, and the notification changed the mood.

Welcome back to Algonquin Valley, Leader.
Level 1 Territory
Current Population: 128
Would you like a rundown of the events that have taken place since you were gone?
Significant events: 2
Minor events: 0

Yes | <No>

He watched as the current population climbed higher. Every individual who passed over the threshold bumped it up, and the system reacted in spurts. As he watched, he continued to move forward but glanced over his shoulder to see people's reactions. Each person who crossed the threshold reacted differently, but all of them seemed surprised for a moment, and then they made strange hand gestures at something in front of them. When they finished, they would look up and around themselves with a wide smile plastered on their face.

They had made it!

Once Joe at the very back of the group crossed the threshold, a corner blinked at him once. He did a quick check of the final population and had mixed feelings. The current population had stopped at 3,992, and while he was happy to have made it back with a large group, he was slightly discouraged by not holding up his promise to himself. He realized that making it back with everyone was impossible, but that didn't make him feel much better.

Rocky closed the welcome message without recapping the significant events. He was already aware of both the rape and the trial that had followed. The reminder only made his teeth hurt as he ground them together. A thought opened up the new notification that had come in.

Congratulations! You have completed a Quest!
Escort Quest
Group Quest
Escort the Ottawa Survivors 1
You have escorted a total of 3,865 of 8,043 to your Territory. As the original quest only specified 10% survival rate and you have managed 48.6%. You will be given an extra 386% Etherience. Great job!
Rewards:
7,563,600 Etherience Awarded.

44,359,549 Etherience remaining until level 23.
—
Ether Protection

Time of Ether assisted protection for Territory: 6 days, 6 hours, 45 minutes, and 22 seconds.

The timer made him grimace. What would happen when it ran out? Would the storms be able to enter the Territory? Would there be a massive monster attack? The storms were unlikely because of what Sela had told him, but the second worry might be possible. He recalled that first day, Sela had definitely explained it was a passive defense that steered sentient creatures away from the Territory, but it wasn't perfect. If the monsters they'd been facing on the way back from Ottawa were going to enter the Territory, Sela was right; they had lots of work to do.

As the caravan continued into the Territory from the threshold, he sent up a prayer for the losses of so many people, but then he forcefully changed his mood, remembering what Sela had just related.

Well, you did just increase the population of your Territory by an extremely large margin. Your goal is to make this place a safe haven and grow it with more survivors. Hopefully, your family will be included in a population increase one day soon.

He refused to consider the possibility that his family hadn't survived. If that was the reality, he would be forced to deal with it when it was confirmed. However, he had firm hopes that his family had been on a University or College campus when this had begun, possibly attending a banquet or awards ceremony.

Fingers crossed. Now stop being maudlin.

Sela took the lead at that point, as Rocky had never been to the Grotto, and she was the only one present who had. The group walked along through Algonquin Valley, crossing paths with lower leveled wildlife that while definitely evolved was nowhere near as dangerous as what the Ottawa hunting groups had been facing. Due to the large group of survivors, even the predatorial creatures just watched from a safe distance.

When they reached the sheer cliff wall an hour later, Rocky assumed they would turn and walk around it. Instead, Sela seemed to walk into a crack that he hadn't initially seen.

The entryway was hidden exceptionally well due to one side of the cliff jutting out and continuing while the other side retracted and stopped. It made an excellent mirage that the cliff face was unbroken. He smiled at this added layer of security for his people; Sela had made an excellent choice, it seemed.

Upon exiting the far side of the passage, Rocky was greeted with a pleasant sight as he looked across a nearly circular clearing which was vast in its dimensions. Near the center, hundreds of logs were stacked and waiting to be processed for building material.

Off far to the left stood the familiar domed building of Arbuckle, an alien metal, that was the shop. As he ran his eyes over the humongous space that could house easily ten times his group's current number, the hundred-plus people spread out through the gorge slowly began to notice the large group of humans entering the Territory and work ceased.

The founding group exuberantly walked over to welcome its newest members. It was both a happy moment and a sad moment as no one knew each other. Rocky could hear questions about family being asked and saw the same moment he'd experienced when people were forced to answer in the unknown or negative.

Tears were shed both in sorrow and joy all around him. The raw emotion nearly made Rocky break down as well. Instead, he forced numb disinterest on himself. He was now the leader of these people, and leaders didn't cry.

He shook some hands of a few people but didn't recognize a single one. Their scrunched noses and quick step away, however, reminded him he desperately needed a shower and chemical de-funker.

He motioned to Joe to get his attention, and they walked to the side. Once away from the group, Rocky looked at him. "I am going to promote you to Captain, the highest rank I can, which should allow you to begin promoting people below you."

He navigated through his leadership screen and added Joe to the same rank Derik held, which soured his mouth as he recalled his first and only interaction with the man. Regardless, as soon as Joe became a Captain, he confusedly asked, "You said I should be able to promote people, right? It seems like that option is grayed out for me?"

"Really?" Rocky asked as he studied his own window. What Joe had noticed made sense in a way because there were only three people successfully promoted on the list he could see: Joe, Smith, and Derik. Jerry Hadfare, the man who'd lost his daughter, had died shortly after Rocky's encounter with him, but Rocky assumed Smith and Derik would have attempted to promote people if they'd been able. It looks like he had made an assumption about people being able to promote under themselves.

The notification had seemed to claim that they could, though? Then he found the boxes beside people's names which needed to be checked. One read approval and the other read declined. All three had it checked declined at the moment, so he went in and gave Joe a check in the approval column. After that change, Joe found that he could approve people and began adding as many people as he could to the ranks below him and the ranks below them.

Rocky was about to walk away when Joe growled and stated, "I can only promote one hundred and fifty-five people in total!"

Sighing, Rocky looked at the new list of people Joe had been adding. Sure enough, there wasn't enough space for the entire military, due to only twenty-five spaces being available in the Second Lieutenant tier and one hundred twenty-five in the Officer Cadet, first tier. This meant that at most they could have one hundred fifty-five members if they included the five third-tier ranks. He would probably need to level his Leadership class to gain more, but currently, it didn't seem active!

There isn't anything I can do about that right this second...

To Joe, he gave a half-smile and shrug before saying, "You'll have to choose carefully who to promote. Extra stats will probably help your fighters more than the admin staff, but that still leaves a huge number that won't get the benefits."

He apologized and excused himself to go to the large river he'd barely been able to make out from the entrance. It abutted the Grotto on the east side. Once he arrived a good fifteen-minute walk later, he noticed that the survivors who had been here for a little over a week had done their best to add a layer of privacy to the bathing area. He smiled at the sign of propriety that still clung on to humans from the world pre-apocalypse.

Forgoing that civilized segregation, he stripped out of his armor and pulled the nanite under armor off back to its black ball composition. Then in his birthday suit, he dove out into the middle of the river.

As he swam and scrubbed, he felt his soul weapon crawl over his skin and smiled wanly. It was an added bit of security for him. While he wasn't really worried about the Ether-mutated wildlife in the river, it didn't hurt to have the weapon always on 'hand'. The fact that it now wanted more human—or rather sapient—essence was terrifying, but he didn't really want to dwell on that too much.

It's not like I am going to be the one converting humans to undead for it... In fact, hopefully, that was all of them.

His last thought rang false even in his head, so Rocky forcibly blanked his mind. He then floated and cleaned himself until the unclean debuff fully fell off, and he was only left with 'Peppy le Skunk'. He assumed that it might take something akin to rolling in talc to get rid of, but his nose had long since gotten immune to the horrendous odor.

Regardless, he exited the water and put back on his self-cleaning nanite under armor. He placed his Chimera Knight's armor in his bag of holding and planned to have it thoroughly cleaned on his visit to the shop later.

Once finished dressing, he made his way towards the construction he could see in the distance. As he neared, he saw a familiar face which was straining to pull on a rope, along with others, to haul a massive cut tree. Rocky jumped forward and put himself into the group. As soon as he joined the rest, a shift in momentum occurred, and the log sped up fractionally in its slide.

Another two hundred fifty feet brought them to the pile, and the group dropped the rope in unison. Smith, the familiar face and one of only three people he'd met who had stayed in the Territory, had his hands on his knees and was breathing heavy. Rocky walked over and patted him on the back, speaking in a tone of gratitude, "Is all this organizing your work?"

Smith lifted his head, sweat trickling down his brow and responded between deep breaths, "Yeah, well, I am… more the… muscle of… the operation." He motioned over his shoulder. "Derik… has been organizing…" He made a motion to encompass everything around them.

Rocky smiled at the Native American man and patted him twice more on the back. "Think you could show me around?"

Smith nodded then took a moment to tell the others helping him that they were done for the day. Rocky smiled at the clear respect the four showed him. As the four walked away, Rocky called after them, "Might want to clean up. We'll be having a party!"

Smith's eyebrows rose before he took on a thoughtful look. "Come on then. We had better hurry. There ain't much to show, honestly."

They walked together to the site of their first building exchanging pleasantries, Smith's Native American lilt comforting to Rocky in its slow cadence. The one and only building under construction was a Longhouse. Smith and Derik had laid out a basic rectangle with trees, and the survivors had even begun attempting to plank some of the wood.

With one hand scratching his head, Smith pointed with the other one at the outline. "The real problem is that no one has any real experience with this." Rocky realized after a slow moment that he wasn't pointing at the whole structure but the planked wood. Smith continued, confirming what Rocky intuited, "No two planks are the same, which means we'll have cracks in the floors and walls. I know you can fill those with mud according to the blueprints Sela showed us, but…"

Smith stopped scratching his head and looked at Rocky seriously. "People are used to a certain way of living, and I think this is going to shock them."

Rocky nodded and asked, "What would make this easier and sturdier?" He looked at the building, then over to the portable forge that stood nearby. "I was already considering getting an automated sawmill."

Smith nodded, and his smile grew larger as he looked over at the Arbuckle shop, "That would be a start. We haven't had access to that yet but heard that it could access some pretty amazing gadgets." He took a pragmatic pause. "You going to give us access?"

As Rocky's mouth drew into a line, while a look of disappointment briefly flickered over Smith's. Rocky opened his mouth to explain, but at Smith's raised hand he paused. Smith put on a half-smile. "Sela told us why when she dropped the thing off, but let's just say there are going to be some… *mixed* emotions about it."

Before Rocky could ask what the heck Smith meant, the man motioned for him to follow him to the woodpile. On the walk over, Smith deftly brought the topic back, "Additionally, people are starting to raise skills that should help speed up and solidify the construction." Smith pointed at his own chest. "My axe cutting is at twenty already and goes up a fair bit each day."

Pointing at the wood, he expanded on his point, "The planking is actually the narrowing point for all this. We might have had walls up already if all of our wood could be converted." Again, he scratched his dark black hair, "I was considering giving it a go tomorrow and converting a good portion of woodcutters over, but if you get a sawmill… that would help a great deal."

After that, Smith excused himself to go get cleaned up and left Rocky alone to contemplate purchases. Creating housing was imperative with so many bodies, and Rocky jumped the sawmill to the number one spot on the shopping list. Thinking about the purchases made him crack a smile when he remembered Garnell.

Garnell was what human mythology would have deemed a Dwarf. He had a stall in the Aretrin Bazaar and seemed to sell building equipment blueprints and materials that would come in useful for a burgeoning Territory.

Don't forget the Dungeon too. If Maximus 'Prickulus Exterious' and I come to an agreement, I am going to have to factor that into the whole picture! What about the economy?

Sela had stressed to him the importance of forming an economy of some sort within the Grotto, and he wasn't sure where to begin. He shook his head, looking at the poorly laid out building as he felt a headache coming on. He blew out a long breath and let the considerations fall for now.

Tomorrow would be for figuring out solutions to Algonquin Valley problems; right now, he wanted to get rid of his Peppy le Skunk debuff and join everyone for a celebration.

I wonder if they have beer and tequila for sale in the shop?

With that excited and uplifting thought, he hurried towards the Arbuckle building with a bit of pep in his step.

CHAPTER EIGHT

Joe looked at Rocky. "Man, you're looking a little pale. You sure you're ready for this?"

Rocky swallowed. Normally, he was an excellent public speaker, but never had he spoken to a bunch of apocalypse survivors. Each person out there in the crowd milling on the other side of this 'stage' had been through a literal hell. Each person had equal rights to despise him or respect him.

Rocky handed Joe his bag of holding and smiled sheepishly. "Thanks for volunteering to stay sober tonight. Also make sure you thoroughly thank the volunteers in the military as well. I will make sure to try to find a way to reward them." He looked around at those present and included them in his broad smile.

Joe nodded. "The fact that you have got this lot alcohol is going to go a long way. Trust me," he quipped and gripped Rocky's shoulder, hard, giving unspoken support while still continuing humorously, "Look, if it gets rough up there, tell them where the food is, right?"

Rocky laughed at Joe's comic relief, then responded, "Not everyone thinks with their stomachs like you do, Joe." He looked over to the smoke coming off the cook fires in the distance. Zippo was over there making sure everything was delectable. "I swear that's why you like Zippo so much!"

Joe laughed. "That kid sure can cook," he retorted. Then with the hand still on his shoulder, he turned Rocky towards the stage. "Just like a Band-Aid, it's best to just get it done."

Rocky felt his heart pound erratically for a split second; then he climbed the jerry-rigged stacked logs they were calling a stage. Once he was visible, some of the voices quieted, but for the most part, the conversations continued as the excitement of making it someplace safe spilled out from people.

He raised his arms to shoulder height and placed his palms up towards the sky, in an inviting gesture, then shouted, "Welcome, everyone, to Algonquin Grotto!"

His words cut through most of the thrum of voices, and a hush fell through the crowd as people heard. He lowered his arms as the silence descended. Those who hadn't initially heard were shushed by neighbors, and before too long, a deafening silence reigned.

Rocky smiled nervously down at everyone, swallowed and continued, no longer shouting but trying to pitch his voice to carry, "Everyone in this valley is a fighter, a survivor!" He paused, looking out at the pride that shone on people's faces. His nerves diminished, and he continued, "What we have all gone through is hard to define—not only challenging physically and mentally but also emotionally."

His hands rose back up, and he yelled, "Everyone in this valley has been through hell and walked out the other side!"

A cheer louder than any Rocky had heard during his sports career echoed through the Grotto. He smiled and motioned to the military men holding recently purchased trays to begin walking through the crowd. On each tray, there were packed cups carrying sweet, alcoholic nectar. 'Cups' was a poor descriptor; these were Cupa Mact Leaves.

Honestly, I can't believe humans wrote a song about the red solo cup! If only they had known about the Cuppa Mact leaf!

The leaf was absolutely amazing and was unquestionably worthy of a few ballads. If they didn't already exist, that was. The leaf itself was a perfectly formed, twenty-ounce, flexible and collapsible cup. As you poured more liquid, it would expand and contain it within the cup-like container, and that wasn't all; the organism chilled liquid. The cup-leaf would use some sort of biological reaction to keep beverages cold.

Eventually, of course, whatever chemical reaction took place to chill the liquid would fail, but each leaf was a single diamond chip, which meant he had gotten them all for three Crystallized Ether!

As the cups were slowly distributed, Rocky saw many people sniffing the contents. The first cup was something called Aguarvo, which he had been told was the lifeblood of any good party. It smelled like a sweeter version of tequila.

Rocky walked back to the back of the stage and was handed up his own cup; then cup in hand, he made his way back. He looked over at Sela, who was standing next to the monstrous Azoth. They were being given a very large berth by most people, despite the fact that Sela was holding a Cuppa Mact leaf for Azoth, who was making sniffing noises loud enough to be heard by Rocky on the stage.

Smiling, he shouted, "As the military is telling you, please hold on to the cup you are given, and please wait until the toasts are made to have a drink." His raised voice successfully brought everyone's attention back to him. His nerves still on edge, he rushed ahead, "Algonquin Gorge is meant to be a safe haven for all. From this day forward, we will welcome anyone who finds their way here and anyone we can bring back with us."

A few cheers went up at his words, but Rocky held up his hand, mostly to stop the people who wanted to try their beverage. He continued, "This place is known as a Territory, and within its borders, we are given certain protections and opportunities," he looked out at the walls and then directly at the half-shod building, "but we also have a lot of work to do. I will not pretend that it's going to be easy or perfectly safe. However, I will ask you now, are you willing to help make this place a home?"

People looked at each other, and Rocky could see the build of the cheer coming. He cut it off, wanting that cheer to come with the toast, "I propose that we strive, together, to make this valley a beacon for humanity." He raised his glass. "Cheers to regaining some of what humanity has lost!"

The cheer was monstrous, and on stage, Rocky grimaced as his heart stuttered again. Then with a tilt to his head, he brought his own untasted cup to his lips and tipped it back, draining it in a single motion.

Aguarvo was tequila on steroids; somehow, the liquid was smooth and sweet but packed the traditional kick he associated with hard liquor. As he stared into the bottom of his cup in surprise, he heard murmurs of approval and exclamations of excitement as the crowd followed his lead. Rocky motioned to the military, now carrying bottles, and they began threading back through the crowd, filling cups.

He turned and got a refill from Joe, who gave him a thumbs up as he approached. "The hard part is done, Rock. Now they'll start to unwind!" Rocky's mouth formed a half-grin he couldn't help; he could already feel the warmth of the delectable alcohol spreading. As he walked back to the front of the stage, his muscles relaxed tension he didn't know they were holding with that flush of heat, and his nerves eased.

Once there, he waited until he saw one of the military men give him a thumbs up. It took about a minute, but everyone who wanted more alcohol got it. The four hundred fifty or so individuals from the military who volunteered to help and keep guard were the real heroes. Rocky nodded to a grinning military woman and smiled broadly, trying to convey that sentiment to her and swept his eyes over the others to share it.

Then he turned back out to the crowd. "Tonight is to celebrate the founding of this home!" He shouted again to capture their attention. This time, it took a bit longer, but eventually, the silence returned. Rocky continued, "Right now, cooks are preparing a feast." He pointed to the rising smoke, and the crowd grew excited.

Another minute passed, and he held up a hand, waiting for their attention to return. "There are drinks enough for everyone," he continued once a semblance of quiet returned.

Then he pointed to a long table with at least fifty military personnel surrounding kegs, bottles, and deserts.

The constant hum grew louder, and Rocky, seeing that it was going to become impossible to keep their attention, raised his glass and shouted, "To all of you and this place of safety for humanity!"

A sound so loud Rocky jumped exploded from the gathered individuals who raised glasses and waited. He looked around, trying to figure out what they were waiting for. Then he saw Sela make a pointed motion of taking her drink and pointing at him.

They were waiting on him, and he didn't disappoint them. In a single motion, he tilted his head back and drank.

As soon as the drinks were empty, Rocky screamed, "Go, enjoy this night. Tomorrow, we get back to work!"

As he turned, a cheer went up, but this one surprised him not in its volume but in what they were saying. "Rockland! Rockland! Rockland!" He turned back, chagrined, blinking at them all and feeling a lump in his throat. He had done nothing to deserve this, and he swallowed against the quick surge of guilt this brought on.

Quickly, he exited the stage, and the crowd dispersed once he was out of sight. Breathing heavily, he placed his hands on his knees and glanced up at a smiling Joe. Joe shook his head and chuckled, "Normally, when people are cheering your name, you don't run away."

Rocky stood up, and just the look in his eyes made Joe reconsider his words. In a quick motion, he grabbed both of Rocky's shoulders. "Don't you ever think you don't deserve what just happened!" Joe paused with tears starting to brim in his own eyes. "I get it, Rock. I do!"

Joe moved a hand from Rocky's shoulder to form a fist and place it over Rocky's heart. Then tapping that fist lightly on his sternum, he entreated, "This is what they are cheering for!

Most people would have packed up and left Ottawa once they discovered a problem like that." Using that same fist, he forced Rocky's chin up so their eyes met. Then he earnestly continued, "We all know you came back to Ottawa to find your family! We all know they weren't there, but instead of running off to continue to search, you brought everyone here!" Joe pointed over Rocky's shoulder at the crowd they could hear behind the stage.

Then letting go of Rocky, Joe stated flatly, "What you're suffering right now is survivor's guilt, and I know a bit about that! I would keep you here and talk to you all night if that would help, but," he paused and pointed at the backs of people walking towards the cooking fires, "I think you'll do better mingling with the people you saved!"

Then he turned Rocky around and gave him a shove towards those fires. Rocky looked back over his shoulder to smile sheepishly at Joe and nodded his head. His chest was still tight, but he trusted Joe. Plus, he wanted to see this feast!

As he blended in with the crowd, he saw people recognize him and nudge their neighbors, but each person kept a distance for some reason. He looked up, trying to see what emotions people were feeling and saw many happy smiles and nods turned his way. He smiled back and felt his spirits begin to lift, but then his eyes met with someone's who wore a look he recognized from opponents on the basketball court.

The eyes staring at him were filled with anger and promised retribution for something that Rocky wasn't sure he deserved. His smile faltered, but he forced it back, pretending nothing was wrong. Coming to a quick decision, he pretended to have forgotten something back at the stage and veered off from the smiling group of celebrators.

Once clear of the throng, he checked over his shoulder and saw ten people veer out of the crowd to follow. Now that no one could see his face, he let his false smile fall away and made another decision. He could trigger Stealth and Dark Cloak and vanish, avoiding this problem, but those looks promised pain, and he worried if they didn't try it on him, they would find another less prepared outlet.

With his slight buzz causing his blood to pump loudly in his ears, he swallowed and chose to keep walking in plain sight. One of the men shouted in a slurred voice, "Stop, you psychotic bastard." In it, he heard the clear notes of intoxication and groaned slightly before choosing to ignore it.

Another voice yelled, "You think you can bring us here and use us as cheap labor! We were safe in Ottawa!" He felt his heart pump louder and fall into his boot.

He quickened his pace, but his battle senses gave him a moment's notice, and he sprang into a somersault as a large, bat-sized tree branch sailed through the space his head had been. Turning the roll into a twist and coming to his feet in one motion, Rocky held up his hands to the men and women of the group. He tried to placate them, "Listen, guys, why don't we—"

Another one jumped at him, and he dodged left, allowing the poorly trained individual to trip over one of his trailing legs and tumble to the ground. He quickly used Analyze on the group, checking for dangerous classes and high-level threats.

Everything he saw was average at best, and he glanced over his shoulder to gauge the distance to the stage where he hoped Joe and some of the military still stood. A swing of a staff nearly took his head off because of his distraction, but he used his shoulder to divert the blow and tilted his head. This caused the strike to sail above his ear and would probably leave a bruise tomorrow, but it was better than getting the weapon to the temple.

In a quick motion, he jabbed at the individual with a quick fist and saw the woman's knees buckle. He grimaced, not having recognized that it was a woman attacker. Then he turned and took off at a full sprint towards the military uniforms he had just managed to make out on his glance back. He heard the group give chase behind him.

Phew, now, I won't have to hurt any of these drunken idiots.

He made it to the military far ahead of the group, and seeing the angry mob behind him, they sprang into action. Within moments, the group was disarmed and down. Rocky pointed back the way he had come and stated, "There is a woman with a staff in that direction. I think I knocked her out." At his words, two men split off and moved towards the direction he indicated.

Joe jogged up, looking worried, and Rocky rubbed his shoulder where the staff had hit him. Joe began to open his mouth, looking apologetic, and Rocky just shook his head at him before saying, "Just keep them under guard until morning. I'm hoping they were just drunk."

With that pronouncement, he turned away from the man, walked up to a military woman holding a mostly empty Aguarvo bottle and smiled. Still smiling, he reached out and pulled the bottle softly from her hands with a crinkle around his eyes. Then winking, he opened the bottle and took a swig, planning to get truly sauced and forget that some of his own people had just tried to kill him.

***

Arggh. Aguarvo doesn't leave a pleasant aftertaste the next morning! Also, who let a horse kick me in the head…?

Rocky grimaced at his massive hangover headache and tried unsuccessfully to produce saliva to wet his tongue and lips. This was far too similar to how he had awoken the day after the first Ether wave for him to not see some irony in the whole situation. At least, this time, he'd actually drank the night before.

He kept his eyes shut tight and recalled the events of the previous evening that cajoled the group of survivors deep into the night. He'd visited the shop first and picked up ten alchemical cleansers for 'pungent, cloying odors'. Those had taken care of the skunky debuff for him and the group that was close enough to be inflicted.

Additionally, while he'd been in the shop, he had queried the Gnome-looking lady, Trixie, about alcoholic vendors. He probably should have realized that her smile was far too devilish, and even prior to that, maybe he could have figured out she knew how to party based off of her name.

Check, don't ask a woman named Trixie her suggestion on alcohol.

Opening his eyes was a task unto itself, but after some furious rubbing and blinking, he managed to scrub out most of the stupid decisions from the night before and could see again. The immediate area surrounding him was littered with sleeping survivors. Some were awake, but anyone he saw who was 'lucid' seemed to be suffering the same problems as him. He chuckled and then winced when the chuckle hurt his head.

A picture of a withered and shrunken, mummified-looking man was sitting on his debuff bar.

Extreme Dehydration

- **Your body has cleansed a poison known as 'Alcohol'. This poison acted as a diuretic and purged your body of a great deal of water. Additionally, the cleansing of this poison has taken more water. You will suffer extreme headaches, nausea, reduced stats, and muddled thought processes.**
  -20% All stats.

These effects will last until you rehydrate your body fully or for your age minus seven hours.

Current time remaining 23 hours, 30 minutes, 27 seconds.

Celebration time! Come on—how does your head feel?

Rocky blinked, seeing the sarcastic and snarky comment at the end. It had been a while since one of his notifications had one. In fact, the last one he remembered had been early, in his Territory…

They all seem personally tailored too. I wonder who's in charge of the notices?

Rocky slowly stood and began moving sluggishly towards the river. Not wanting to talk to anyone who was there, he went to a free area and dunked his head under the surface to cool off and clean the alcohol-induced sweat from his face. Once he was done scrubbing that off, he took a few mouthfuls of the cool, refreshing water and came up for air.

Then he sat back on his heels and looked around him at the Grotto. Again, the size of the space made him blink, and he considered the future of everyone present. A few moments later, a recognizable figure in military fatigues striding his way made him wince.

Joe strode up to him a few blessedly silent moments later. "Rocky, what would you like us to do with the captives?" His voice sounded like concerned gunfire. Rocky winced, held up a hand, and tried his best to hold back the nausea. He doubled over on the ground, and to contain the vomit, he chose to dunk his head back under the surface of the water.

He had completely forgotten about the group of ten individuals who had tried to attack him last night. Thinking back on the night, he found it ironic that they had tried to attack him just after he had made his speech of welcome and safety, which they clearly hadn't listened to!

He took a few more large gulps of water before his stomach settled enough for him to resurface. When he was no longer dizzy, he shook his head sadly. Then he looked at Joe before speaking softly, "I remember the ten people who attacked me. Where did you end up keeping them?"

"Ten? Rocky, this morning, we have closer to seventy people under guard behind the shop," Joe claimed with shock clear in his booming voice. Rocky wanted to strangle the man when he smiled at Rocky's newest cringe at what appeared to be an intentional decibel assault.

Rocky blinked and whispered delicately, "Seventy! What in the hell? When did you gather up the others?"

Joe explained while raising the volume of his voice further—if that was possible. Rocky shushed the man and got a smile in return. Joe did lower his volume, though and told him a good portion of the detained were because of drunken antics. At one-point, Joe even looked skeptically at Rocky. "You were also almost detained a few times. Do you remember much of last night?"

Rocky shot to his feet and groaned as Joe began detailing a few of his rather embarrassing moments from the night before. He attempted to flee the persistent man and make his way towards the shop, hoping Joe would take the hint.

He didn't. He followed and continued his recollection of the night before.

As they walked, Joe detailed more to him, and Rocky sheepishly began recalling portions of each. His face flushed beet red, and Joe seemed to be enjoying his impromptu torture. Rocky groaned again when Joe recalled for him, "Then I thought you and Sela were finally going to kiss and get over that awkwardness between you. Instead, you chose to bet her that she couldn't shift from form to form without becoming a human in between." Joe paused and looked at Rocky more seriously. "Honestly, did you know she only had two charges left?"

Joe waved his hand and chuckled. "Well, she won the bet."

Rocky felt cold sweat break out on his skin at the reminder. He had barely averted kissing his Ancestral Guide, emphasis on ancestor!

He had flip-flopped back and forth a bit with what Sela being his ancestor really meant. If she was really a distant relation to him, she had lived over a billion years ago. In his very limited understanding of the human race, this most likely meant that the bloodline had diverged so significantly that to call her a relation was a stretch. On the flip side, the system had termed her an Ancestor, which implied a closer relation than he felt comfortable with. She also was the person he usually asked about these sorts of quandaries, so this left him in quite the emotional limbo on the subject.

I wonder which form she ended up being stuck in. I don't fully remember this.

Joe was chuckling to himself, and Rocky looked at him sternly before whispering, "I think that's enough amusement at my expense for a while. Go wake up anyone still sleeping and have them gather somewhere centrally. When I am done with the detained individuals, we'll have Meditation training for everyone."

Joe continued to laugh as he saluted, handed Rocky back his bag of holding, did an about-face, and then strode off. Rocky frowned at his departing back, not seeing the humor in the situation. Then again, he didn't remember everything about the situation…

A short walk later, he spotted the seventy people all sleeping or sitting in a circle with military guards surrounding them. Immediately, Rocky knew some of them were there because they had gotten a little too drunk and done something stupid. The shading of the eyes with hands was a dead giveaway.

Yet, there was a contingent of about twenty who glared daggers at anyone around them. Rocky's brow furrowed in thought.

Some of these people chose to attack me or others only after they got to the Territory? Either they are secretly part of Corsair's contingent, or something else set them off. Was Sela right? Am I really going to regret teaching them those skills?

Continuing his walk, he saw many of those glaring eyes change targets and begin tracking him. Still unsure what to do with these bad apples, he Analyzed the guard in charge and then opened his mouth and addressed him, "Good morning, Letty. Could you please run through what each person is here for from least severe to most severe?"

Letty saluted and then, in a pure business tone, began listing the severity of problems that people were detained for. The first twenty barely would be considered problems in the old world they came from, and in this world, when small bruises and injuries could heal in minutes, Rocky didn't think a drunken fistfight or shove should count for much more than they had already suffered through. On top of that, each name that was called were the people who seemed to be in the worst shape physically from the alcohol. He held up a hand after the guard began listing people who had tried to steal weapons from the militia.

"Alright, everyone listed up to Jayden, get up and go get some water. We'll be meeting for training in an hour." After Rocky announced this, many groans were heard, and the group of misdemeanors stood up and stumbled out of the remaining individuals. One even disregarded any shred of dignity he had and crawled away. Guards checked their names as they left and told them to not get into fights in the future, which made Rocky chuckle. The guards looked like parents scolding children, but the children were all grown up.

There was a strangely silent moment as the entire group watched the crawling man make his way past the guard, mumble his name, and keep crawling.

Some people just can't hold their Aguarvo!

Turning back, he grew immediately serious and felt some cold anger rise up in him. Turning to the lead guard again, he stated, "Send the rest to me by severity. One by one or if they were in a group when apprehended, all of that group at once." Rocky then walked a short distance away towards a pointed tree stump. Since he wanted somewhere to sit, he formed his slithering Soul Blade into a sword and sliced the stump into a flat top with one smooth motion.

The act caused a few gasps to be heard from the guards and the prisoners, and Rocky blinked in surprise before shrugging and sitting down. He chose to sheathe his sword this time to keep it visible in hopes it might deter any particularly dense individuals from doing something stupid. A group of five young adults was walked up to him, and he tried to blank his face. Instead of speaking, he just stared at the five people casting Analyze on each until one of them spoke up.

"Sir," a young, very pretty girl named Bailey, who looked no older than twenty years, stuttered out, "I am sorry. My friends and I were a bit drunk, and we were playing a game of truth or dare that… umm… led us to try to take a few of the guards' weapons."

He raised an eyebrow, and she continued, "We had dared each other to take one, and then I might have insinuated I would kiss the man or woman who did it." She coughed into her fist but forced herself to continue while blushing red, "Umm… then… I tried to take it and stop them from arresting the others."

He looked at them sternly, but inside, he could feel his anger fade slightly, "What do you five plan to do now that you are in the Territory?"

Bailey looked at the group, and at their nods, she continued, "We want to be adventurers like you and your team!" This answer made Rocky tilt his head quizzically before looking at the guards who were smiling proudly.

For some reason, they seemed proud of the young adults who had committed a minor crime the previous night.

He did a quick Analyze of the members of the group. None of them had an NPC class, which meant that farming and hunting was definitely within their wheelhouse.

Rocky suddenly felt awkward and conflicted at the sudden change in the mood. "Okay then. Well, yeah. Then go get cleaned up and meet in just under an hour for training." He had responded clumsily; how does one punish young adults anyway?

The next group was similar and had tried to see who could catch the largest nearby monster but had run away in fear after attracting the massively aggressive Elk herd's attention. They had luckily only led a group of five creatures back to the Grotto, and a few shots had been enough to deter the Elk from continuing into the area. This foolish action had also happened when drunk, and Rocky shook his head, glad none of them had been hurt. He let that group of ten individuals go with a similar message to the first after they sheepishly claimed they wanted to be hunters for the Grotto.

That was when the rest of the people were all led to Rocky, and he clenched his teeth in anger, recognizing some of them as the ones who had attacked him after his speech yesterday. With his hangover and current mood, he considered killing all of them. He had already made the mistake in the past of letting enemies live, and it had cost him two young men who were nearly family.

"Give me a reason why I shouldn't exile all of you!" he spat out and didn't even recognize his own voice. Even the guards, who the question wasn't directed at, flinched, and seemed to step back accidentally at his tone.

One of the individuals stepped forward with an ugly sneer, and Rocky Analyzed him before he began talking.

Jeremy Brown
Level 11
Apprentice-Sailor
Health Points 120/120

"The people in your Territory told us of your tyranny when we got here! We traded one dictator for another, and we won't stand for it!" Jeremy spat the words out with vitriol that couldn't have been faked.

Rocky's eyebrows had climbed steadily during Jeremy's quick and entirely baseless accusation. He could see all the survivors nodding along with the man. Rocky felt his anger putter and die instantly when Jeremy compared him to Corsair. The fact that the rumors were started by the people he and Sela had saved and allowed to live here was... surprising.

The people took in his shocked look, and as a group, he watched them hesitate, blinking and perhaps thinking over what they'd heard. Rocky blinked a few times in quick succession and whispered confusedly, "I've been in Algonquin Valley for a grand total of two days now, and I haven't interacted with more than three people who lived here through the intervening time." After speaking, a silence fell over the delinquent individuals and military. Rocky allowed it to linger.

After he felt it had been long enough, he cleared his throat, "Do you remember who told you this rumor?" His voice, while quiet, held a menace the survivors widened their eyes at. After a time, they nodded, and he motioned for the military to escort him and the group of twenty people through the camp to find this individual.

Rocky, who had been planning on killing the instigator, was lost a moment later. The problem was that each person had heard about it from a different individual, which left Rocky with a frustration that clenched his jaw and hands. How was he going to rectify this problem?

The military gathered up each individual who was pointed out, and Rocky questioned each one. Each man and woman he questioned looked confused at the accusations. Then each one of them pointed out another individual they heard it from, and each one of those pointed to another. After twenty minutes of this, Rocky was at the end of his rope. The fact that everyone had now gathered for training also played a factor.

If I make a speech about that rumor, will it help?

"I am going to ask you all," Rocky looked at the hundred-plus rumor spreaders before continuing, "to remain under guard for the moment and stand beside the stage."

The reaction of the group was startling as many of them began to cry, and a few even lost the ability to stand unassisted. Seeing their fear, he quickly continued, "Don't worry. I realize you have all been misinformed and your reaction, while very stupid and impulsive, was done only after a few drinks." He looked over everyone and forcibly softened his eyes for a moment before finishing, "However, if anything like this happens again, you will not get the same treatment, drunk or not!" He met each individual's eyes before articulating, "I can't have people attacking me or others because of rumors. Do. You. Understand?" He clipped the last bit out with pauses in between, transferring his gaze back and forth across the group.

They all nodded, and most still seemed to think he was going to reconsider and kill them now. Shaking his head sadly, he made his way once again to the pile of cut trees.

As soon as he stepped on stage, all conversation was stifled quickly. The moment was surreal for Rocky, but he forged ahead, "The people you see before you attacked me or the military that surrounds you." He boomed out these words and pointed at the guarded group of one hundred. He moved on quickly, "They did so because of a rumor that was shared with them."

Rocky stopped and looked over the gathered crowd and saw guilt in a few more eyes. He met those people's eyes, but in them, he didn't see any emotion that gave away anything more. Each person he saw seemed sheepish, like they knew better. He took a deep breath, having hoped he would find the de-facto leader of this dissent.

Disappointed, Rocky projected into the continued silence, "The rumor that I am a dictator is unfounded and strange. First, if I was a dictator, would I let people who attacked me go with just a warning?" Rocky made a motion to the group, and they walked into the crowd to join them.

Smiling, Rocky continued, "Secondly, I have not been in this Grotto myself before yesterday and have only spent a single full day in Algonquin Valley. So, whoever told you I was a tyrannical leader couldn't possibly know me personally."

He looked to the group where Smith stood. "I only met three people who live here during my brief stay. So, if you hear the rumor I am speaking of, please think about that."

Rocky scanned the group again, taking a long, pragmatic pause. Then he finished, enunciating every word in hopes this time it would stick, "Lastly, everything I announced last night about making this a place of safety and growth for all humans still applies."

Then he clapped his hands together. "Now, let's get to training the Meditation technique that many of you already know. For the rest of you, pay attention and ask one of the Ottawa survivors why this is so important!"

Rocky sat down to begin his instruction on Meditation. As he lowered himself, he saw Sela, who was no longer trapped in a druidic form since midnight had passed.

Her eyes flashed for a moment before she turned and strode off towards the entrance to the Grotto, changing into her cat form as she went. As his eyes tracked her leaving, he saw Frankie and Joe standing at the back of the clearing. Frankie was scribbling notes in his journal, and Joe was shaking his head looking between Rocky and the retreating tail of Sela.

Why do I feel that Frankie is psychoanalyzing me?

CHAPTER NINE

SELA

Sela stalked out of the Grotto.

That man! How can he just let people who attacked him live? Then teach them a priceless skill that I would have killed armies to obtain in my previous life! Where did he even go last night?

She had woken up frustrated and less hungover than she would have liked. Somehow, as the festivities were just getting good, she had used her final two charges to change through her druidic forms, ending in her current cat form. If she was remembering right, it was because of a bet from Rockland. He had made the bet, and then the next thing she remembered, he was gone.

Now though, she worried that he had gone missing because of the survivors who had attacked him. That thought made her even angrier. Why would he let the traitors live? Not only had they attacked him, but they had ruined a good night of celebration! She had been having fun with Rockland the previous night, at least she thought they were…

She ran through the forest, trying to find the other group of humans who had been let off from a punishment she believed they deserved. Smith had told Sela they'd been leaving food at the entrance to the Grotto every morning and were working extremely hard to make up for their part in Arti's despicable crimes.

Sela didn't believe that people could be forced to do something that they didn't want to do. In the world she knew, all you had to do was put in some extra work, and you would gain the power to stand against tyranny. Work a little harder, and you could create your place, write your future, or sign your name on the annals of Gaian history. While there was something to be said about the family heritage of classes, skills, wealth, and the like, they weren't insurmountable advantages. She had always lived with the motto of her grandfather, "Hard work beats talent when talent doesn't work hard."

She prowled the expanding forest of Algonquin Valley, looking for signs of the four individuals and quickly discovered signs of human passage. As she followed them in Stealth, she continued to consider some of the oddities that this world seemed to latch on to. Immediately, her mind recalled how people who met her for the first time seemed to immediately think she was fragile. It was mostly the male populace, but there was a definite shift in the way she was regarded by people because of the way she looked or her sex. What in the hell had happened to make males think that women needed to be protected? For that matter, what stopped those women who Arti had abused from getting their own vengeance?

Sela tried desperately to understand it from the way Rockland described it. According to him, women had been less physical in the world 'before' the return of Ether, which was still naturally true in the new world. However, to Sela, that didn't mean they were 'weaker' which was what seemed to be the implied correlation. She clenched her jaw and narrowed her eyes, thinking of what she would do if someone tried to tell her that she was weaker than someone based on her sex. Women may not be as physically imposing naturally as men were, but in her time, they had always had greater spiritual stats. It had been obvious to any researchers that men at the age of eight would have slightly higher Stamina, Agility, and Strength, but women would have slightly higher Intelligence, Wisdom, and Dexterity. It was usually a single point swing in either direction, and based on how hard one worked, any disadvantage could be turned into your greatest strength.

It was with this mindset that she stumbled on to a clearing that was occupied by the four men she had exiled from the Grotto. From Stealth and the shadow of the trees she Analyzed each of them.

Brendon Forgis
Level 12
Apprentice-Shielder
Health Points 180/220
Strong-Analyze has failed to reveal further information.

—

Frank Futis
Level 12
Apprentice-Windrunner
Health Points 120/120
Strong-Analyze has failed to reveal further information.

—

Guy Jilles
Level 11
Apprentice-Lurker
Health Points 135/185
Strong-Analyze has failed to reveal further information.

—

Jack Estra
Level 13
Apprentice-Strengthener
Health Points 130/130
Strong-Analyze has failed to reveal further information.

Three of the men stood guard over Jack as he skinned their most recent kill, an antlered animal that Sela didn't fully recognize. Analyze told her when it was alive, it had been called a Deer, and it had been level 10. The men chatted amiably as she watched.

Guy, a tall, skinny man with deep-set eyes and dark hair, smiled at Frank. "It was amazing to see so many people join the Grotto. I wonder where they all came from."

Brendon sneered, "We would know if they hadn't exiled us!"

Frank, still with his back turned, shrugged, and in a tone exactly opposite Brendon's hostile one, corrected, "Well, if we can join our families back in the Grotto, we can ask them ourselves." He glanced back directly at Brendon. "Let's keep working as hard as we can. At least we aren't dead!"

Jack, a muscular, shorter man, wistfully stated in his baritone voice, "I wish I had known how easy it is to get stronger. Maybe we wouldn't be in this mess."

Brendon chimed in again, anger lacing his voice, "Arti was a real Blue Jay." Sela could tell his last system-adjusted word was a swear word and without thinking, reported the language.

She immediately grimaced to herself; what did language matter in this present world? While it was definitely true that in the Silver Spire, people made a point of not swearing and it was commonplace to report violations to better others, in this world, she doubted it mattered. However, that reminded her of Rocky's hilarious reaction. She felt her feline mouth attempt a smile and clamped down on her emotions, returning her attention to the group.

The men no longer had smiles on their faces, instead replaced by grimaces. Jack, who was deftly and quickly skinning the corpse to Sela's appraising eyes, spoke up. With determination and regret lacing his heavily accented words, he intoned, "We can't change the past, gents. All we can do now is what we are doing and hope to make a better future."

Sela's mouth fell open, and she looked around the clearing to try and see who these men were putting a show on for. While they still held animosity of some kind, it seemed the vast majority of that hate was directed at Arti and not the residents of the Territory. To Sela's surprise, her senses told her that it was only her and them in the area. She stalked away somehow more annoyed after being shown that particular scene. How come this world kept forcing her to question what she knew?

As she prowled the forest aimlessly, she continued to consider. What were the chances that someone from her world hadn't known the skill of Ether Manipulation? The skill that quite possibly could have saved her life from the deadly Martian poison. It was very hard to believe that no one in Cathodiem had known a skill that Rockland had discovered in a few weeks.

In addition, she'd grown up in the Silver Spires, which was the strongest Cathodiem Territory. If the leaders, one of which was her grandfather, hadn't known about Cardinal Dungeons, she would eat an entire tree. The fact that she had been told to find and eradicate Dungeons her entire life was odd. What reason could leaders have to justify the destruction of something that could be so beneficial?

Everything is so twisted. Cathodiem seemed to be at war with all Dungeons; we were even sent in to 'save' Territories from 'invading' Dungeons, but now, I think those were those Territories' Cardinal Dungeons! What in the abyss weren't you telling me, Grandfather?

Depressed, Sela mentally contacted Azoth, as she couldn't speak directly to Rocky unless she wanted to waste a charge to change back, and she didn't yet.

She could always use a Vial of Gambler's Charge to regain a form shift, but she only had two of those left, and they were extremely expensive; each one would cost a full day or more of farming. Unfortunately, they also had a ten percent chance to remove a charge, which had happened to Sela already. This was a huge waste of the five crystals they cost. Sadness in her mental tone, she sent, "Azoth, tell Rockland we need to meet tonight. It's about the shop."

Azoth jubilantly sent back, "It done. Sela okay? Is Sela hunt?"

Sela felt her bad mood gradually begin to evaporate as Azoth joined her, and together, they hunted creatures and critters inside of the Territorial boundaries.

She would get to the bottom of her controversial discoveries about her past… but that would come later.

ROCKY

After the Meditation practice, Rocky left the stage and searched out Derik and Smith. They were looking for him, it appeared, so he found them easily and quickly.

"If it isn't our abandonment issue leader!" Derik sneered as he saw him approaching, and Rocky shook his head while simultaneously sucking on his teeth but let the comment slide.

Still not one hundred percent okay with Derik and his attitude, Rocky strode up and shook Smith's hand before emphasizing speaking only to him, "Morning, Smith. How has everything been since moving to the Grotto? How are we doing on food and other resources?"

Smith glanced at Derik once and briefly shook his head as well before starting into a report-like tone, "It would seem that we're going to have to greatly increase the number of hunters. We were easily supporting the hundred-plus individuals here prior, but if the numbers Joe mentioned to me are accurate, then we now have four thousand hungry mouths to feed."

He paused, took out a pipe, and began to pack it with tobacco as he continued, "As far as resources go, there seems to be a lot of helpful plants that grow in the Territory. Many of the groups with a miner swear that there seem to be metal deposits in areas that a day prior didn't have any. Almost like they're growing or popping into existence." He finished packing in tobacco and pulled out a metal match that he struck on the case and lit up.

After a brief puff and exhale, he shrugged and whispered, "Our group has noticed the same strange effect with monsters, almost like they're growing rapidly or every time we kill one, a new one is born and grown so fast it makes no difference. At current, I don't think we have to worry about overtaxing the surrounding environment, at least." Then he pointed to the trees and nodded his head, making it clear that they were abundant and growing back as well.

Rocky put a hand to his chin in thought at what Smith had just explained. That was definitely good news and did bode well for the people within Algonquin Valley. Additionally, he would like to possibly try to mark up a map of some sort from the Grotto to create hunting zones for groups and resource gathering crews. If Smith was right, that would require some coordination by the leaders—so him. He blinked. "Smith do you think you can take me on a tour and show me where you traditionally have been running into what monsters?"

Derik sneered and cut into the conversation in his annoyingly high octave falsetto, "We have been marking locations for a while in the dirt. Follow me, and we can show you everything we have gathered. Not that you deserve the help of people you abandoned!"

Rocky swallowed and looked at Smith who shook his head and rolled his eyes, clearly not feeling the same way as the eccentric and dramatic Derik.

With his lips pressed tightly together, he answered as politely as possible, "By all means, Derik, please, lead the way."

Smith and he followed Derik to an area on the ground that was covered with a large drape of interwoven leaves. He examined it, and his eyebrows rose; whoever had made the tarp-like device had done a marvelous job and must have also been the one who wove the bathhouse dividers.

Derik saw Rocky admiring the tarp and smiled falsely. "I created this tarp to try to keep the rain off and people from walking on our rough map. It would be really great if our esteemed leaders would provide a roof over the heads of the people and maybe some damn paper!" Derik pontificated in such a rude, obnoxious way that Rocky thought he felt his blood begin to boil.

Dammit, I just praised Derik. At least it wasn't out loud. Just calm down—it really does look like Derik did a good job. Don't let him get to you.

Interrupting his inner mantra, Derik continued, "The places I have marked with miniature mountains denote some of the places we've found veins of minerals. I placed a star next to the ones that we've only found on rare occasions. The dividing lines I've roughly drawn seem to denote areas within the Territory. I can't be sure, but I think that each species I listed within those lines are most likely to be found in those areas, which could mean that's where those creatures reside or procreate?" He pointed out each area as he spoke and looked at Smith on occasion, who nodded along. "Finally, Smith marked places where he found some of the more useful plants on the map, and the squares with neat rows are meant to denote high fertility of earth that he believes we could use as farms." One of those farms was right on the other side of the river from the Territory. Derik looked at Rocky as he finished his detailed summary and was met with an open-mouthed stare.

Derik stood up and sniffed disdainfully. "Honestly, I knew how useless you seem to be, so I started thinking of things to help the people here. I will continue to do so because I don't trust you or our little, sadistic, resurrected princess!"

That was the tipping point; Rocky had punched Derik before he knew it. The man sprawled sideways, luckily not ruining the rough map. Smith reacted instantly, putting both of his hands on Rocky's chest and holding him back with as much force as he could.

Honestly, it felt like someone was simply standing in his way. If he wanted to, he could be by Smith in an instant, but he already felt he had gone too far. Derik was a complete jerk without question, and perhaps if he had stuck to insults directed only towards him, Rocky wouldn't have punched him. However, insulting Sela set him off, triggering his Dark Cloak simultaneously with a thrown punch.

I'm probably lucky that my sword didn't materialize. At least I had some restraint.

Thinking quickly as Derik collected himself out of the dirt. Rocky snapped a picture of his map on the regulated Knowledge Tablet. Then he disengaged his Dark Cloak and stepped back, nodding to Smith, who looked at him to gauge his emotional state.

Derik stood up, holding his mouth. Rocky was surprised to see what looked like a broken jaw. Grimacing, he cast a quick Dark Mend on Derik and saw his eyes lose some of the pained expression before opening wide in a look somewhere between madness and seething outrage.

Derik took off, walking right through his map. Luckily, he didn't mess it up too badly, but Rocky shrugged, knowing he had captured the map on the Knowledge Tablet. Turning to Smith, he sighed. "I will try to purchase some useful items from the shop later today. If you can think of anything, let me know. I also will try to get one of these," he held up his Knowledge Tablet, "for everyone."

Smith eyed the electronic tablet, nodding. Then he grimaced and drawled, "You're probably going to want to make things right with him; he's been pretty helpful with organizing and starting projects in your absence. I'm not saying he goes about handling it in the right way, but I am saying he will be a valuable ally to have on your side if you truly plan to make something of this Grotto." Smith turned to watch Derik walk into the distance and then looked back to Rocky. "Would you like to go hunting with my group and see what we can do? Since Derik doesn't really hunt as often as us, I should add a theory of my own to the monster areas." He took another drag of his pipe. "We've noticed that as we leveled the people in the gorge higher through controlled hunting and finding safe areas, it seemed the monster levels grew. I'm unsure, but I think that the average level of the people who are living within the gorge has a direct effect on the monsters' levels. Want to go check that out?"

Rocky nodded, and together, they moved off to meet the rest of the famous A-Team Sela had told him about. They walked to the entrance of the Grotto in silence. Smith smoked his pipe, and Rocky examined the places in the Grotto as they passed them. At the entrance, Smith pointed his pipe stem at a group, and they changed their course towards them. "This is the lovely Miss Amber." He'd moved the stem of the pipe from the dark-haired, muscularly built Native American woman to a dark-haired, largely rotund, exuberantly smiling man. "That there is Jack and finally Mr. Pips." Smith ended on a wiry man whose hair was so blonde it was nearly white. The lanky man was all hard, bony angles, and Rocky wanted to feed him something immediately. After the introductions, Smith looked at the group. "This is Rocky, the leader of the Territory." He took a deep breath and paused before adding, "We shouldn't expect Derik, but where is Bart?"

Amber smiled, which turned her from homely to beautiful and punched Smith in the arm. She quipped playfully, "I don't know about lovely, Smith! As for Bart, he took out a group of people this morning to help them stay safe. So, he won't be joining us."

Then for the remainder of the day, Smith, Rocky, and the three other members of the A-Team hunted and stored unbutchered corpses in the Territorial Inventory. Once that was full and the group was ready to turn back, Rocky showed them the bag of holding and suggested they continue for a bit longer today. The bag interested Smith greatly, as he had been using the Territorial Inventory to store corpses, but the area he had access to was limited. He wondered if there was a possibility of all the hunting groups getting a bag themselves or if it was possible to organize the Territorial Inventory into a butchering storage and yard.

Rocky considered this and added it to the discussions for the night. If they created a team of butchers who had access to the same area of the inventory as the hunters, perhaps they could have all the hunter groups dumping kills and the butchers pulling them out. Then the butchers could have another area for butchered meat and prepared foods. He doubted that he could get each group a bag of holding—as his was the only one he had seen, and the circumstances in which he got it weren't exactly repeatable. Again, that left him thinking of LFD and how the eccentric, curb appeal obsessed Dungeon was faring. Not to mention discussing this whole Cardinal Dungeon business with the Dungeon, LFD was much easier to get along with than Maximus had been.

For the remainder of the day, the group hunted, trying to stock up on food and plants that would be beneficial for the Territory. As they hunted Rocky asked further questions, "How are the ten job categories?"

Mr. Pips pointed down at some deer tracks and answered, "Helpful but many of us are unsure how helpful. Bart is in charge of them and he has been adding people all morning who are interested." Mr. Pips paused for a moment and finished, "I think we have hunting to level three currently which allows thirty people?"

Rocky opened his territory screen and scrolled the jobs.

Territory Job Categories
- **You are able to have ten job titles total. Ways to unlock additional job titles is currently hidden.**

Reach Territory Level two to unlock additional information.

- Job titles increase over time as actions and quests are completed that fall under each category, or you can have the job skill level doubled by having it occupy two available job title slots.
- Job titles can be reallocated once per quarter, current job reset counter = one. Counters cannot be stored. If they are not used, they will be reset at the end of a quarter. Current time remaining until next quarter. Five days, fifteen hours, two minutes. Dismissing a job will reduce its level back to level one.

Job's Chosen

- Alchemist II – Alchemy, Herbalism, Chemistry, Ether Properties
- Farmer I – Cultivation, Seeding, Crop Fertility, Harvest
- Hunter IV (Doubled) – Accuracy, Tracker, Skinner, Butchering
- Lumberjack II – Axeman, Planking, Debarking, Lumber
- Builder I – Architecture, Engineering, Materials, Creativity
- Researcher I – Research, Discovery, Progress, Invention
- Crafter I – Tools, Creativity, Discovery, Craft
- Cook II – Knives, Cook, Palate, Ingredients
- Soldier I – Shield, Spear, Training, Endurance

"It is actually level four currently. How did you guys manage to raise it?" Rocky asked wanted to know why some had leveled up faster than others.

Smith was the one who answered this time, "If you are a hunter, you are offered a daily quest to gather meat for the village. I know each hunting group completes it every day." Stroking his chin he continued, "People from other groups show me their quests and they are nearly impossible right now. The quests don't give us any Etherience, but we think they add to the level of the job category and often give levels in skills as rewards."

Rocky nodded and made a mental note about it for later. Then said, "Bart will make sure all job openings get filled for now?"

Amber smiled, "He has been doing a good job so far, but complains it is harder than it seems."

Later that night, as midnight approached, Rocky stood and surveyed the smithy and checked its progress. It would seem that some bars had been created of what looked like copper and possibly tin. However, if that was the case, then the smiths hadn't yet been able to figure out the process of smelting bronze. He could even see some raw iron and other questionable minerals accumulating in a pile off to the side. He used Analyze to identify some of the rarer ones he didn't recognize on sight. Aluminum, silver, nickel, tungsten, and cobalt were a few of the ones that he hadn't been able to identify by sight. However, he stared at the screen of the last piece he had just used his Analyze skill on.

Arcanium Ore
- **A metal that is particularly soft but great at holding Ether or converting Ether to other energy sources.**

There wasn't a ton of the aforementioned ore, but it was a metal that he didn't recall ever seeing on the periodic table. He had to assume that smelting and forming ingots of most of the metals that he was staring at currently would require a higher skill level for the smiths or he may be able to purchase them some skills or knowledge scrolls.

He pulled out his Knowledge Tablet and made a few notes to check prices for knowledge scrolls in the shop. His first priority needed to be a sawmill or something that would help the builders stay on top of the construction of housing for nearly four thousand individuals. While they were all very happy and excited now, that would wear off if he couldn't keep the rain off their heads. Derik's mutterings from that morning bespoke an issue that would build rapidly if not addressed. As he left, he noticed multiple buckets filled with nails made of copper. At least they had something to use, but copper nails would bend and flex a bit too easily, he figured.

Bronze jumped up in priority quite a bit when he saw the copper nails. Yeah, it wasn't steel, which would be pretty good, but bronze was actually a far superior metal to iron, copper, and tin. It was a common misconception that iron was better because knights in Medieval Europe used it. Rocky, however, had read that the European countries had been blessed with an abundance of the mineral and that was why it was so prevalent in history—not its superiority but its availability. Currently from the stocks he could see on hand, copper and tin were his two most prevalent resources, and bronze was made by mixing those two if his memory served.

That was pretty common knowledge, and he wondered what the trouble was with just mixing the two. Was the process more complex than he thought, or had the people who were learning to smith just not attempted the mixture yet?

He made a note to make sure they began experimenting and to have them re-smelt the copper nails back to ingots. If they used the copper nails, those structures would be subpar, and he truly believed in building for longevity where possible.

That's when he walked by the cooking area and groaned. The smiths had made some massive copper pots that seemed to be hanging on makeshift erected tripods made of uncut wood. It seemed like this was another problem that needed to be addressed. Someone had cleverly created a large portion of clay bowls and spoons, but there were only perhaps fifty of them in total. Which meant that the initial survivors had been sharing and taking turns while eating. If he wanted morale of his Territory to remain high, he would need to have enough cutlery and utensils to allow everyone to eat simultaneously. Humans are social creatures, after all.

Unsure what the priority would be here, he added to his growing shopping list and grimaced. He currently had around eight hundred Crystallized Ether, which was the primary currency of this world. Four hundred of the eight hundred crystals were from his group's personal stores, and the other four hundred was what was left over from Corsair's Ottawa stores. Eight hundred was actually a ridiculously huge sum for one person to have. Considering that he had stolen near three thousand from Corsair, who'd been stealing it from a hundred thousand and change Ottawa survivors, and the problem became apparent. Rocky would not be able to get this large of a sum again. So, each purchase had to be thoroughly considered.

Here, in a Territory, the shop came with some pretty awesome functionality. First, you could set up a tax function for every purchase made. The shop would automatically add it to every purchase made within and keep it for collection. Second, the leader could set the shop's parameters for who could and couldn't enter. Rocky was tempted to leave it off-limits to everyone, but that was too similar to what the sociopath Corsair had done. He jotted down more notes to try to find a way to safeguard the Territory but allow access to the shop.

Why not allow everyone access to the shop? Because inside the shop, there were people from all over the Etherverse, and many, if not all of them, would be overjoyed to learn about Gaia. Most just because it would be considered a new, untapped resource, but if they learned the truth that Gaia was one of the oldest planetary gods and that she was currently in a very weakened and vulnerable position… Rocky couldn't even guess how many expeditions would be sent to capture her.

Considering his last thought, he looked at a note he'd made on the trek back to his Territory. The note read, "Start Researching Upgrades for Intergalactic Ships." He had desperately wanted some sort of shuttle or flying ship that could transport survivors more safely. When he'd brought it up to Sela early in the journey, she'd laughed. It would seem that the ships themselves would be available, but they were all base models and absurdly expensive.

The top tier technology and research available was all guarded by the individuals who discovered it. The base model starship itself was available but out of their price range. The technology to make it safe during travels was jealously guarded by the creators, guilds, or planetary governments to hold an edge if conflicts ever arose.

This phenomenon extended to any shuttle that could accommodate large groups of humans. With the monsters in the air and on the ground, any shuttle would need to be well defended or absurdly fast. Yet, the technology to make them safe fell under starship patents, which left anything that was purchasable light-years behind even Earth's primitive jet fighters. Rocky had explained those to Sela, and she had just asked him how the most advanced tech from his world would fare against any of the monsters or golems he had seen.

Unfortunately, I thought and still do think they would be worth little more than the material they are made from. Not to mention they use an even more expensive resource to fly!

Of course, he was thinking of oil, which was actually Gaia's personal Essence and was worth far more than humans had ever suspected. The amount of oil the world had consumed as Gaia slumbered was vast, and Rocky knew now that she was awake finding the substance was going to be much more difficult. After he finished his quick perusal of the camp, he flicked his radio to notify Joe and Zippo of the meeting Sela had set up. "Guys, let's meet up and plan a trip to the shop."

Joe and Zippo arrived carrying an entire pot of stew between them. Joe smiled at the group. "Only way I could get the kid to come."

Zippo still didn't look happy to be present at the 'boring' meeting. However, he sat down with a bowl and sipped away. It was well after midnight, and Rocky hoped that the two had stolen leftovers only. However, to be on the safe side, he dumped all his personal butchered meat from his bag of holding into the Territorial Storage area to make up for anything they might have 'stolen'.

Once everyone was sitting, Sela surprised all of them.

Selaphelia Ardensai would like to begin a meeting and has invited you.

\<Yes\> | No

Once Rocky clicked yes, a blank window popped up in front of him, and Sela looked pointedly at him. He shrugged his shoulders, not sure what she was expecting, which forced her to sigh. "Just think what you want to put on the screen, and it will share it with the screens in front of the rest of us. If you have anything written on the tablet you can just open it and transfer it over as well."

His eyebrows rose. He had been wanting to find some functionality like this, but here, Sela had just displayed a much deeper knowledge of the system so casually. It made him realize he was probably missing huge numbers of opportunities the system had at his fingertips. He pulled out his tablet and shared his spur of the moment shopping list.

Shopping List
- **Sawmill**
- **Knowledge Scrolls (Bronze)**
- **Construction tools (For more squads)**
- **Industrial Kitchen Equipment or Dining Establishment**
- **Blueprints as needed**
- **Crops**

Sela smiled wanly at Rocky for the briefest of moments, then disappointedly emphasized, "You have a very utilitarian view on what is needed, Rockland. I agree that we need something to speed up the construction on the Longhouses, and the sawmill is a great start. However, I think that after food or some sort of dining hall, you are really going to need an economy with luxuries that can be purchased and a guildhall."

Joe nodded his head. "Rocky, I grudgingly agree. I know that in a perfect world, everyone is going to work together, and income would be split. However, everyone here has grown up with capitalism. How many people do you think will go out and hunt for meat every day when they get practically no benefits for themselves and their family?" He paused and looked around the fire at the people present. "Also, from what little Sela has told us about guilds, a guild will be essential for our Non-Power-Class citizens and their leveling."

Zippo clenched his jaw, then got himself another bowl of soup. Rocky grimaced. "I can see your point about the guild, but what do you mean about luxury items? We're all in this together.

I am not looking for money or gains by saving people. Are you, Joe?"

Sela shook her head slightly. "The government for ruling this Territory will not work as a full democracy. I agree we do need to have the people involved and having a say in the decisions, but at the end of the day, final decisions need to be made by a single body who is aware of the entire picture." She gestured to Rocky and herself, making him feel a little uncomfortable.

Sela highlighted the funds Rocky had listed with a mental command. "If I am not mistaken, these are all the funds we have. Correct?" At Rocky's nod, she continued, "Then we need to put aside at least half of it to pay wages. Then we need to set up an economy within the Grotto. Otherwise–"

"For Totto's sake. If this is what the meeting is about, I don't need to be here. I am not Oliver!" Zippo cut off Sela and stood up suddenly, simultaneously throwing and breaking his clay bowl.

The entire group was stunned into silence as he stormed away from the three others. Rocky pursed his lips as he also stood up, and at Sela's look, he held up a hand. "I think I should have that chat with him." Sela nodded somberly, eyes filled with tears, and he wondered if Sela would be the better person to comfort the young man.

Knowing he was trying to avoid the awkwardness, he pursed his lips and followed after Zippo, hoping he could do or say something that would help. He let the kid walk for quite a distance, each step taking them further from prying ears and others. He assumed that Zippo would want to have this conversation in privacy, but Rocky didn't actually know where the conversation would go.

"Rock. Please stop following me!" Zippo called back from up ahead, and Rocky seriously considered turning around and going back but just shook his head and continued.

A moment later, Zippo's hand lit up with a Fireball, and he rounded on Rocky. "I asked you to *stop*! If you don't... I will... I will..." Rocky had kept walking towards the mage. The Fireball, while menacing, wasn't meant for him, and even Zippo knew it deep down. The last few steps, as the boy stuttered, Rocky had taken deliberately and closed the last few feet before embracing the young man in a hug.

Zippo's body tensed up, every muscle rigid and trembling. A moment later, the Fireball at his side shrank, and he seemed to along with it. Within moments, Rocky was holding the sobbing and trembling child he had befriended just a few weeks ago. In fact, Zippo had been sobbing similar to this the very first time they'd seen each other. That time it was because of the immediate loss of his family, and this time, it was that and the further loss of something more. Rocky waited, feeling that he would need to say something soon but also knowing that he himself wasn't ready to speak just yet.

After a time, Zippo let go of him. Rocky took that as his cue and stepped back, holding the young man's shoulders and trying to look into his downcast eyes. Then he started using his softest voice, "Jason, I know how you feel, buddy. I lost them too." Rocky's voice carried their joint loss, and Zippo looked up into his hard-sad eyes, first with anger at hearing his name but then softening as he saw the mirrored pain.

Somewhere along the way, Rocky had changed, and just like Rocky saw it in Zippo, Zippo saw that change starkly in Rocky. The kind, empathetic man was almost entirely gone, and while he was seeing a glimmer of it now, he could also see a sharp edge behind it.

"I don't want you to take any blame for what happened," Rocky continued, staring at Zippo with a clear war raging internally. "I was the one who trained you kids and brought you into a battle that you had no business being a part of. Hate me if it helps! Despise me! If I could change places with them I would, Jason…"

Zippo shook his head sadly, already having had his anger at Rocky for his part in their deaths falter and die on the hellish march here. Rocky had tried his best and made mistakes, but they were no larger or smaller than his own. At least that was what Zippo had concluded.

When Zippo began to speak in a stuttering sob, Rocky snapped his mouth shut, "Listen, Rock, you weren't in that school. I panicked, and when the bomb went off, I covered myself in my shield. I could have covered a group, but in that split second, I showed my true colors. I showed myself to be a coward. I'm not like you, Joe, or Sela. You're all so strong, and I'm nothing more than a coward."

Rocky blinked rapidly at the change of direction, not having expected it. Never would he have expected Zippo to be so blind, so wrong. When the words finally computed, he felt something grip his heart.

He wanted to respond immediately with anything and everything he could think of, but he managed to rein in that gut reaction. Instead, Rocky sputtered, "Zippo, you're so far from a coward, it's ridiculous. How many monsters did you challenge on the hike here?" He paused then continued pointedly, "Do you even realize that you barely survived that explosion yourself?" Another pause. "When I found you, your shield had barely stopped your own death. Expanding it weakens it greatly, right?" Rocky looked down for a moment, then quickly back up to meet Zippo's eyes. Then he pulled the boy into a hug again. "It wouldn't have saved more than just you!"

He continued to grip Zippo tightly and willed his words to be what the kid needed. Using one of his hands, he cupped the back of the boy's head and ruffled his hair. In his most earnest of timbre, he intoned, "You need to let this guilt go." After a moment he added, "I need to let this guilt go."

Zippo hugged Rocky back hard and asked earnestly, "And what, Rock?" Then after a pause, he croaked out, "Should we just forget them? Forgive ourselves and let their memories die with them?"

Zippo choked back another sob. "My family deserved better... They deserve better."

Rocky squeezed the boy tightly, which cut him off; then he softly reassured, "They do deserve better, Jason." He felt Zippo's shoulder ease slightly at the admission. "You knew them best, so if they were here right now instead of us, what would you tell them?"

Zippo blinked and slowly pushed back from Rocky. After a long look into Rocky's face and eyes, he looked up to the stars. With confusion lacing his words, he whispered, "I would want them to live. I would want them to become strong and work to save others... I think?"

At the question, he looked down into Rocky's face and saw him smiling paternally at him. He nodded at Zippo, hoping he knew that he was loved. He hoped the kid realized he had a family still, maybe not the family he would have chosen but a family all the same.

The conversation continued for a short while, and Rocky responded as honestly as he could. Admitting he was afraid most days, almost all the time, seemed to assuage the young man. Confirming that he didn't know what came next, that he didn't have a grand plan, brought a smile to Zippo's lips.

With each question and response, the boy seemed to straighten slightly. As Zippo ran out of questions, Rocky knew they had a long way to go to truly heal the young man, but as they walked back to join the group, Rocky swore on everything he held closest to his heart; he would continue to try. He wouldn't ever let this young man wander this painful path alone.

CHAPTER TEN

Once a cried-out Zippo and Rocky returned to the group, the discussions started in earnest. They had a lot to cover, and everyone wanted to get started quickly. Zippo didn't look like he would add much, but he did seem a little less dark and brooding to Rocky.

Joe gave Rocky a raised eyebrow, and Sela tilted her head when they returned. For his part, Rocky nodded a few times in quick succession, conveying that they had talked. This brought a smile to Joe's and Sela's faces.

The initial planning was primarily between Sela and Rocky. First off, of the eight hundred and three Crystallized Ether they had, they were going to change approximately two hundred into gems, marks, and chips. This would be the city coffers, and Sela suggested paying individuals from it. This would be an investment into the Territory that would hopefully grow as the NPCs began crafting items and consumables that the hunters could spend locally on.

This, of course, meant that they would have to put in place prices and taxes for luxuries in the Grotto. So, suggestions were bandied around for what those might be.

For food, it was decided that some cooks would specialize in luxury meals, and they would be sold for a set price. Surprisingly to everyone, this was Zippo's idea, and Rocky smiled, remembering how good of a cook the young man had become—especially in comparison to himself. Stew would be free for everyone who lived within the Grotto, at least in the beginning. As would accommodations, but after those two necessities, they chose to make a few buildings priorities that would return money to the city coffers. One would be a restaurant, another an actual bathhouse with heated water, and most importantly, some sort of bar with alcohol. Rocky had made beer before in his garage, and as long as they could buy some tools, yeast, wheat, or grains, they would be able to make that here.

He also knew the shop sold multiple types of liquors from all over the galaxy after his most recent trip. That, however, would be an investment once a bar was set up, and they found an individual to run it. Joe had been the one to point out the necessity for alcohol and perhaps even tobacco—after seeing Smith and his pipe. As an ex-soldier, he argued that not many people knew how to deal with the loss and stress this world seemed to pile on. With alcohol, people would have a nice release and easy method to gripe about problems while feeling like they had an excuse. At Rocky's initial reluctance, Joe pointed to the distant figure of Frankie sitting with a crying woman. It was well into the night, and the fact that Frankie was still up surprised everyone except Joe. He clicked his tongue. "That man has been working around the clock. I know it isn't easy to see past the immediate problems we face. Yet, I will tell you right now that every individual in this valley has experienced loss on a scale unheard of before the crash."

Joe pointed to himself, Zippo, and Rocky, then expanded further on his point, "We have each other to confide in, and a lot of our loss and resentment is vented during fights." He took a deep breath in through his nose. "We have found a purpose—to protect the people around us, to create a Territory, and to grow stronger."

Rocky nodded his head, finally seeing what Joe meant. He glanced over to Frankie who had his notepad out and was clearly in session. "Frankie is trying to help others find a purpose, then?"

Joe looked back as well. "Yes and no. It isn't all so black and white, but we need a few more people offering what Frankie is offering—a listening ear. Then we would need a bartender that we've trained to spot signs in people. In this way, we can help people integrate into the new world, into our Territory."

Knowing that they had to go investigate Chalk River and the nuclear meltdown, Rocky put Joe in charge of finding someone to begin looking further into this project. In a week or two, they would meet again and move it forward.

A guild was the next big topic of debate. This was for a few reasons, but first amongst them, according to Sela, was the proprietary ability that guilds could impart on learned skills. If Rocky understood the proprietary ability correctly, the guild could teach all its members skills like Meditation and Ether Manipulation, but if they ever left the guild, Ether would somehow remove those skills from their minds while also not allowing them to teach those skills to others. The fact that the system had so much power over individuals made Rocky and Joe shudder, but it wasn't like there was an option to opt-out.

The other reason a guild was a priority was for level equality. It would seem that members of a guild could contribute a set portion of Etherience gained as a tax to the guild. This Etherience was then able to be given out on guild quests. So, if an individual needed a new set of armor, for example, they could order it and pay an individual, but additionally, the skilled individual who crafted it would be given Etherience, which helped offset the cost somewhat. Sela explained this as commonplace, making it clear that this was how all guilds and societies functioned in the past.

The crafters could also populate quests for materials that would award additional Etherience to parties who collected them. This helped keep Non-Power Classes safe and awarded hunters who were willing to put in a bit of extra work for the betterment of all. The amazing parts came because guilds also increased the amount of Etherience that groups could earn by small percentages. Usually, at level one, that Etherience increase amounted to one percent, but considering that they would be taxing everyone's Etherience gains, Rocky wanted to have something to balance that particular scale.

Rocky touched his chin and asked a question that had been on his mind, "Do you think we can ask for a large shipment of Regulated Knowledge Tablets?"

Sela glared at Rocky, probably recalling that he had spent money on the free item. "Yes, we can. However, that does create a problem. If we're cavalier about the whole thing, everyone in the shop will know we own a burgeoning Territory. That rumor would best be avoided, or people will start asking questions."

At the questioning looks from the men around the fire, she elaborated, "A new Territory is extremely rare on already settled planets. Usually, all Territories are already captured and cataloged. This means that most new Territories are on new planets, and during my life, literal races and wars were undertaken to secure new planets."

She raised a finger emphasizing the next few sentences and continued, "Obviously, merchants and factions are aware of the major players in these conflicts. So, if a new faction is suddenly in possession of a new Territory, questions will be asked. Furthermore, since we can't control all the shops that exist on Gaia, eventually, answers will be given. To put it bluntly, the longer we can delay Gaia being rediscovered, the less slim our chances are for repelling invasions."

Joe asked the obvious, "How are we supposed to stop star fleets and armies filled with Master classes? Even given time, that seems impossible; it's an insurmountable advantage." Rocky felt goosebumps rise on the back of his neck and down his arms. Fighting Master class monsters was bad enough, but fighting an organized military foe with tactical usage of Master class fighters would be a nightmare.

Sela nodded. "Exactly. Right now, we are fighting for every day, each extra moment we can use to increase the strength of the human race. For every second, we can use to find allies and learn the mysteries that caused Gaia to slumber."

Then she smiled, leaned forward, and excitedly continued, "While the high levels of Ether on Gaia can be seen as a negative because it is causing extreme monster mutations and a massive casualty rate, it is also a fantastic boon. Master class monsters were never common, as most were killed long before they could reach past journeyman. Now, however, we have an overabundance of the creatures, which means we can raise ourselves in levels over an extremely short period of time. I also believe Gaia has provided us fodder in the way of non-intelligent golems. Once trained, humans will find the basic golems are rather dense and easy to kill, at least without a golem leader around."

Rocky blinked, having not seen that silver lining before. Then he shook his head. "Sela, we can't take on a starship from the ground!"

Sela's excitement died. She blinked and pursed her lips, nodding her head, then shrugging. "I guess it's something that I never had to consider before. While I lived, no star fleet ever compared to the Gaian Military's. It was one of the reasons we were so successful in campaigns. While most fleets had to drop combatants planetside with a quick support bombardment, we were able to set up in orbit and tactically support as needed. The only reason we were so successful was our Leviathan class ships and their space mage pacts."

Sela looked around, seeing blank looks, so she spoke into the silence and shook her head in clear exasperation, "They existed from a time before I was even born. I don't know much about them. I didn't even ever set foot on to one of the living creature's legendary hulls. All I know is that they were somehow alive and able to cast devastating offensive and defensive spells in space. I don't even remember a laser or torpedo ever breaching their mage shields, and that isn't even counting the raw firepower they could bring to bear."

The stunned looks on everyone's faces made Rocky realize that they had gone completely off the current topic. To be sure, he asked one final question, "Sela, if some of the other planets found out about Gaia today, how long would we have?"

Sela wobbled her hand in the air. "Complete guesswork on my part, but I would say at least a year, possibly less depending on how far technology has advanced since I was alive and how far the planets of origin are located from Gaia."

After that, they got back to a much-subdued discussion about their fledgling Territory, everyone thinking similar thoughts. How were they going to get from here to there?

The list ended up being finalized as:

Shopping List

To Buy
- **Automated Sawmill**
- **Distillery**
- **Kitchen**
- **Cutlery and Plates / Bowls**
- **Skill Scrolls**
- **Research Unlocking Equipment**
- **Blueprints**

To Build
- **Residences**
- **Guild Hall**
- **Meal Hall**
- **Town Hall**
- **Restaurant and Bar**
- **Crafting Hall**
- **Local Shops**

They had mostly decided that they would try to buy the first three on the 'To Buy' list and wait until they had built the first three buildings; then they would sit down and re-discuss.

The group wanted to rush them off to go to the shop right away, but Rocky pulled out the magazine which Jesse had given him that first visit, what felt like ages ago. While Jesse had turned out to be a true slimeball, the times for merchant hours within the book were accurate, and while he didn't have a watch, Sela had learned that the shop was approximately twelve hours in front of the time it was in this geographical location on Earth, meaning that it was somewhere near seven in the morning in the Grotto and seven at night in the shop. Garnell had listed hours that he would be in the shop. Currently, he was out of the shop for at least a few more hours and maybe as much as six hours.

The shopping trip momentarily on hold, they turned to any advantage that might help them progress faster for obvious reasons, which of course, meant the Dungeon needed to be dealt with. So Rocky pulled off his backpack and removed the softball-sized glowing stone.

"Alright, Maximus. How do we do this?" was Rocky's awkward question. The stone didn't respond, and Rocky noticed how faintly it was glowing. So, he panicked for a moment, thinking he had killed it.

It turns out that Max, the Dungeon, was merely deep in thought. Sela screaming at the stone woke it up, to her smiling satisfaction and pleased, crossed-arm victory pose. She had definitely succeeded in startling both Max and Rocky with her outburst.

Rocky repeated his question, and Maximus got serious, "If you choose to enter into negotiations, Gladiator, all you must do is place my core on the ground. Once I am on the ground, a menu of options will arise, and we can begin to negotiate between us for my place in the Territory."

Rocky looked at Sela, who shrugged and then flippantly interjected, "If the Dungeon is lying to us. We will just be forced to kill it."

Rocky shook his head and tried to hide a smile as he placed the Dungeon core on to the ground within the Grotto. Sela may one day get over her intense dislike of Dungeons, or perhaps, she wouldn't, but that comment might help the negotiations. As he stood back to his feet, a green menu box appeared in front of him.

Maximus, the Arena Dungeon, has been grounded in Algonquin Valley.

Would you like to begin negotiations with Maximus, or is he an invading Dungeon?

<Negotiations> | Invader

Rocky mentally selected negotiation, and a new window popped up.

<u>Terms of Cardinal Dungeon Contract</u>

<Standard> | Customize

<u>Standard Terms</u>
- **Dungeon receives 2.5% of Territory-generated Essence**
- **Dungeon receives at least one tribute in the way of valuable items or monsters sacrificed to its depth per moon.**
- **The Dungeon is not held responsible for any deaths of citizens who enter willingly.**

- **The Dungeon is not held liable for any injuries on premises.**
- **Dungeon attempts with all due haste to reach the Tectonic Dungeons.**
- **The Dungeon will work together to meet this goal with all other Cardinal Dungeons.**
- **Territory Leaders shall never be harmed within Dungeon.**
- **The Dungeon will increase the fertility of lands in the cardinal direction of its placement.**
- **The Dungeon will defend and notify Leaders of invaders from said direction.**
- **The Dungeon can call on Leaders to defend it from invaders who seek its heart.**

Offer | \<Back\>

Looking at the standard terms, Rocky's eyebrows shot up because he understood a grand total of zero of its clauses. He looked at Sela who was reading the same list as him. She shook her head and tilted it quizzically. Rocky turned to the core. "What exactly is this Tectonic Dungeon? Also, what in the hell is going to attack you?"

Maximus took a pragmatic pause, which was probably the only way he could convey gravity to a situation since he didn't have any appendages or features. Then he spoke, "Gladiator, Tectonic Dungeons are the deeper seven. They are the place of legends, and Territories who gain access to their halls are granted power beyond compare. To be able to challenge the strength of the Seven should be something that any Champion would aspire towards! As for attacks, if you accept me into this position, other Dungeons and monsters may attack me and the other three Cardinal Dungeons to delay or prevent our progress to the Tectonic Dungeons. According to records, at present, only one Tectonic Dungeon was ever entered. Dungeons fight jealously for the honor of challenging the Seven."

Rocky shook his head and considered if Maximus had just implied what he was thinking. Tectonic only related to one thing in his mind, and that was the tectonic plates. Conveniently, he believed that there were seven of those. Rocky chose to ignore that as it was an eventuality that was too monstrous and distant to fathom. He assumed that these seven Tectonic Dungeons would be far more powerful and nasty then Maximus was letting on.

"Alright, so let's talk about what you as a Dungeon want? Cause the only one I understand is the Essence and sacrificed monsters," Rocky continued, trying to understand the depth of this contract. Even understanding the Essence was a stretch, since from what he could deduce, it was some higher form of energy than Ether.

"Dungeons need to be strengthened. We are constantly threatened by travelers, such as your homicidal druid over there. Everyone wants to kill us, and even our own don't want us to reach the Seven. So, we want stronger monsters and Essence to be able to build defenses and armies. In addition, we would like people to challenge our depth to learn and grow," Maximus gushed excitedly, like challenging the Tectonic Dungeons and evolving strategies was an imperative for him.

The poker player in Rocky perked up at the emotion in the rant, and he smiled. Rocky didn't care at all about these Tectonic Dungeons currently, and that gave him leverage since Maximus clearly did. To confirm this suspicion, Rocky opened a customized contract and added a few lines while removing a few others.

Customized Terms
- **The Dungeon will not kill any of the citizens who venture within its halls.**

- **The Dungeon will receive 2% of Territorial generated Essence.**
- **The Dungeon will receive a new monster corpse one time per month.**
- **The Dungeon will drop loot at each wave of the Dungeon for explorers and give them the option to exit the Dungeon between waves.**
- **The Dungeon will increase the fertility of lands in the cardinal direction of its placement.**
- **The Dungeon will defend and notify Leaders of invaders from said direction.**
- **The Dungeon can call on Leaders to defend it from invaders who seek its heart.**

<Offer> | Back

Rocky had taken the last three from the standard contract verbatim thinking that they should be fine as listed. He clicked "offer" at the bottom and waited.

Maximus went silent, and a moment later, the screen popped back up with a counteroffer.

<u>**Customized Terms**</u>
- **The Dungeon will not kill any of the** *guild members* **who venture within its halls** *if they are not competing.*
- **The Dungeon will receive** *5*% **of Territorial generated Essence.**
- **The Dungeon will receive a new monster corpse one time per** ~~month~~ *moon.*
- **The Dungeon will drop loot at each wave of the Dungeon for explorers and give them the option to exit the Dungeon between waves.**

- *The Dungeon is not held responsible for any deaths of citizens who enter willingly.*
- *The Dungeon is not held liable for any injuries on premises.*
- *Dungeon attempts with all due haste to reach the Tectonic Dungeon.*
- *The Dungeon will work together to reach the Tectonic Dungeon with all other Cardinal Dungeons.*
- *Territory Leaders shall never be harmed within the Dungeon.*
- **The Dungeon will increase the fertility of lands in the cardinal direction of its placement.**
- **The Dungeon will defend and notify Leaders of invaders from said direction.**
- **The Dungeon can call on Leaders to defend it from invaders who seek its heart.**

Accept | <Revise>

Rocky smiled because he knew he had the Dungeon after the counteroffer. He immediately saw his bargaining power and wasn't going to let it go. They went back and forth and spoke often. Maximus seemed shocked when Rocky told him he didn't care at all about reaching the Seven. In addition, after many back and forth exchanges, it turned out that the Dungeon couldn't distinguish if people were citizens and had to change it to guild members because then through some feature of the system, they were tagged for the Dungeon to recognize.

In the end, they reached an agreement that Rocky thought was ideal for his population. Maximus, on the other hand, felt he had given away access to something that Rocky should have wanted to begin with.

You can't start planning for the distant future when you have no foundation set in the present.

Strangely, what ended up assuaging the Dungeon's feelings was the 'donation' of human excrement. The North Dungeon, Maximus, was going to create an area in the northern part of the Grotto that would absorb human waste. Rocky was ecstatic about this boon, but the Dungeon had fought for it. According to Maximus, human waste of any kind had some Essence and Ether still present. If you put enough of it together, then it amounted to something.

The Dungeon had also wanted to create bathhouses, which would be able to absorb filth and human skin cells from the wastewater. Rocky really wanted to accept that offer but felt like it was a good bargaining chip for later or one of the other Cardinal Dungeons. Thinking of LFD, Rocky was strangely contemplative on giving this Dungeon too much.

Customized Terms

- **The Dungeon will not kill any of the Guild Members as long as:**
  - **If a Member would have 'died', they will be notified and forced to leave the Dungeon, and 'dead' Members cannot return until after Resurrection Day—Voskresenie (Sunday).**
  - **On Saturnday (Saturday), the Dungeon will tally each spared Member and will be awarded accordingly.**
  - **A Member can choose to enter after they have 'died', but then all above protections are void.**
  - **If a party has cleared past the final wave, they also must wait to re-enter until after Resurrection Day.**

- The Dungeon will reset to wave one for all parties on Mōnandæg (Monday).
- The Dungeon will receive 2.5% of Territorial generated Essence.
- The Dungeon will receive a new monster corpse or equivalent Crystallized Ether one time per moon (month).
- The Dungeon will drop loot at each wave of the Dungeon for explorers and give them the option to exit the Dungeon between waves.
- The Dungeon is not held liable for any injuries on premises.
- The Dungeon shall attempt with all due haste to reach the Tectonic Dungeon as long as it doesn't hinder other clauses.
- The Dungeon will work in conjunction with all other Cardinal Dungeons for the betterment of the Territory.
- The Dungeon will increase the fertility of lands in the cardinal direction of its placement.
- The Dungeon will defend and notify Leaders of invaders from said direction.
- The Dungeon can call on Leaders to defend it from invaders who seek its heart.
- The Dungeon will create a sewage system to receive human excrement from the Territory for absorption.
- This agreement is subject to change and will be re-negotiated once per full rotation.

<Accept> | Revise

Rocky had added in all the parentheses to make it more understandable for himself. Sela had to try to explain what the days of the week were, using the second day and matching it to Mōnandæg before he had understood. While one moon equated to twenty-nine and a half days, Rocky had affixed month on to it more because that was the time delineation he and every human would be used to seeing. The Dungeon at first had fought desperately to be allowed to kill humans or travelers who entered if it had the opportunity. Rocky, who needed a safe training ground, had racked his brain for a solution to this problem.

Between Joe, Jason, a somewhat smug Sela, and himself asking questions of Maximus, they had begun to understand the Dungeon's desire. The conundrum, as Rocky understood it, was that a Dungeon, when absorbing a corpse, consumed all the accumulated Ether in the corpse. This was a great boon and equated to much more Ether than usually looted in the form of Crystallized Ether. Additionally, most people had some Essence accumulated in their bodies as well, which seemed to be an order of magnitude more potent than Ether.

In the end, he had discovered that the Dungeon would accept something in place of a human's accumulated Ether. One Crystallized Ether per 'kill' was accepted after much grumbling—or something of equal value, which Rocky assumed would be a monster corpse or the like. Shaking his head, he mentally pushed accept. He wasn't sure he had made a good deal with the Dungeon, but he had added the final addendum for just that possibility.

Rocky carried Maximus over to the North wall of the Grotto and held him up against the stone. As if the stone wall was water and Maximus was dropped into it, the wall sucked in the Dungeon core and rippled back to normal. According to Max, it would take approximately four days to get set up, and he would open on Monday, and just like that, in an offhand way, Rocky had found out it was currently Thursday or Thorsday as Sela had informed him.

I will try to do a better job of keeping track of the day. You 'retire' and suddenly don't know the day of the week. Old man!

He chuckled to himself and walked towards the training area. Sela followed along with him, while Joe and Zippo left to go organize the militia into both a defensive force and a temporary administrative one.

That had been another discussion from the night before. The military being one of the few organized groups in the Grotto, it was going to have to pull some double duty for a time. They would need to run some of the backbone of the administration jobs until a government was properly set up. The military's jobs still included regular police work, Grotto security, and the like but extended to creating a list of people and classes present, what skills each person had acquired, and crafting needs.

Sela distracted his thoughts as she sped up her pace to get in front of him and put up a hand. "Are you sure about adding the Dungeon to the Territory? Also giving it Crystallized Ether seems like it will get costly." In her words, Rocky heard her intense dislike of all Dungeons, and it continued to worry him.

"Sela, you forget a few things. I did specify that it had to drop loot and confirmed that it could create the three currency stones." Sela was obviously confused, which was indicated by her narrowing eyes. So Rocky smiled and continued, "We may be giving away a Crystallized Ether early on to strengthen our population, but the loot they will receive will include items to counter this loss. If we choose not to allow the Dungeon to absorb any other form of currency, we will either be receiving gear, meat, or Emerald Gems. Do you see?"

Sela's eyes widened, and she pointed a finger at Rocky in disbelief. "You were planning this the whole time?" Her voice couldn't contain her disbelief with Rocky's ingenuity. She continued, "And as our population gets stronger and doesn't 'die' as much. We will be counting anything the Dungeon drops as pure profit?" Rocky smiled, confirming her thoughts, and she shook her head, truly surprised by the plan. After a thought struck her, she frowned and confusedly asked, "Why did you put in the renegotiations, then?"

Rocky frowned. "I am kind of hoping that the first bit looks so unfavorable to us in the deal that I can get more out of Maximus. Then lock in a permanent contract before the odds skew back. In truth, if we continue to increase our population numbers, it may never really skew fully in our favor. It's all just theoretical at this point."

Sela shook her head again but moved out of his direct path to the center of the Grotto. They had worked at the meeting and subsequently dealt with the Dungeon through the night. It was time for the daily training, and then they would go to the shop.

They had almost chosen to skip the daily training to go to the shop, but Rocky had felt it was important to get the populace used to a routinely scheduled training session, and he needed to lead it. He was trying desperately to make this an every morning routine that they could adjust on the fly based on what the Territory needed. He would have to find others who could lead it for times when he was away, though.

They walked in silence as Sela considered how to break Rocky of his aversion to leadership, and Rocky considered how to break Sela's aversion to Dungeons.

CHAPTER ELEVEN

After the morning training, in which Rocky taught Meditation and Sela directed people in hand to hand combat, Rocky's and Sela's projections phased into the familiar mountaintop of the Aretrin Bazaar. Rocky looked around and considered where to start. There were a few merchants he really wasn't looking forward to visiting. Mainly Jesse, the man who ripped him off on his first visit, then handed him a magazine to let other merchants know he was a sucker. Unfortunately, the other merchants who sold skill scrolls and the like were nowhere near Jesse's equal in what they offered. Regardless, he chose he would visit all of them before he graced the Elf's stupid blanket.

As his eyes roamed, he swore he saw a red mechanical humanoid disappear, and he blinked rapidly.

That had looked a hell of a lot like Corsair!

He looked over at Sela, who nodded. She had seen it too, which at least confirmed he wasn't imagining things. Sela stated in a whisper, "I assume they are looking for humans that enter. Considering that they were probably meeting with Corsair or one of his goons most days. Now suddenly, no humans from Corsair's contingent have entered in almost a week."

Rocky nodded his head and moved off, hoping to get away from the place where most Bazaar visitors phased into. It would be much harder to find them in the Bazaar itself. Not that the 'Mechano-Lords' could do anything to them in the shop, but after their late-night meeting, Rocky was on edge. Add in all the trouble the Mechano-Lords had caused in Ottawa, and they made his blood boil.

As planned, they headed first to Garnell, who specialized in construction materials, building blueprints, and special orders. Rocky really enjoyed the straightforwardness of the man, who reminded him of a blue-collar working man. Approaching the

Karacy, or what could be called a Dwarf by Earthen standards, Rocky smiled, and Garnell matched it.

"Rocky! Great to see ye again. How are all ye tools and materials working out?"

Rocky tried to pat Garnell on the shoulder and unbalanced for a moment as his hand slid through the projection of the merchant. Muttering as he righted himself, he grimaced. "Hey bu– Damnit! I am going to get used to that! Sorry, Garnell." The Dwarf was giving him a bit of a worried look. Rocky continued, "The tools, materials, and forge are working very well, thank you for asking. Can we make this conversation private by chance?"

Garnell raised an eyebrow, then fiddled with invisible screens in front of him.

Garnell BoulderCad has offered you to use a Private Sales Room.

Cost is one Crystallized Ether; would you like to be transported along with Garnell and Selaphelia to the room?

Yes | <No>

*If you spend over 20 Crystallized Ether, the room is automatically compensated by the shop.

Rocky looked at Garnell, then queried both Sela and the man, "If we use this room, can we invite other merchants into it after Garnell?" Sela shook her head and began fiddling with her screens. Suddenly, one of his corners began blinking yellow, and he ground his teeth, still disliking notifications that appeared on his interface in this way. He minimized Garnell's and opened the new yellow notice.

One day I am going to figure out all of these stupid notifications that cause blinking corners and phase them out!

Selaphelia Ardensai has opened a Private Meeting Room.

Cost is five Crystallized Ether; would you like to be transported along with Selaphelia and Garnell to the room?

<Yes> | No

*If you spend over 100 Crystallized Ether the room is automatically compensated by the shop.

Rocky shrugged and rejected the first offer to accept the second, assuming that this was Sela's answer to his question. As soon as he mentally selected yes, the world around him shifted, and the three of them were in an indoor, opulent space. The round room was dominated by a massive mahogany meeting table. The furniture was so lush and posh, Rocky's eyes widened unbiddenly. The table itself was made out of a single tree that, on closer inspection, he didn't actually recognize, despite the mahogany he had associated with it. He could see numerous rings that denoted the tree's age, and it was so dark and glossy he couldn't quite tell what sort of varnish had been used.

The carpet under his feet was deep, earthy colors and seemed so opulently fluffy that he wanted to lie down and go to sleep on it. The walls were all adorned with paintings that depicted magnificent landscapes that either were pure fantasy or the worlds they came from were beyond human understanding. Shaking his head, Rocky pulled out a massive leather chair and sat down. Garnell did likewise, lowering himself slowly as he looked around. "Been a while since I've been in one of these!

Usually, a settlement owner books one of these when they come in to stock up for the year!" Rocky tried to show no response as he turned to look at Sela who tapped her fingers on the table twice.

That was the symbol she told me before entering. One tap for yes and two for no. I am guessing that Settlements and Territories are the same thing, but Sela doesn't want to reveal ours just yet.

"Well, we have some spare cash and plan to purchase quite a bit today if the prices are right," Rocky interjected to cover the momentary lull in the conversation. Then he placed his Regulated Knowledge Tablet on the table and began diving through the Dwarf's wares with occasional comments from Garnell.

"That kitchen is good for feeding approximately a hundred people an hour, and yeah, that's the larger version for a thousand. If you're going to get the next size up for ten thousand, you need to order it and have it ported into location. It's too large to have a compact version that can fit into the shop."

"That sawmill needs to be loaded for each log individually and can plank an entire tree in thirty minutes… That more expensive one is the top-of-the-line model, and if felled trees are in the vicinity, it will automatically load them into the mechanism. In addition, the unused portions of the trees are chipped and turned into plywood."

After looking through the items they were deciding between, Rocky stumbled upon a wide array of tents of all sizes. The options they could provide for his population were extremely beneficial. In fact, one, in particular, made him change his plans slightly because it spoke directly to something Sela had been adamant about.

"This Guild Tent, what is the difference between it and the regular military tent?" Rocky asked, not really needing to know the answer but trying to hide the fact that he wanted it for a Territory. Based on the fact he had just perused through a kitchen for a thousand people an hour and a second kitchen for one hundred people an hour might have already given it away. Not to mention the top-of-the-line sawmill. Those three items were extremely expensive, and he didn't know how he could keep the fact hidden if they kept going.

He somewhat trusted Garnell, but Rocky needed a way to hide who he was from the next merchants they met with. As he internalized these problems, he listened with half an ear to Garnell. "Yes, the military tent will allow you to sleep under cover, conveys a full eight hours of sleep in seven hours, and sets up a perimeter spell at a fifty kilometers radius out from itself. I can open up their properties for you. Honestly, not a lot of people consider these items... unless they have an army in the field." Suddenly, the screen that he was looking at gave quite a bit more information, and Rocky raised an eyebrow at Garnell before reading it.

Guild Tent
- **This tent will act as a guild headquarters, and if placed in the field or a settlement, it will allow a guild to be founded or act as a mobile guild headquarters for expansion. This is not a true building however, so all guild benefits are halved until a more permanent structure is completed. This building is more of a stop-gap to allow the guild to begin growing on new planets or in new Territories before the Territory has access to the construction blueprints and materials to construct a true guild house.**

Cost 100 Crystallized Ether

"Why did you keep the information hidden?" Rocky asked, confusion written plainly across his face.

Garnell shrugged, seeing Rocky's look. "Most people come to see what the exact quality of the items are, and then try to replicate them and sell them at a discount. Most merchants will keep some parts of the crafted gear held back for serious buyers only."

Immediately after his last word, Garnell paused and looked sharply at both of them. He then leaned forward, growing serious, "Listen, let's talk honestly, you two! Do you have an army ten thousand strong and are preparing to march, at which point I cannot in good faith sell to you under the merchant laws of neutrality, or…?"

He let the final comment hang in the air, and Rocky looked at Sela, who was looking back and waiting for his decision. Rocky sighed and looked at Garnell. "Are there any laws that would stop you from revealing information shared with you?" Garnell's stoic demeanor didn't change much, but his mustache and beard twitched, which indicated to Rocky he had shocked the man.

Garnell fiddled with some unseen windows, and suddenly, a black screen appeared in front of Rocky, which had white letters adorning it.

Garnell BoulderCad has suggested a mutual Ether Binding about any information shared in the last thirty minutes and for the remainder of your meeting. If any of the parties involved share information that is spoken about in this meeting and was deemed confidential, then the other party will be informed.

> **To mark information as confidential, speak the words, "This is in confidence," before speaking or simply state all information shared is in confidence. Everything before this contract is signed is deemed confidential if not otherwise specified.**

Accept Ether Bound contract?

<Yes> | No

Sela's eyes had widened slowly as she read to the end of the message and then read it again. After a few quick blinks she nodded to herself then focused her eyes back to him when the screens closed. When Sela nodded to him, Rocky smiled and accepted as well. Then he opened his mouth, "I notice this doesn't stop you from sharing the information outright? I assume that this means that it is more of a reputation loss with me if you do break it?"

Garnell's beard twitched, and Rocky heard a smile in his next words, "That is correct. A Duangar who breaks his word loses his clan and hearth not long after." Rocky blinked. He had obviously never heard that particular idiom, but he could easily figure out the meaning behind the words, so he nodded once.

"Okay, before we get into the discussion, is there a way for me to hide my identity better from future merchants that I meet?" Garnell just shrugged and pulled two fox masks out of thin air and followed them up with something that looked similar to a Japanese kimono.

Garnell shrugged. "I have seen people use something similar to this, and it works relatively well. In conjunction with the Ether Binding we just signed, usually individuals get an idea of who is to be trusted and who to be wary of."

Rocky inspected the items which had instantly gained a bubble that indicated they were not his but were currently accessible and Analyzable by him. He Analyzed one of the masks.

Ceremonial Fox Mask & Ceremonial Kee-chu of the Fox

- **These are expertly crafted items that are often used by the Children of Chaos of Kareet during ceremonial festivals to honor deities.**

Price 1 Gem per set

Purchase 2 sets?

<Yes> | No

It was next to nothing per set of clothing that should help keep them slightly safer moving forward. Rocky accepted, and both Sela and he wrapped the Kee-Chu around themselves with a few directions from Garnell about sashes and buckles. Once they were finished donning the kimono-like garment, they resumed discussions with Garnell.

They told him their current situation and all about being a brand new 'Settlement' just starting out. They made sure to begin discussions with "This is all in confidence," and completely avoided telling him what their planet's name was. Garnell, for his part, nodded along as if he had expected something like this.

Once Rocky finished explaining everything, Garnell nodded once. "This is in confidence, but if you are looking to start a Settlement, then I do have a reserve list of items that I can show you. Keep in mind, some things from this list will have to be brought to the seed shop on my end. So, you have to order them. Then on your next visit, you will pay and receive the items. Also, the first item on the list is something of a necessity for larger purchases. It keeps its location entirely shielded from merchants but allows us to port purchases directly to them."

Sela blinked at this information, which told Rocky that she wasn't aware of Garnell's reveal. A flick of some invisible option and the screens Rocky was looking at changed.

Garnell BoulderCad's Wares

Each item on this list is specific for Territories (Settlements).

Shop Add-ons
- Untraceable Shop Warehouse
- Populace Accessible Shop and Accompanying Assistant
- Purchased Item Tracker
- Shop Tax Storage Vault
- Merchant Room

Territory Blueprints and Temp Buildings
- Housing Tent
- Guild Tent
- Townhall Tent
- Food Hall Tent
- Blueprint – Two-Sided Meal Hall
- Blueprint – Crafters Pavilion
- Blueprint – Training Hall
- Blueprint – Barracks
- Blueprint – Hunters Hall
- Blueprint – Research Library

Page 1 of 12
(1) 2 3 4 5 6 7 8 9 10 11 12
~~Previous~~ - Next

Rocky needed to understand what the Shop-Add-ons did. So, he mentally selected them in turn.

Untraceable Shop Warehouse
- This shop-addon building folds down into a box six-feet by six-feet and will unfold next to the shop if equipped.
- Allows merchants to port in larger wares to Settlement Owners that normally will not fit into the seed shop proper.

- Building hides its location from all merchants and shop owners.

> This item is prohibitively expensive due to its small amount of Arbuckle but grants the owner anonymity.

Cost 300 Crystallized Ether

—

<u>Populace Accessible Shop and Accompanying Assistant</u>
- This shop-addon building folds down into a box three-feet by three-feet and will unfold next to the shop if equipped.
- Allows Settlement owners to grant access to the entire populace for selling and purchasing items without granting access to the shop proper. The assistant that runs the 'Population Shop' will be granted access to a running list of purchasable items the shop has access to through current merchants. It will then allow sales or purchases by individuals. It has minimal negotiation abilities.
- Artificial intelligence will not reveal anything about the customer to a merchant.

Cost 100 Crystallized Ether

—

<u>Purchased Item Tracker</u>
- This AI add-on will keep track of all purchases made and allow individuals to peruse them at leisure.
- Only useable if Populace Accessible Shop and Accompanying Assistant is purchased.

Cost 10 Crystallized Ether

—

Shop Tax Storage Vault

- This shop add-on will keep a certain percentage of purchases and sales as taxes inside the vault. This allows specified individuals to access the vault at any time.
- This item can be used in conjunction with AI from Populace Accessible Shop and Accompanying Assistant. If stored here, the taxes will be counted, and a running total of what's available will be presentable by the AI.

Cost 30 Crystallized Ether

—

Merchant Room

- This shop add-on is a necessity for storing larger merchant wares. This building will store and allow the shop access to items that have been sold, transferring out said items into designated seed shops of the main shop.
- This item is prohibitively expensive due to its moderate amount of Arbuckle and Accompanying Smart Storage System.

Cost 1000 Crystallized Ether

Rocky was stunned first by the items and then further by the prices. It would seem that, in time, he would need to have all of these add-ons. However, at current, he really needed one or two. Stroking his chin, he looked over at Sela, who was also looking through the lists. He let her finish and look up before he asked, "Did you go through everything or just the shop add-ons?"

She glanced at him and then Garnell before she responded, "Garnell, I assume these prices are set by your guild or planetary alliance? At least for the shop add-ons." Garnell nodded, and Sela nodded in confirmation. "I figured. One does not simply come by Arbuckle easily. As for your question, Rocky, I went through everything briefly and think we could use a few items if the price is right."

Warning:
Five sapient creatures have entered your Territory.
They have marked themselves as non-hostile and have requested a meeting with the leader.
Would you like to mark them as enemies?

Yes | <No>

Rocky blinked rapidly and looked at Sela whose eyes had widened, and she had half stood from her chair. Rocky placed a hand on her shoulder and stood himself. "I think one of us should stay here and continue this discussion. Since you are the more knowledgeable, I think that should be you. I will go take a look at what has entered our Territory. Azoth should be able to contact you if needed, or I'll simply mark them as hostile."

Sela first shook her head and looked ready to protest, but when she looked at his hard-cold eyes, she saw a dark, swirling cloud that made her shiver. She saw in them the man she had glimpsed that fateful night they lost two young men, the man she had seen a few times on their journey back to the Territory, and she smiled before nodding. A moment later, Rocky ported out of the shop, leaving her and Garnell to continue.

CHAPTER TWELVE

As soon as Rocky found himself in the room inside the seed shop, he looked over to his guide and friend, Sela. She was statue still, serene, but still somehow commanded respect. Chagrined, he shook his head to clear it of the momentary, albeit beautiful distraction. A moment later, he exited the room by placing his hand on the inside wall, which opened a door.

Once he was outside, he mentally called Azoth, who surprised him by chuffing right behind him. Rocky jumped before laughing and patting the giant Chimera, who had been resting near the shop, probably waiting for Sela or himself. Rocky touched his ear and sent to Joe, "Joe, there's something that entered our Territory to our southwest. They have somehow signaled they're friendly, but just in case, rally the army and march in that direction."

Rocky winced when the first notes of Joe's response were overlaid in group chatter, "Roger, Rocky... That might take me a bit longer than normal. I just told a few squads to get breakfast assuming that we were going to meet after you were done in the shop. Over." Rocky was surprised Joe hadn't given him a hard time on his radio etiquette, but maybe, he was finally realizing Rocky was a lost cause.

Shrugging, Rocky mounted up on to Azoth, and they took off. Using his knees and mental connection, he directed Azoth to follow the gold threads towards the southwest edge of Algonquin Valley. The gold threads were his Territory's way of letting him know exact locations within. Together, Azoth and Rocky made a pass over the indicated area, and mentally, Rocky confirmed that neither of them had noticed anything. They had made multiple passes and still couldn't see a thing.

Reluctantly, Rocky told Azoth to land farther back from the clearing in question, and once grounded, he left the Chimera's back to activate Stealth and Dark Cloak. Then together, they stalked the clearing, still looking for anything they had missed from the air. Expecting a group of humans who had seen their tracks or some stragglers from Ottawa, Rocky jumped from branch to branch in the trees that surrounded the marked area trying to locate anyone. After fifteen frustrating minutes, Rocky dropped his two skills and cautiously walked out into the open.

The other party has been indicated of your arrival and is en route to the meeting area. Safety is guaranteed for both parties for the next hour. If your party attacks, ramifications will be enacted as per Statutes of Atlantis: Diplomatic Immunity IX (III)(A).

Rocky looked around the clearing and shook his head, realizing that he still had a lot to learn. Somehow, these people had indicated and set an area for a meeting. Now, they were protected and had been waiting to be informed that he had arrived. Rocky began to sit down, not sure how long he would have to wait. The plan from the previous night's long talks was to meet after the shopping trip and create a council that included more people from the Territory.

Hopefully, by doing this, it would expand the understanding and new world concepts through the burgeoning society. They wanted to limit the number at first to try to control the meetings more, so only Derik, Smith, Amber, Jack, Mr. Pips, Bart, Joe, Rocky, Zippo, and Sela were going to be in attendance at the first session. So basically, the A-Team because it had built a strong relationship with the first settlers and Rocky's group which had a strong relationship with the Ottawa survivors. In time, they would add others to make the group as inclusive as possible.

As soon as he fully sat down, through his hands and butt, he started to feel it—a vibration that was too subtle to feel through his boots' soles but obvious with his bare hands and through the thinner fabric of his leather pants and under armor. It was gaining in intensity the longer he sat, and eyes wide, Rocky shot back to his feet and drew his sword.

What in the Atlantean hells is going on? The frequency of those vibrations make it seem like multiple huge creatures are approaching—

Rocky was proven right as a gigantic, green-armored foot exited the foliage between two trees. A moment later, a green, armor-clad, humanoid body of a massive golem followed suit. Within thirty seconds, four more gargantuan frames of familiar-looking golems entered the clearing to form a line all facing Rocky and Azoth. Then all of them moved in sync, raising high their weapons. Rocky stepped back, but they seemed far too distant to attack him.

These are the golems from Ottawa, the five I saw in the distance. They were sitting where the parliament buildings once resided.

In a fluid motion, the first golem on the left sunk his spearhead and part of the shaft into the ground. Then down the line, one after the other, they sunk weapons into the ground. A battle-axe, followed by a naginata, long-sword, and lastly, two short swords. Then in unison, they all stepped forward two gargantuan steps and kneeled down, resting on their heels.

Azoth growled menacingly at the seated figures but remained at Rocky's side as he mentally sent, "Azoth sees them in place we travel from. Why they here? They do a following? Azoth confused. Are they attack-ees?"

Rocky placed his hand on Azoth's chest and mentally sent, "They seem to want to talk only. Calm down and follow me, then sit when I do. Okay?"

Azoth nodded his head, and Rocky activated the radio in his ear, "Joe, when you get here, set up a perimeter. Do not attack unless I give the order. Understood?"

"Copy," was Joe's response, this time with no background noise, which probably meant they were en route or massing.

Rocky raised his sword above his head and then drove it into the ground; he felt slightly reassured he could summon it to him if needed. Then he and Azoth walked forward a fair distance before sitting down on the ground as well. Feeling slightly out of his element, he just looked at the massive, medieval armored figures that sat placidly in front of him. He used Analyze on the one on the far right, the one who sat in front of the dual swords.

Omega
Master-Knight of Gaia
Level 72
Moderate Analyze has failed to provide additional information.

Rocky would have kept Analyzing them all, but the figure in the middle, the one in front of the naginata, began to speak. Rocky's wide, surprised eyes shot to him instantly when the deep, booming voice broke the silence, "Greetings, human, we would like to speak with you peacefully, and we are quite glad that you have chosen to come and negotiate with us."

Strangely, the expressions on the Knights' faces betrayed the speaker's words. One of the Knights smiled broadly, including the speaker—two seemed impassive, one frowned at him, and the final member was sneering. Tilting his head questioningly, he first Analyzed the speaker, wanting to know his name before responding.

Epsilon
Master-Knight of Gaia
Level 72
Health Points 9,319/9,319

"Hello, Epsilon. I am not exactly sure what we have to talk about. Pardon my skepticism, but the only other talking golem I met tried to kill me and a village of people—"

Three of the golems shifted and looked at each other with obvious excitement, which cut Rocky off mid-sentence. "Brothers, do not believe the words of this tiny man. You trust easily!" the golem in front of the battle-axe angrily spat out. Hearing the anger in the voice, Rocky instinctively used Analyze.

Gamma
Master-Knight of Gaia
Level 72
Moderate Analyze failed to provide additional information.

Epsilon clapped his massive hands to regain the attention. "I apologize. Some of us are just very excited to hear that there are others like us. That can speak and think. However," Epsilon glared at Gamma before continuing pointedly, "*some* of us are skeptical." He took a deep breath and looked away before regaining his neutral tone, "In general, we weren't sure what our purpose was after being born, and without guidance, we have all gone slightly separate ways on the issue. We followed you in hopes of discovering more, and then Gaia confirmed our path–"

"Slow down! Hold on, you followed us, and somehow, Gaia has confirmed that it was the right choice?" a flustered Rocky cut off Epsilon, not sure he was understanding the relatively religious worship he was hearing. It was pretty hard for him to associate human emotions to these creatures as well, but they had clearly indicated they had each felt something upon waking up and that they each were struggling to make sense of their individual existences.

"Yes, Gaia asked us to protect your group on the final leg of the journey. She personally offered us a Red Quest." Epsilon looked at the other five and then pointed to Rocky. "We ensured that you and your group made it home safely and also avoided our own demise in the raging Ether Storm that followed. The quest was from Gaia herself, despite some members' protests to the contrary." Epsilon glared down the line at Gamma again, who looked straight ahead scowling.

Rocky stopped himself from smiling at the byplay for two reasons. One reason was that despite how nice Epsilon seemed to be, they could slaughter him and his entire fledgling populace without much effort. The second reason was because he didn't want Gamma to think Rocky was laughing at him. Based on the current conversation and the interplay between the two, Gamma seemed like the quick to anger one in the group.

Epsilon looked back to Rocky expectantly, and Rocky blinked into a deepening awkward silence before starting, "Umm… well, I mean, thank you… but what do you plan to do now?"

Epsilon looked left then right down the line of his brothers. "After much discussion, we wish to help build a place of safety here. Then we can perhaps search for others like ourselves and have them join us? We wish to try to possibly create a community akin to yours."

Rocky shook his head confused; he felt Epsilon was misunderstanding something. "Epsilon, humans seek community for a fair number of reasons, but currently, it's because of safety, as you mentioned." He looked at all the golems then raised an eyebrow skeptically, "What in the Atlantean hells do you all have to fear?"

I am rather proud of my new swearing substitute!

Gamma answered instantly, anger lacing every word, "Well, in the way you humans seem to fear every creature around you, nothing! Do not presume to understand us greater beings! We have quite a few more important fears."

Epsilon shook his head sadly. "With the rate of growth, you humans have shown, we will one day be overpowered by your race. We have no way of reproducing, and while we can gain power by attacking wildlife and perhaps even killing the pale, lifeless golems as well, we have no ability to capture Territories; if we are hunted by humans, we will one day be destroyed."

The group went silent, and an angry voice cut in, making Rocky's head snap back to Gamma, "Or we could just eradicate all humans before that happens, like I suggested." Rocky's mouth dropped open, and the only thing that stopped him from summoning his sword was that three of the creatures were shaking their heads.

The Knight on the far right, in front of the spear, opened his mouth to speak, and Rocky Analyzed him for a name.

Delta
Master-Knight of Gaia
Level 72
Moderate Analyze failed to provide additional information.

"As the quest indicated, Gaia does not wish for humans to be entirely eradicated, Gamma. So, unless you wish to displease our creator, there must be another purpose or reason for our creation." Delta's voice was cultured and calm. The golem seemed to inflect no emotion. Instead, he gave off a vibe of serenity and intelligence. He even touched the bridge of his nose as he spoke, almost seeming to push up an invisible pair of glasses.

Rocky, who also had no idea what possible reason Gaia could have had for creating sapient golems, pursed his lips. He responded flatly, "Honestly, I really don't know how people will handle golems living with or near us. This is quite a lot of information to digest, and I am not sure how to help you five. If I choose to let you stay, it could cause everyone in the Territory to live in fear and hate you for the deaths of those close to them."

The golem on the end in front of the dual swords, Omega, had been smiling the entire time. For some reason at that moment, his obvious excitement became too much for him, and he finally chose to interject. After his first word, Rocky felt his head tilt and eyes widen in confused shock. In clear, California beach boy tones, Omega exclaimed, "Also, dude… we would like totally want to try some of the other creature comforts that you humans seem to enjoy. Like food and drink, dude. While we don't have to eat—"

Epsilon shook his head and held up a hand that interrupted the buoyant Omega. "I am sorry for him. He doesn't always sense the mood." The sudden change in direction to the conversation had caused Rocky to blink more rapidly as he listened to more byplay between the two. Epsilon continued, "He has a fascination with the smells and food he has seen. It didn't help that many of our lesser brethren absorbed strange pictures as they grew for other exotic and delectable looking foods."

Smile widening, Omega 'Santa Cruized' some more, "Yeah, bro, especially 'pizza'. How does one call the displayed number?"

Rocky sat still eyes wide for a few long seconds. Looking around, he saw the golems were all staring back at him intently. So, Rocky tentatively divulged, "Unfortunately, those were called advertisements, Omega, and the number you were considering calling will… definitely be out of service?" He finished slowly.

The group of golems looked at each other, a few going as far as sighing deeply; even Gamma! Epsilon nodded once sighing deeply. "Sorry, this has gotten a little off track. I apologize for being blunt, but can we stay?"

Rocky felt whiplash from the change in direction again; he slowly drew out his answer. "I honestly don't know. I'm going to discuss this with my people. For now, you are welcome to stay on the edge of the Territory and enjoy the protection from the Ether Storms, and then let's meet tomorrow afternoon. Is that acceptable?"

Rocky heard the pleading in his own voice and knew that he had no power to back up his words. If these creatures chose to stay, they could simply destroy everyone and take the Territory. So, his only option was to pander to them and hope that through discussion, perhaps a mutually beneficial agreement could be reached. Otherwise, he was pretty confident Algonquin Valley was the least defended Territory in the world! Having only experience in the strength of monsters that had guarded his Territory and the Ottawa Territory, Rocky assumed that it would be one of a small portion of Territories captured by humans.

"We will set up a meeting area for tomorrow and await your decision," Epsilon spoke flatly. Then all of the five bowed in unison. Rocky followed suit and caught Azoth attempt a bow out of the corner of his eye. The fact that the jumbo-sized cat-bird needed to use his wings to balance himself made Rocky chuckle.

Or maybe that was supposed to be a flourish?

Smiling, Rocky continued to sit there as the five Knights stood and moved back to their weapons. He cast Analyze on the final member he didn't yet know. Delta was walking towards his spear; Epsilon his naginata; Gamma his battle-axe; and Omega picked up his dual swords. Rocky Analyzed the individual who picked up the longsword.

Tao
Master-Knight of Gaia
Level 72
Moderate Analyze failed to provide additional information.

Rocky watched the five Knights retreat and shook his head as they almost instantly vanished into the trees. Then he stood up, collected his sword from the ground, and clicked his radio. "Joe, we've had a… development. Mind if I catch a ride back with you on one of the tanks?" He let go of his radio button and turned to Azoth. Patting him on his chest, he cooed, "Go hunt, buddy. I don't think I'll have much time left for fighting today. After I'm done with Joe, I should join Sela back in the shop, if she isn't finished."

Azoth pushed his massive head into Rocky's chest, and his two goat horns grated against his hardened leather armor. Then the massive Chimera took off and mentally sent back, "What pizza? Azoth also want try all food. Azoth like-d Omega."

Rocky chuckled and mentally sent to Azoth, "Just bring back your leftovers, birdbrain!"

Joe's voice crackled over the radio, "Affirmative. I believe we're just east of your current position. Over."

Rocky began walking and contemplating all of the things he still had to do with the current day.

CHAPTER THIRTEEN

"We should accept them right away!" was Joe's response as Rocky finished relaying the story from moments ago.

Smith had come along after hearing of the possible danger and was walking beside them. He shook his head. "I've barely faced these creatures, Mr. Joe, but I've heard nothing but anger and fear from the mouths of survivors. Every person who has lost someone in our Grotto would have to confront it all over again, come face to face with a representation of the creatures who did it. If we bring in a group as powerful as this, even if they mean us no harm, can you truly say that we mean them no harm?"

Some people have already tried to kill me. I doubt we can offer the golems a better reaction.

Zippo surprised Rocky by interjecting in a voice that leaned towards amusement, "Guys, we already have a meeting planned, and Sela is going to be there. She might have a better idea or something to add on the subject. Once we get back, Joe and I will go to procure a pot of stew from the cooking area. Then I'll put in the finishing touches when Rocky goes to get Sela from the shop." Rocky smiled; hearing Zippo's voice without the sullen and depressed overlay made him want to dance a jig. The young man was still looking serious, but even the fact he'd joined the conversation unbidden was improvement.

The group continued to chat amongst themselves about the pros and cons of having the creatures, and Rocky seriously considered possibilities for the powerful golems. It didn't take long for the military column to return to the Grotto, and by then Rocky had started to consider a plan he thought might work.

As Zippo added meats and spices to an already simmering stew pot, Rocky had entered the shop to finish up or finalize any transactions and collect Sela. Even though it had been about an hour since he left, Sela was still with Garnell, and they were discussing some of the finer points of certain tents. He'd entered the shop and had a few moments of fiddling with the shop screen before he found the meeting room that Sela had prepared for the group. Rocky was happy to see her negotiating and questioning every piece of information she was told when he phased in behind her once again.

"Sela, we have to wrap this up. There's been a development, and we have that 'council' meeting coming up," Rocky stated simply, hoping that he wasn't interrupting something important.

Sela nodded and turned to Rocky, eyes sparkling. "I think we should get three items now. The problem is that they will burn through most of our savings and some that we hadn't planned on using." She paused, and Rocky didn't say anything, so she continued, "The Guild Tent, the Autoloading Sawmill, and the Populace Accessible Shop. All totaled, that will come to six hundred crystals, but Garnell has offered to discount the sawmill to half price with such a large purchase. So, we can get them all for five hundred and fifty crystals."

Rocky saw the dilemma instantly; with approximately two hundred and fifty crystals left, they would be left with little money to buy any of the other items they considered necessary. Considering that they wanted to convert two hundred crystals to gems, chips, and marks for wages that made it even less. Knowing Sela had a reason for this Rocky asked, "Please explain the reasoning for these three and why you have ignored the residents' tents, kitchens, or Meal Hall?"

Sela nodded her head, explaining, "The shop access is going to go a long way to helping the people from Ottawa to see a big difference between Corsair and us. However, while it should bring up morale, it also allows us to set a tax for goods purchased in the shop, which means that we can start earning crystals that can then be reinvested into the Territory." She pointed to Rocky's bag of holding, "Additionally, people can sell loot drops, plants, minerals, and the like to the shop assistant. Again, we would make some money on those sales." Sela had been gesturing with her hands at the tablet in front of her, so Rocky had moved forward to see a web diagram on the page she had hand drawn.

The major point in the center of the web was 'Economy', which was drawn with a snake eating its own tail. The next layer out from the center had four bubbles: Luxury Goods and Services, Guild Hall, Shop, and Producible goods. Two of them had been circled, but all of them had small notes coming off of them.

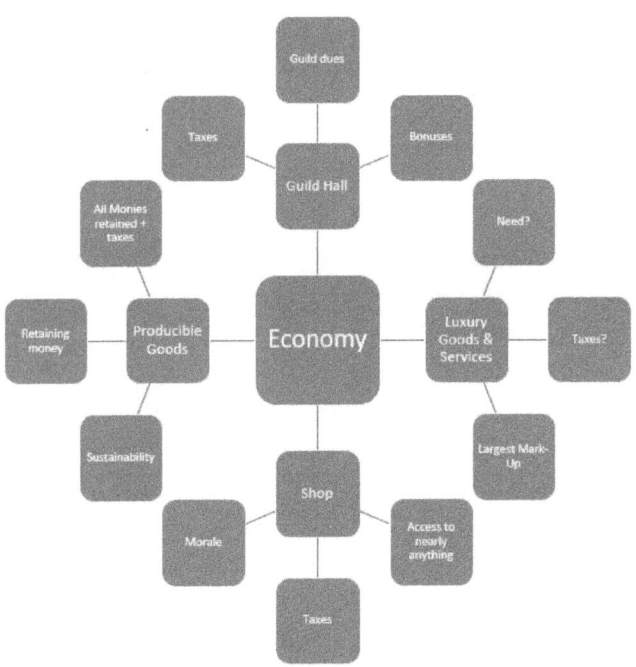

Sela had clearly thought this out, and Rocky was pretty convinced at this point. Sela saw him studying it, and she pointed to Producible Goods and Luxury Goods & Services. "These two are going to be something that we are going to want to foster and grow, but there isn't much we can do right away about them." With that, she pointed to the other two. "These two we can jump-start now and begin earning some money that can then be injected back into the Territory. Unfortunately, as you pointed out, we're ignoring the Residential Tents this way, but two things come to mind for that. With the sawmill and additional bodies, we should be able to greatly increase building speed. Also, the Guild Tent can sleep two thousand comfortably and maybe everyone if we want to crowd in close."

Rocky instantly saw the dilemma as well. So, he turned to Garnell. "How much do you sell a single tent for? Standard issue, just to keep the rain off."

Garnell forwarded the description of tents to Rocky quickly through the ever-present screens of the system; a tent to sleep two was a mark, to sleep eight was a gem, and to sleep twenty was a crystal. Rocky continued, "Sela, I think you are right, and with access to the shop, people can purchase tents or buildings if they don't like this solution. While I wanted to meet other merchants and browse their goods, I think this is as much as we can do today. Let's do it. Can Garnell also change the crystals for pay and salaries?"

Garnell smiled. "Of course I can, and be sure to mention to the people that they can have the assistant come directly to me to avoid cheap knock offs of products. I will be sure to give your assistant the best deals I can." Rocky smiled, finally seeing the merchant in the man.

Luckily, his bag of holding was able to carry objects of any size. The tent was folded down but was still extremely heavy and huge. It was easily the largest item, even more than doubling the sawmill. The sawmill was similar in size to the portable forge and had just as much metal accompanying it. In contrast, the shop addon was a box of metal about the size of a small moving box.

Once he had placed all the items into his bag of holding, he was forced to remove the bag to stand back up after his rump quickly hit the chair. Even with all the weight reduction, the bag was too heavy to just be casually worn. Once Sela and he exited the virtual shop and were in the pie-shaped interior of the shop building, they both placed their hands under the bag and lifted it together. They managed to get it outside of the shop, and the few people who were watching as the two of them exited sweating and straining with a tiny pouch suspended between them gave them some very odd looks.

A few steps from the shop building, they placed the bag down, and Rocky dumped out all three items, then reattached the bag to his belt. Sela picked up the moving box-sized shop addon with ease and walked it to the side of the shop before placing it down. As soon as the similar-looking metals touched each other, the box began to rapidly expand and grow. It was odd because it was extremely hard to see where the shop was getting the larger mass from. Rocky assumed it had been something like solid metal on the inside, and now, the metal was looking somewhat liquid as it grew and thinned out.

As it continued to grow, Rocky bent down and swept the two other items into the Territory Inventory, knowing that using it this way would allow them to place them wherever they wanted without having to carry the awkwardly shaped and large items around.

People from the Territory began to stop and stare, starting with the ones who saw the two of them straining under a heavy weight, then more joining the few as a building unfolded from a tiny square.

Smiling, Rocky looked out over the forming crowd, then looked back to the shop, realizing it was done. He continued his turn to Sela. "Want to check it out?"

Not even answering, he sprinted inside to Sela's laughter at his excitement behind him. The interior of the shop was surprisingly large. The walls must have been slightly thicker than paper but made out of a similar metal to the shop—only much shinier and less chromatic. Upon entering, Rocky was greeted by a female voice with just a hint of a robotic intonation, "Welcome, currently the shop and myself, the assistant, are setting up and downloading information on the 'Aretrin Bazaar' seed shop we are joined to. We will be ready for business in a few hours. Please return then."

Some of the crowd stuck their heads in the door and looked around. He could even hear a few relaying what the assistant had just robotically intoned back out to the group.

Chuckling, Rocky walked over and saw a holographic image of an amorphous, gray shape on top of a wheeled robotic platform. He smiled, thinking that this meant the assistant in the shop would be able to float around and may also create a shape once the set up was complete. Unsure, he turned to Sela. "Have you been in a shop like this before?"

Sela looked around and nodded slowly. "Yes… I have, but I didn't realize at the time that it was actually a shop attached to a seed shop. It was melded into a storefront and had décor that covered most of the metallic walls." She paused for a moment, looking around. "I wonder if the seed shop it was attached to was deemed unsavory by the leadership of the guild?"

Rocky shrugged and turned to the assistant not having an answer; that was all in the deep past, and they wouldn't be able to answer that particular question, probably. "Can you please keep all taxes and track the purchases made by anyone who comes in here? Then keep both available for only the leaders of the Territory?"

"Apologies, the required components to track purchases do not exist in the shop currently because this is a personal upgrade, I can search for them now?" The amorphous, gray holograph asked without moving at all. It was quite disconcerting to see a human shape but not have it act human in any defining way.

Rocky nodded and added, "Please go right to Garnell." An extended pause followed, and he hoped the computer registered the nod.

He was about to open his mouth and verbalize his affirmative when the shop chimed, "Object found. Would you like to purchase it for ten crystals?"

Rocky looked over to Sela, and she shrugged sheepishly, realizing that they had forgotten that particular add-on in their excitement. So, Rocky nodded and pulled out ten crystals from his bag of holding before holding them out and looking around. A silence stretched, and Rocky looked at Sela, who was trying to fight down laughter. A moment later, the robot voice broke the awkwardness, "Please place your payment on the counter."

Damnit! I may need to request a manual for things in the future. I hate looking stupid…

Sela burst into laughter behind him, and he glared at her as he placed the crystals on the metal counter that separated the gray hologram and himself. Once that was complete, the computer woman piped up again, "Purchase is complete. We will install the device along with our current setup routines. Please come back in a few hours for any other purchases you might require."

As the two moved back to the entrance, the people retreated back outside, and Rocky took the moment of privacy to whisper, "Does it have an automatic rate for taxation, or do we set that somehow." Sela shrugged but started flipping through her screens, looking for it.

A moment later, she furrowed her nose in disgust. "It is locked until we have a Town Hall. It is probably set to a certain amount currently. Assistant, what is the current tax rate on incoming items from the shop?"

"Currently, the shop has its tax rate set at ten percent. If you would like to make a non-shop related purchase, please come back in a few hours when I am done with my current setup."

Rocky frowned, getting sick of the repetition and motioned to the door. They exited to find a crowd of excited people looking anticipatingly at them. He smiled and opened his arms before joyously projecting, "In a few hours, anyone can access this shop. Right now, the assistant is setting up, so please stay out until," he motioned to two military guards in the crowd, "the military guards here say it's okay."

He motioned the two forward and Analyzed them. Then in a clear voice meant to be overheard, he asked, "Barry, Samantha, do you two mind being stationed at the front door and maintaining order to any line that may form?"

They saluted, and he nodded to them as they took up positions on each side of the door.

He expected the crowd to stay and begin making a line up to the entrance of the shop, but most of the group followed him and Sela as they left. Eyebrows raising, he made his way towards the center of the Grotto. He shrugged to Sela when she looked back and sheepishly commented, "Let's set up the tent and the sawmill, then head to that meeting. Maybe people would like to see more."

On the way to the center of the Grotto, they passed by the pile of trees, and Rocky pulled out the portable sawmill from the Territory Inventory. The crowd made noises of astonishment, and he blushed.

Come on now, guys! No need to be surprised by this.

The push of a button saw the sawmill unfold from around the myriad of circular saws that were hidden in the center of the blocky, metal contraption. Once the building clicked its final pieces into place, a mechanical arm reached over and placed two grippers around a massive cut tree.

The crowd, seeing the dangerous appearance of the saws and mechanical pieces, stepped far back from the machine. Rocky motioned to more military who were walking by and they jogged towards him. They stopped with a salute and a, "Commander?"

He saluted them awkwardly. "Please watch this machine and make sure no one tampers with it or gets too close to get injured." Then he looked at it. "Well, not unless you are told they can. Like right now. I'm going to try to fix it." The machine was stopped with its grippers clamped on a tree.

Damnit, I broke it already… but it isn't whining like an overloaded electric motor.

He walked around the rather large, unfolded, portable sawmill; the building had a two-hundred-foot-long inverted wedge in the center that had rotating grinder blades in the middle section. It was clear that the log could be pushed backward and forward over this section as it spun to remove the outer bark and branches. Rocky wanted to understand the rest of the machine but first had to find why it had failed to start working. A blinking light caught his attention, and he walked up to a screen.

Resource located, confirm resource pile location. All resources left outside of pile location will not be processed.

<Yes> | Rescan | Manual

Rocky clicked yes, and the machine loaded the first log into the inverted wedge trough. A moment later, the machine confirmed his notion for the grinder blades, but somehow gravity and the rotary blades themselves pulled the log over the grinder blades while simultaneously spinning it. Once all the bark and tree branches were removed, the grinders retracted slightly, and the screen flashed again.

Size of resource scanned. Please select the cutting method for the resource.

2x4 Planks – 40%
2x6 Planks – 16%
2x10 Planks -12%
4x4 Support Beams – 8%
8x8 Support Beams – 4%
Other Cuts <Specify> - 5%
Plywood – 15%

<Economical> | Manual | Focused

<Edge Grain> | Flat Grain Bark Down | Flat Grain Bark Up

<Confirm Settings> | Change Settings

The quick work of the automated sawmill had the crowd jostling each other, and he saw more military guards appear to make a larger ring around the machine. He smiled at the ones who joined before turning back to the screen.

He blinked. "Sela, do you know anything about the list of construction materials needed for the Longhouses?"

She came over while flipping through a floating window. "Not off the top of my head, but I think it is listed in the Construction Page." As she arrived, she looked at the machine's display screen and flipped a few more of her own personal ones. Then she sidled up beside him so they could both compare the two. Sela had clearly zoomed in on a corner of a larger drawing that Rocky would have to look at later, but it reminded him of an architectural or structural CAD sketch.

Longhouse Blueprint Details

- **This Longhouse blueprint will create a two-story rooming complex. This building does not provide individual kitchens or personal relaxation areas. It is a basic level building that provides one hundred total rooms with a single bed in each room. This provides a modicum of privacy for the occupants and helps reduce the chance of spreading disease.**

Materials Required
2x4 – 600
2x6 – 200
2x8 – 0
4x4 – 100
8x8 – 75
Nails / Screws Assorted
Plywood – 1000 Sheets
Drywall – 400 Sheets
Shingles – 500 Squares
Foundation – Assorted Amount and Material

For best results, place a solid foundation under the building. In time, the Longhouse can be converted into a Small Apartment / Condo Complex. This will require doors to be created between rooms and individual kitchens installed. If, in future expansion, more floors are likely to be added, use greater number of 8x8 supports in optional locations mentioned in Blueprint.

Rocky looked over the two and clicked Manual on the screen for the Automated sawmill. He removed the percentages in the other cuts—2x8 and 2x10 categories. He then did some simple math by converting the total number of logs needed in the Longhouses into percentages of each type. In the end, he put those numbers into the machine. He assumed he would have to adjust this again in the future as they changed their building priority, but for now at least, it would be working, and the pile only had about fifty logs anyway. They would need a lot more than that for the five thousand plus people they had in the Grotto.

Turning to Sela with a raised eyebrow, she answered his unspoken question, "We will get someone who knows more about construction to be in charge of this in the future. At least for now, they will have some materials ready and waiting for Longhouses today." Rocky clicked 'confirm setting', and as they walked away, the machine whirled to life behind them. The sound and smell of cut wood brought a smile to Rocky's face as he felt the proverbial first step of his burgeoning population being taken.

The group that surrounded the machine parted to let the two through, and Smith surprised them by falling in beside them on the way to the next stop. Rocky blinked and asked, "Everything okay, Smith?"

Smith nodded but made a sour face with his mouth. "I'm here to show my support of you as a leader. I feel that any decisions you make are going to be questioned, so it's best to have as much support as possible." He looked like he was about to continue but shut his mouth quickly before smiling at people in the crowd.

As they kept walking, Rocky looked at Sela, who had her eyes squinted at Smith, sensing as he did that something was being left unsaid. He sighed deeply and put a smile on his face like Smith, hoping he wasn't in for a surprise later.

The last thing they attempted to find was a clear area for the massive dimensions of the Guild Tent. Garnell had mentioned to Sela it would have a diameter near three hundred meters.

Unfortunately, as Rocky scanned the central area to the Grotto, there was no space that was clear enough to place the Guild Tent. The entire floor was littered with tree stumps and rocks, and they were forced to delay the set up of the Guild Tent. He chose a good place, then marked an area in the dirt where they would start clearing a large circle around. Right now, they had delayed the meeting long enough.

Slightly disappointed, the crowd that had followed them dispersed as they made their way over to an area of the Territory near one of the cliff walls. Someone had clearly used a tank, as evidenced by the tread marks, to drag over four logs to sit on and had even started a fire in the middle of the square. As they walked up, he saw that Zippo was tending a pot of something that was suspended over the fire, Joe was sitting and talking to a beautiful, dark-skinned woman, Derik was hovering like a helicopter parent over Zippo's shoulder, and the rest of the A-Team that Rocky had yet to meet was sitting while talking congenially to each other.

All eyes tracked Rocky and Sela as they approached, and once they sat down, the group all moved in closer to the two of them. Zippo continued cooking but circled the stew pot to be able to more easily be included. Amber was the first to chime in, "I don't think we ever thanked you," she directed this statement at Rocky and Sela, "for saving us from that massive bear."

The other A-Team members all nodded, except for Derik, who sneered and added in a quip, "Yeah, like he did it for altruistic reasons…"

Mr. Pips, who somehow was still a massively obese man even after the system changes, scolded, "Derik, we're alive, and that means quite a bit more than whatever fictitious, underhanded ulterior motive you have cooked up." Mr. Pips then smiled at Rocky and Sela, conveying that Derik was the only one who felt that way.

Bart, who they hadn't seen earlier, was the spitting image of a Hell's Angel biker. He had a bushy, white beard, and his long, white hair was tied back in a ponytail. He wore a leather jacket with a stylized picture of the Roman god Bacchus on the front. This was only clear because the letters Bacchus were spelled out on the back above the depiction. The persona and his obvious altruistic actions from earlier warred with each other and reminded Rocky never to judge a book by its cover.

With everyone but Derik's seal of approval, Rocky began telling the story of what had occurred that morning, and he summarized their purchases in the shop. Derik's scowl grew larger as he spoke, and his quick, angry glances at Smith weren't missed by Sela.

CHAPTER FOURTEEN

Helion Resistance Headquarters – Deep Cave

Flowing, silver nanobots flew into the room like liquid metal and began piling up on top of each other to create a viewing monitor in front of Amelia Nanospark. "What in the Helion depths was the urgency?" she thought as she mentally commanded her nanobed to help her rise from her previous prone sleeping position to receive the message. A garment sailed through the air from her closet, and she stepped forward as more of her bots wrapped the garment around her pale nakedness. She was a Helion, which meant her appearance was of pure, white, alabaster skin; silver, orbed eyes; dark black, chitinous hair; clawed fingers; and sharp-pointed ears. While there weren't many of her people remaining, they had always preferred the deep depth of their world, so being forced deeper by the invading guilds hadn't been the primary cause of the genocide of her people.

No, her people had been slaughtered ruthlessly so the guild's alliance could capture their first planet. Traditionally, one of the elder three planetary god's military captured newly discovered planets and took them under their flag. While this wasn't exactly a perfect situation for a new planet, it was still much preferred to the massacre that had occurred on Helion. It would seem that this was the third such endeavor orchestrated by the allied guilds, and they had learned their lessons from their previous two failures. In all other cases, the resident populace of the conquered planet had been left alive to join the guilds or been enslaved to serve them, but in both previous cases, that had led to their power being overthrown because of the massive support of the superpowered god planets. This time, her people didn't have enough of a foothold to mount a serious rebellion. At least not yet…

This time, they hadn't even tried to enslave or offer the populace of Helion anything. They had flown in with ships the likes of which Helion residents had only heard rumors of in shops and decimated ninety-five percent of the population. The only reason the genocide hadn't been one hundred percent effective was her people's lucky capture of the deep settlement that her rebels currently resided in. Waking up the next morning to the flames of a world that had barely had time to breathe had been a brutal truth Amelia and her remaining people could have done without.

Since then, they had scraped by using the boons of the Settlement, what her people called the Deep Cave, to survive. Organizing her people into hunters, seekers, builders, and deceivers, Amelia had desperately fought against extinction using her class of Nanospark to the best of her ability to help her people remain undetected as they leveled and planned a coup. Now those extremely powerful nanobots, came rushing back into the Deep Cave urgently.

The screen showed a flashing beacon on a deep space map. Amelia blinked, not seeing the significance of the blinking light or the need for such haste. Then she saw the solid red line that delineated an anomaly that had been a subject of vast study since her conception nearly four hundred years ago. The beacon was quite clearly on the wrong side of that line. She narrowed her eyes as she read the name of the beacon, "Starlight III." She glanced over at the second blinking light, the beacon that she expected to see over on that side of the line. "Starlight DII."

She shot forward out of her bedchambers and practically glided to the Deep Cave headquarters. Her nanobots disassembled their urgent screen message and flowed behind and under her feet, propelling her far faster over the stone floors than she could walk without their increased speed. She burst through the main doors to see a group of her people surrounding a single screen but looking up at its projected image on to the main monitor of the headquarters.

As she watched, more dots began to blip to life, starting off as faded, pale things before stabilizing into bright, blinking lights. Soon, near on five hundred dots were blinking at Amelia from the monitor in front of her. Her people slowly turned their wide eyes and open mouths in her direction.

"This is what we've been waiting for. This is our chance. My nanobots will have given us approximately two hours of advanced warning over even the most well designed Mechano-Lord beacons that were sent into the Etherless Void. Send them an order to stop the main systems of the research drones from coming to life for as long as they can! We need time to plan!"

Helion Prime – Guild Collective Castle – Alchemy Wing

Hectar stared at the multitude of tests that he had just run and shook his head, not sure if he should be excited or upset. His mood really depended on if someone was playing a trick on him or not. According to these tests, he had just found the most powerful Planetary Essence ever recorded. However, that in itself lent argument to someone playing a trick on him. Probably someone over in the Biology department. Those guys were a bunch of bottom feeders.

He picked up the results and began walking through the castle towards the guild head's office. As he walked through the monitoring room, he overheard a conversation between two low-level members. "The battery on Starlight DII has been steadily climbing for the last few weeks. It's now reading fifty percent, which is up from the four percent it had remaining. This is a really weird glitch."

"You know that Garef told us that its systems are probably going haywire this close to Ether depletion. It will just blink out in a week, and we'll launch the newest model in hopes of reaching the other side of the Etherless Void."

Their conversation continued as he walked by and entered the elevator, the first one picking back up the conversation. "Yeah, Garef would know too. He helped build the last thirty that were launched. What are your thoughts on the zone?"

The doors hissed closed as he heard the second individual barely begin talking about theology. Must be a member of the Tenant guild with the level of excitement he mustered into his words. A brief pause later, the elevator began speeding upwards into the central tower of the highly advanced Technological Castle. As it ascended, Hectar considered if he was making a mistake bringing this to the leader. If he was wasting Dario's time, his guild's favor may fall, and that wouldn't be ideal. Dario had just started his first five-year term as elected Guild Prime, which meant the worst-case scenario was he could piss in the waters for his guild for the next fifteen years. On the other hand–

The doors opened before he could finish his line of thought, and he walked carefully towards the Guild Prime office entryway. The AI secretary asked if he had an appointment, and he began to sweat profusely. Before he thought better of it, he used his guild clearance level to override the need. He was quickly informed to enter the room and report his emergency findings.

He shuddered at what felt like a wave of cold water wash over him from head to toes. He swallowed hard and stood stock-still, trying to firm his resolve.

Unfortunately, to get a regularly scheduled meeting with the Guild Prime could take weeks. While it was not ideal to use his guild's emergency code, which would be removed if the Prime deemed that it wasn't an emergency, it was his only option. Hectar brushed his science robes down, swallowed a forming lump in his throat, and took a deep breath. This was a classic damned for and damned against situation.

If he didn't report this and it turned out to be legitimate, he would be in trouble. If he reported it and it was a falsified finding, he would still be in trouble. But if it was a legitimate finding, he would be praised. He stopped brushing down his robes when he saw that he was leaving wet streaks from his sweaty palms.

Breathing out a mild curse, Hectar strode into Dario's, the ninety-fourth Guild Prime, office. As he entered, three other heads turned his direction, and he felt his step hitch for a moment. Dahrix, the head of the Mechano-Lords; Geb, the head of the Bio-cult; and lastly Tirahnya, the head of the Mage's guild were all present. He was in esteemed company, and he was only a Lieutenant-Captain in 'Alchemy is the Basis of All'.

Trying not to faint, he fixed his eyes on Dario and studied the man who was currently reading something on his desk. The man had risen from the Martyr's Chaos guild and had been their second in command before he took the high seat for his first term. Everyone gossiped he was a fair man and wasn't quick to overreact. However, the robes of the Guild Prime didn't seem to suit the wildness of the man.

The man radiated some sort of animal ferocity which spoke towards his prowess as a fighter. This was further evidenced by the robe's tightness across his muscular chest, back, and arms. His dark black mohawk and full, wild beard added even more to the machismo of the man.

Dario looked up from his desk, and his vibrant purple eyes glowed in his gray skin. His lips pulled, flattening into a line, before he commanded, "You used your emergency beacon and have interrupted a meeting of some import. You have exactly two minutes to explain the situation!"

Not wanting to waste any time, Hectar began speaking at a fast clip, starting by handing the report to Dario. The three leaders attempted to catch a glimpse of the report as it passed by them but then went back to sitting quietly, waiting to see this particular piece of drama unfold. It had been millennia since someone had used an emergency beacon, and surely, a sheet didn't warrant it!

Hectar finished his story about the Flow Ridians and their claims of having a great deal of this gas substance, and the room was in utter silence. The three leaders looked between Hectar and Dario. Dario looked up again with a brow cocked. "How many times did you run this test?"

"Ten times, Prime," Hectar whispered, quickly hoping that he had made the right choice. The silence in the room deepened and added more worry to his mounting stress.

"What does it say, Dario?" Dahrix seemed to shout into the silence. Even though his voice was its normal pitch, everyone jumped at it. Dahrix had always had a fiery temper, which was strange since his entire body, besides his brain and perhaps a few other fleshy apertures, was mechanical and should have perfect chemical balance. As Dario blinked at the intrusion, Hectar examined Dahrix's black, sleek metal, which had stress lines of perfect silver etched into the metal in a pattern that transfixed the gaze. His eyes were a blood-red and never blinked, making it clear that even though they may appear fleshy, they had long since been replaced with a mechanical counterpart. His face which was of the same dark metal seemed stuck in perpetual calm, despite his voice and tone.

Dario pointed to Hectar and nodded, asking him subtly to do the unveiling of the paper's contents. Hectar swallowed hard and wiped his brow, the sound of the sweat striking the stone floor proceeded his awkward stutter, "The gasoline the Flow Ridians had… had contained a rather large amount of planetary essence… That planetary essence is by far the… the strongest concentration ever… tested on record."

Tirahnya stood up in her white gown and pointed at Hectar, which made his world spin; then she exclaimed, "Youngling, the mage's guild personally handed your guild a vial of Gelthisar's planetary essence not one year ago!" She was a Mertill, which was a relatively short-lived race, at least compared to the other known races. On average, her scaly, fish-like race only lived to an average age of approximately one thousand years. Tirahnya was young then for her position. She was lithe and fit and had recently celebrated her hundredth birthday. Her strange habit of calling people young despite them being older than herself was frustrating, but no one could deny her magical prowess.

Hectar, who was older than her by at least a few centuries, felt his fear recede slightly at this realization. Confidence growing, he responded, "Yes, Guild Leader. The comparison between the two is on that page, and the newer sample is far more concentrated. Nearly doubly so."

Geb, who was a blue-skinned Iranarian, stood up. His tall, skinny body loomed over the other two as he sucked his overly large, square teeth for a moment. The love between the biology and the alchemy guild was well known, and luckily, Dario forestalled whatever scathing response Geb had planned. Dario simply stated with a clinical air, "Please describe these Flow Ridians," as he motioned to an open chair.

As Hectar got underway describing the multiple skin hues of the Flow Ridians he had seen and the striking similarities to the powerful human factions, the other three members in the room started to seethe. He felt his sweat glands begin producing buckets of the stuff as he literally saw the recognition and then thunderclouds rolling across their faces.

ROCKY

"We could use them for everything from helping us build to defending the Territory if it was ever under attack! Not to mention our current predicament with the Irradiated Ether!" Sela clipped out, trying desperately to make her point again. "You can't hate a race or group just because some of them have hurt you, Joaquim!" She finished pointing directly at Smith who was sitting, placidly nodding along with her points. Sela had a strange habit of using people's full names, despite what others called them. In fact, she was one of the few who still called Zippo Jason and got away with it. Somehow, during the discussion, Smith had become the opposition to her vote of allowing the golems to stay, even though he was all for having them join as well.

He opened his mouth and replied, "I completely agree, Sela. However, as I claimed, the people will not like it. I personally went around to a random group of one hundred people and took a poll whether they would be comfortable with peaceful golems living among them. Seventy-five of them were strongly against it. I have no grudge with these golems and have barely seen more than three of them." He took a long pause, then sighed. "I'm afraid that is different for the vast majority of the four thousand present in this Grotto, though."

Before Sela could respond, Rocky stood and motioned her to sit down. She did so with a sigh. "I think the real issue here is that the only golems that any of us had seen before these five were considerably more violent…" He let that statement hang in the air because it was an obvious understatement. Then he continued, "I have been considering this issue since you first brought it up, Smith, and I think we can make a compromise. What if we were to let just one of them stay with us to begin acclimatizing our population to the idea?"

"What would the other four do, Rocky?" Zippo asked, curiously nodding with Rocky's first point, then tilting his head in confusion.

Amber chimed in a quick, "They can go do whatever they want! If they want access to our Territory, they have to abide by our decisions." In the intervening conversations, Rocky had noticed that Amber was a bit hot-headed and struggled to see the larger picture at times. If those five golems wanted to, they could eradicate everyone in this Grotto, so Rocky wasn't going to be telling them to piss off in such a manner.

Rocky shrugged and shook his head at Amber, then reminded her, "I have already told you all how strong they are." Then he looked at Zippo to answer his question, "I was thinking of trying to convince them to go to nearby towns. If my car is still intact enough, I should have maps of Ontario in the glovebox. We could ask them to check towns for survivors in a direction away from Chalk River. Maybe send some of our military and tanks with them?"

Smith nodded. "Would the Knights be willing to accept this compromise—"

Derik interrupted him, "Compromise! Stop trying to please everyone and just let them all in. No one is going to be able to hurt them, and we could use them for Tony the Tiger's sake!" The clear vehemence in Derik's voice made Rocky clench his teeth then recoil when the system adjusted his swear word. The system's choice of word replacement made him hold back a smile, but Derik saw his laughter in his eyes and grew red in the face.

He shook his head as he realized that Derik hadn't been present when everyone had discovered the system's flagrant invasion of their minds. He considered telling him but then, with a quick shake of his head, chose to let him sound like a disgruntled Mormon child for a while. Rocky had sounded like one himself without knowing, and Derik deserved it, at least from his point of view.

Rocky raised his hands to Derik, not wanting to start a fight. "Sorry I'm smiling because I think that allowing all of them in is probably the best idea. I just don't like agreeing with you!"

Derik wasn't sure what to make of that statement and eyed Rocky sideways as they continued.

CHAPTER FIFTEEN

Despite trying to keep the filter a secret, Zippo had blurted it out to the A-Team during the continued discussions. Mostly because Derik kept trying to swear and was growing more and more agitated when people laughed at the system's choice of replacement words.

Zippo... What a goody-two-shoes. Who knew? I guess it was only a matter of time.

It was weird that everyone who was upset at not being able to remove their filter changed their tune when they heard how long Rocky would be under the censor. The longest any of the A-Team would have to go without swearing was a month, and that was in Derik's case. It was a bit of a slap in the face for him until he heard that Rocky wouldn't be able to swear for a full year. Then he laughed uproariously like the others. Rocky's dislike for the man had increased slightly.

Once Sela had seen the hurt on Rocky's face again, she'd managed to calm her laughter and explain it slightly, "Rocky, I truly started reporting you because of habits that were left over from my previous life. It was considered beyond abhorrent to swear. Probably because, as children, we never picked up the habit, and as adults, those lessons stuck with us. Friends would make fun of us for weeks as children if you swore and said something ridiculous instead." She paused and looked around the group.

"Once I met other people, I realized how common swearing had become." At this point, she looked back at Rocky, and a small smile was on her lips. "It didn't mean that I wasn't offended and amused simultaneously anytime you swore, though." Rocky blinked at her for a few seconds as she finished. He had expected her to keep talking, but that was the extent of her 'apology'.

After the distraction of the expletive filter was surmounted, the group got back to the discussion at hand. While most of the people disagreed and still wanted all five of the powerful golems present in the Territory, Sela made a point that supported the decision slightly. It turned out that the levels of Ether in the Territory were based on an averaged level of everyone present. So, if all five of the creatures were accepted and became citizens, then the level of many of the creatures would jump up in turn. It wouldn't be a lot probably, considering that it would be five Master classes and four thousand apprentices, but she did say that it always weighted higher levels far more than low levels.

After that point, the group wasn't convinced, but they did agree to talk with the Knights about the decision. In addition, Rocky, who had sat rather quietly during the follow-up discussions, pointed out that they needed teams out and searching for more human survivors in the area. They couldn't hope for a stronger escort team than the Ottawa Knights.

The remainder of the meeting was about the Territory and how they were going to feed, organize, and manage four thousand people.

Rocky stood up at this point and started a shared screen through the system meeting feature like Sela had shown him. He began, "I think the breakdown needs to be heavily skewed to builders and hunters at first. Considering that on average, I personally have been consuming at least two hundred percent more food in a day, I have made the assumption that means that as people level, they will need more food. I'm sure you have all noticed this as well in yourselves."

He paused momentarily and put up the first figures on the board. As he queried the A-Team how much meat they usually could gather in a day.

Food needed for four thousand plus civilians. Based on estimations.

Assumptions:
Average healthy calorie intake per human before Ether: 2,000 calories.
Average calorie count for a flank of meat: 220 per 4 ounces.
A-Team's average haul of meat per person: 50 pounds. (50 ~~pounds~~ x 16 ounces/~~pound~~ = 800 ounces)
Number of calories needed for entire population of settlement: 4,000 ~~individuals~~ x 2,000 ounces/~~individual~~ = 8,000,000 ounces
Multiply need by 300% due to appetite increases: 8,000,000 x 3 = 24,000,000 calories
Individual hunter haul in calories: 800 ounces / 4 ounces * 220 calories = 4,400 calories per hunter
Number of hunters needed: 24,000,000 / 4,400 = 546 hunters

He left his notes there and looked around the group's stunned faces. Amber stood up and looked around. Rocky Analyzed her again confirming her class for himself.

Amber Dell
Level 14
Apprentice-Fencer
Health Points 130/130

She looked around at the group nervously, and her long, dark hair flung itself around as she did so. Smith gave her a parental nod, and she stood up as straight as she could, which accentuated her tall, lean fencer build. She queried confusedly, "You want us to convince one in eight people of the current population to be hunters? We also have been steadily increasing the amount of meat we pull in. Can't we lower that number?"

Sela smiled at the woman and stood to walk over beside Amber. Standing beside her, Sela reassured, "Those numbers are just a basis for discussion, and a lot of the assumptions can be adjusted. Personally, I don't know what calories are, but I can deduce they have something to do with nutrients inside the food?"

At Rocky's and the group's nodding heads, she continued, "Alright, first off then, most of the meat will have been enhanced by Ether, so the amount of 'calories' per piece of meat will increase. However, that also means that the two hundred percent more actually increases. So those numbers will remain somewhat similar. However, Rocky, you are forgetting cooks and what they will be capable of doing. Not to mention vegetation and the fact that we are cooking stews primarily at current."

Rocky nodded. "I didn't know how to calculate stews and vegetables. I think we can lower the number and have many of the hunters learn to be herbalists to further lower this number." Then he pointed across the river. "Not to mention if we get some farmers to grow some sort of grain or start a grove on the other side of the river. My larger concern is how the Territory is going to keep up with such a huge demand on the wildlife and fauna."

Amber sat down next to Jack, who patted her on the shoulder as if to say, "Way to go saying that politely." Again, Rocky Analyzed him for his class, trying to see what the A-Team was working with. Perhaps other classes would be better hunters, for instance.

Jack Wareham
Level 15
Apprentice-Trapper

Moderate Analyze has failed to reveal additional information

Sela distracted him from Analyzing the final four members of the A-Team because she answered his question, "This Territory is huge, and the wildlife and fauna will be grown based on the need of the populace. It will need a basis to grow from, which means we can't hunt a population to extinction and will need a good rotational hunting strategy. It also means that as long as we don't decimate the existing population or fauna in an area, we can expect for growth rates to increase based on our activities."

Rocky breathed a sigh of relief and then queried her for more specific numbers, "So, do you have a suggestion for an exact number of hunters?"

Sela sighed herself and grimaced. "Unfortunately, even though I think we can lower the number needed for the amount of food, I don't think we should." Amber tilted her head at the woman, and Sela used her interest to make her point. "Amber, how much Crystallized Ether do you currently have on you?"

Amber reached a hand into her pocket unconsciously before pulling it back out filled with softly glowing crystals, "Umm, I didn't really count it, but I think around ten maybe." She quickly counted. "Sorry, thirteen."

Sela nodded and looked around the group before she emphasized, "Each of you probably has around the same amount. Since we will have to pay anyone who isn't a hunter for their work, it is better to have more income coming in from outside sources. In my time, hunter groups were paid the crystals they collected. Often, hunters were even in the highest classes because of how much they could potentially earn. Only merchants and very successful crafters would surpass them."

Derik shot up, "Wait, we won't get paid to hunt! That's ridiculous. We're doing work for the Grotto just like anyone else!"

Rocky glared at the man, and Sela raised a hand to stop his protest and smiled devilishly. "You are more than welcome to ask for pay for hunting, but if we pay you, you will be required to pay us to hunt in the safety of the Territory grounds. I assure you, the price of that privilege is far higher than what you would get for a wage and would have to be made up for with the crystals you loot. Of course, you can hunt outside its boundaries and make a 'killing'!" She air quoted the last word in her speech, and Rocky nearly guffawed when he saw her use them. At her words, Derik's face paled, and he sat down quickly.

Rocky smiled and considered the point Sela had just made. He hadn't even considered the boon the Territory was giving hunters by keeping them in a much safer environment for leveling and earning. While the work was still difficult and dangerous, Sela had used the stick of the outside environment perfectly to cow the greedy weasel. Not that Rocky would have actually forced anyone to pay to hunt on the Territory grounds, but it sounded like Sela wouldn't hesitate to.

Sela continued, "Another great addition we have is the Territorial Inventory. If we are going to be creating an economy," she pointed at Zippo which made the young man tilt his head, "we will want cooks that make specialized meals. Those cooks will buy the meats from the Territory and prepare them for a profit. I can assure you that good cooks are a necessity for the growth of our budding city. They can create meals that will increase stats, Etherience gains, recovery rate, and so much more!" She paused for a moment and then finished, "While stew is a good starting point, we need to consider the future and that we will hopefully be growing our numbers."

Derik stood up and spat out, "What about houses and roofs for people! If we focus that much of the population on food, how long will it take to build rooms for everyone?!" He wasn't really asking questions so much as being his usual confrontational self. Rocky, who had had enough of the man, stood up, and Sela, who had been about to respond, saw his face and shut her mouth before calmly walking back to her seat with a smile.

Rocky strode forward, pointing his finger at Derik and shouted, "A tent that sleeps twenty is a single crystal, Derik! Sela and I have also just explained we bought a massive Guild Tent that should sleep a good portion of the population!" He took in a deep lungful of air then continued, "Everyone who doesn't become a hunter will be building, and hopefully, we can have many houses being constructed simultaneously. Could you stop being a prick for a moment and try being constructive to this meeting?"

It was probably the wrong way to handle the situation as Derik started shouting back. Smith and a few others managed to calm the situation down quickly, but words that couldn't be taken back had already been uttered. Derik made his exit and strode off into the distance, abandoning the meeting entirely. Rocky couldn't even remember what he'd shouted at the man, but Sela was holding up three fingers at him. She mouthed, "Three more," while smiling devilishly.

Honestly, if she was anyone else, I would probably try to kill her!

He felt his blood boil at being reported some more, but for some reason, her smile and belief he could do better made him hesitate. He shook his head angrily and wanted nothing more than to storm off as well. Instead, he sat down and told himself he would be leaving soon.

Get everything organized and then go scout the land towards Chalk River. Just get it started.

He repeated that to himself over and over as he took a deep, calming breath. He remained there and listened as more pieces of the future plan fell into place steadily. At first the A-Team would break up and teach individual groups of up to ten people how they had been hunting in the valley. Smith personally would teach everyone who was willing herbalism. Hopefully, they could then teach others, and the number of vegetables and helpful plants would grow vastly in the Grotto.

A group of about two thousand more were 'volunteered' for construction, at least for now. They needed to create a large list of buildings, and of primary concern was housing for women and children. Strangely, Sela got rather upset at the prospect of women needing any special treatment, and when she was instantly joined by Amber, the group relented. It would seem the only special consideration then would be children. Sadly, Rocky recalled that children of an age under eight years old had been decimated by the Ether Crash. The fact that they hadn't had access to the system seriously hindered their survivability, and in most cases, their family's survivability.

From that bitter note, they moved on to crafting. The hope was that they would have some skilled individuals in the Grotto who would have experience in tailoring, curing hides, blacksmithing, construction, carving, farming, and many other areas. These people would probably pick up the skill quickly or may already have it. They could then teach others, and more of the hides currently stored in Rocky's bag and the Territory Inventory could be used to begin outfitting hunters and soldiers.

Sela insisted that it would be at a fee, as the hunters would be the wealthiest individuals in the valley, and since the military could also go hunt in their free time, they would be just as flush. The crafters would need to eventually begin paying for the hides and other material they used, but it was decided that at first, those costs would be absorbed by the guild they would form. Additionally, hides and other materials would, in time, need to be purchased by the guild and then purchased from the guild by the crafters.

There were two questions Rocky had and quickly voiced, "First, is the equipment that's made just sturdier clothing, or will it be like the gear from the shop?" He looked at Sela during this question and then asked his second, "Won't the guild, acting as a middleman in all transactions, cause problems with people who want to sell directly to other merchants?"

She smiled and nodded sadly. "The gear is just a blank piece of clothing that will offer better protection than most of what people are wearing, but no, it needs to be enchanted before it will be like the gear in the shop."

Sela didn't have any idea how enchanting was possible and had resigned to selling the blanks, as she called the un-enchanted equipment, to the shop, but Rocky still had an idea on that point. He refused to elaborate currently as it was just a theory, but he planned on studying some of his equipment, as well as the locked equipment from the arena Dungeon, to see if he could extrapolate from it and his few visits to the shop.

Then Sela answered the second question, "Direct sales between individuals in the Territory are tracked and recorded. At least, they will be once a Town Hall is erected. People will be expected to pay taxes on all sales, and we will need people to manage all of that." She paused then pointed in the direction of the shop. "And if people sell to a shop, then it takes a cut for the Territory as well. Regardless, the guild needs to act as a middleman to make money. Then that money is reinvested into the populace. The Territory, on the other hand, will act like a central government that uses funds strictly for growth and management of the Grotto. The guild will also be able to one day purchase a vendor's attachment for the shop or multiple shops if we find more. This will allow people to sell through the guild for higher profit in the future."

The discussion sped up from that point, as they decided most other problems would be dealt with as they came up. There was a general consensus that a few Longhouses could be constructed simultaneously, and after the first ones were finished, they would consider having a group make a Town Hall or Eating

Hall. The main purchase that needed to be bought in bulk was cement for the foundations, and Rocky gave that task to Joe.

Zippo looked unhappy, and Rocky assumed it was because they didn't have a kitchen, which was probably going to cause some problems in the long run. However, for now, it was the state of things, and they would have to buy a kitchen with the next available funds.

After that, the group spread through the Grotto and started organizing as Rocky, Azoth, Sela, and Zippo started gearing up for scouting. With the time left on the countdown of the Ether protection, Rocky felt a mounting pressure to get started. He was unsure what would happen when the countdown reached zero.

Ether Protection
Time of Ether assisted protection for Territory: 4 days, 11 hours, 58 minutes, and 32 seconds.

If they didn't get a progression to the quest after scouting or at least a source of more information, he wasn't even sure where to start on the next steps. He brought it up to Sela for the first time, hoping she might alleviate his fear about the timer running out. "Sela, what do you think will happen when the Ether Protection buff runs out?"

Sela sighed and looked Rocky in the eyes, then shrugged before she spoke. "I can't say for sure. I think there will still be protection from the storms, but if there are any creatures like the Irradiated Ether Zombies we faced in the Arena Dungeon, I am pretty sure they will be able to cross into our Territory. I guess the good news is that there didn't seem to be any intelligence in the creatures?" She finished with a grimace, realizing she hadn't answered the question well or alleviated any worries for either of them.

Rocky groaned and then just kept walking as Azoth bounded over to the two and mentally bombarded them, "We do a scouting? We foughting?" Rocky chuckled and tried to correct the creature on his tense and language use. It always got worse when he was excited.

Zippo, who'd run off to get his Staff of Focus, was waiting at the Grotto exit for them as they walked up and fell into step with them. "So, are we hoping to get to Chalk River today?" Zippo asked from behind Rocky.

Rocky tilted his head as he considered. "Honestly, I think another storm went by this morning, so this is probably the best time. That being said, we don't know much about what's in that direction. If there's an abundance of wildlife or mutated creatures, we're going to have to play the situation differently. Let's just start by seeing what we're dealing with."

The rest of the walk continued in silence as they slowly approached the northeastern edge of their Territory. They saw some groups of creatures they decided not to attack, as this was just a quick scouting trip. Rocky hoped they would be back in a few hours with a better idea of what they needed to do or what enemy they were facing.

As they approached, that same clear line of delineation could be seen as trees turned a dark brown and green that was so dark even in the sunlight it looked black. Rocky touched one of the trees, and it felt almost soggy. He pulled back his hand and shook it, disgusted with the feel of oil it left on his skin.

"Rocky," Sela called his name as he examined the tree. "Rocky!" she tried again at an increased volume level, but he was distracted trying to figure out if these trees could be saved. "Rocky!" she screamed, and it finally got his attention. He turned to look at her and Zippo, but they were both looking at something in front of them. Rocky turned and saw a mound of rock pockmarked with a great deal of caves covering its surface.

That looked exactly like the entrance had to LFD; the only difference was that the rock was black and stained with what might have been watermarks.

Oh no! I hope that isn't the Little Friendly Dungeon!

CHAPTER SIXTEEN

Sela and Rocky stood just inside the largest cave's entrance and looked back at Azoth. The massive beast kept trying to squeeze in and join the two. It was an extremely humorous sight, as Azoth kept tucking his wings in and then moving forward, expecting a different result.

Each time he neared the entrance, he would inhale and try to suck in his belly, but the problem wasn't his slim hindquarters, it was his shoulders. He backed out of the cave with a piteous wine and mentally sent to Rocky, "This clearly not same place! Azoth fits last time! Silly caves."

Rocky looked over at Sela, who had one hand on her stomach and another over her mouth, trying to cover her giggles. He then chortled, "Sorry, buddy, we need to check this out. Can you bring Zippo back to the Territory? He needs to tell them where we're going."

They had tried the radio to get back in touch with Joe, but either they were out of range, or there was interference in this area. Either way, they couldn't just explore the Dungeon and possibly be stuck down there for days without having the people who were running the Territory in their absence appraised of the development.

Also, maybe I want to protect Zippo a bit. I kind of like the kid.

Azoth whined and sent back, "No, Azoth fits. Wait for Azoth!" He then tried a few more times, even pushing in far enough to get himself momentarily stuck before pulling back in a bit of a panic and ruffling a good portion of his wing feathers. Looking at the feathers, his head fell. "Tell stupid Dungeon make bigger for Azoth!" Then he let a sulky Zippo, who had also voiced complaint, mount up, and flew away back to the Territory.

Rocky, who still wasn't one hundred percent sure this was LFD, turned to Sela, who had stopped laughing and looked thoughtful. "He really just wants to be included, I think," she spoke softly before turning to Rocky. "Let's get this over with so we can hopefully continue on to the site if there's time!"

Shrugging, he turned and walked further into the cave. A couple meters later, a resounding boom sounded, and he was greeted by a very familiar message.

Welcome to the Long Forgotten Dungeon
>   **You have entered in a group of two, suggested group size 5-10.**

Good luck!
>   **Level: 1 ++**
>   **Age: 28 Days**
>   **Floors – 12+**

To exit the Dungeon, you must defeat the final boss.

Rocky felt his eyes narrow. He was extremely happy to have found the 'Little Friendly Dungeon' but that welcome message had changed pretty drastically since the group's last visit. First was obviously the age, which had increased by twenty-six days. Second was the number of floors the Dungeon now contained, which led Rocky to believe this was going to take a lot longer than a few hours. Finally, the Rank had two pluses beside it? When they had cleared the Dungeon before it had been given a Rank of Level 1, mostly because the only monster inside had been a level one bunny rabbit named Thumper, who Rocky had cut in half.

He focused on the two plus icons, and a new pop-up window overlaid itself on to the Dungeon notification.

* **+ Dungeon has possibly gained strength enough to be classified as a different level since last clear.**

- **++ The Dungeon has been visited by an entity or group that failed to clear it, and Dungeon has possibly gained strength enough to be classified as a different level since last clear.**

Rocky knew that LFD had gotten stronger since his last visit, as he had personally traded the Dungeon ten creatures' corpses for his dimensional bag. However, who had tried to clear it and failed? Did failing to clear the Dungeon mean that LFD had killed humans?

LFD has been in the area around Chalk River the whole time, though, hasn't it? That also brings up the question of why it's right outside my Territory.

Not feeling the greatest about the possibility of LFD killing people, Rocky looked at Sela. Her face was solemn, and she just nodded, seeming to have come to similar conclusions or at least preparing herself for trouble. As they looked at each other, Sela pulled two daggers out of her bag, and Rocky mirrored her when he saw the action to form his liquid sword into a thin longsword. "Not going to transform into your cat form?"

Sela shook her head and turned to slowly stalk away, entering Sneak and Stealth. A disembodied voice of Sela called back through the darkness and was repeated on the radio, giving a strange double to the conversation, "This way we can discuss enemies we see after each fight. I will go first. Enter Stealth and Dark Cloak and radio in whispers if you see enemies."

Rocky initiated both of his skills and crept along the hallway until he saw the walls slowly branch outwards and form a large, circular room. A mound began to materialize into his view as he got closer to the entrance for the room. The creature was slumped into a lump in the middle of the room. At first, Rocky thought it was already dead because of the Boar's bleached white and paling skin. However, he used Analyze.

Irradiated Wild Hell Boar
Level 18
Apprentice-Tusker
Health Points 490/490

This definitely didn't bode well for LFD, and Rocky felt his heart sink as he whispered, "It looks like the Dungeon might be infected. This might mean we will have to destroy LFD. I'll attack the Boar first; you go second."

The radio clicked once in response, which Joe had taught them would mean affirmative in covert operations. Rocky struck from Stealth with his sword at the back of the mound's neck. His sword cut deeply, and as the Boar squealed and raised its head, Sela materialized with two daggers, taking the beastly-sized Boar in the throat. It slumped over dead, and Rocky looted the creature but received nothing. Rocky was debating about skinning the creature when he heard noises reverberating down one of the exit hallways.

"What is that?" he whispered and looked over to Sela, who'd gone pale in the face.

She hissed out, "The Dungeon is sending everything against us! It's just like I am used to! Go into Stealth and communicate under radio silence! Left exit out—go!" She took a step, breaking into a jog and vanished in the middle of one step towards the left exit away from the noises coming down the passage on his right.

Entering Stealth, Rocky moved quickly to the left exit hallway, which didn't have any noise he could hear. Three quick clicks made Rocky hug the wall as four simian rats flew by him in a frenzy. Again, their hair and skin were bleached white.

Irradiated Rat Monkey
Level 15

Apprentice-Winged Monkey
Health Points 315/315

One radio click after the monkeys passed told him Sela was continuing. He glanced back and saw that the room they had just vacated was now slowly filling with all types of monsters. He felt his eyebrows rise as he saw more streaming in from other corridors.

Blinking, he turned and moved as quickly as he could to follow Sela. A few moments later, he clicked his own radio four times, requesting Sela to flash out of Stealth. Her form flashed momentarily in front of him, and they continued lightly jogging through the darkness. They reached the next room, and Rocky was beginning to believe this first floor was a similar honeycombed setup to what they had navigated the previous run through.

Once in the next room, Sela exited Stealth in a dark corner and stood still for a moment until he joined her. As soon as she saw the dark fog touch her hand, she smiled. "Unless you want to take on every creature in here at the same time, it would be best to do this as a Stealth run." Rocky looked questioningly back the other way, but sensing the question in the silence, Sela continued, "I really don't think we can take on the monsters in here. The ones back there weren't that strong, but traditionally, every floor gets stronger until the last one!"

She took a deep breath and looked deeply into the fog where she thought his head might be, then continued to whisper, "If we bring this whole place down on us, I feel like even we will be in trouble."

Realizing he hadn't said anything and Sela couldn't see him through the shroud, he softly answered, "I'm following your lead, Sela. You have more experience in this."

She smiled and crinkled her eyes before softly asking a question herself, "The issue is how to coordinate better than the radio clicks we are using. Any ideas?"

He didn't really have any great plans for this situation. He'd thought about it before, but the need for absolute invisibility ruined his initial thought of using his clone to lead the way. They, unfortunately, hadn't purchased any sort of tracking devices. Rocky scanned the room they stood in and saw a pile of white on the other side of the room. With a smile, he instantly remembered a great many childhood memories playing with the white rocks. When he grew older, he'd never looked into exactly what the rocks were made of, but assumed it was either limestone or some sort of metamorphic rock.

Regardless of its components, he walked over and picked one up to test it out. "Where are you going?" Sela called in a whisper as the fog moved away with him. The rock left a white line on the wall just like he remembered from all those decades ago. Smiling, he placed ten in his bag and then walked back. Sela saw the return of the dark fog and relaxed. "Did you think of something?"

"Follow the white line on the wall. The creatures shouldn't have the intelligence to follow it," was his whispered response to raised eyebrows from Sela. Then he walked along, dragging the chalk along the rock every so often. The grating of the rock on rock was the only thing not beneficial with this plan. In the future, he promised himself to carry something like a laser marker or something that would be silent. However, for the current purposes, it would have to work.

Rocky led the way and kept his eyes peeled for any traps that might exist. Last time the two had been in the Dungeon, there'd been a few basic false floors and swinging rocks. This time, it seemed that no traps existed as the two of them navigated around the honeycombs, avoiding the monsters that had gone back to idling in the middle of each room. Each creature was clearly infected by the Irradiated Ether, and the further they traveled, the more worried Rocky became for LFD's core.

Before too long, they reached a room that had a balcony with a railing that overlooked a spiral staircase that circled its way down along the wall. Rocky began to descend and finally noticed a few traps on certain steps. They were clear as day to him as the stairs on each side of them had clear wear from foot traffic, but these stairs were accumulating dust and also were very rough stonework. To indicate the stairs to Sela, he put an 'X' on the step above each one and below, but a snort told him that Sela wouldn't need that in the future, as the signs were far too obvious, and she may be better at seeing traps then he was.

Maybe in the future, she should lead…

The stairs continued to go down with options to exit on to each new floor every level they climbed down. However, unlike Dungeons he was used to in games, this one didn't force him to leave and find another staircase to continue further down; the stairs just spiraled down into the darkness below. After the fifth level and the fourth trap stair, Rocky felt his eyebrows rise as he thought of something and clicked his radio to whisper, "Who is traveling up and down these stairs?"

"I didn't even—" Sela was cut off by a very alien-like scream from above them. It echoed through the hallways and reverberated from rooms all around them as they stood statue-still on the stairs. The screams had a very eerie feeling to them; they sounded so animal-like, but the noise was also familiar in a way Rocky couldn't place. A moment of hesitation was all it took before they began sprinting down the steps, jumping them two or three at a time in their haste.

Now that they were traveling fast, Rocky used his radio to notify Sela of any trap stairs he saw, ignoring pure silence for speed. The stairs were so obvious that he easily saw them even two or three steps away, but he knew his vision was much better than hers in the semi-darkness that the glowing moss failed to completely push back. When they reached the bottom floor, they heard a great cacophony pressing down the spiral staircase. A moment's pause and a loud splat sounded in the center of the room followed by a few more.

Rocky blinked and tilted his head, trying to understand what he was looking at. What followed was a moment of horror so profound, he froze as more and more twisted shapes crashed into the floor. Luckily, Sela's questing hand found him through the Stealth and Dark Cloak and reefed his arm hard towards the doorway. As they exited, the haunting sound of falling human corpses chased them through the exit on to the eleventh and final floor.

Rocky exited Stealth and dropped Dark Cloak as he felt his mind stutter. Sela exited Stealth in front of him and slapped him hard in the face. "They are already dead. They were dead long before they hit the ground. They probably aren't even human but creations of the Dungeon! Let's go!"

She reached into his pack and pulled out a mine in each hand and threw one right at the bottom of the stairs. As Rocky started moving, she threw another a few feet into the hallway they were now sprinting down. As they saw the telltale brightly illuminated archway that had depicted LFD's final room the last time, Rocky stopped and dropped out his final four MKZ Goblin Turrets that he had from the shop. They each had just over a half charge, and he didn't expect them to last for more than fifteen minutes.

As soon as he mentally commanded them to target any enemy that approached, he turned and sprinted into the final room to the sound of the first mine exploding behind him. Dank, stale air peppered his back as he froze a few steps into the room. "Thumper?" he managed to squeak out.

Ether Corrupted Thumper
Level 18

Apprentice-Undead Basher
Health Points 1,337/1,337
Boss

The creature that stood in front of him was closer in size to a workhorse than the tiny, cute rabbit that he had killed on his last visit. He got a single glimpse of its twisted, mutated form before it sprang off massively powerful hind legs directly at him. Rocky's eyes widened as the massive, sharpened front teeth flew towards him, and he pushed hard to his left. The Dark Cloak saved his life for the hundredth time as it helped him move farther and faster than he could on his own. Even with its help, he felt three stripes of fire bloom into existence on his chest.

He attempted to swipe his sword at the creature, but it flew by him so fast, his sword whooshed through the air instead. Out of the corner of his eye, he saw Sela transform into her Predatory Cat form and wink out of sight.

I get to be the tank. Thanks, Sela.

Rocky turned around and had another instant to take in the massive rabbit's form crouched on the wall before it was bounding back at him. Rocky pushed off the wall as hard as he could, and this time managed to fully avoid damage as he rolled and came back to his feet to follow the rabbit's path across the room.

Oh, come on—it's using the walls to move faster; gravity, you are a cheating Succubus!

"LFD!" Rocky screamed as he began his next dodge. A second explosion went off behind him, and he felt sweat break out across his back. They didn't have time for this. Additionally, to make a bad situation worse, his commitment to a dodge in a direction was noticed by Thumper, who adjusted course and jumped choosing a path that would intersect his. Rocky plunged his sword into the ground and felt his arm jerk, and his momentum came to a jarring stop.

As the rabbit flew towards the spot that Rocky would have occupied, Sela appeared in the air above the beastly creature and dug her claws into its back, followed by her long, vicious sabretooth canines. The rabbit let out a growl and hiss that was deep enough that Rocky felt it and heard it simultaneously. As the creature attempted to get up, he charged.

With Rocky closing in and Sela clawing at its back, it still managed to get back to its feet. It swiped at him with its front claws, attempting to keep him back as it bunched its legs and got ready to spring. Rocky avoided its front paws and ran his sword down the side of one of the offending limbs. Suddenly, the rabbit bounded backward directly at the wall behind it. "Sela, drop!" Rocky managed to scream out in desperation.

She let go, fell off of Thumper's back, and fell straight down. She managed to get even with the creature's bottom legs as it slammed its back into the wall with a loud, thunderous boom. Sela's health dropped, but it wasn't drastic, thanks to her quick reaction. She quickly began clawing and biting at any piece of exposed undead bunny flesh in an attempt to free herself.

As Rocky pushed off hard and worked up to a full sprint, he heard the next line of defense, the MKZ Turrets, start ionizing and discharging behind him. If Sela wasn't in the way, he would have cast Dark Blade, but as it was, he created a Shadow Clone and felt it fracture off of himself mid-sprint before it entered Stealth and vanished.

Honestly, I am getting really sick and tired of being the bait.

Surprisingly, his clone popped back into existence, and he realized he'd better be careful what he thought in the future, as it assumed those were orders. However, this particular decision was much better for him. So Rocky traded Dark Cloak for Stealth and ran through the front of the black cloud, which now hovered in a roughly humanoid shape where he released it.

Thumper touched back down on to the ground, and Sela disengaged and rolled away, snarling at the rabbit.

Weighing his options, he chose to drop an 'alpha strike' on the creature and end it if he could. He charged his Dark Blade with five charges and released it from about ten feet away. His Shadow Clone had the creature's attention, and it attempted a two-handed clobasaurus slam on to the clone's head. Committed to this action, the explosion of Rocky's skill caught Thumper completely unaware and tore through both his Shadow Clone and the beast.

Smiling smugly, Rocky stood there as the dust settled, breathing hard. No notification window popped up? He was further surprised when from the cloud in front of him, he heard a hiss and snarl. Thumper was still alive?

Come on, that's my most powerful skill!

He glanced at his Ether bar and realized he only had a third remaining, so he chugged an Ether Draught. The taste of electric blue, sickly-sweet energy was now just a regular companion for him. The dust finally fully settled and showed him a very different version of Thumper. Its skin now entirely black, and its eyes bloodshot and red. Where Rocky's skill had hit it, a massive crisscrossing of open wounds mangled its once patchy fur.

Vines began to creep out of the walls and floor, encircling the creature before snapping tight as Sela, who must have shifted back to human, shouted, "It's an Enrage skill, which means it's very low on health! Attack it with everything, but don't let it hit you!"

Glancing at his Ether bar, which hadn't yet reached halfway, he knew he could repeat his previous five charges of Dark Blade, but that would bottom him out. Last time he had done that, he was unable to stand or fight for a good fifteen minutes because of Ether depletion. Instead, he chose to re-cast Shadow Clone and sprinted forwards, entering Stealth again. His clone also winked out of existence but not before it gave Rocky the finger.

Hmm, I guess it didn't like me sacrificing it like that. Honestly, I am a little worried about how independent the thing is.

Changing course, Rocky approached the struggling Thumper from its side. Sela was sweating, trying to restrain the creature as it constantly snapped the new vines she summoned to attempt to hold it. All of that happened in a blink, and Rocky struck from Stealth, activating Dark Cloak and a single charge of Dark Blade as he swung. In a previous fight, against a fast healing troll, he had seen that using Dark Blade as a melee range option increased the damage of his Soul Blade and acted almost like a poison.

Simultaneously, his Shadow Clone sunk two daggers into the hind end of the creature, and together, they continued to hack and slash, furiously hoping to bleed away whatever remained of the massive beast's health pool. Sela's sarcastic voice broke them out of it, "Yeah I think you have killed it already. Stand down, tiger."

Rocky felt his cheeks flush as he realized it hadn't moved since their first attacks made from Stealth. The adrenaline and continued ionized fire of the MKZ Goblin Turrets were making him a little jumpy. Rocky let his sword turn into black liquid metal, shouting, "LFD, are you okay? Answer me!"

A small pulse of green light from the center pedestal was all he got, and he raised his eyebrow at the pulse of ominous red that preceded it. Looking at Sela he insisted, "We have to save his core or destroy it if it's tainted." Sela nodded and made a motion with her hand that seemed to indicate he should hurry.

Reforming his Soul Sword, he hacked at the pedestal until he found the crevice that LFD's core resided in. His stone was a muted green, and it was surrounded by a pulsing thread of red that looked like a living artery. Rocky used Analyze, and as he read, he felt his face drain of blood.

Bathilnda's Heartstring

- **This tiny fragment of the Dragon Bathilda's heart carries with it immense power—power to control or dominate nearly any will in existence. This string only remains powerful as long as the Dragon still lives. Each string taken from a Dragon reduces its magic significantly, and thus, it is one of the rarest items in the Etherverse to find a functioning part of.**

Rocky motioned to his clone, who gave him a look that told him it didn't like what he was thinking. Then the clone reached out and picked up the Dungeon core before unwrapping the Heartstring from it. Immediately, the Heartstring pulsed violently and attempted to coil on to his clone. Rocky felt something try to press into his mind, and he narrowed his eyes in concentration as his clone flung the string into his dimensional bag. His clone puffed out of existence after it accomplished the task, and Rocky felt his legs shudder.

"What the hell was that?" Sela asked, sounding worried.

It was LFD that answered, "That was a stolen piece of Bathinda's Heart! It was really strong, and I couldn't fight it. Honestly, whatever that explosion unleashed, it's been attempting to subvert the Dragon ever since. It has managed to contain her to the ground and pry off a few Heartstrings, but she is still not under its control." Rocky winced as LFD began rapid-firing answers at them the same way it had spoken to him last time.

Sela walked over, helped Rocky stand, and shouted at LFD, "Enough, we need to get out of here. We probably have four minutes left on those turrets with the increased rate of fire they have been exhibiting. Also, LFD, why were you so close to our Territory?"

"I was trying to escape the massive horde of Zombies! But no one was here to accept me into the safe area. I tried my best to dig deeper and hold them off but some sort of Necromancer—"

"You dare to interfere with the great Apep's work!" a voice followed by a massive blast of red came from down the corridor, and the turret fire cut off very abruptly. LFD's color paled, and he stopped talking, which Rocky found even more disturbing.

I thought it was impossible to shut LFD up.

"Back door, LFD! And close the entrance to this room?" he shouted at the stone. Two grating sounds started, and Rocky looked down the hallway to see a man walking calmly towards the room. He was covered in a blood-red robe so dark it was practically black. If it wasn't for the glowing red staff, maybe it would have been black. However, the staff pulsed with a red light that mirrored the Heartstring. The staff's focal point was what seemed to be a rod, and if Rocky's gut was right, it was one of the nuclear rods from the plant. Down the length of the staff, someone had wrapped another Dragon Heartstring. Just before the door closed, he managed to use Analyze.

Devoted of Apothis
Level 26
Apprentice Irradiated Necromancer
Health Points 425/425

Perhaps by himself, the creature wouldn't be a problem for the two of them, but with the army of undead it had behind it, this was a time to flee. They probably only had a small amount of time before that wall was going to come down. Rocky picked up LFD and sprinted for the back exit. Sela followed, and they ran through the tight, confined tunnel with reckless speed.

On the climb back to the surface, he desperately tried the radio over and over again. Until finally, a static response came through, "Rock, it's Zippo. What's going on?"

He felt a huge wave of relief wash over him, and he clicked his talk button. Then he shouted, "We need some fire support, buddy! I want this tunnel to be sealed tight once we get out of here!"

A moment later, Zippo queried, "Can you send up a signal or something? I don't see an open tunnel from up here!"

They reached the surface, and Sela placed her hand on the ground to begin concentrating. Rocky could see Azoth circling in the sky and started crossing and uncrossing his arms above his head.

Note to self, get flares.

Zippo landed and started forming a massive Fireball between two hands as he slid off Azoth's back. Azoth mentally asked Rocky, "What come?"

"Hopefully nothing—" Rocky started but was cut off by Sela.

In a strained voice, she cried, "Jason, just wait one moment. I have almost loosened enough stone to cause a cave-in from your blast."

Then she flopped back on her butt and nodded to the young man. He released his skill, and the ensuing explosion, wave of heat, and clear sounds of a collapse was a beautiful chorus to Rocky's senses.

Sela, who was now sprawled on the ground, ruined his moment, "Yeah, I think this problem just got a lot larger."

CHAPTER SEVENTEEN

"You know leaving me behind was stupid! I could have helped," Zippo continued to cook over an open fire as he complained to anyone who would listen.

Rocky had already told him they had chosen not to have him accompany them because they needed the people of the Territory to be told about LFD and them checking it out. He held back telling Zippo that his presence would have probably made rescuing LFD impossible. However, despite his tact, it seemed like the boy still wasn't over it.

Chuckling to himself, he was currently moving around the folded-up Guild Tent and placing his hand on one massive stump after another. Each time he reached a stump, he would mentally call it into his bag of holding and then dump it back out a short walk later. It was a surprisingly efficient way to remove the stumps and entire root network of trees without much effort on his part. He kept leaving the large, eerie-looking tangle of roots in a massive pile near the Automated Sawmill. Later, he would change the settings and have it turn them into firewood or plywood.

When they had returned, Sela and Rocky had decided to put the conversation with LFD on hold and tackle putting up the Guild Tent before having a meeting with the A-Team. It was already in the waning hours of the day, and soon, the shelter would be helpful for people to sleep in. Not to mention that Sela believed that they would be able to set up and initiate everyone into the guild once they created it. Creating a guild was a pretty large priority for his Ancestral Guide, and she had a good reason for it.

It sounded useful to Rocky, and he also felt that having a roof over some of the people's heads might help with morale issues. The people who stood watching on made him even more aware of their excitement at the prospect. After they had begun removing the stumps and roots, people had slowly made an area which they used to sit and watch the two. He would have been annoyed, but almost each person was eating stew while attempting to figure out what was happening.

At some point, someone put the massive fabric pile and the ground clearing together, and some real, genuine excitement had begun that he and Sela had paused to listen to.

Clearing the ground had taken an hour of walking back and forth, but he placed his hand on the last stump and whisked it into his bag of holding, seeing Sela do the same on the other side of the clearing. Looking at the torn-up and uneven ground, Rocky groaned audibly then shouted to Sela, "I don't think this torn-up, uneven ground will make a good floor for the tent!"

Sela shook her head and knelt, placing her hands on the ground before donning a look of concentration. Rocky felt the ground under him buckle and shift, making him stumble a bit. Then he saw a wave of undulation begin at one edge of the large circle they had cleared and finish at the other. A moment later, the ground packed itself down as if a giant, invisible stamp had been lazily pressed into it. Sela fell on her butt, sweating but smiling.

The crowd cooed with excitement, and a few people shouted encouragement and praise in Sela's direction. Rocky walked towards her, smiling as well at the antics of the crowd, who were all now sitting down but watching with rapt attention.

"That was impressive! You're getting stronger with that ability," Rocky exclaimed with surprise. She had just used it to cave in a tunnel, but he wasn't able to physically see that act. Plus, this circle was massively more extensive, he thought. Instead of rushing her recovery, Rocky walked over to the sawmill and deposited both of their final stumps into the pile since Sela had been using the Territorial Inventory, and he had access to both of them.

As he walked back, Sela huffed out breathlessly, "If I had been stronger in this ability during the trip, that worm…" She faded off, and Rocky caught a glimpse of her own guilt for the deaths that night haunted them with. Sela then turned to him, and her face grew even more worried. "Apep is a name I hadn't heard in a while. I feel like someone just told me the boogeyman is real, and I am a child again." She shrugged to him at his raised eyebrows. "I was trying to remember everything I knew about him before I said anything."

He looked over his shoulder to see if anyone was close enough to be listening, then queried, "And?" a bit impatiently before sitting on the ground next to her. Zippo walked through the crowd that had formed, coming over with some meat and veggies on a clay plate for all of them. The crowd patted him on the back, and a few even stood up to move around at the signal that his appearance gave. It was time for a break, and everyone in the Grotto loved the kid. Zippo was getting even better at cooking, which people were beginning to know him for. Rocky felt his mouth water as soon as the smell reached his nose; somehow, the young chef had created a salad and even dressed it.

Sela smiled and accepted a plate, sniffing the salad openly. "Is this Ardon's Vinaigrette dressing?" At Zippo's chagrined nod, Sela's smile widened. "Two things now that are a blast from my past." Rocky smiled, realizing that Zippo had bought a mass-produced dressing from the shop, then tucked into his food like a barbarian. It was delicious and tasty, and to his surprise, a buff popped up into his top corner. A little focus later, it opened into a notification window.

Well Fed
- **You have eaten a meal that is particularly well cooked and designed.**
    - **+2 to Stamina and**

+20% Satisfaction for the next four hours.

"You can get buffs from food!" Rocky exclaimed in confirmation of what he already knew. Zippo looked proud, and he deserved to be.

Sela smiled and nodded, too engaged with her food. The evidence was in front of all of them anyway. Instead, she just kept eating and reached the end of her plate before the other two. Once she was finished, she took a big swig of water before starting, "As your Cooking skill levels up, you will be able to create more impressive buffs with rarer ingredients. It's the level of Ether the specific ingredient holds that can transfer some strength to the person who eats it. It's the skill of the cook that doesn't destroy it as he cooks and prepares it for consumption."

She pointed to Rocky, emphasizing, "We have all seen what you do to food and the little care you put into preparing it. Now, look at the care Zippo gave the food and see how he manages to keep the food at a much higher grade, thanks to it." She smiled, trying to take the sting out of the words. "Now, for who or what Apep is."

Sela paused and looked off into the darkening sky. "Keep in mind that these are all stories I heard in passing from a time before I was born." She shook her head sadly before continuing, "My mom used to tell me bedtime stories about him right along with those of Ether Storms. Apep was made out to be pure darkness. He was some sort of giant snake at times, but every story made him out to be despicably evil." She stopped again and looked at Rocky. "Actually, your ancestor Azrael was the one who beat him, supposedly. That's how he got his famed title, General of the Darkest Night." Seeing the two men's confusion, she clicked her tongue. "I am doing a poor job of explaining this. Let me start at the beginning."

She smiled sheepishly before beginning, "Apep was known for sending his minion Apothis to worlds through Dungeons. If his minion, who is reborn by the corrupted Dungeons on the new world, is able to subjugate the Planetary God, then they would use the conquered planet as a base to invade the other surrounding planetary gods of that galaxy through coercion or destruction. Apep uses a minute amount of his energy to conquer a Dungeon and give birth to his minions." Sela pointed towards Chalk River. "Once Apothis or one of his minions successfully conquered the solar system, he would call Apep. Then Apep consumes the Star God of the weakened system, bringing that entire solar system into the Darkness and his domain."

She pointed at Rocky again before continuing, "The story has it that Azrael graduated the academy during a horrible time for our Planetary System. According to stories, it was on the verge of falling to Apep. Without going into the long campaign that Azrael undertook, he was able to conquer Apep across every planet, across the entire system, pushing him out and stopping Apep from destroying Odin, our Star God. He destroyed him with the armies of the Cathodiem Guild. It is why Azrael became so renowned across the entire galaxy."

He raised his eyebrow. "How is Apep so strong? I thought Gaia was insanely strong, but Apep definitely sounds like he's on a different level."

She nodded. "He isn't a Planetary God but something more on par with a Star God. It is theorized that he is the reverse of a Star God. The name we used was Void God; he has no body but exists and draws his strength from the darkness of space. Because he is so spread out, his power is sometimes weaker or stronger depending on the conditions."

Rocky blinked and asked, "How did Apothis and Apep return now then, if they were defeated?"

Sela shrugged and tried her best to answer the question, "My mother used to say that the evil in the hearts of mankind lets him in. She used it as a lesson for why to act honorably and pure of heart. So perhaps something to do with that explosion was a perversion, or could it have been a weapon that people would link to something terrible or evil?"

Rocky tilted his head, considering how best to answer that. "Not specifically, no. What exploded was an energy plant that was used to supply our world with electricity. However, the technology that is utilized has other much more menacing origins. It was originally created as a truly effective weapon. Would that count?"

Sela looked at Zippo and saw his grim look. "I am assuming if every human on the planet feels that way." She pointed at Zippo's blanched face. "Then perhaps that's exactly why."

Rocky felt his heart stutter, and his lungs clenched tightly. "That won't be the only explosion of its nature on the planet. We had many such power plants that utilized that same technology; we called it nuclear technology. Unfortunately, we also had many more times that number in weapons as well. However, those would be much more stable and probably didn't explode. I hope!" He took a deep shuddering breath. "Honestly, as far as the rumors say, the world had enough to destroy every living creature on it several times over."

He held up a finger for a moment, showing he was going to continue but wanted to collect his thoughts. Then in a voice that was more somber, he emotionlessly intoned, "That isn't the worst part of these weapons either. These weapons leave behind some sort of radiation." At Sela's confused look, he clicked his tongue, searching his mind for a better descriptor, then chose to explain it differently, "It's like a massive, poisonous cloud that occupies the land around one of these explosions. The problem is you can't see it without the proper tools, and it lasts for centuries before it begins to dissipate." He took a deep breath, then spoke the last point, "That cloud was nearly a hundred percent fatal."

Sela blinked rapidly at this new knowledge. After a time, she looked like she was going to be sick, but her hand raised up to her chin, and she responded quietly, "That does sound like something that people would consider evil." She shook her head sadly before continuing, "If this isn't the only disaster site, we need to take care of it fast. We don't want Apep to get a good foothold on the planet when the inhabitants are so weak, and we definitely don't want him in control of a Dragon."

Rocky stood up and raised his hands in surrender; he wanted to be done with this depressing topic. "If it isn't one thing, it's another. Let's set up the Guild Tent, have our meeting, and try to get those Master Knights on our side, at least!" He made a pointed gesture all around him. "This is all on a pretty huge level. We don't have the strength to save the entire world, Sela!"

Sela stood along with Zippo and they all walked over to the bundled-up tent. There was a tab that made Rocky pause. "Maybe stand clear? This pull tab is a bit ominous." They all walked back to the edge of the cleared area. Then Rocky summoned his Shadow Clone. When it arrived, it crossed its arms and was clearly not happy with him.

Rocky looked helplessly at Sela and Zippo who were laughing silently. Since they were of no help, he looked at the clone sheepishly. "Will you please go pull that tab over there?" The clone raised its eyebrows and stuck its tongue out before it was forced by his mental intention to walk over and pull the tab. As soon as it pulled the cord, the tent began to unfold, and the clone began to dash away. The clone was nowhere near fast enough as it was overtaken quickly by the expanding fabric, and the tent continued growing at an explosive rate.

Rocky stuck his tongue out as the clone disappeared. Yeah, it was childish, but the clone was really starting to get on his nerves with its antics. The tent kept expanding until, suddenly, it was fully set up, and massive anchors shot out from multiple spots, burying themselves deep into the tilled earth. They all stood there marvelling at the gigantic circus tent that now stood before them. Rocky opened his mouth to speak but was cut off by a massive roar from the sky.

He turned his head and saw Azoth dive-bombing the new tent, "Azoth, no!" he mentally screamed. It was too late, and the birdbrain tore a hole through the top of the tent. Rocky ran inside and screamed at the creature to stop its attack.

Come on! This thing was brand new. This is why we won't be having nice things!

Looking at the hole that Azoth had created, his head dropped, and he groaned. Still staring at his pet's work, he blinked as the hole began to repair itself slowly. The fabric must have some sort of self-repair added in, and he breathed a sigh of relief before putting a hand on Azoth's massive chest. "Okay, buddy, this is our newest guild building. Can you please not tear it apart anymore?"

"Azoth sorry. Azoth saw tent eat dark Rocky. Azoth protect Rocky." Rocky smiled, shaking his head as Sela and Zippo entered the tent behind him. Then he noticed the moving mound of fabric that was probably his clone. He quickly dismissed the skill so it wouldn't stay trapped or pull an Azoth and cut its way out...

He glanced again at the shrinking tear in the roof and noticed that even though it was repairing, he could easily tell that it was a damaged section of fabric. So much for a flawless, new Guild Tent.

Despite looking through his interface thoroughly and having Sela also look, they still hadn't discovered how to completely remove the blinking corners. A bright orange blinking was dominating his bottom left corner, so he glanced at it before it gave him a seizure.

Congratulations! Your Territory has erected a Guilt Tent!
Due to this being a non-permanent building, you will only receive 50% of the benefits associated or derived from this building. Create or join a guild to discover more.
Would you like to join an existing guild?

Yes | <Create New Guild> | Postpone

The option for the new guild was definitely what he was looking for, but he was curious if there were any guilds available that he could join. So, he clicked 'Yes' and was rewarded with a blank screen and a back button. He hadn't been hoping for an existing guild, but it sure would have been nice if some of the old, powerful guilds from Sela's lifetime were still around.

He looked over at Zippo and Sela and asked, "Any ideas for names for our new guild?" Zippo smiled broadly, but Sela frowned.

She ran her tongue along her teeth before entreating, "Did you–"

Rocky, knowing she had been hoping that her Cathodiem guild would be an option, cut her off with a sharp nod of his head, and she dropped her gaze once again before turning her back on the two of them. Zippo, not knowing what was wrong, looked at Rocky and gave a few suggestions, "Maple Leafs? The Nice Guys? Algonquin? Humanity?"

Trying to take his mind off Sela's pain for the moment, Rocky smiled at Zippo, responding, "I was thinking something that could be a beacon for anyone who was going to join. Maybe call it Hope?"

Zippo tilted his head and immediately tried to make it cooler as children often do, "Last Hope? Humanity's Hope? One

Hope?" Sela started laughing at Zippo's exuberance, and Rocky, who had also begun smiling at Zippo's antics, felt a weight lift from his chest when he heard the musical sound of her laughter.

I'm very glad she's so strong.

"Meliora was part of a common saying from my era. It was Ad Meliora and meant 'toward better things.' I think it would be appropriate now." Sela chimed in after she was done laughing, and her mood began to sober again.

The way she enunciated the words sounded foreign but also beautiful and uplifting in a way Rocky didn't know how to associate. He chose to go with it and typed it into the box requesting a guild name. A moment later, a new notification window popped up.

Congratulations! You have founded a new guild! Meliora is officially founded.

Would you like to add all members of the Territory to the ranks of Meliora?

<Yes> | Select Individually | Postpone

Would you like to deem any knowledge proprietary to the guild?

<Yes> | No

Would you like to change guild settings?

<Yes> | Postpone

Would you like to write a guild welcome message?

<Yes> | Postpone

Confirm and Save all Settings | <Save and Exit> | Advanced Settings

Some of the options were easy, like inviting everyone to the guild, and Rocky, along with Sela's input, made them quickly. When he pushed the button, it lit up green on the blue background, saving his choice for when he confirmed all decisions. However, when he pushed yes on the guild settings, a different window popped out overlaying the first, and he realized that the input of more people would probably be needed for those decisions. Zippo was sent to gather up the A-Team, who were acting as a de-facto council of sorts, at least currently, while Sela and Rocky examined options that the setting windows provided.

CHAPTER EIGHTEEN

To everyone's surprise, the meetings continued through the night, with a brief, one-hour break for everyone to take an Elixir of Shortened Sleep, but they then continued. It probably shouldn't have been much of a surprise considering that this would be the first step for an entire community, and everyone wanted to ensure it was in the proper direction. They had vacated the guild tent and taken the meeting outside pretty quickly. Almost as soon as the massive tent sprung up, people had been milling around inside and outside of it. Near what seemed to be bedtime, the members of the council left the interior to allow the civilians who wished a roof over their heads to utilize the Guild Tent and to gain a bit more privacy.

From the very start of the meeting, Derik had been irate with Rocky about a couple of things. He was not happy that Rocky had spent a vast majority of funds on the Guild Tent instead of buying something more appropriate. When Sela questioned Derik on what might be more appropriate, he had indignantly sputtered, "What about defenses for the Grotto or tents for the people who will be forced to sleep outside?" like it was an obvious choice.

Rocky responded a little hotly, "Almost everyone is going to be focusing on building houses until we get roofs for everyone. As for defenses, while those tanks that are parked near the entrance look intimidating, they are truly pitiful in the face of the creatures that are outside of Algonquin Valley!"

Perhaps he should have tried to be more political in his answers because Derik had become a greater nuisance all night, contradicting almost anything that was discussed. The only way to deal with the man had been to switch out his Elixir of Shortened Sleep with an Elixir of Dreamless Sleep that Smith had offered Rocky circumspectly. Rocky knew that Derik and Smith were actually very close friends and had hesitated to switch the potions at first, mostly because it would only exacerbate the problem in the long term. However, Smith had taken the initiative anyway and explained to the A-Team, Rocky, Zippo, and Sela after the short hour break that it was his choice.

Even after Derik was absent from the meeting, it had hiccups. It wasn't nearly as bad, but it had taken the group right up until morning training to fully agree on the initial course of action which included how they would allocate Guild Etherience for quests, how they would allocate salaries, how they would choose others from the Grotto to join the 'council', and who present wasn't interested in further politics and planning. There were so many other things that they decided on that seemed less important but might turn out to be extremely important down the road, like that hunters kept the crystals they earned and all loot, but the butchered food was the Territory's.

Sela told the group that it was extremely common to place Territorial lands under an Atlantian Contractual state known as 'The King's Forest'. These areas were illegal to hunt in without express permission of the governing body or the ruler of them. If you were hunting them illegally, then the system would notify the leaders of the Territory. Sometimes, the strongest Territories had the kills locked, so the killers couldn't loot or gain Etherience. In those cases, only the meat and hide were available to the perpetrator, but it was only the truly desperate that hunted King's Forests without permission.

I still wonder if that is where the tradition had come from in our medieval histories.

After that realization, some members of the group had started back up the argument, wanting to take the Crystals from the hunters' loot and use it to pay wages evenly amongst all citizens, creating something like a communist society. Sela had again stepped in, "Those were tried with some success in my time. In the long term, they were proved ineffective though, due to the lack of motivation for people to improve or grow. Yet this study was provided by a democratic ruling body so it could be biased, but I truly think that we should be attempting to force people to grow at all costs." She had pointed at the Guild Tent. "We do not have the luxury of ensured safety that was afforded people in my day. So, making hunters more appealing will perhaps give us stronger defenders and fighters."

While many had grumbled about it, they had all seen Sela's point in the end and agreed on that at least. Another oddity and the second reason Derik had been irate was that Rocky's initial founding of the guild had added all current individuals inside the Territory to the guild automatically without any choice on their part. Rocky hadn't known that it wouldn't offer people a place in the guild, instead enlisting them automatically and agreed with Derik on that point. However, he had suspicions that Sela had known the system would act that way. The fact that people could leave if they chose didn't appease the ornery, middle-aged hothead. Rocky clung to that tidbit to help his conscience with what he saw as a massive breach of privacy by the system.

Rocky shook his head to clear it of the night's reminiscing and stepped up on to the cobbled-together stage to first address his people and then lead them in Meditation. Once he was in the center of the stage and in front of a very rough-looking podium, he cleared his throat. Then using his loudest voice without actually shouting, he projected, "Good morning, everyone! I know it has only been a couple of days, but much has happened, and you should all hear about it. First, we have established a guild, and I welcome you to the ranks of 'Better Things' or Meliora." It had taken Rocky a great deal of coaching by Sela to finally be able to say the Latin word without butchering it.

The vast majority of the crowd erupted with cheers, and Rocky smiled, waiting for silence to return. Once it did, he continued, "Another great addition to our Territory is our first 'friendly' Dungeon. I encourage everyone to challenge themselves in its sand pits, as Maximus, the Arena Dungeon core, has guaranteed our safety as long as we follow the rules. The rules are posted inside the Guild Tent and must be read and verbally agreed to before you will be granted access to the Arena Dungeon. It will open on Monday, which is in two days!"

Rocky had raised his voice in excitement at the end and clearly signaled that this was the end of another announcement. A few scattered claps and cheers were all he received however, and he nervously held his smile, realizing that many people had absolutely no clue what a Dungeon was. The ones who had cheered his announcement were likely the gamers of the group and had 'experience' with the phrases that this world had made common overnight. The ones who didn't cheer were likely just lucky that they had found a school early on and that they'd been escorted to Algonquin Valley. He hoped the gamers would help the others in the days to come. In his days of playing online MMORPGs he'd come across gamers who were some of the friendliest and most accommodating people he had the pleasure of meeting. Unfortunately, he'd also come across almost an equal number of elitist pricks who wanted to lord their superiority in the new made up world over him. He hoped that those people weren't here, but he felt in his gut that they eventually would be as they collected more people to Algonquin Valley.

The silence stretched and forced Rocky to clear his throat again. "I realize that many of you are unaware of what that means, and I hope that the people who do know will take the time to answer the questions of others after our training. Yes, I am looking at the gamers amongst you. The rest of the people need to know what you have learned playing video games... finally!" He smiled and heard a few people chuckle at his lame humor.

He continued quickly, trying not to detract too much from his message, "Finally, today, everyone will be able to pick up a Knowledge Tablet," Rocky held his up to show everyone, "from the shop. These tablets allow you to download books about the current world. I'm asking for some volunteers to dedicate themselves to reading books and teaching us a bit about what they read every morning before we train, Montessori-style learning where you learn the subject before teaching it to everyone."

He turned to look at the A-Team beside him and gestured in their direction. "If you are interested, please talk to any member of the council and we will make sure that all volunteers are in contact with each other."

Some scattered applause and conversation broke out so Rocky paused to let it die. Then he continued, "Finally, we'd like to have people join the council that are chosen by the majority of you. If you're interested in having a hand in the decisions and governance of the Territory, please make yourself known to a current council member, and we'll inform you as per the rules and timeline for running your platform." Many people began looking around at this point at their neighbors and friends, wondering who might choose to run. Rocky smiled when he saw this high school like reaction and finished, "That's all the announcements for today! Let's get down to Meditating!"

A few hours later, after Meditation and martial training, Rocky was negotiating another deal with a Dungeon. This deal was much stranger and more humorous because of the entity he was dealing with. "If you make me the East Dungeon, I would be on the side of the water, which isn't ideal. Maybe I can be the West Dungeon? The Grotto wall has plenty of places for entrances. I need to have my curb appeal if I plan to be the most traversed and popular Dungeon in the world!" LFD finished saying in his rapid-fire exuberance.

"Look, LFD, if all you want is to be the most popular Dungeon in the world, the Territory can help you with that. Taking the east and having one large, glorious entrance on the other side of the river will give you more curb appeal than multiple entrances. Think about it! One beautifully sculpted entrance designed to appeal to adventurers!" Rocky was, at this point, saying anything to have LFD accept the modified terms that Maximus had already accepted. The fact that it was stuck on which cardinal direction it would occupy was bothersome to say the least. Rocky needed the Dungeon in the east to help protect against invasions from the current threat of Chalk River.

Customized Terms
- **The Dungeon will not kill any of the Guild Members as long as:**
  - **If a Member would have 'died,' they will be notified and forced to stay in room of their death while kept in a cage. A quest will be placed on the guild boards for rescue of any dead adventuring teams. 'Dead' members cannot return until after Resurrection Day; Voskresenie (Sunday).**
  - **On Saturnday (Saturday), the Dungeon will tally each spared Member and will be awarded accordingly.**
  - **A Member can choose to enter after they have 'died', but then all above protections are void.**
  - **A party can clear the Dungeon as frequently as they are scheduled to enter. However, from the second floor on the Dungeon will attempt to scale challenges to the party's skill and level.**
- **The Dungeon will receive 2.5% of Territorial generated Essence.**
- **The Dungeon will receive a new monster corpse one time per moon (month).**

- The Dungeon will drop loot for each floor boss of the Dungeon and give them the option to exit the Dungeon at the completion of each floor.
- The Dungeon is not held liable for any injuries on premises.
- The Dungeon shall attempt with all due haste to reach the Tectonic Dungeon as long as it doesn't hinder other clauses.
- The Dungeon will work in conjunction with all other Cardinal Dungeons for the betterment of the Territory.
- The Dungeon will increase the fertility of lands in cardinal direction of its placement.
- The Dungeon will defend and notify Leaders of invaders from said direction.
- The Dungeon can call on Leaders to defend it from invaders who seek its heart.
- The Dungeon will create three bath houses that are for the use of the Territorial inhabitants and visitors.
- The Dungeon will create a retractable bridge leading to its entrance that will withdraw if Territory is under attack from the cardinal direction.
- This agreement is subject to change and will be re-negotiated once per full rotation.

Offer | Back

"You're not listening, Rocky! I read multiple entrances is the best for curb appeal. Why have one gaudy entrance when you can have many entrances of all shapes and sizes? Clearly, you need to read up on your real estate knowledge," LFD countered, sounding like a child trying to condescend to an adult.

Rocky groaned and tried a different tact. Earlier in the conversation, LFD had gotten very excited about having each group confined to a floor until the next group had either 'died' or cleared the following floor. For some reason, the game of escorting a captured team to the end of the current floor was exciting for the Dungeon, almost like a perverted game of capture the flag. "LFD, if someone enters one of your entrances, do you not close all of them? If what you said about having a single group in your Dungeon per floor is true, won't that be the case?"

There was a long moment of silence while LFD's core pulsed; then the Dungeon babbled, "As I was saying, the east side is the ideal location for my Delving Dungeon. I think one extravagant entrance is the best for appealing to your Territorial inhabitants and adventurers. I will get started on everything right away! I will need a few days to regain my lost Essence that was left behind when we fled my previous body."

Rocky felt his eyebrows shoot up, and his teeth clicked together as he closed his hanging jaw. Sela, who had been practicing knife throwing, collected her blades and rolled her eyes as she turned around mouthing, "Finally." Then they hopped on Azoth who had descended from the skies to join them at a mental signal from Rocky and made a short hop over the river to place LFD on the ground as centrally to the river as they could manage.

Once the Dungeon sunk into the ground, he clicked his radio. "Just completed negotiations with the Dungeon. Have the golems arrived at the clearing yet?" Rocky joined Sela back on Azoth's back as he waited for a response.

Sela punched him in the shoulder. "You didn't say over. You know he is going to correct you. Honestly, being a leader is about making everyone as comfortable as you can, and saying 'over' on the radio with military folk isn't that hard. Get it right!"

As soon as she finished, Joe's voice chirped, "This is negotiation perimeter. The golems and the council are both present and are just awaiting Leadership. Please remember to use your radio moniker and to say over. Over!" The way Joe stressed the moniker they were supposed to be using, Leadership, made Rocky wince. Honestly, he almost pulled the radio out of his ear and left it on the ground as Azoth took to the skies to make the quick jump over to the clearing where they would negotiate with the golems.

The only thing that stopped him was that he may need to order the perimeter troops to save the ass of the council if the golems chose to get violent. Not that he thought the golems would, after his last meeting with them. Derik was probably the biggest worry, but he was still passed out for a few hours under the effects of Smith's Elixir swap.

They flew into the clearing directly and watched as the golems slowly grew and resolved into the towering and imposing figures that Rocky remembered from his last meeting. Omega was cheerfully waving at him, and Rocky smiled, remembering the surfer dude persona of the massive golem. It reminded him of Azoth in some ways, and Rocky immediately hoped that they would be able to come to an agreement, mostly because his Territory desperately needed the protection that these five could offer.

They stayed atop Azoth until they reached the ceremonial line of weapons that were placed on the ground behind the council. Rocky, who hadn't seen any of these weapons yet, glanced over many of them, only recognizing Zippo's staff and Joe's laser rifle. As he added his sword and Sela added her knives, he glanced at a pair of stylized spears that looked far more powerful than he had been expecting to see on the ground.

Spear of the Fishes and Eels

- **These spears were what the Algonquin derived their namesake from and embody their strong ability to survive by hunting and fishing.**

Soulbound Weapon Level 2
Quality: Relic / Soulbound
Ether Pool: 110/110

Rocky felt his eyebrows rise and looked at Sela who was also examining the spears. They both looked to Smith at the same time to find the man calmly regarding them. When their eyes met, Smith nodded once acknowledging their suspicions, and Rocky smiled sheepishly. That was very interesting, considering that he was also an Ancestral class. He briefly wondered if there was a way to change people's classes that had already chosen, then dismissed it as something to consider later after this meeting.

Add it to the list to ask Sela.

They walked up and kneeled in the center of the assembled humans opposite the hulking golems and both bowed. Rocky then explained, "We apologize for our lateness, Epsilon and the Knights of Ottawa, we were negotiating with our newest Dungeon." Epsilon bowed respectively back, and the other Knights followed his lead except Gamma, who ducked his head as little as possible. Rocky winced seeing the angry Knight who had suggested killing everyone during their last meeting. He hoped that he wouldn't say anything like that during this one, or this negotiation might turn.

When Epsilon exited his kneeling bow, he boomed out, "We were not waiting long, Rocky, and we got to meet some of your council while we did. I must say, speaking to these members here has really allowed us to see the diversity each human possesses." Rocky looked around, and no one would meet his eyes.

Oh great—something already happened?!

Sela cleared her throat. "I, on behalf of my people, promise on my faith that I will deal faithfully with you, not cause you harm, and will observe this oath to you completely against all persons in good faith and without deceit during our negotiations."

All of the golem's heads turned to Sela in unison, leaving a node of stunned silence hanging in the air as they all regarded the young woman. Surprisingly, Tao, who had not spoken during the last meeting, was the first to find his voice, "I, for myself and my order, pledge upon our sacred oath to do no harm, treat with you without deceit, and honor the pledge you have offered us during our negotiations."

The moment hung, and everyone looked between the two speakers as they held each others' gaze unblinkingly. Then they both nodded simultaneously, and the moment passed.

Azoth mentally sent, "They doing a dominance dance? Who win if neither blink first?"

Rocky responded mentally while trying to maintain a straight face, "No, Azoth, that was some sort of ceremony to begin negotiations between Knights, if I'm not mistaken. I think Sela just put us well on the right foot again."

Azoth scanned across the Knights and chuffed once into the mounting silence. "I think I could make them submit to dominance!"

Rocky shook his head and sent back, "Not today, buddy. Please just sit down and relax!"

Epsilon broke the silence, and Rocky's internal conversation with Azoth, "We did not expect to hear such an oath in this place. Please explain how you entered the order, little one?"

Sela turned her head and smiled at the massive and imposing form of Epsilon. "That is a rather long story, but let's just say I was inducted into the order of the Knights of the Lighted Path well before anyone present was ever born."

Gamma made a sound of disbelief but was cut off by Tao instantly, "We will look forward to hearing your tale one day, honored elder." Gamma looked at Tao, who had begun a full, deep-seated bow, and his green copper eyebrows shot up before he followed suit and mimicked the motion precisely. The other golems also bowed to Sela who seemed to sit up a bit straighter as her lips pressed into a thin line at the gesture. Then she rapped her knuckles twice on her hardened leather, and the Knights straightened up, ending the surreal moment.

Sela, who knew the goal of the meeting as well as Rocky did, continued to take the lead, "We have considered your situation and would offer you refuge here and a place to build a home for friendly members of your race. In exchange, the threats to Algonquin Gorge become threats to you, and a call to defense becomes a duty all who take our offer must fulfill."

Epsilon bowed his head apologetically. "Circumstances have changed slightly for us. We received another quest from Gaia last night and wish to accept your offer but also complete the quest for our creator."

Rocky blinked and asked the obvious, "What is the quest?"

This time, Omega responded, removing a great deal of levity from the conversation, "Dude… Gaia has tasked all golems with protecting humans. Any surviving humans are to be protected and provided for as best as the unintelligent golems can manage. Gaia has tasked us with going to collect the nearby groups of humans and bringing them back here."

Rocky felt himself jerk back as this so closely resembled his initial plans for the golems that he wondered if Gaia had been listening in to their first meeting. Additionally, that meant any remaining survivors were probably going to be a lot safer than they were previously. He took a moment to picture golems ringing human settlements of schools, hospitals, and libraries and smiled to himself, hoping that meant his family, if they were still alive, would remain that way.

Epsilon looked to Tao before speaking; Tao nodded once, which seemed to give permission to Epsilon who declared, "However, we will leave two of our order with you to help prepare the Territory for the arrival of survivors. We have decided that Tao and Gamma will remain behind to help you build up your settlement."

Rocky felt blood drain from his face and saw a similar reaction from the members of the council around him. His earlier assumption that Gamma had done something threatening was all but confirmed by the group's reaction to the names called. Rocky cleared his throat, "I thank you for your consideration, but we wouldn't want you to be left without Gamma—"

Delta cut him off clinically, stating, "Do not fear Gamma. He will make an oath to not harm any human without permission to do so by someone who you deem to be able to give that order." Delta looked pointedly at Gamma and scowled "Won't you, Gamma?" he finished.

Gamma began to stand before Tao placed a hand on his shoulder with a very menacing smile plastered on his face. Gamma gulped and stated, "Yes…" before he returned to kneel, and the fight drained out of him.

Epsilon smiled. "Gamma is, in fact, our best builder, and his axe will be of great help to you while you gather and construct your settlement. Don't worry, Tao is more than capable of keeping him in line…" Tao nodded and turned his wicked smile to the group. Clearly, Gamma didn't want to be the one left behind, but also just as clearly, Tao was going to enforce that decision despite Gamma's dislike of it.

Rocky looked around at the council members present, wondering if there was going to be an issue with two golems staying instead of one. At their accepting look, he wasn't sure what else there was to discuss. The two Golem Knights were already chosen and would stay in the Territory, helping them build and defend it. That thought made him ask a question to clarify, "Will Gamma and Tao help us defeat the cause of these storms?"

Tao shook his head vigorously, and Epsilon insisted, "No, they will only defend the Territory if it is attacked and will follow orders during such a defense. Otherwise, they will help build and train your people, but will not attack any enemies of the Territory until our return. Is that acceptable?"

Rocky nodded, expecting that answer but still disappointed in it. Sela saw his face fall and whispered in his ear, "Don't worry, that gives us the ability to go all out on attack while depending on them for defense. It is still a great benefit to us!"

He nodded once at her words, understanding her sentiment entirely. Right after this meeting concluded they were planning to try to make their way into Chalk River and the site of the explosion, after all.

CHAPTER NINETEEN

Rocky and Sela had mounted Azoth and sped ahead of the party to return to the Grotto to prepare for their scouting excursion into Chalk River. From the air, it was an inspiring sight to see the two golems accompanying their military and pseudo council towards the Grotto. Additionally, once high enough, they could see the people of the Grotto hard at work looking like ants in a colony. Each member was moving around to collect material and return to building one of the ten construction projects they currently had on the go. They got occasional glimpses of the hunting parties that were out trying to target individual prey safely as well, each group accompanied by a tank and two soldiers who tried to stay out of the fight entirely to not impede on Etherience gains while still keeping the groups safe from death.

The scene was uplifting to Rocky, seeing so many people who had lost so much hard at work to create a new home for themselves and provide for each other. This was why as they neared the landing point, Rocky was quite shocked to see a group of approximately thirty people moving ominously to greet them, at their head a red-faced Derik. Rocky sighed deeply as Azoth touched down and slid off his back after Sela hit the ground softly.

Derik didn't even say a word as he launched his attack at Rocky, who wasn't even truly aware of what class the man possessed. Three bolts of purple energy soared at Rocky, who dodged sporadically and triggered his Dark Cloak as he shouted, "What the hell, Derik?!"

Sela transformed into her cat form as she got hit by a few projectiles from the charging group, but Azoth took the worst of it as he let out a roar that could easily be heard for miles. Rocky felt the Chimera's roar course over him and even felt stronger as a buff notification climbed up into the top left of his vision.

Call of the Predatory Pact

- **Your pet has been wounded and called for your aid.**

  Increase to all stat points by 20% for two minutes as you rush to his defense.

Not sure why Derik and this band of people were attacking them, Rocky jumped into action. He could feel Dark Tidings craving the souls of these individuals but forced down its whispers as he closed with Derik. Just as he attempted to pommel the man in the temple, Derik vanished and appeared forty yards away from Rocky behind the charging group. Rocky felt his blood boil, and he continued his rush to intercept the other ranged damage dealers.

His levels easily dwarfed the group around him, and he dodged and weaved through the melee strikes with the aid of his Dark Cloak, only being scored by a few glancing blows that were mostly absorbed by his armor. He retaliated when he could, trying to incapacitate his mute attackers wherever possible, which counteracted his advantage, putting him at more of a disadvantage than he thought it would. The people who closed with Sela and Azoth were not so lucky, and out of the corner of his eye, he saw a man get torn in half by the enraged Chimera.

Screams erupted around him as people of the Grotto realized that this was not a demonstration but something far too real as internal organs and blood flew into the air after Azoth's vicious strike. Rocky renewed his effort attempting to work faster to try and save more of the men before they fell victim to Sela or Azoth. Not that they deserved saving after this ambush, but something inside Rocky sensed the wrongness in this fight.

He shouted as loudly as he could, "Try to incapacitate or wound. Avoid killing them!"

They attacked us head-on and haven't said a single word.

He moved as fast as he could throughout the remaining attackers until he reached Derik just as the red-faced man finished a spell. Derik bent down and placed both hands on the ground under him. Arcane energy pulsed and wove, attempting to create some sort of glyph in the dirt. Rocky sliced through part of the forming symbols with his sword just as it grew bright enough that he had to look away. Then he felt a massive force punch him along the entire front side of his body, and he was suddenly airborne, flying away from Derik, who was also speeding away from the destroyed glyph. Rocky tucked into a ball as he hit the ground and felt the momentum carry him end over end as the damage mounted. A moment later, he uncurled his bruised and beaten body.

What in the hell was that all about? I know I needed to do laundry, but I didn't need to be put in a spin cycle with the clothes. I feel like the rug that gets hung up and beaten clean of dust.

He stood up and almost fell back over from the dizziness and disorientation that blast had caused him. He glanced at his debuffs and saw a great many new symbols he didn't yet recognize but even more that he did. Sela loped up to him, and he nearly fell into her horse-high back. In the wake of the fight, a broken, bloody, and disoriented Rocky leaned heavily on Sela, as Azoth walked over, bleeding and angry. "Why Derik attack Azoth?" he shouted into Rocky's mind.

The volume caused him to wince, and he held up a hand as he fished out a health elixir and cast Dark Mend on himself. After he had downed the liquid, he responded out loud for both Sela and Azoth, "Let's go ask him, shall we?"

There were eight of the thirty torn in half and another eight dying from vicious wounds Sela had inflicted upon the attackers. Rocky, who was limping his way along using Sela's cat form as a crutch, grimaced and cast a few Dark Mends on the worst cases to hopefully prolong their lives until he had answers at the very least. As they approached Derik, Rocky realized that the man wasn't far from death himself. He had landed near a tree trunk and had unceremoniously careened into it a few bounces after.

If they didn't do something quickly, he would definitely die. Rocky pulled out a Health Potion and poured it down the man's throat and then cast a few quick Dark Mends on the dying annoyance, nearly bottoming out his Ether pool. Looking down as bones popped and crunched back into place, Rocky felt sick but not as sick as he did a moment later when he saw a strange, glowing, red pulse under Derik's shirt. The rough landing had nearly torn the shirt entirely off, which revealed the necklace that had not been visible on Derik during the fight. Snarling, Rocky bent down and ripped it off, mentally throwing it into his bag of holding in the same instant. He felt the familiar presence on his mind from Bathilda's Heartstring for a split second before it was gone.

As Derik healed, he walked around gingerly, inspecting the other survivors to see if they had Heartstrings as well, but he didn't find any. He did, however, find a strange, pulsing handprint on each of them in different locations. When had Derik been affixed with the perverted thing? Rocky tried to think back and realized that Derik had been an asshole since the first day he met him, so it was going to be very hard to pinpoint a change in his demeanor.

Who was controlling them? Was it Derik?

Sela, now human again, came up behind him somewhat angrily. "Why are you healing them? Do I need to remind you that they just attacked us out of a cloudless blue sky with no provocation or warning!" In answer, Rocky pulled out the Dragon Heartstring, using an old shirt to keep it entirely away from his skin. He showed it to Sela discretely before looking around at the growing crowd of people around them. The small crowd looked scared and confused, having just witnessed a large amount of senseless violence; Azoth's kills were particularly disturbing as they were still in multiple pieces.

Rocky took a moment before the crowd grew larger to walk around and place as many of the dismembered corpses into his inventory, and he saw Sela follow suit a moment later. A few people looked very disturbed by what was happening, but luckily, the crowd was small. Within a few minutes, the only evidence of the death and violence was blood pooling on the ground and on Azoth's claws. Rocky handled the second by asking Azoth to go hunt for his lunch.

"Did Azoth do wrong? Azoth not sure…" Rocky felt his heartbreak from the confused tone his pet used, and he could honestly say he was lost for what to say to the soft-hearted companion. Azoth had simply defended himself and had done nothing wrong at all; even Rocky hadn't known that these people were somehow infected. He had recognized some of the attackers as the same individuals who had assaulted him on their first night here, which had given him even more reason to kill them. Yet something about the method of their attack, the lack of communication, had immediately felt perverted and twisted to Rocky.

Rocky turned to the big, black Chimera and placed his hand on the beast's chest before looking directly into Azoth's black eyes. "Azoth, you did nothing wrong. They attacked you, and you reacted. In no way was that something bad." He saw Azoth glance around the valley before his wings flapped open with a gust of wind.

"Oh, okay! Azoth go find meatier treats!" When Azoth responded, all the hurt of his previous confusion was entirely gone, replaced by childish exuberance, and if his mental words were interpreted right, he had considered eating his kills. Rocky blinked and covered his head as the massive Chimera took off and winged away to find a more appropriate meal. He sighed and wished his mood could swing as abruptly as his pet's could. Also, he made a note to discuss with Azoth to never eat humans.

That sure would change the story of Clifford the big red dog.

Once Azoth was gone, he did feel a bit of the tension in the air leave, and he cleared his throat, "I need some help to gather all the survivors of that attack and put them together, please." At his words, some of the hunters who were more accustomed to the sight of blood stepped forward and gingerly moved the remaining twenty survivors into a rough circle. Rocky continued as they worked, "Does anyone know why these people attacked Azoth, Sela, and I?" He made sure to stress the word attack to ensure anyone just arriving realized that this was an unprovoked assault by the unconscious people currently being dragged into a tight group.

One of the hunters dragging a body spoke, "This guy's name is JF, and he wasn't at training this morning. I can confirm that his team," he pointed at two others and briefly glanced at the blood on the grass, "were absent as well. We were going to talk to them about hunting an area together today."

Rocky Analyzed the man who spoke.

Terry Crew
Level 13
Apprentice Hoplite
Health Points 303/310

As Rocky read, he heard more people in the crowd begin noticing the same pattern amongst the unconscious people being dragged around. Soon, it was quite clear that each individual had missed the morning Meditation and martial arts. What good that knowledge was, Rocky wasn't sure.

Great, we can clearly see they didn't believe in the group learning and training I had initiated, which only highlights further their dislike of my leadership, or they felt that the danger from the Irradiated Ether that mediation—

Rocky felt his brain begin working furiously as he considered the possibilities of his last thoughts. Clearly these people were somehow being manipulated by the Dragon's Heartstring or some kind of magic. Did the Meditation that he had all the survivors training somehow prevent it from working as effectively?

He knew that it definitely stopped the Zombie-like mutation that the Irradiated Ether could cause. Perhaps this form of manipulation was something similar, something that worked through the Ether Channels in its target's bodies.

He looked at Terry and ordered in a very loud voice, "Gather everyone in the Territory. Stop them from anything they are doing and have them meet at the stage!" He looked around the clearing and shouted, "If you know anyone who has missed morning meetings, go to the military immediately and inform them. Someone is trying to mind control our people, and I think that people who are missing the meetings are more affected!"

The crowd scattered, either going to spread his orders or tell the military about people who missed training. The fear was evident on their faces. He wondered if his face held the same sort of expression. Having your mind invaded was one of the most heinous, disgusting actions he had ever considered. The Atlantean System and Etherience had a lot to answer for ...

Then he turned to Sela and met her eyes with his fear filled ones. "If you missed that, I think someone is attempting to manipulate our people, and the Meditation is preventing it to a relatively large degree. Do you have a signal to get the hunters back?"

Sela nodded slowly. "Yes, I do, but I have to be in my bird form to accomplish it, which means we probably won't get to Chalk River today." Rocky looked up to the countdown for the Ether Protection of the Territory.

Ether Protection

Time of Ether assisted protection for Territory: 3 days, 12 hours, 12 minutes, and 14 seconds.

While time was counting down on the Territory's protection, they would still have time; they definitely needed to get to the bottom of this problem, or they could expect to come back to a Territory that was subverted. That didn't mean that they shouldn't get something done on both fronts though, so Rocky nodded at her. "Give them the signal to return, and then contact Azoth and do a fly-by of Chalk River. Try to see what we're going to have to deal with, but don't engage."

Sela transformed into her Raven form and winged away without a word.

SELA

Sela flew in ever-enlarging, concentric circles, cawing at the top of her lungs and feeling rather silly. When she had made this signal, she assumed that she would only have to use it for attacks on the Territory, but now, she was up here because Rockland thought he was attacked due to some sort of manipulation by the enemy. She stuttered one of her caws as she considered how many times, she had been attacked by groups of people who hadn't warned her during her time. It was a normal occurrence, and that was why she hadn't held back at first.

Often after such an attack, they would find anyone connected to the individuals and round them up as well, imprisoning them for conspiracy. Now, their screams of innocence and disbelief that their significant others, sons, daughters, or close friends were capable of such a betrayal had become an accusation in her memories. Could it be that she had condemned innocents to punishments that they hadn't truly deserved? Why wouldn't someone have checked the attackers for marks of manipulation then?

She kept cawing, relieved when she remembered that she had checked thoroughly through many such groups specifically because she had felt the same wrongness Rockland had felt from his recent ambush. However, none of the groups she had fought had borne any such mark, and she knew that none had been wearing a Dragon Heartstring. There had only been one Dragon on Gaia, Smog, and he had been so utterly powerful that even the Leviathans that the Gaian Military possessed avoided his ever-resting home on the mountain. Due to his immense power and age, he rarely woke, and nothing on the planet could truly sustain him anymore. So, once a month, he would make a circuit into deep space to capture and kill one of the myriads of monstrous creatures that lived there. Then he would return and slumber. Every rumored attack on Smog had been destroyed to a man, and anyone foolish enough to steal from him would bring destruction on an entire continent when he returned.

That thought led her back to the one thought that kept rattling around in her head lately—could the Ether Manipulation, Meditation, and Ether Channels be the reason that the force manipulating the population left a mark? It clearly needed the power of a Dragon's Heartstring to control Derik, and that was quite a bit more than was warranted for a single human. The Dungeon made sense, but Derik? Derik really wasn't even that big of a factor in the Territory; he was on the council, but most of the group barely listened to him anymore because of his constant negativity.

Sela finished her final circle and saw the council and the two Knights running toward the Grotto under her for just a moment as she winged by. The council had heard the signal and informed the Knights. She chuckled to herself; they were going to be surprised to run into the clearing only to be told to sit and Meditate. She wished Rockland luck with explaining that one.

"Azoth, it's time to go scouting," Sela mentally sent, hoping that he was in range of her druidic ability to talk to animals. He was the only animal she knew that could talk back currently, but she did get many hungry or angry feelings from other wildlife.

Azoth responded almost immediately, "Azoth above you! Come up, better breezes." Sela felt her bird beak open as her muscles attempted a wide smile. It probably looked rather sinister, but she began winging up above the clouds to meet with the joyful young Chimera. Once they were both level, Sela blinked a few times, looking towards their destination. Another storm was forming in that direction, and she clenched her beak in anger at the sight. This would be a much more dangerous scouting mission if they got caught by that when it released.

Azoth, who was already a much better flyer than she was, guided her to a slipstream of wind that was moving in the right direction, and together they took off towards Chalk River. The flight was very quick for them with the aid of the wind at their backs, and soon, she was starting to see the destruction and perversion around the immediate area. It was the worst at the site of the meltdown and subsequent thermal explosion. All the plant life in the area was black and oily, giving off a sense of violation to her druid senses. In fact, she realized that on the trip in, she got less and less of a signal from Gaia, and now, it was as if this entire area was completely cut off from the planetary god as if this was a different planet entirely.

Sela shuddered as she banked her wings slightly to ease out of the slipstream they rode. Once they dropped the builtup speed, they began circling the center of the epidemic. Near the blackened and melted earth, Sela saw eight black-robed figures all holding twisted, gnarled, black staffs adorned with a molten glowing rod at the top. The eight figures ringed a massive creature easily as large as Draksus had been in Ottawa. This creature had wings, and the scales Sela could see initially were the utter black of a moonless and starless night. Yet on the ground immediately surrounding the creature, many such black scales were littered, and most of the underside of the creature was now filled with a bleached, sickly, white-looking scale. It was clear that the eight Necromancers were casting some sort of spell to weaken and perhaps even corrupt the majestic creature. For a moment, she wondered why they didn't move closer and touch the beast, having learned from personal experience in her past life that physical touch amplified these disgusting types of spells.

Then she saw the five broken and desiccated bodies of long-dead Necromancers ringing the beast and nodded to herself. The Dragon clearly was putting up a fight. A closer look told her even more; none of these Necromancers had a Heartstring around their staffs, which was a very good sign if the message about each removed string reducing the Dragon's magic and strength was taken into consideration. If her suspicions were anything to go off of, Apep was slowly trying to convert Bathilda to its service. The weaker the Dragon got, and the more Heartstrings that Apep managed to harvest, the faster the conversion would take place. It was a maniacal plan and something right up Apep's twisted, dark alley, which meant that it was easily something one of his minions would be capable of.

On the other side of the valley, Sela saw another group of about sixteen Necromancers. This group was sitting in a large pentagram that seemed to be roiling to her druidic senses. Her chest clenched, and she immediately felt sick. This was the cause of the perverted Irradiated Ether and also the cause of the storms if the relationship of its placement and the center of the forming blueish-black storm cloud was any indication. The Necromancers were the only creatures on the surface that were visible from the sky, and they were entirely defenseless.

Not defenseless, if the one in the Dungeon is any indication. He wasn't the least bit worried about attacking Rockland and I head-on.

Yet this seemed like a perfect opportunity to disrupt some of the perversion to Gaia. If they could stop the corruption of the Dragon or put a stop to the perversion of the Ether, then they would deal a massive blow to Apep. The question was which one would be a greater blow to the two. Sela deliberated and came to a decision in an instant as her war training had instilled in her long ago.

In her mind, without the storms, Rocky, Sela, and Azoth could return here without a time limit; without the corruption of Ether, the conversion of the Dragon would slow down further. So, with her mind made up, she mentally projected to Azoth, "I need you to be ready to get me out of here as soon as I am finished destroying that pentagram. Can you get us out of here quickly?"

"Azoth hold back on flight here to let Sela keep up. Azoth protect Sela." Sela met the loyal shiny, obsidian eyes of the deadly creature and felt her heart melt for a moment. What she and Rockland would do without the beast, she didn't want to contemplate. She held his gaze for a moment before motioning with her avian head to follow her.

They descended as surreptitiously as possible, alighting behind a crumbling wall about one hundred meters from the sixteen Necromancers and their pentagram. Sela transformed into her human form and knelt on the ground as Azoth stood vigil. "What Sela doing?" Azoth mentally queried like a child needing understanding of something that they didn't really have the comprehension to grasp.

"A spell," Sela growled at the birdbrain, hoping he would get the hint.

A few moments later, she was sweating, and Azoth asked another question, "Sela done yet?" It took every ounce of her considerable willpower to not change the location of the pit she was digging to under Azoth.

Instead, she huffed, "No, Azoth, Sela is not done yet! Now stop asking questions!"

I feel like I am babysitting my nephews or something. Do you think he is doing it on purpose?

Azoth looked around as she continued to exert her new gift to dig a massive hole under the ceremony. If she was closer, it probably would have gone faster and would have been far easier, but this was the only cover within a kilometer of the two groups that she had seen. "Why not just land on robies?" Azoth asked another question that made her teeth clench together as she pushed her power to the limit. She chose to ignore this question and thus seemed to invite a barrage of others.

"Azoth could just go tear robies in half! Azoth not see anything happen... Azoth waiting... Azoth is bored..."

Honestly, by the end, she barely heard the childish antics as the mental pressure of what she was doing built. The problem was that she had to dig the pit deep enough that when she initiated the collapse, the Necromancers had a really high chance of dying from the fall. She, of course, planned to collapse the pit on top of them to add to that surety of their death, but if it wasn't deep enough, she might only bury the somewhat undead creatures, which she wasn't entirely certain would kill them.

It took a long time, but once the pit was about one hundred feet deep and ended in very hard and jagged rocks, she felt she had finally accomplished the feat. Unfortunately, when she tried to begin the collapse, a spike of pure pain nearly made her cry out, and holding in that impulse made her fall flat on her face. Azoth pranced around her looking worried. "Sela okay? Nothing happens Sela!"

I am definitely going to slap him when I can move.

Once he was beside her, she dragged herself towards him as he knelt down to sniff at her. "Sela smells of sweat and exhaustion, but Sela do nothing?" Luckily, he was kneeling down, so she vindictively took hold of his fur and feathers in each of her hands and began dragging herself on to his back. The flinch he made when she pulled his feathers and hair was immensely satisfying.

"Azoth, could you please divebomb the pentagram and then fly us back to the Territory as fast as you can?" Sela mentally panted in a sickly-sweet voice. When the pentagram broke, it would unleash the built-up storm, and if they didn't hurry back to the Territory, it was going to end badly. With leaden arms, she tied herself into the saddle, using the same contraption Rocky had utilized during the hell hike to the Territory. Her muscles felt like mush, and her hands were numb on the ropes, but she managed it. Then she was pressed into the Chimera's back as he launched into the air.

"Azoth tell Sela he could just land on them!" he mentally returned, and Sela grabbed a handful of feathers a little harder as she clenched her fists in an apoplectic fit at him. He flinched and maybe finally got the message because he did shut up.

Once they reached about one hundred meters, Azoth folded his wings and dropped directly into the center of the pentagram, only opening his wings at the last minute to make the landing manageable on his four powerful legs. The landing knocked the breath out of her lungs, and she felt her ribs groan in protest to the treatment.

The crash was more than enough as a massive boom echoed down the chasm she had painstakingly dug, and then the entire circle and more buckled and vanished, forcing Azoth to pump his wings desperately to not follow the debris into the pit. A few shouts of panic sounded as the meditating Necromancers plummeted down the massive hole. Then as she had hoped, based on her construction, the tapered walls began to crumble on top of the falling perversions.

Azoth winged away from the sight, her limp body strapped to his back, and she smiled for just a moment before he gushed, "Did you see that? Azoth make big hole in ground with super stomp!" She groaned, and a massive boom of thunder and lightning signaled the release of the Ether Storm.

ROCKY

People began streaming into the Grotto, many of them panicked with weapons drawn and gazes wild. Rocky did his best to calm everyone down and get them to join him and guard the somewhat recovering prisoners who were currently tied up. Derik had woken up and began immediately teleporting all over the Grotto, and so Rocky had taken a bit of pleasure in hitting him in the head with the pommel of his sword when his Ether had run dry. He had drawn blood, so perhaps he had struck the man a tad too hard.

Whatever. He deserved it after the massive pain he has been—even more so if he's the culprit!

Derik had spoken as Rocky approached, demanding to be let loose from the ropes, but he couldn't be sure if Derik wasn't the perpetrator of this whole ordeal. Additionally, Rocky might have wanted to hit the man too because, during the fight, Derik's failed spell had taken that second chance away. The others who'd woken up were confused, upset, and were spitting vitriol, but they were also speaking, which might mean they would try to Meditate with the group. If not, Rocky was dreading what he would have to do.

They had checked everyone for the marks that the captives sported and found another seventy-five people who were afflicted and nearly just as nasty as Derik usually was. Immediately, Rocky had asked them to begin Meditating and searching for anything amiss in their Ether Channels. Within five minutes, one of the group's eyes had snapped open, and he had haltingly described some sort of slimy, angry, snake-like creature that was inside his Ether Channels. Rocky felt his stomach rumble from the description alone, but he quickly guided the conscious individuals along with everyone present on how to attempt to remove the unwanted Ether. It was one thing to know how to do it and a whole other thing to actually do it. The first afflicted citizen finally had some success just as the council and two massive golems entered the Territory.

The moment of absolute silence that descended was filled with such obvious preparation to flee that Rocky immediately shouted, "Wait! They're our friends, and are here to help! Don't panic!" A few people took that as the signal to bolt still, their nerves clearly frayed past the point that they were listening to his words. The vast majority, though, seemed to calm down slightly but didn't let their eyes waver from the two imposing figures.

Once Tao and Gamma realized that there wasn't an attack, they both sat down to appear less intimidating, which did stop the fleeing people some hundred meters distant. Once the fifty or so people who had fled replayed Rocky's words, they sheepishly turned back around and rejoined the group. It turned out everyone on the council and the vast majority of the military were infected with whatever this manipulation was. Soon, the entire population of the Territory was Meditating under Rocky's direction, and each time someone managed to displace the snake-like Ether creature from their channels, he would see a body shudder and collapse. Whatever these things were, they were dug in deep.

Derik woke up thanks to some particularly smelly herbs that Smith waved under his nose. As soon as he woke, he looked angry and confused until he saw the entire population sitting calmly around him, most sweating and a few being carried off to the Guild Tent to recover from successfully cleansing themselves. Rocky cleared his throat in the silence. "Derik, you have been infected by something or somebody." He held the Dragon Heartstring up in his t-shirt and showed it to him. "Who gave you this?" Rocky asked pointedly, letting some of his anger at the man creep into his voice.

Derik blinked and then looked around before a sneer crossed his face. "It was one of the people you brought with you from Ottawa! He said it was a very powerful item that would improve my mage abilities!"

Rocky felt his eyebrows shoot up in surprise, then sputtered, "You didn't Analyze it?" With the shocked looks of some of the people around him, Rocky realized that it wasn't common knowledge yet. "Okay, let's all learn how to Analyze things, right now!"

I need to stop taking things for granted. Next Montessori lesson...

He spoke of how he initially got the skill of Analyze, and a few people pulled out items they held to stare at them intently. Other people nodded and turned to help neighbors learn the skill. Before long, Rocky was relatively sure that everyone had accomplished the task, so he turned back to Derik. "Have you Analyzed what I am holding yet?"

Derik's face had gone as pale as a piece of flawless, white paper, and he nodded and gulped, looking like he was holding back vomit. "It was a man named Frankie; I didn't get his last name. Can you talk me through Meditating to remove whatever was affecting me? Please!" The last word was almost a sob, and Rocky almost felt sorry for Derik for the first time.

His anger at Derik, at himself, at the whole situation wouldn't let him sit down at this point. Instead, one of the others in the group of citizens sat in front of Derik and began soothingly guiding the man in exactly what Rocky had instructed them all on. Joe approached him in the silence and whispered angrily, "Frankie Cocozza is missing, and he was supposed to be on duty here in the Grotto."

Rocky sneered, then opened his interface. He was going to put a stop to this. He navigated to the guild menu and ejected Frankie from the guild. Then he banished the man from the

Territory. When the notification asked if he wanted to give Frankie time to vacate the boundary, Rocky selected no, and immediately, a quest notification popped up.

Law Quest
> **Bounty Hunter**
> > **Detain Frankie Cocozza**
> **Frankie Cocozza, a banished member of Algonquin Valley, is treading upon Territory grounds. Capture or kill this individual to receive a reward.**
> > **Rewards:**
> > > **10% of Guild Ether Pool**
> > > **1 Crystallized Ether**
> > > **Possible additional rewards from Territorial Leaders**

> > **Do you accept this quest?**
> > **<Yes> | No**

Rocky selected yes, and a gold filigree pointed in the direction that Frankie must have fled. His devilish smile widened, and he sprinted to the river and launched himself in, swimming across the length before sprinting out the other side. As he exited, he noticed that Joe and Smith were both with him along with Jack from the A-Team. They all sprinted, and he saw a few others jogging to the river as they too accepted the quest.

Pretty quickly, the group of four with heightened stats left the others far behind, but that wouldn't matter as each individual who accepted the quest could see the direction through the gold line the system projected into their vision. Sprinting with all his speed, Rocky led the way and outdistanced the other two as his anger fueled his legs. Frankie, the psychologist who was in charge of treating and talking to people. It made sense; he had easy access to everyone. In hindsight,

Rocky even recognized the wristband that Frankie had been wearing and twisting at the campfire. And that damn journal!

He pumped his legs as fast as he could, eventually leaping to the massive trees and taking his favorite route of the squirrel highway through the treetops to avoid the dense ground foliage. As he went, he saw many creatures scatter away from his mad dash. A herd of massive deer bolted in all directions as he flew above them in the shaded trees. Amazingly, many of them leaped straight at tree trunks and turned mid-leap to plant four legs on the tree and then bound off of it in an entirely new direction. Their legs ate up ground even faster than his, and he watched a few dash ahead of him in the direction he traveled. A moment later, one of the creatures was pounced on by a massive cat. Rocky was certain that cats hadn't resided in the park previously, so this must have been some sort of mutation or migrant to the area. The purple eyes of the cat glared at him as if to say, "You almost lost me my meal," before it took its catch and pranced off, tail waving high in the air as Rocky careened away.

Pssh. Cat's are just so frigging judgy. Your new name will be Purple Princess, and I so hope you're a male cat!

The moment at least lost him most of his anger as he slowed his pursuit a bit and began planning for what he might do to try to catch this man. Hopefully, without letting Frankie touch him—not that he thought the man could control him that quickly, but it was probably better to avoid it. Just as he thought that, his filigree blinked out, and Rocky realized Frankie must have just exited the Territory. He sped back up, and was notified a moment later that he had also left, indicating he was right behind the man.

Rocky stopped and scanned the open area in front of him as the trees were less healthy and grew far sparser after the delineation point of his Territory. A moment later, he spotted Frankie running in the direction of Chalk River. Since he was still within skill range, he double charged his Dark Blade ability and sent it flying towards the man.

The noise as it cut through corrupted, soggy trees was evident, and Frankie dove behind a rock as his skill approached. A massive boom of thunder and the continuous lightning strikes drew Rocky's attention away from Frankie for a brief moment as his gaze fixed on the freaky nature show. He saw a small, black dot backlit by the lightning with each new flash, and he just knew Azoth and Sela were behind this. Wind struck his face hard, and on it, he could smell the rot and perversion of the trees he had just sheared down, as well as the storm wall behind it all.

Returning his attention to the rock, he used his Shadow Clone and told it to sneak up on the man. The clone winked out of sight as it turned to follow his thoughts. That's when Frankie stepped out from cover to gloat, "That's right, Rockland. You can't come get me, or you risk getting trapped in the storm! Apep's priest Apothis gave me immunity to its effects, so you will just have to watch me walk away from the safety of your Territory! I can't believe how stupid you are, just taking everyone from Ottawa with you! Initially, my mission was to create an army of willing humans for my master, but you put an end to that!" Rocky felt his jaw crack from the tension he placed on it. Frankie had just confirmed he was the one responsible for all that perversion in Ottawa! Rocky had always thought something more was at play than Corsair. He hadn't wanted to believe that one man could subvert so many good people so easily without something more sinister in the mix. Now he was staring at that perverted cockroach.

Frankie Cocozza
Level ~~11~~ 17
Apprentice ~~Psychologist~~ Apep's Ether-Manipulator
Health Points 110/110

There was some sort of effect going on that Rocky hadn't seen before when he Analyzed the man's information. It only took a moment before he realized that the thing in front of him wearing the smile of a psychopath and the face of a human had been hiding his information. He assumed it was a skill he could choose from his skill tree, and Rocky vowed to find a way to see through things like it in the future.

Frankie sneered and shot out a red cloud behind his back. It hit Rocky's clone who blinked back into vision and curled in on itself in obvious pain. "You think an Ether-Manipulator can't see a creature created by Ether!" Frankie shouted and drove a dagger into the clone, which destroyed the construct. Rocky felt himself stutter; he wanted to yell, he wanted to scream, but he just glared at Frankie while keeping an eye on Sela and Azoth in the distance, just ahead of the storm.

Since he waited too long, Frankie continued into the silence, "I hope my welcoming party wasn't too much for your little brain to handle. You just killed ninety-one—oh, make that ninety-two people—all because you're too naïve. Honestly, I would have had control of your whole population if it wasn't for your stupid nameless skill!" Frankie paused for a second, blinking and then tried again, "Your nameless skill?" For a brief moment, he looked confused. Then he stared blankly in front of him, reading something that Rocky couldn't see.

He thinks we are killing the people currently purging his influence! At least I have a number for how we are doing with that.

"Oh, you kicked me out of your guild, which stops me from using or naming the skills you placed as proprietary. Clever, but that won't matter. I'm sure Apep will bestow upon me skills far superior to your parlor tricks!" He held up a hand that glowed with the red of a Dragon Heartstring, and Rocky groaned. If only he had remembered seeing it that first night sooner!

He stepped forward, wanting to charge the cocksure man, but unfortunately, Rocky could already see the rain behind Frankie, and it was speeding up. He definitely wouldn't have time to get to the psychotic creature in front of him. Rocky growled and mentally contacted his pet, then shouted, "How did Apep contact you?" trying to distract the psychotic Frankie.

Frankie looked at the bracer and kept it raised in front of him. Then he crowed back with delight, "As soon as I selected my class, I could hear the whispers. I had heard them all my life, but now, I could hear them more clearly! They gave me purpose, and finally, I understood what I was, who I served. Finally, I had a purpose!" With the last word, he pumped his fist higher into the air, holding a position of a prize-winning boxer. That was when the blur of Azoth and Sela struck. Unfortunately, Frankie seemed to sense that something was coming and managed to lean away from the blow, but that didn't save his arm.

Azoth hit the ground running with a mutilated arm clenched between his teeth. His legs ran for all he was worth, just barely outpacing the blue rain that fell behind him. Rocky smiled when he heard Frankie's scream; it rang out, echoing over the trees but soon morphed into something far creepier, and Rocky's smile faded as shivers ran down his spine. Frankie's scream went from hurt to angry and then finished in a laugh that ricocheted all around them.

A moment later, he realized that Azoth wasn't going to outpace the storm. He mentally shouted encouragement at his pet, but he could tell that in the storm winds, Azoth couldn't get off the ground. At the last moment, Rocky entered the Territory with tears in his eyes and a curse. They had to make it!

He stared at the dividing wall as he heard Jack, Joe, and Smith sprinting up behind him. He held up his hands, and they stopped, having heard the storm approaching.

The storm raged against the barrier, and he mentally sent out pleading signals to his pet. He felt his head drop and thought his world would shatter a long heartbeat later. Then just as he started to feel his body going weak, Azoth bounded through the barrier of water and instantly dropped the mutilated arm before beginning to shake violently.

Energy coursed into Rocky, and he ran over to untie a weakened and blue splattered Sela. Azoth continued to shake violently, the convulsions forcing him to lay down and close his eyes, his breathing beginning to even out. Rocky hoped that meant he was Meditating and turned his eyes on Sela. "Come on, Sela. Listen to my voice and use the skill we've been practicing." Her shaking intensified, and he cast as many Dark Mends on her as his Ether allowed. Then to his relief, he saw her body begin pushing out the blue, irradiated water. Her shaking continued to intensify, however, and he hoped she could remain conscious long enough to succeed in cleansing the Ether Storm water.

He glanced at Azoth, who also was expelling water from his feathers and fur as well. He mentally sent encouragement to his pet, and verbally continued to bolster Sela. They might be okay after all!

He kept holding Sela long after she was back to her normal complexion and no longer shaking. Finally, once he was sure she was sleeping and okay, he deposited the arm into his bag and lifted her up in his arms.

He mentally sent to Azoth as he went, "Once you've rested enough, join us in the Grotto, okay?"

Azoth, who had been keeping up a constant mental mumble for the last five minutes, responded with, "If that was bath, Azoth never taking again!" before his mental voice went quiet in the tell-tale way it did when he slept.

CHAPTER TWENTY

Aretrin Bazaar – Seed Shop – Deep Cave

Amelia entered the shop and took off from the landing area quickly, running to a shadow of a tent, acting her part as an iridescent Kobold. She had discovered a while back that her nano-bots could manipulate the seed shops and create an image of a different race. It was strange to be half again her normal height and be so colorful, but the disguise made it very easy for her to go relatively unnoticed.

While it was unfortunate for her people, she had been forced to limit access to the shops proper because she was the only one who could be seen in them, albeit with the disguise she now wore. Amelia wasn't here on her usual Territorial errands, and most of her people could buy things using the Populace shop from the assistant when they needed. Those rarer items meant she made a trip occasionally to get some of the merchants' select wares, but today, she was here to speak to one man.

She flitted from tent to tent, trying to pretend to stay hidden but just playing her role as best as she could with the timer that was counting down in the back of her mind. As she approached the stall of the one man who knew her for who she truly was, she took a deep breath and paused out of sight as he finished some transactions. Once the coast was clear, she ran up to him and immediately sent an invite for a private room. She was loathe to spend the crystal, her inner miser disliking the need, but the pragmatist inside her forced that feeling down.

A moment later, she flickered into a small stone room with two chairs surrounding a rather shabby looking table. She had theorized that this place was meant to be unappealing to push trades along faster, but the stone and cold reminded her of home, the safety and comfort of the deep cave. She smiled as the man she was here to see phased into view in front of her.

"Amelia, twice in a month. I hope this be a pleasant surprise, but from your expression, I art be assuming this is somewhat urgent?" Garnell conversed in his sturdy, dependable Karacy lilt. Of all the races, the Karacy were Amelia's favorite as they too loved to spend time underground, and while they were most well known for their excellent craftsmanship, they were also known for their honesty and perhaps their facial hair.

Amelia attempted a smile but failed miserably. "I apologize for the promptness of this meeting, Garnell, but I have another five contacts to meet today, and you are just the first." She paused for a moment and mentally commanded her nano-bots to allow her regular projection to be cast. A moment later, she felt her perspective shoot up towards the ceiling and immediately felt more comfortable. "What I say next is privileged information, Garnell. Please keep it between us."

Garnell nodded and leaned forward after those words. He hadn't heard her speak them in a long time, and she wasn't one to casually throw them around either. Amelia continued into the avid silence, "The Etherless Void has changed. It is too early to tell why, but I can say with certainty that Ether has returned to the perimeter and quite a bit farther since the drones are coming back online."

Garnell felt his mouth fall open, and he rebuked, "Is that the confidential information? Because ye know full well, I will need to eventually let my people on Gelthisar know of it…" Amelia waved a hand acknowledging the Karacy's plight. Then she made a motion touching each one of her foreclaws to her thumb; in the language of the Endarkened, it meant somewhat.

Amelia spoke, clarifying her meaning, "Yes and no. I ask that you please wait a week to share that news and honor this information in the manner it was given. I did not charge you for it, so ask that this be part of the price you pay for it now." At Garnell's slow nod, she continued, "Good! Now, what I need your help with and what is the true secret is that I have been holding this information away from the Guild Collective. My nanobots can probably only continue to disrupt the functionality of the drones for another two weeks at most." Amelia held up two fingers and then shot two claws further out, emphasizing a rather meaningless point. She had always been a bit dramatic in Garnell's opinion, but the information she had already shared with him was so large he didn't blame her. He was a bit worried about what she would ask for, of what remained of the vast majority of the payment.

"I have discovered that the Mechano-Lords failed to create a beacon to a new world, and I have suspicions that the reason for this is because it isn't a new planetary god." Garnell felt his eyebrows rise at her implication. "Yes, Garnell, I believe that the rumors of the Etherless Void being older than any planet alive are true and have procured some evidence from the Alchemy guild that speaks to that fact. So, I ask you, in payment for the information I have willingly gave, have you seen or heard of anything strange in the last few weeks?"

Garnell felt his mouth open and close like a fish as he blinked rapidly. Amelia was not someone to over exaggerate, at least not to this degree. She was dramatic, proud, devious, and even a little scary at times, but this claim he never would have expected from her. In fact, they had discussed theology at length in previous meetings, and he strongly remembered that she believed that the Etherless Void was just an anomaly. Now she was suggesting something far different.

Garnell felt his mouth slam shut, and his eyes widen when he connected some odd dots in his head. Humans were rare creatures, and he had only encountered them in their own shops before. While he had found it odd that two of them were walking around the Aretrin Bazaar, he hadn't considered it implausible. He had assumed they were a force conquering a new minor planetary god and setting up a Settlement for the Aesir, the Seraphian Seven, or one of the multitudes of other powerful human factions. The reason his mind connected these particular dots was that all of his research into the rumors of the Etherless Void had always come back to the Humans or Martians.

Amelia saw his look change, and she felt herself grow excited; she knew Garnell well enough to know he had thought of something. "I can see you have thought of something particularly odd. I don't think I have ever seen you this out of sorts before!" she crowed.

Garnell gave a chagrined smile. "That was a lot of information to have thrown at me in a relatively short amount of time, Amelia, which I assume was yer strategy all along." He ran a hand over his face trying to regain a bit of composure. "I may have some idea of who ye are looking for and may even be able to set up a meeting. I will post a request through the channels I have available and let ye know in the same way?"

Amelia smiled. "I will expect a message in my Populace Accessible shop then?"

Garnell nodded and rose from his chair, extending his hand. He cleared his throat as she extended hers, but before they clasped, he stated, "I cannot guarantee that they will meet with ye. I can only extend an ore vein and hope that they will swing the pick." She grabbed his hand and nodded once as she began shrinking back down to her Kobold form. Then they both winked out of the room to complete the rest of their remaining tasks for the day.

Rocky

Sela was in a pretty deep sleep, but healthy if what he Analyzed was anything to go off of. He left the Guild Tent and walked outside into the night. He'd been walking back and forth the remainder of the day, checking on her. He knew it was a bit overkill, but that didn't change his need to check. He wanted her to have a familiar face there either right when she woke back up or shortly after. He assumed it was a hang-up from his own time in hospital after sports injuries, but honestly, the need to check was there, so he just kept going back.

The council and all citizens had undergone Meditation for a large portion of the day, even being joined by the Knights, Gamma and Tao, who surprisingly were able to move their internal Ether around outside their bodies, creating patterns and figures. Supposedly, it was quite the show to watch, and Rocky was disappointed he had missed it. That being said, in time, he would be able to match it. He'd been gaining ranks in the skill pretty consistently if his character sheet was any indication.

Rockland Barkclay Level 22
    Class: Apprentice-Dark (Azrael) Revenant, Level 1 Strategist
Leadership Class:
Class Skills: Dark Blade, Dark Mend, Soul Blade, Dark Cloak, Shadow Clone
    Health Points = 270/270
    Dark Ether Pool = 210/210
You have 0 stat points and 0 skill points to distribute. (Assigned and awaiting confirmation.)
    Stamina – 27 (Strength of Body +6)
    Strength – 31 (Strength of Arms +5) (Strength of Arms +12)
    Agility – 38 (Speed of Arms +5)
    Dexterity – 31
    Intelligence – 21 (+1)
    Wisdom – 28
    Charisma – 30
    Luck – 10
Weak Skills

Non-Class Combat Skills: Combatant –
22, Ether Channels – 18 (+5),
Ether Cleanse - 4 (+3), Ether
Manipulation – 17 (+6), Stealth –
26 (*Rank up?*), Swordsmanship
– 29 (+3) (*Rank up?*)
Common Skills: Barter – 8 (+3),
Camouflage – 7, Endurance – 25
(+3), Perception – 28 (+4)(*Rank
up?*), Tracker – 16, Trance
Meditation – 19 (+4)
Profession Skills: Actor – 5, Butcher – 22
(+3), Cook – 2, Herbalist – 19,
Miner – 1, Skinner – 22 (+2),
Teacher - 10 (+9), Trader – 5

Moderate Skills
    Non-Class Combat Skills
    Common Skills: Analyze – 12 (+2), Sneak
      – 13 (+1)
    Profession Skills

The skill point he had dumped into his Shadow Clone skill, bringing it to two of five and increasing the stat transfer to his second self, despite it being a bit of a jerk lately. As for the stat, he placed it in Intelligence, as it seemed to be the stat that was flagging behind the farthest. He'd also bottomed out on Ether a few times on the trip and during the healing after the previous ambush.

Rocky raised his eyebrows as he reached the bottom of the page and saw that he could rank up a few skills. It was frustrating because some skills allowed him to rank up sooner than others. He thought about each skill he could rank up and realized he understood a new concept in each that he hadn't before the rank up option had become available.

Swordsmanship, for instance, he'd focused primarily on his wrist and grip for much of the apprentice rank. However, in recent one-on-one training with Sela and her Seraph sword, he realized that concise, compact motions were highlighted. While many Hollywood movies made a sword fight showy, the Seraph sword style was much more about positioning of the blade and minimal movement to do the maximum damage. Was it that lesson that gave him the ability to rank up?

Swordsmanship
- **A quantifiable number for your ability to use a sword.**
   Weak - For each level of the skill, you are four times less likely to cut yourself when using a sword.
   Moderate - For each level of the skill, you increase the chance to strike accurately by 2%.

—

Perception
- **An ability to notice things that others may miss.**
   Weak - Increases chances for you to notice obvious abnormalities in your surroundings.
   Moderate - Increases chances for you to notice conspicuous abnormalities in your surroundings.

Symbiosis:
   Moderate - Analyze - Increased chance to observe hidden information about objects and people.

As for perception, he'd spent the rest of the day after discovering that information could be hidden glaring at everyone and casting Analyze on them, trying to see if he could find any discrepancies in the information provided. He discovered one person who changed the spelling of their first name. When he saw their name the way it was given by their parents, he immediately understood why they'd wanted it to change. His original name was Ben Tweener, and he'd changed it to Benjamin Tweener.

Rocky couldn't wait to have a chuckle with the man about it over a beer one day; parents could be so cruel. During this process, he noticed that if something was altered about the person, it could be distinguishable by a slight distortion around the information in the notification window. It was so subtle he'd quite honestly missed it and moved on to the next person the first time. It was when he was examining Phoebe Cathe's information that he noticed a difference between hers and Benjamin's and returned to examine the man.

Luckily, they were both busy with construction projects. If they had seen me glaring at them, they may have questioned my sanity or intentions.

Finally, Stealth was a bit of mystery. The number for the skill hadn't changed, but now he could increase its rank. He thought back and realized that he learned something watching his Clone. During one of the numerous times he had popped out of existence, he had noticed that the Stealth skill often took time to reach the centerline on his clone. He'd since been focusing on starting his skill at center and the edges simultaneously; perhaps it had been working.

Hard to tell without a mirror.

Stealth
- **The skill of manipulating light waves and becoming mostly invisible as a result.**
    Weak - Use your own internal Ether to manipulate the surrounding light waves and Ether to hide your presence.

Ether cost: 10 personal Ether per second. Increased by the amount of noise made. Moderate - 8 Personal Ether per second. Small noises will draw ambient Ether to cover.
Symbiosis:
Moderate-Sneak: Decreased by 25% + 2% per level.
Dark Ether: Reduces cost by 90% on the value after initial deductions.
Dark Cloak: Reduces the Ether cost of this skill.

Azoth had recovered far faster than Sela, and in his disjointed childish way, he had relayed the two's adventures to Chalk River. It was impressive that Azoth had managed to collapse a spell glyph and sixteen Necromancers into a massive pit with an aerial stomp. Rocky suspected that Sela had a huge hand in the endeavor, but he was still going to ensure he told Azoth's side of the story, maybe even embellishing it a little. Rocky gave a small chuckle and hoped that this meant they'd seen the last of the storms for the time being.

Azoth was particularly furious about the treatment of the Dragon, Bathilda. Rocky could sense in his mental sendings the anger and hurt that he felt for the trapped beast. There was something unnatural about holding creatures against their will. Rocky didn't believe pets were part of this category, taking Azoth as an example. However, to capture and hold a creature that clearly belonged to itself and amongst a different setting entirely was wrong. In a way, Azoth communicated in emotion rather than language.

I think we'll need everyone to have a chance against what might be lying in wait for us. Frankie could travel in the storm, which lasted hours, and would have warned them already, which means they'll be prepared!

Tomorrow at the latest, they would go and assault whatever forces were detaining the Dragon and try to return the three Heartstrings to the beast. Perhaps not if it was aggressive and an enemy, but regardless, Rocky was hoping to negotiate with the thing to get another powerful ally. He wondered if Sela had Analyzed the creature or if she'd been forced to stay out of range to not attract unwanted attention and then realized it was likely the latter.

Rocky watched Tao and Gamma return to the Grotto, fording the river with four massive trees. Both monstrous golems only sank to mid-thigh in the river and easily carried two trees each, one over each shoulder. He shuddered at their show of monstrous strength, then smiled, remembering they were on his side. The two worked tirelessly, and since they'd arrived, the sawmill didn't have any downtime. As he watched them dump their loads, he remembered Tao's insight.

Tao, in his wise and soft-spoken way of speaking, had listened to Rocky relay what Azoth had seen in Chalk River while sitting with the council and observing. Then as if to himself, he deliberated, "Dragons are by far the most ill-treated of all races. Most Dragons birth five to twenty offspring every century, and rarely does a single one make it out of adolescence. Unfortunately, their bones are too valuable, their blood too potent, and their scales too resistant to ignore." Then he went silent and looked to the sky.

Where the 'young' golem had heard this rumor, he didn't know. Rocky glanced at Gamma to gauge his reaction right after the uncharacteristic speech, but Gamma, too, was looking up at the stars, both looking reverent and contemplative.

As Rocky sat remembering the scene that had occurred a few hours ago, the two golems turned and headed back across the river to bring more trees and resources back. By morning, the bottleneck of cut wood would be entirely removed, and the builders would be the new stone in the road. He looked at the mostly completed first Longhouse and instantly felt like things were going to be better. Today as he had moved around, Tao and Gamma had lifted massive pieces of wood into place as humans worked around them. It had sped the construction of the building up drastically, making the need for widgets and coordination between teams nearly meaningless.

Here's hoping the other three bring back more Sapient Golems! Each one of them is worth a hundred humans when it comes to feats of strength. Heeaavve…

After the two were across the river again, Rocky walked over and attempted to lift a side of the log they had been carrying. It didn't even roll over, and he felt his face go red. He casually placed his hands on his hips and turned to walk away. Smith was standing there, smiling. "Yeah, I did the same thing after their first load. They made it look so easy!"

Rocky dropped the nonchalance and laughed uproariously along with Smith. The Native American man sobered after a time and looked after the two, "I saw them change a lot of people's minds today. Especially the quiet one. He reminds me of a Native Elder—or a grandfather if you prefer. He has a way of speaking to himself but conveying wisdom through it." His face morphed into a fatherly smile, and he continued into the silence, "I hope you know I wasn't against bringing them in and am glad that the people's minds seem to be changing now that they've arrived."

"I was just thinking to myself that I hope they find some more like themselves when they're out saving humans!" He smiled back at the man. "I will feel a lot better about the safety of everyone and this Territory with more of them around."

Instead of buoying Smith's mood, Rocky's comment made the man grow serious. "I've been meaning to ask what you plan to do with Derik. I know he can be an ass, but honestly, I truly believe he was under control since we all returned. If what you said about Frankie is true, he was a huge part of what you all went through in Ottawa as well."

Rocky nodded somberly, but his voice was hard and somewhat cold, "I don't plan to kill him, if that's what you're thinking. However, I can't just let what he did go unpunished, Smith. I know he's your friend, and you'll see the best in him, but from his own retelling, he wasn't truly under full control of the Dragon Heartstring until after you dosed him with your potion." Smith's face fell further when he was reminded of his own part in the man's fall to madness.

It would appear that the Meditation every morning had managed to ward off a large portion of the effects of the necklace for Derik, and it had done the same for the others Frankie corrupted. They were, in fact, lucky that it seemed Frankie's skill possessed some sort of cooldown—at least Rocky assumed as much—or they would have been attacked by far more people when they returned. In fact, Frankie assumed that they'd been forced to kill ninety-plus citizens to rid them of the corruption he worked.

Rocky took a deep breath and softened his tone a bit, "I think if he and the others are willing to switch places with the four exiled members until they too have proven themselves, then that's what I'm leaning towards." He motioned towards the entrance of the Grotto. "I know that the four out there were in a similar situation as he was, and I think allowing them to rejoin their families will give the surviving twenty who are going to be 'exiled' hope." He air quoted exiled because he felt that it was a very tame exile to allow them to remain in the protective safety of the Territorial borders.

Smith opened his mouth for a moment with a thoughtful look on his face but never managed to respond because Joe came jogging up. "Rocky, according to my men, the shop AI has a message for you from someone. It will only deliver it to you." He paused as he noticed Smith. "Oh, hey, Joaquim, sorry to intrude. Didn't see you behind Rocky." Smith smiled and made a dismissive gesture at Rocky with his hand. Rocky had to assume that meant he was satisfied with his decision or that he would hear more about it later.

Chapter Twenty-One

The message was from Garnell, and Rocky felt confused as to why he would want to meet him in the shop at his earliest convenience but figured it was best to wait for Sela to wake up. While he felt relatively comfortable making a trip to the Bazaar himself, he had a strange feeling that Sela would be rather upset she missed it if he went without her. Instead, he'd gone into the Guild Tent and tried to keep a wakeful vigil on Sela using his trusty camping chair that he picked up on that fateful first day of the apocalypse but never really used. He quickly discovered that sitting down in something as comfortable as a chair gave his body an excuse to promptly fall asleep.

He woke up to find Sela gone and that he had the entire Guild Tent to himself. He sat up and ran outside to discover Tao leading the Meditation that he normally would have led—not that it bothered him in the slightest. He sat down beside the nearest person and joined in as he contemplated why they'd let him oversleep. Were they really that sick of his poor instructions?

I mean, with that giant leading the Meditation, it is easier to see him. Even sitting near the back, I can make out his dour expression.

Rocky stuck his tongue out at Tao and saw a slight smile touch the corner of the golem's lips. It was probably his imagination that Tao had noticed his childish antics; his eyes were closed after all. Instead of dwelling on it, Rocky closed his eyes and dove into himself. Once he became aware of his first Ether Channel, he immediately became aware of something else. Due to the most recent events in the Territory, the strange feeling almost broke his concentration as he freaked out and worried that it was some sort of attempt at manipulation.

His skin broke out in a cold sweat, and he attempted to wrestle with the strands of Ether that touched his channels. As soon as he touched it with his projected consciousness, he heard a chuckle low and deep, followed by a familiar, angry voice,

"Relax! You lazy sack of flesh!" Gamma's unmistakable voice sounded in his mind.

A moment later, Tao's calm voice took its place, "Gamma, he was not present to hear the instructions. The others chose to let him sleep after how hard he's been pushing himself. If he takes but a moment, he will see that we are guiding the apprentices in the art of Ether Channeling and Manipulation."

Rocky heard a physical grunt that shook the ground and could only have been Gamma's response to the chastisement. He, however, relaxed after Tao's words and sunk back into his calm, meditative state that he taught his guildmates was best for Channeling and Manipulation. Once he'd accomplished the proper mind space, he felt the subtle direction that Tao, and surprisingly Gamma, were offering.

He allowed the small dendrite in and followed it through his channels in a pattern he hadn't known existed. Every loop he created made endless figure eights forming around the central point of his heart. Within fifteen minutes, he had something that looked like a daisy in his mind with his heart at its center.

The dendrite began to withdraw, and Rocky unconsciously continued to follow it. The moment it left his channels, his manipulated Ether tried to follow, but as soon as it exited his body, he gasped and lost focus. For a millisecond, he had felt everything so distinctly in the small space his Ether had touched. It was like he knew every nanobot that made up his under armor, every follicle that made up his skin, the denseness and flexibility of his leather armor, everything! He only knew about a piece the size of a quarter for each of those, but it had been absolutely shocking to see without seeing.

To his surprise, Gamma stood up and told everyone to get to work. Rocky put a hand on the man's arm beside him as he rose and asked, "What about the martial training?"

The man smiled. "That was done first on Tao's instruction; he said he wanted to build up a sweat and then give our bodies time to cool back down and absorb the teachings." Rocky felt his eyebrows rise as the man patted his hand and moved away with the crowd.

He was overjoyed that the man had treated him so normally, and he couldn't stop the massive grin that split his face as he walked to join Sela, Joe, Smith, and Zippo, who were all converging on Tao. A bump in his back made him turn to see a massive lion head, and he turned to walk backward as he scratched Azoth everywhere he could reach.

When they both arrived, Azoth mentally sent with his usual childish excitement, "Tell Tao he much better at that than you!"

No more scratches for you! Traitor!

He turned to Tao and instead claimed, "Azoth says you're very good at that!" Azoth gave Rocky a shocked look, and Tao chuckled deeply from inside his chest as he winked at the massive Chimera.

"He knows you is liar," Azoth crowed in victory at him as he left Rocky's side and wound around the much larger golem's legs in mimicry of a house cat. Rocky felt his eyebrows rise at Azoth's choice, but also found it funny to see a dump truck-sized Chimera treat a converted four story-ish building as a rubbing post.

Tao reached down and patted Azoth on the head before looking to Gamma, and in his stead, Gamma awkwardly rehearsed, "We would like to thank you also. We both learned a bit more about stat ellipse capping and chaining from your Mont-iss-sorry group." Rocky felt his eyebrows climb higher at the news. How long had they let him sleep in? He looked at Sela, who opened her hand in a placating gesture and pushed it down in a sign he interpreted as 'calm down'.

Joe smiled at Gamma and responded for the group, "I'm sure it's currently more valuable for people of your impressive strength and levels. It will be a while before we reach the exponential breakthrough points, but I do believe it's a good piece of knowledge for growth. Perhaps it speaks to a strategy of pushing a single stat with the free stat points we receive." Joe finished with his hand on his chin, and Tao seemed to look thoughtful as Rocky looked up at his massive, aged, copper face.

Zippo grew excited and whispered something in Joe's ear. Joe smiled and then excused himself and Zippo with a quick, "Thank you again for the training, Tao and Gamma. Zippo wants to walk and talk about the lessons learned this morning. Would anyone care to join as we go to inspect the construction?"

At his words, Tao gave a meaningful glance to Gamma, who was surprisingly smiling at Zippo.

Could the angry golem have a soft spot for children? Too bad Zippo is the only teenager we brought back from Ottawa.

That thought sobered Rocky, and he felt his shoulders climb towards his ears as he heard Gamma grumble, "Tao and I will join you; we have work to be about as well." He somehow made the sentiment upset even though Rocky had just seen him smiling.

What a Negative Nancy.

Rocky spoke up then as well, "Joe, we're going to have to deal with Derik and the other survivors of the failed ambush now. You sure you can miss that?"

Joe looked surprised and then nodded sadly before indicating Smith; then he responded, "I talked with Smith earlier, and what he has to say is both well thought out and the best course of action. However, the final decision is yours. I'll be around if I'm needed." Then he turned and continued away with Jason.

A cleared throat sounded, and Smith awkwardly intoned, "I've asked for a bit of privacy during your pronouncement." He took a deep breath in and then gave one of the most awkward smiles Rocky had ever seen before continuing, "This morning we asked for nominations for the new citizen appointed council, and the name that came up the most was

Derik's." He held up two hands to forestall Rocky from bursting in. "I know, I know. I just want to point out, I spoke to the people who did the nominating. Derik and I have been the only members of the current council," Smith motioned around at the group and seemed to make it larger with that same gesture, "that have been going around and speaking with everyone to find out how they are feeling, what they need, and how to make their lives easier. I'm not saying he doesn't deserve the exile you've suggested. I just want to perhaps try to minimize the publicity of it." He finished lamely, and Rocky blinked at him.

"Do you mean that you think people would be upset with him receiving a punishment?" Rocky asked dumbly as he tried to understand what Smith meant.

Sela nodded with a look of utter approval on her face and elaborated the question, "You want to minimize the shock and give people time to hear the rumor and ask questions about why Derik is in exile?"

Smith tilted his head back and forth and then smiled. "Well, not in so many words," he started sheepishly. "I just know that while most people have heard about the attack he made yesterday, I don't think everyone has, as evidenced by his resounding support amongst some of the people for him to hold a council seat."

Rocky looked at Sela, who was nodding along and looking right back at him. "Good... thinking?" Rocky fumbled, feeling he had to say something but unable to think of anything better than that. Somewhere during the conversation, Joe, Zippo, and the two golems had walked out of sight towards the site of construction. So Rocky shrugged. "Well, let's rip the Band-Aid off then..."

As Smith took the lead towards the shop, Rocky asked Sela about the lesson that occurred this morning. She shrugged but answered, "It was overly complicated to point out something relatively simple. There are points, stat markers that, once reached, will create a breakthrough effect." At Rocky's puzzled look she shook her head and chuckled. "Okay, I realize that isn't enough, now that I said it. For example, the first breakthrough point is at fifty points in any stat. Essentially, if you graph increases to your body, you will see that from about one to twenty-five points in a stat, you have exponential growth. Each point placed in a stat at this point will increase the associated characteristics by more than a single point will later."

She made a motion of a steeply rising curve with her hand then held her finger at the point she finished at in the air. "Then from twenty-five to thirty-five, you will have something closer to linear growth." This time, she made a flatter line of increase with her hand and again held her finger at the point she reached. "During the linear period, think of every point added to the stat increasing the characteristics by a factor of one, at least in comparison to the exponential portion. Finally, from thirty-five to fifty, you have an inverse exponential, where every point placed into the stat is less effective than the one before it until you are placing stat points but they are almost doing nothing. With me so far?"

Rocky nodded and swallowed before asking the obvious, "And after fifty?"

"That's why they are called breakthroughs, Rocky. After fifty, you have a steeper exponential increase for every stat point entered, then a higher sloped linear relation where one stat point gives you two, and finally, another inverse exponential leading to the next breakthrough, which is at one hundred and fifty." Sela continued with a bit of exasperation in her voice. She made the motion of the strange curves joining each other over and over again in the air, "This pattern was dubbed Stat Learning Chains because of the unique S shape they make. Before you get too hung up on it and choose to base decisions off of it, please realize it is a purely theoretical notion that was put forward in my time. It was never proven—"

Sela cut off as she realized Rocky had stopped listening to her. From her explanation, he realized most of his stats were about to reach the slower growth period. Sela frowned when she realized she was being tuned out and rolled her eyes seeing that her warning had been pointless; Rocky was clearly going to try to create a strategy based on the knowledge she just shared. A moment later, she smiled as he mumbled strategies to himself, and she shrugged; it was better to make plans for the future, after all, and while unproven, the theory was widely believed to be true.

Should my focus be on pushing a prime stat to fifty to gain the increased growth? Or should I try to get all my stats to thirty-five to maximize my current growth?

Rocky was so consumed by statistic strategy, he didn't even realize when they arrived at the prisoner holding grounds and accidentally ran into Smith's back. He sheepishly apologized before looking around and noticing the military guards and tanks on duty in the clearing. His eyes then fell on the twenty-two prisoners before he turned and met Derik's defeated slouch. He felt somewhat bad for the man, as he truly did believe the attack was not entirely of his doing. However, he knew that a lot of his negativity and elitist attitude was entirely of his own design. Perhaps the exile would help him.

As Rocky looked over the group, Smith whispered in his ear, "Do you mind if I tell them? And lead them to the other group of four?" Rocky, who'd been dreading the pronouncement, really wanted to let Smith be the bearer of bad news, but a glance at Sela reminded him that he was the leader here, and he better get used to that fact.

He shook his head sadly at Smith and stepped forward to address the people present, "What happened yesterday was regrettable. Each person present harbored ill-intent towards me or my team, and because of it, people lost their lives." He paused and looked at the military surrounding the prisoners, then back at the Territory.

Turning back slowly, he added, voice starting soft and gaining hardness as he continued, "Your violence wouldn't have stopped at me and could have injured one of the men you see around you. If not one of them, then one of the innocents in the Grotto because you attacked right in the heart of it!"

He took a deep breath to calm down before he spoke again, "I'm going to give you all the same opportunity that was given to the people who aided Arti during his disgusting deeds. You will be exiled from the Grotto—"

The outcry from the individuals present cut him off, and a lump formed in his throat. He looked over at Sela, who was stoic, and wondered how she remained so steadfast in her determination. With her as his example, he hardened his resolve and dismissed any turmoil over the situation.

He continued monotonously, "Smith will lead you to the other four exiles and will ask them to spend three days teaching you how they survived outside of the protection of these natural defenses." Rocky opened his arms wide, indicating the natural bluffs and river that surrounded them on all sides. "After they've shown you the ropes, they're welcome to rejoin us here in the Grotto. However, now that we have a guild, a few changes will come about in your treatment. First, you will be placed on the limited hunting list for the King's Forest. This means that during your exile, all your loot will be taken and held by the guild. You can keep the meat and pelts, but that's all."

Rocky saw a few grow agitated and angry in the group, so he raised his voice, "You're welcome to hunt outside of the Territory and keep everything you kill, but there are no protections in place out there," he pointed up and away, "to limit the levels of creatures!"

He took a pragmatic pause, meeting eyes with the angry individuals in the group he had seen. Once they lowered theirs, he continued, "Second, Smith or someone from the military will come meet with you daily to guide you all in Meditation training.

If you have any extra supplies you wish to send back to the Grotto, that is your choice, and they should be sent back with the individual who meets with you."

After a brief pause, he looked over the twenty-two souls that might contain a few innocent members and asked loudly, "Do you all understand?"

More crying broke out at this point, but no one seemed to have any questions for him. After a time, Smith placed a hand on Rocky's shoulder and nodded once before his voice cut through the muted sobs, "Please follow me."

Rocky stood there, watching the military and Smith escort the exiles out of the Grotto. While he frowned, Sela stood stoic and straight-faced. He tried again to emulate his Guide and couldn't manage it, as he couldn't feel nothing for the poor people.

He turned to her after a time. "Shall we go meet Garnell?"

Sela shook her head. "We will visit him tonight after we have rescued a Dragon!"

CHAPTER TWENTY-TWO

A few hours later, Rocky and Sela were standing at the front of the army. They'd decided to take all the tanks and military with them. The Territory was still under Ether protection, which admittedly wasn't a complete protection, but it also now had the two Master class Knights, so they might as well use this opportunity to attempt to beat the enemy with everything they had. Looking at the tanks and rifles, Rocky worried that they were going to be useless, except against Zombies. If the trip here had reinforced anything, it was that inherent Ether protection trumped the firepower of the mass-produced weapons; even the simplest of Ether-infused armor cut the damage significantly.

That being said, everyone in the military was level 15 or above now since they'd been running training drills and hunting simultaneously in groups of ten. This meant that many of them had gotten a third or even fourth skill, often strengthening their attacks. Hopefully, they would all soon be able to afford their own individualized weapons. Rocky's greed menagerie growled at him when he remembered all the weapons he'd destroyed in Corsair's office at the hospital, they were definitely of significantly better quality than the mass-produced ones, and his army could have used them now.

Just within himself, he could feel his inner menagerie building to a crescendo of indignation. He had yet to buy anything specifically for him from the shop. He'd spent a huge sum of his own money to help others over himself, and that was completely counterintuitive to his inner zoo of cupidity. He shook himself and promised some sort of special treat after this was all over to try and appease them.

Attention outward again, he could see those groups prevalent now as each unit of eight surrounded a single tank that had two members inside. Joe discovered on day one in the

Territory what the limit of the system was for a party before you started to lose Etherience due to what Sela called 'risk reduction penalties'. They fooled around until they noticed that the same level of creature they killed gave them the optimal amount. Something else Joe noticed was that if the military trained against hordes of ants or in situations where the opponents' numbers were greater than five, it seemed the Etherience limiter was removed.

When the military gets stronger, Joe wants to run some tests against more powerful enemies. The level of the creatures around the Grotto averages around thirteen, so it makes sense that they've started losing a place to effectively level for now.

Sela informed Joe of something that she had already told Rocky—that the level of the monsters would depend on the average level of the citizens. Which, of course, meant that with almost twenty-five hundred citizens sitting around level ten or eleven, that the average level was about twelve or thirteen. Rocky was hoping that the Dungeons would help speed along the leveling of everyone once they were finished setting up.

Additionally, he noticed that many hunters and others were commissioning quests in the guild hall to craft reagents, make clothes, and a few even asked for armor. Rocky knew that the armor wouldn't be complete until he finally had time to experiment with enchanting, but at least the quests would mean experience and crystals to some of the crafting classes in camp.

Rocky waited as Joe got everything organized for the march to Chalk River. They were already at the edge of the Territory, and from that point on, everyone needed to be on the lookout. Each tank was still equipped with a radio emitter, and Joe had tied them into the devices that the A-Team, Sela, Rocky, and Zippo all wore. That way, they could pull heavy hitters to areas that might need them. According to Joe, the standing order was to retreat to the Territory if anything was too hard to handle. This excursion was going to be a foray to essentially test the enemy; if they could win, they would push it, if not, then not.

Five minutes later, Joe walked up and nodded to Rocky, who began walking along at the speed that the army could muster. Azoth leaped out of nearby foliage impatiently and began flapping his massive wings, kicking up a dust and grit storm in the infected and plague-ridden area just across the Territorial line. "Fine-ale-easy." He mimed in a clear imitation of Sela, who Rocky was forced to glance at with a wide smile on his face.

Sela shook her head minutely and wore her own smile as they both watched the creature take to the skies. "Couldn't have said it better myself, Azoth," she exclaimed while continuing to chuckle as Azoth flew over their heads.

The tanks, which could move around forty kilometers an hour, were actually the bottleneck when it came to speed now. While they could move at a good pace, the humans that surrounded them with enhanced stats could move faster if they chose to go all out. However, some of the tank pilots had some pretty devastating skills and abilities that they could pair with the clattering machines to truly great effect. Additionally, the tanks gave quite a bit of defense to the teams in any sort of ranged fights. They were mostly used now as moving cover; well, moving cover with a massive turret that could spit death a few times a day.

Thirty minutes later, Azoth sent a confused mental signal, "It clear one second. Now ground spits out pale creepies." Rocky received a mental image of what Azoth was seeing simultaneously and felt his hair stand on end. There was undead spewing out of cave mouths in front of them. From the air, Azoth could see twenty-five or more caves, and each one was spitting out a horde of the creatures. Additionally, clear from the sky, on top of each cave, a Necromancer stood with a rod of twisted wood in hand.

Something about the Necromancers made Rocky ask Azoth to send him another image with them as the focus. Once

Azoth complied, Rocky instantly saw what had bothered him about the dark wizards on top of the caves. Each one was standing in a natural fortification that was getting higher and thicker as Azoth watched. The only upside to a closer view of the Necromancers was that he didn't see any staff topped with red rods or Dragon Heartstrings.

At first, I would have thought this was something LFD did, but unless those Necromancers have geomancers with them, they still have an active Dungeon on their side!

"Prepare for contact with the enemy," Sela commanded to Joe.

Joe nodded and then touched his ear. "Contact imminent. Form up." Letting go of his earpiece transmit button, he turned to Sela and Rocky. "Any ranged fighters amongst them?"

Sela answered, as she too had received the images from Azoth, "The vast majority of the enemy are Zombies similar to what we saw in the Arena Dungeon, but yes, there are approximately twenty-five Necromancers; they are fortified and dug in. Haven't seen them in action yet, so be prepared for anything as we close." Rocky felt a bit helpless in this situation. He wasn't a war leader like Sela or Joe. He was entirely out of his depth and wondered what he could do to aid them. He was the highest leveled and arguably the strongest fighter here, so what could he do that others couldn't?

As Joe got back on the radio, Rocky turned to Sela. "I'm going to try to remove some of the entrenched enemies. Can you keep the main forces busy?" Sela frowned at his suggestion, looking at him with a bit of concern showing in her eyes. He felt that formerly caged part of him raise its hackles at her concerned look. He didn't need to be protected; he needed to protect, and he was going to be the best at it!

The competitive surge surprised him, but he was very familiar with its intense need to be the best at any cost. He tried to tamp down the rising heat of frustration he felt; it wasn't like

Sela had done anything wrong. Her concern for him should be touching, and he knew it. His attempts to get his anger under control only fueled it more, and he clenched his teeth as he felt the need for action grow to unbearable levels.

Sela watched as the myriad of emotions flitted over his face, and she narrowed her eyes, trying to understand what had just happened. She had only wanted to confirm he wasn't going to do anything stupid and reckless. She nodded to him and stated, "Be smart and deadly," the same words she had used with many covert agents in wars past. Rocky's smile was terrifyingly predatorial, and Sela felt a quick jolt of exhilaration rush through her chest and flush her face as dark, cloying smoke oozed from his body.

Rocky sprinted away from the group, easily outdistancing the clattering tanks and formations of the men that accompanied them. He entered Stealth on the run and took a few deep breaths to center himself. Once he was sure he wasn't dripping black smoke, which would give him away in the afternoon sun, he continued. A short sprint later, he felt himself nearly miss his next footfall as the forming undead came into view. It was much more intimidating to see the thousands of pale, lifeless creatures from the ground than from Azoth's point of view.

He increased his speed, aiming for a slowly filling gap in the lines between two of the cave mouths that kept spitting out the Zombies. As he neared the hole, he considered where all of these undead were coming from. There was no way there had been this many people in the area of Chalk River before the apocalypse. As he got closer, he glanced at the cave mouths and remembered Sela had claimed they were Dungeon born creatures.

I kind of see what Sela dislikes about Dungeons right now.

Once through the forming line, he turned left and ran directly towards the first mound of earth that housed the cave exit or what he now was nearly certain was a Dungeon entrance. Once his back was pressed into the rocky outcropping, he summoned his Shadow Clone and sent it to the right. The Shadow Clone looked around briefly then gave a rare sardonic smile before vanishing.

Good to see it is over the whole bait and sacrifice thing.

During his run, he had heard a few more orders from Joe or Sela over his radio, but he had turned the volume down now that he was acting autonomously. However, Joe's next radio transmission made his heart quicken a bit, "Barrage formation. Wait for the order to open fire." The need for cover suddenly jumped to the top of his priorities. He activated his Dark Cloak and began jumping and climbing up the back of the protruded earth the Dungeon had forced up to create an entrance. At the top, he found the Necromancer looking out over its Dungeon-created army.

Rocky formed his sword and struck, not giving the abominable creature a chance to truly defend itself. His sword easily cut through the woman standing there, and he felt nausea rise for a moment. Then a concussive blast of force hit him in the chest and threw him from the top of the cave.

Honestly, I am getting really sick of spell backlash! I am going to have to look out for these glyphs in the future.

The current blast was nothing compared to the one Derik had produced, and a moment to orientate himself was all Rocky needed to flip in the air and land on his feet fifteen feet below and twenty feet away. In a moment, he was sprinting back toward the mound and climbing back up to his new vantage point. As he looted, he also scrutinized the lifeless corpse he had just murdered and sighed. Was this Necromancer a Dungeon creation as well?

Apep's Void Shroud

- **This armor was created from a dungeon under the control of a Void God.**
    Quality: Normal
    Stats: Unknown

Apep's Void Stick
- **These staffs are rumored to be all that is left of an entire planets vegetation after being consumed by a void god.**
    Quality: Good
    Stats: Unknown

Under the corpse, a burnt-out glyph resided, which must have been the source of the backlashing spell.

They are standing on and powering something, but what was it?

He looked from left to right and saw that the entrances were spaced pretty evenly at about five hundred meters apart. He looked at the ranks of undead in front of him and saw that they were as thick as twenty deep in places, usually in front of the cave mouths, and then they thinned to about four deep in the gaps. It was clear the enemy didn't have perfect control of the creatures.

"Fire!" was the one-word command that was barked out over the comms before all hell broke loose in front of him. He saw a tank muzzles flash, and the laser bolts blurred forward before turning into five identical shots spread out by about ten feet each. Laser rifles triggers were depressed a fraction of a second later, adding a kaleidoscope of skill-induced color to the barrage. The first wave of ionized laser fire struck the ranks of undead to his left and fizzled on contact. In front of him, ranks of undead were mowed down, however, and he blinked at the disparity for a split second.

He glanced to his right and saw a similar shielding effect occur down those ranks. Between himself and the next cave, he saw the creatures were being cut down with ease, but past that cave, the creatures were defended and unharmed. Rocky groaned and stepped back to study his Dungeon-created cover and the burnt-out sigil more closely. His killing of the resident here and his clone's apparent success had succeeded in removing the source needed to maintain it. He made sure to memorize the pattern, hoping it would help him in his future enchanting endeavors.

An eyeblink later, Rocky disengaged Dark Cloak and jumped from his vantage. He sprinted the five hundred meters to his left as he touched his ear. "Working on it!" he stated simply into the torrent of other conversation that was going on over the comms.

A confused torrent of, "Working on what? Who is this?" answered him and gave him his first realization for the need for monikers and radio etiquette. He hoped Sela and Joe would recognize his voice because the Necromancer in front of him wasn't facing the army. It was facing the cave he had just come from, as he too must have seen the disparity in reverse from the assassinations he was undertaking.

A red wave pulsed out from the Necromancer, and unable to avoid it, Rocky ran right through it. He winced, expecting a spell to take hold, but all that happened was that the wave of red warped and curved around him. It lingered around him like a strange blood bubble. "Atlantean hell!" Rocky cursed and activated Dark Cloak, realizing that the spell was highlighting his position. He bolted left and right, beginning to weave. A pure black bolt struck the ground he had stood on a split second after he activated Dark Cloak and spun violently into the earth before imploding and then detonating outwards. His eyes widened at the destructive force of the spell as dirt and debris peppered his body and face.

Yeah, I definitely don't want to get hit by those.

He ducked and weaved through more spells from the Necromancer as he approached. Unfortunately, the closer he got, the less time he had between the cast and the contact point, which forced him to begin strafing around the ranged caster. In all of his maneuvering, Rocky noticed one thing. The Necromancer refused to move from his spot on top of the cave.

They need to be in contact with the rune to power it!

A frustrating few spells from the Necromancer later, Rocky was no closer to him. He weighed options between a long-distance Dark Blade that may not succeed or if he had another option. His mind fell on his bandolier; he threw a few daggers at the man who stood on top of the cave. While his knife throws were entirely ineffective in the damage department due to his lack of skill, they did have the desired effect as the Necromancer was forced to interrupt a cast and erect a hasty shield that the daggers clanked off of, hilt first.

Rocky grinned wickedly and leaped towards the snarling Necromancer, closing the distance and charging his sword with Dark Blade. The black-robed figure hissed one word and knelt as Rocky closed in, "Apothis!" Then he touched his hand to the ground. A massive, black king cobra head shot from the dirt towards him, and he hastily released his charging Dark blade into its approaching maw. His Dark Blade sparked, screeched, and ground against the spell but finally tore the conjuration in half before continuing on to do the same to the Necromancer. Rocky landed a moment later, with his heart in his throat as a small explosion from where the dead caster had stood showered him with more debris but failed this time to displace him from his spot ten feet away.

He clicked his radio. "Eagle Eye here. Another shield down. Moving on to the next. Over" Then he sprinted, removing his Dark Cloak and engaging Stealth once again. This was going to be a long day.

An hour later and many grueling fights, clone resummons, and Zombie meat walls later, Rocky had cleared all of the caves in his direction. He turned back a grisly smile on his face as his forces continued to bombard the fragile undead from range. He checked his connection with his clone and felt that it was far away in the other direction, most likely attempting to clear Dungeon entrances still. Rocky received a mental image from Azoth and saw that his clone had three such Necromancers left to clear.

None of the Necromancers had carried Heartstrings, which meant that there were definitely more powerful creatures lurking somewhere either in the depths of the Dungeon below or further ahead guarding the Dragon. Rocky gulped down a Health and an Ether Potion, looking to replenish himself after his most recent fight. While there had been a few easy kills of Necromancers who were 'less aware' of their surroundings, the vast majority of the sixteen he had ruthlessly slaughtered had turned it into a life or death fight. The massive hole in his Chimera leather pants reminded him of how close it had been in some of those encounters. He had a robe and staff from each corpse in his bag of holding though to help offset the cost of the repairs. He would Analyze them after the fighting.

But now victory is—

He stopped instantly when he saw the piles of unmoving undead begin sliding towards each other like groups of puppets being dragged by cut strings. As each one joined a central point, they began to melt together, flesh crawling and bones cracking. Rocky felt his stomach give a heave from the noises that they were emitting but forced down nausea as he clicked his radio. "This is Eagle Eye. Do you guys see this? Over."

Sela's voice responded, "Selaphelia Ardensai here. They are forming Abominations. It's a common Necromantic Champion. We must retreat. Over." Rocky pursed his lips at the woman's words. She was the expert in situations like this, but what the hell was an Abomination.

In answer, the first blob began to take on a humanoid form but aberrant and bulbous. Its head was a ball of flesh with hundreds of eyes facing all directions. Its mouth was a grotesque, hinged apparatus with thousands of human teeth placed haphazardly on any surface inside the gaping crevasse. Its long, thick, blue tongue even had human teeth covering it like scales. Its arms formed next and were entirely fleshless, made only of bones shaped into a hook on the left side, and a massive, three-fingered claw on the other. Its belly was bulbous and round like the nightmare had overeaten, making it all the more abhorrent and hideous. The legs were utilitarian and stunted, which might be the only thing that would save the retreating army as the first blob finished forming a twenty-foot-tall, aptly named Abomination.

It shambled forward in a freakish hobble, and Rocky shuddered at the sight. Immediately, laser bolts began striking the creatures ineffectually. He wanted to go help with the retreat but realized that he was already behind the creatures. He and his clone still had a chance to complete the mission. "Eagle Eye is continuing with the mission. Over."

Radio chatter went deathly silent before Sela whispered, "Be smart and deadly, Rockland!" In her voice, he heard restraint. He heard something unsaid, but he couldn't be sure what it was. A background disagreement from Joe on Sela's radio com was heard before Sela released her depressed mic button.

Rocky adjusted his mic's volume then turned to face Chalk River. He mentally sent to Azoth, "Keep an eye on the retreat of the army and the path in front of me when you can!"

Azoth sent back, "Will watch and attack if needed. Sela says to keep the dumm-mee safe. Sent it with image of you. What dumm-mee, Rocky?"

Smiling to himself at the birdbrain, Rocky ran, leaving the question unanswered as he charged headfirst into danger; he wasn't sure if he truly was a dummy for this, yet.

Azoth had sent Rocky a mental image of the Dragon from the sky, but it wasn't until he actually saw the Dragon begin growing from what looked like a small lump far off in the distance to something more akin to a natural hill that he considered a question that had gone unasked. What had raised those Abominations? He almost turned around on the spot, considering that there must be a very powerful enemy behind him possibly wiping out the army.

Yet the radio still was clipping out muted orders and sounded like an organized retreat, so he didn't. Instead, he kept up the jog and considered what he might be able to do to free the quickly growing and quite intimidating creature in front of him. It turned out that this particular Dragon was simultaneously like every story Rocky had ever read and different than all of them.

Yeah, it was a massive lizard with wings, a long sinuous neck, and a barbed tail. Sure, it was beautiful and majestic with equal parts of colon clenching fear and awe-inspiring majesty. It was actually the eyes and emotions that clearly rolled off the creature that Rocky hadn't been expecting. The thing was massive, probably bigger than the Albino Crocodile Draksus had been, and even at a distance of at least five kilometers, Rocky could feel waves of anger coming off of it. Mixed in with that anger though was a clear fear and a sad inevitability that made his heart clench with injustice. This powerful, majestic, graceful, and deadly creature was resigning itself for an inevitable fate— the death that it thought it had beat all odds and overcome as a whelp but now knew it was staring into the jaws of.

Tao said that these creatures are some of the most hunted in all of the universe.

A confused array of emotions struck Rocky in the chest, making his heart stutter and then beat out like a war drum. If he could help it, this injustice, this systematic slaughter, this game-hunting would not stand. Maybe Dragons were deadly creatures, and perhaps policing their numbers was a necessity if you wanted any sort of population to thrive on a world, but to see the intelligence in its bright blue eyes and simultaneously see its kicked dog, shaking form set something off inside of Rocky. He allowed the cold magma and his inner demon to seep into his veins as he felt his mouth click shut and form into an angry line.

He continued to close the final few kilometers and activated Stealth as he dismissed and re-summoned his Shadow Clone. His clone entered Stealth almost instantly, seeming to flash like a flickering light in the corner of Rocky's eye. Around the form of the Dragon a group of eight Necromancers still stood with staffs planted firmly into a small spell circle that surrounded their feet. Each one was spaced out around the Dragon evenly, making a circle with a circumference of a kilometer. If he wasn't so angry, he might have taken some time to come up with a better, safer plan, but with his blood pumping hot, he pulled out and transferred four recently purchased plasma grenades to his clone. He literally lobbed each grenade into the air beside him, knowing that empty space was where his clone ran.

These, too, disappeared as his invisible Shadow Clone juggled and caught the things. In his mind, Rocky formulated a plan and calculated spacing between the Necromancers and the Dragon. It would appear there was little to no room for error on their throws. He smiled grimly and Analyzed the Dragon first and then the cultists.

Bathilda the Darkscale
Level 112
Epic-Firespit
Health Points 13,102/55,405

—

Devoted of Apothis

Level 24
Apprentice Irradiated Necromancer
Health Points 175/175

Seeing the level of the Dragon made his eyes widen as he circled around to the left and again sent his clone to the right. The level of the Necromancers, though, was what he expected after his recent fights, so once he reached a position that he had clear line of sight on four of the eight minions of Apothis, he quickly depressed the activation button on two of the four grenades. Then he lobbed one to his left at the farthest chanting minion and one to his right at the mirrored position. Trying to have everything trigger as simultaneously as possible, he quickly depressed and threw his final two at the translucent-skinned Necromancers closest to him.

As soon as he finished, he activated Dark Cloak and dropped to the ground, hoping to avoid the shrapnel and flying debris that the grenades were likely to dislodge.

As the explosions chimed off with a split-second delay between each one, Rocky felt a wave of superheated air buffet his back and press him into the soft soil. As soon as the pressure was released, he had pushed off the ground and was trying to survey the damage. As the smoke cleared, it was like a nightmare slowly resolved itself. First, the bottom of four black robes began to materialize out of the ground as the smoke ascended, and then the Dragon behind them began to slowly take shape, his eyes fixed on Rocky's position.

The four Necromancers would have been enough to make him quail normally, but a Dragon's eyes made it even worse. He sure hoped that the Dragon wouldn't join the fight on the enemy's side, or he was already dead. He bunched his legs and sprung forward towards the four figures who he had only succeeded in moving slightly off of their spell circles. They must have had an outward protection in place!

One yelled out from amidst the group, "Defend Apep's prize. Smite his enemies into his eternal darkness!" His voice carried all of the tones of a dying toad's last croak and made Rocky's skin prickle with goosebumps as he charged. He loosed two throwing daggers from his bandolier and let them fly, hoping to distract them like he had with many of the other single Necromancers he had fought earlier. Two of the creatures held up hands, and the daggers vanished in a puff of smoke; Rocky heard himself curse under his breath.

He felt his Dark Cloak react to something that attempted to strike him from behind a moment later, and his own thrown daggers flew through the air, just missing him before clinking off of the ground in front of him. "Seriously?" he groaned. Two hands of the other Necromancers extended, firing shadow bolts in his direction. He careened left. The two bolts hit the ground, and he simultaneously felt his Shadow Clone die. His anxiety doubled. If he didn't finish this soon, he would be facing eight instead of four.

The next barrage from the two who had teleported his daggers came as two shadow whips that attempted to wrap around him at the shoulders and waist. His Dark Cloak gave him a split second that he used to drop straight down and roll while simultaneously releasing his protective Dark Cloak skill. The whips closed around themselves, making the fog look like an exploding shadow ghost, and Rocky sprang back to his feet while reactivating the skill. He was right to do so as one of the four canceled his shadow bolt and lanced out with a blood field that highlighted his invisible form.

He was going to have to take some hits if he wanted to close, and he split his Soul Blade into two short swords as he heaved himself forward, heading straight for the four at a half sprint. As soon as the whips cracked behind the group's back and launched forward at him, he pounded his feet into the ground and increased his pace to his full sprint. His tactic succeeded and allowed him access to a deeper part of each shadow whip. He brought each hand down, aiming his short sword at the conjured whips and saw sparks of shadow flare to life where they made contact. In haste, he powered both of his swords with a single Dark Blade and released them, managing to sever the spells just in time as the pivoting tails of each whip fell lifelessly behind him.

A quick glance told him his Ether pool had just dropped past the halfway point, and his brow furrowed in concentration. These next two attacks would decide everything. Did he go up or roll under? It was a gamble, and he knew it, but it was his only option. He chose to go over for one reason; in the air, he would still have some small ability to contort his body. Just as hands shot forward, he launched himself into the sky and formed his sword into a single long blade again. He had guessed right, it seemed, as two bolts flew just under his rising body.

With a smile of triumph, he spun around his center and dropped another three charges into the blade, which consumed just over three-quarters of his remaining Ether, seventy-five points. The three blades of the skill pressed the four Necromancers' bodies first into the ground and then ground them up, mixing the gore in with the soil underneath in a disgusting, churning display. It looked like a farming accident as it tilled the earth in evenly spaced rows. Rocky, who hadn't fully been paying attention, landed directly under the Dragon's head. Its mouth opened, and Rocky saw what he imagined would haunt him in the afterlife as row upon row of razor-sharp death stared into his soul.

How in the hell did you forget about the Dragon!

"There are far more than eight of them! They take shifts, you better have a greater plan than killing the eight to release me. They possess my contract item!" The Dragon's voice was deep and old but smooth and buttery. Rocky stood still, dumbly staring at its unmoving mouth, trying to piece together how it had spoken without moving its 'lips'. The act was alien to him, and during the next words, he noticed its throat contracting to form the words as its vocal cords moved.

Like a giant parrot! Oh no! I hope I didn't say that out loud!

Luckily, he hadn't, and the next draconic words snapped him out of his momentary stupor, "Stop staring at me and do something before you die during a rescue attempt!" He blinked and saw four approaching Necromancers kicking up dirt as they closed in. Knowing he couldn't kill another four with twenty-five Ether he did the only thing he could think of; he pulled the three Heartstrings out of his bag and pressed them to a scale on the creature's lowered and cowering chest. As his hand glowed, the Dragon sighed in ecstasy as it murmured, "Oh!"

A moment later, its tail whipped out, and the four Necromancers turned from a threat to bloody mist floating in the air. Rocky swallowed, and the sound his throat made was loud in his own ears.

Then the Dragon's head whipped to the side, and it breathed a beam of blue fire down a hole in the ground. The sound was like a jet engine starting beside Rocky's ear, followed by a sucking in of air and then a massive 'whoosh' as it went down the tunnel. The Dragon kept at it for ten seconds before she closed her mouth and ran her tongue along her snout.

Then it glanced down at him and attempted a smile, but to Rocky, it looked more like he was about to be dinner again. Bathilda didn't eat him, however. Instead, with her mouth still closed, she 'bellowed', "Thank you for your timely aid, but I fear you have only prolonged my conversion."

Rocky might have sounded stupid as he asked the only question he could think of, "Can't you just… umm… fly away now?"

A deep chuckle, or maybe a growl, sounded from Bathilda as she shook her head. "No, little man. They have my contract item. When I formed the contract to come to your world with Gaia, it was given to me, and I wore it proudly.

Unfortunately, when I landed here, my pride got the better of me as one of these," she paused, punctuating her anger-filled tone with another blast of fire down a newly opened tunnel and took a long pause as she pumped more fire into the cave mouth. "Sorry about that. This is how they got me the first time. You should get out of here now! They will keep opening entrances until I miss one. I should have flown away and regrouped, but I couldn't fathom losing to a bunch of smelly undead!"

Rocky blinked stupidly up at her as she spoke. Not much of what she was saying made sense to him, but he did put together that she couldn't leave because she needed something that Apothis or his minions now held. So, after she blasted another tunnel with fire, he asked shakily, "What is your contract item? Maybe we can get it back for you."

"Necklace," she started and surveyed him up and down, "but you are too weak to go against the head cultist, unfortunately." She bashed a tunnel that had formed too close with her agitatedly waving tail and simultaneously bit another forming cave, crumbling both, but a moment later, they continued to push up along with two others. "Youngling, you must go now! I thank you for allowing me to fight on, but I cannot hold them for much longer! Take this." A massive ring landed on the ground beside him, and he realized it must have been on one of her teeth. "Now, get out of here and come back with a weapon that can kill me if you want to help!"

He quickly bent down and wanted to examine the ring, but the formation of two additional bumps made him reconsider. He placed his hand on the Dragon ring and as many fallen scales as he could before whisking them into his inventory. Then he looked sadly up at the Dragon as it continued to fight a losing battle. "I will be back, and I will save you! Hold on!" Then he sprinted away and asked Azoth for an update.

As he ran away from the majestic creature, he could hear a deep bellowing, sardonic laugh reverberating through the air and earth.

Chapter Twenty-Three

Sela

Sela grimaced as another man yelled from somewhere, "Loading my last battery pack!" As soon as she saw the undead army forming up, she realized that this attack had been a mistake. After she and Azoth had made their surgical strike into the enemy's base, it should have been obvious that they would have plans to stop an invasion or another such strike. She cast her vines again on an Abomination that had finally ripped itself free. Then used Analyze on it to see how the army was managing with this particular beast.

Abomination
Level 31
Journeyman – Necromancer's Pet Horror
Health Points 1,250/2,142

They were managing to whittle the creature's health down, but often, it took multiple shots to remove a single point of health from the creature. The tanks had long since run dry and were using what they had left of batteries to act as the vehicles for the retreat. Joe had been rather ingenious when he thought of this tactic for the squads of ten. Each member now rode on a tank as it slowly retreated from the oncoming constructs.

One of the Abominations to her right lit up in a massive conflagration, and its skin began sluffing off as the fat underneath boiled. That would be Zippo securing their right flank. To her left, a massive soundwave buffeted a creature as its skin rippled, and a faraway, high-pitched screech wailed. That would be Joe securing their left flank.

A full five minutes later, the two creatures expired, and Sela let out a breath as she cast another Nature's Thorny Embrace on another freed Abomination. They only had fifteen of the remaining twenty-five to deal with, but the time between Zippo and Joe's attacks was steadily increasing, showing that the constant chugging of Ether Potions was stacking de-buffs on to them faster than they could kill the Abominations. She looked behind her and saw that they had another two kilometers to go. Her spells were the least mana intensive, and she planned to recast and order a full retreat at the kilometer mark, hoping the Territory boundary would repel the stupid, undead creatures.

Unfortunately, it wasn't likely since their master was probably pushing them on. However, the Ottawa Knights would be forced to join the defense at the border.

Ionized bolts flew from all directions, striking the fifteen creatures that remained, and she growled deep in her throat. One of the dead creatures suddenly had a shade rise from its corpse and charge its compatriot from the back, showing that Smith was somewhere in the fight using his Spirit Walker skill. Again, it proved to be only marginally effective as the lower leveled shade, it seemed to be capped at Smith's level, managed to shave off five hundred health points before being ripped apart.

Unfortunately, while this was a relatively orderly retreat, the three tanks and a few mangled corpses of soldiers told the story of a few mishaps. In some cases, someone had closed in to release a skill and failed to keep a close eye on their enemy. In the case of the tanks, an overeager gunner had fired too many shots and overridden the safety protocols, allowing the turret to pull Ether from the engines. Often, the tanks had been empty, but in one case, the two soldiers inside had drained the battery so utterly that the electronic locks on the hatch had seized shut. That being said, of the nine hundred or so she had led to battle this day, only about twenty-five had fallen. Those numbers were the dream of any general, and Sela held her head high knowing her tactics now would keep more alive to shine tomorrow.

Jack and Amber from the A-Team stood by and waited to see if their close combat skills would be needed. They both, unfortunately, had no ranged attacks that they could add to the mix. Even Smith was using but one of his three skills because it was the only one that had the range needed.

Suddenly, one of the fifteen Abominations with low health stepped forward and was punched in the face by a massive arcane ball. The ball detonated and ripped the creature's stomach apart, leaving behind dragging entrails as the Abomination continued to stagger forward a few more steps before falling flat in death.

Another Abomination suddenly was fighting a mud man that had risen from the trampled earth in front of it. At first, the Abomination was winning until the mud man got hit in the back with four spells Sela recognized. With each hit, the mud man grew larger, gained ghostly green armor, moved faster, and finally enraged. After its reinforcing, it pummeled the creature in front of it into the ground before throwing the corpse at the nearest Abomination and flowing across the ground in its direction. Well, this was unexpected!

They could win!

Sela looked beside her to see Derik give her a curt nod before casting another massive ball of arcane power. The other twenty-four exiles around him were adding their own class skills to the battle. While some of them were definitely NPCs, all of them stood together, showing a unified front in the face of the advancing death magic. Before the army even reached the kilometer mark, they had managed to down all of the remaining injured creatures, as the army was bolstered by Derik and the fresh exiles.

Smith trotted up and patted his friend on the shoulder. "Good to have the big guns show up," he drawled with his

Native American lilt before pulling the man into a hug. Yeah, Derik was an ass to Rocky, but Sela knew Smith had been his friend since they were both young men.

She looked away, scanning the group, looking for the real heroes of this battle and found them. Staring back at her pridefully stood the four men she had exiled outside of the Grotto. She nodded to them in appreciation, knowing that the mud man with the reinforcing buffs had done the majority of the work. They had been training alone outside the Grotto every day constantly, and it showed. If nothing else, this showed her the need to train herself!

Sela simply ordered the army to continue its retreat to the border after acknowledging the four men. They wouldn't be able to handle anything else today without waiting for the recharging of Ether batteries. As they turned to leave, she heard Azoth mentally say from above, "Sela, they go liquid again!"

She growled in her throat as her body shot around to look, startling everyone around her, as all of the dead Abominations flowed into a single, roiling blob of white skin, innards, fetid blood, and cracking bones. She felt a dread well up inside of her at the familiar sight and what it had led to an hour ago.

She Analyzed the blob to try to get an idea of what they were about to face.

Hulking Abomination
Level 65
Master – Necromancer Champion
Health Points 9,112/9,112

As it grew its body and accompanying bulbous belly, Sela ordered a full retreat to the safety of the massive Territory trees. The army wouldn't be able to hold this creature back as easily as its lesser brethren. If she was honest with herself, this creature could and should be able to wipe out the entire group in minutes. Her only hope was that if they got to the Territory, it might choose to leave them alone. She doubted it, but if it entered the Territory, the two Ottawa Knights would be obligated to join the fight as well.

Warning! Someone has touched a place of power under your Territory. This has contested your leadership for Algonquin Valley. To cancel the contestation, destroy the force holding the Altar of Michabo. If you fail to destroy this force or to offer the altar a worthy sacrifice, the Leadership of the Territory will be transferred in six hours!

5 hours 59 minutes and 45 seconds remaining.

Now that your Territory is under contestation, all Territorial buffs, Territorial effects, and Territorial systems are currently unavailable to your population or you. To remedy this, capture the contested place of power before the enemy.

She felt her body whip in the other direction, eyes wide as she looked in the direction of the cave, she had exited weeks ago. The altar she had laid upon was a place of power?

Places of power aren't real! They are stories told to entice adventurers and treasure seekers!

A massive, bellowing, multi-toned roar sounded, and her body whipped back again, making her look like a kid playing with a Barbie doll as her blonde hair streamed behind her. Her vision was entirely filled by a Hulking Abomination in all of its fetid, ghastly atrociousness.

She screamed, "Retreat," and saw the line that denoted the start of the Territory but not the Ottawa Knights that should be there to support them.

ROCKY

Warning! Someone has touched a place of power under your Territory. This has contested your leadership for Algonquin Valley. To cancel the contestation, destroy the force holding the Altar of Michabo. If you fail to destroy this force or offer the altar a worthy sacrifice, the Leadership of the Territory will be transferred in six hours!

5 hours 59 minutes and 45 seconds remaining.

Now that your Territory is under contestation, all Territorial buffs, Territorial effects, and Territorial systems are currently unavailable to your population or you. To remedy this, capture the contested place of power before the enemy.

What now?!

He whined internally as a notification for something he didn't even fully understand floated in front of him. There was a place of power below his Territory? And how in the fires of damnation was he supposed to stop the takeover?

How the hell did they get by the boundary without it warning me of an invasion?

With the army out of the Grotto, did that mean that someone had attacked the Grotto? How could they have taken it with Tao and Gamma present? Rocky increased his pace and checked his Ether pool to see it full once again. According to Azoth, the army had just managed to defeat the last of the Abominations before another bigger one took all of their places.

Currently, the army was fleeing to the safety of the trees, which denoted the Territory line, as the thing formed. A massive, bellowing, multi-toned roar sounded from a good distance in front of him, and he clenched his jaw as he felt the ground shake under him. At first, he thought it was his imagination, but another quick tremor rattled his teeth together, causing them to grind due to his clenched muscles. He forcibly relaxed his jaw after that unpleasant sensation and continued sprinting forward as a hulking white humanoid shape came into view. He Analyzed the creature and froze stock-still; it was a damn Master class. Checking again with Azoth, he confirmed that Tao and Gamma weren't at the Territory line as expected.

In desperation, he rifled in his bag of holding, trying to find anything that might help. He had two remaining plasma grenades and five gravity grenades. If he could force the grenades down the creature's throat, he might have a chance. As he pulled items and dropped them back into his bag scanning its contents, he was suddenly holding the massive tooth ring from the Dragon. He blinked and watched as it shrunk in size to something that he could wear on his wrist before shrinking further to the size of his index finger. He Analyzed it as the creature began picking up speed towards the trees.

Come on, be good this one time!

Dragon's Eternium Ring of Spell Storage
- **This ring will store one spell or skill up to Legendary rank within itself. The wearer can expel the charge on the ring to cast the spell or skill, costing themselves nothing as the initial charge giver must pay the Ether or Essence price of the spell or skill stored.**

Current spell stored:
Liquid Blue Fire Spit
Charges: 1

The Dragon had been breathing blue fire in the fight he had seen. While Rocky couldn't be certain, he really hoped that this was the same destructive spell or skill he had seen Bathilda using. If it was, he could definitely use it to fry the creature in front of him. The problem was that if he did use it for that, he wouldn't have it for whatever was trying to take over his Territory. His inner greed menagerie was going wild, and he was forced to fight with his desire to hoard the ring and never use it.

He slipped it on to his finger regardless, for a situation was destined to come where he would need the thing. Then he asked Azoth to come to pick him up. It was time to take down a Hulking Abomination, and he didn't want to climb the thing's rotten-looking flesh if he could avoid it.

Azoth took a moment to circle overhead and while he did, Rocky clicked his radio deciding to use his time wisely. He interrupted whoever was speaking, "Eagle Eye here. Everyone okay?" There was a long pause after his words, and Rocky assumed it was because he hadn't finished with over. Azoth started descending towards him.

"Selaphelia Ardensai. We won't last for long once that thing reaches the trees. Where is the Dragon? Over," came Sela's voice in his ear, and he nearly threw the device away in a fit of rage.

Then he mumbled to himself, "The Dragon was stuck in place because it didn't have its pretty little necklace!" He didn't send that over the radio as he realized that it wouldn't be the greatest for morale, so instead, he blandly stated, "Otherwise detained."

Azoth thumped down beside him as the chatter of the retreat continued, no longer addressed to him. The Hulking Abomination was picking up speed as it moved, and its sixty-foot, fat body would soon be crashing through the healthy trees of the Territory and the army they hid if he didn't do anything. "Let's distract the giant, fat toddler!" he mentally screamed at Azoth as he tied himself in. Azoth didn't hesitate and launched himself into the air with a tooth-clattering leap.

As they approached, Rocky saw three black circles on the ground with nothing inside them. From the air, he couldn't be sure especially against the black of the contorted foliage, but it looked like Zippo had been at play. He shrugged as he continued speeding towards the disgusting form of the beast.

It turned out that it was easy to distract the creature but much harder to avoid it once you did. Azoth zoomed by ten feet from the Abomination's nose, and Rocky saw its black eyes lose focus, then track the Chimera as it swung its arms to bat them from the sky. Luckily, Azoth was moving very fast, and an arm whooshed by. The displaced air was enough to force Azoth into a barrel roll due to turbulence.

Steadying back out with a white-knuckled Rocky on his back, Azoth watched as the creature came to a sliding stop and glared at them before throwing a bone chain affixed to a hook that Rocky had failed to notice. The hook would have skewered Azoth if Rocky didn't bat at it with his sword and all his strength. Even then he only managed to move it a few feet, which when combined with Azoth's banking, avoided the projectile.

Rocky ordered Azoth to dive again and tightened the straps on his legs that tied him into the saddle. Azoth swooped back as Rocky brought out plan A. He linked together all five of the gravity grenades and got ready to launch them into the thing's open mouth as it tracked them. Just as Azoth reached a point over its head, the Abomination looked up, unhinging its jaw and opening its mouth wide as it did so. Rocky dropped the payload and depressed the pin on one of the grenades. The hook the enemy fired passed within centimeters of Azoth's rear end as he sped by, and luckily, the grenades hit their rather massive mark and ricochet down the creature's throat.

This may need to become my signature move!

"Bank!" Rocky shouted in celebration as the payload hit a tooth before sinking into the massive basket of a throat. Nearly instantly, he saw the creature's stomach begin roiling and sucking inwards. Azoth continued to speed away as distant squelches could be heard as the creature's skin, fat, organs, and other body parts liquified in the blackhole blender. Rocky watched as it sat down, no longer having the muscles needed to carry its skeletal structure. Then he flew over to the trees to find Sela looking on and smiled at her. "That seemed to take care of it!" he exclaimed cockily.

Sela's answer was a shake of her head and a mute point backwards. Rocky whipped around and saw that flesh was re-affixing itself in place in much of the creature's body. He used Analyze.

Hulking Abomination
Level 65
Master – Necromancer Champion
Health Points 4,523/9,112

"Oh, come on!" Rocky exclaimed and thought about the rest of his grenades or making an Azoth-assisted trip to the shop. However, he knew that the thing would be in their Territory and wreaking havoc if he did that. Rocky looked at his new ring and sighed, hoping he wouldn't have to use it but feeling deep within himself that it might be inevitable.

In the heartbeat he had spent contemplating, the bones of the creature had suddenly shot erect, and twenty small chains with hooks erupted from the creature in a wide arc. One wrapped up Jack who was standing right beside him. All across the trees, silence descended for a heartbeat, then screams erupted from twenty throats as the chained people flew towards the creature. Rocky thought desperately, trying to see a way to save the people who were now chained to one of the creature's rib bones.

He considered trying to charge it and break its bones, but then watched on as Jack unleashed his full range of skills on the creature to no effect. Amber screamed out her rage from where she stood, not four feet from where Jack had been, and began to glow a golden color. Sela placed her hand on Amber's shoulder. "You cannot help him now. Charging in there will only increase the butcher's bill." She turned to Rocky and screamed, "We need to destroy that thing now! As soon as it is done digesting those twenty, it will probably grab another twenty to continue healing from the damage you did!"

As he watched, skin began forming over the struggling Jack, and his bellowing screams told them of the pain he was in. Rocky jumped on to Azoth's back, and they leaped back into the air. His only option was the ring, and his only chance to save the rest of the army was to use its charge. It was no longer a question.

Once they reached a point above the reforming creature, Rocky leaned far out from Azoth and held his closed fist out, aiming it at the Abomination beneath the hovering Azoth. He could see Jack still screaming and the other nineteen people looking up at him with pleading in their eyes. He closed his own eyes, trying to not see them, then unleashed the charge in the ring. A pillar of blue fire burst to life, blinding Rocky through his closed eyelids and anyone who was watching from the trees was forced to look away. Through his blindness, he heard a wailing hiss from beneath him, and he felt a scorching heat wafting up from below.

Azoth asked, "Why you blind Azoth?"

Ten seconds later, the world was still white, and the sounds of evaporating flesh were gone. Rocky heard the radio in his ear click on, "What in the tarnations was that?" Joe had forgotten to use radio etiquette, and a blind Rocky normally would have felt vindicated, but all he could picture was the struggling twenty people he had just put to the torch.

When his vision began to clear, he realized that he and Azoth were far higher than they had been when he unleashed the Dragon breath charge. The superheated air had most likely created a powerful updraft that had made Azoth's constant flapping raise them instead of holding them steady. Azoth shook his head a few times, trying to clear the vestiges of his vision as they both looked down at a smoldering, blackened pit where a monstrous form had stood moments before. Anything left of the creatures seemed to have been converted to carbon before blowing away on the cleansing wind.

Rocky directed Azoth to join the army in the trees, and the Chimera obliged, only mumbling mental oddities again that Rocky didn't fully understand, "Azoth was above... creature burnt dead... Azoth use new ability?" Rocky wasn't sure, but he thought perhaps his pet was trying to understand what had just happened, and he thought it might be slightly more humorous to see what he came up with than trying to explain the truth of it to him. Right now, he needed that humor.

The group in the trees had begun forming back up and heading back to the Territory. Only Sela, Zippo, and Smith were still present and waiting on the two to rejoin them. As they landed, Sela immediately asked, "Did you receive the notification?" Rocky nodded to her, his eyes sad and distant. In response to his look, she overdramatically stated, "I am worried that Tao and Gamma didn't arrive to provide aid. I have already sent the army back, but we should return to the Grotto ahead of the army!" She put a bit too much emphasis and volume into her announcement for him not to understand what wasn't being said.

She thinks that it could be Tao and Gamma who are contesting the Territory?

He hoped she was wrong because the only weapon he had that might have damaged the two Master class Knights had just been used to save the majority of the army from a Master class pet. Also, he rather liked Tao and Gamma.

Rocky looked seriously at Smith. "Get back to the Territory quickly! I am going to fly back with Zippo. Sela, you good on transformation charges?"

Sela nodded and began shifting to her bird form in answer. Zippo jumped up on to Azoth's back and started giving the cat-bird lots of scratches as he waited for Rocky. Smith nodded and soberly exclaimed, "I was the one who told Derik about the mission today. I accidentally said it in passing as I walked him to meet with the other exiles, but I still indicated the event. I just wanted you to know why they all showed up."

Rocky blinked, not having known that they had shown up at all. Zippo piped up from Azoth's back, "Yeah, and they saved our behinds! Rocky won't be upset at you for that, Smith." Feeling the wind flow right back out of his sails from Zippo's words, Rocky just nodded at Smith and hopped on to Azoth's back once again. They flew to the Grotto, and Zippo filled him in on a lot of what had happened to the army, talking about it like it was a grand adventure and not something that could have easily killed him. Rocky pointedly tried to ignore his own thoughts and nightmares from killing twenty people.

As soon as they got in view of the Grotto, Zippo went silent, and Rocky forgot all about the previous fight as he leaned forward in his seat, trying to get a better idea of what he was seeing. The two Knights stood on the west and south of the massive Guild Tent, weapons drawn and in clear battle stances. Three of Algonquin Grotto's newly outlined Longhouses had been turned into splintered woods, and the ground was littered with Zombie and Abomination corpses. Every so often, a group of the corpses would liquify and begin creating a new Abomination pet, but as soon as it got into range of Tao or Gamma, it would unceremoniously be chopped in two.

Rocky felt himself begin to panic when he saw corpses of residents scattered amongst the bodies of the Zombies. His skin broke into a sticky, cloying sweat when he realized that he didn't see anyone alive down there other than the two Knights. Zippo saw the dark smoke that signaled Rocky's anger begin coalescing from his pores and asked, "Are the people in the tent?"

This did have the accidental effect of calming Rocky back down, as he immediately flushed and realized that was the obvious answer to the conundrum his brain had ignored when it saw a few additional dead corpses. Azoth flew in and landed at the entrance to the Guild Tent, which faced east towards the river. As soon as they landed, people screamed from inside before a group yelled out, "It's Rocky, Zippo, and Sela!" Then cheers and cries could be heard as a palpable bubble of anxiety broke with their return.

Rocky walked around to Gamma and blurted, "Thank you for protecting them!" Getting his emotions under control, he continued, "What happened here?"

Gamma swatted a newly formed Abomination with the flat of his axe, which blew it apart into tiny pieces. With a quick glance at Rocky, he rumbled, "They broke out of the cliff walls and seemed to have no end. However, fifteen minutes ago they changed tactics and started raising these fat, disgusting Abominations at regular intervals. I don't think they expected us to be here!"

Rocky nodded to himself. How would Apothis know that he had recruited two Master class allies? This must have been meant to be an ambush to wipe out whatever they left behind in the Grotto during the attack on Chalk River. Sela walked up beside him and nodded to Gamma before speaking to Rocky, "I think I know where the place of power is. I also think that the attack we just made was just to hold our attention when this was all put in motion. That's why it was so 'easy'!" She attempted to make air quotes when she said easy, but the gesture was all wrong; instead, she accidentally gave herself wolf ears that she twitched around rather cutely.

Rocky snorted accidentally but responded, "We should restock at the shop and attack the place of power. Where is it?"

Sela tilted her head in consideration. "The entrance I used is outside the Grotto near a small lake, but the actual alter is below us in a large network of caverns and tunnels. I think I was reborn on it." Rocky blinked at her rather disjointed answer. Why hadn't she told him about this sooner?

She continued, "I was planning to go down there and examine the place with you, but there was always something else that was coming up. Plus, I had no idea it was a place of power. As far as I knew, places of power were legends that adventurers told each other in taverns. How there is one here and why it is so far underground, I don't know."

Rocky put a hand on her shoulder, seeing the wildness in her eyes. "We'd better hurry. Will Azoth fit down there?" he asked her to try to get her back on track. She shook her head, and he turned to the Chimera, who had been lingering on the edge of the group. "Go get Smith and Joe! Bring them here. Now!"

Azoth attempted a salute with his front paw, but because he was a cat, it looked more like he was trying to cover his eye and play peek-a-boo. Rocky snorted again; if they all survived this, he was going to take a day and explain to Azoth and Sela what they were trying to mimic, what it meant, and how to do it properly!

He looked at Gamma. "Can we leave the defense and possible retreat of this place to you?"

It was Tao who responded, "Nothing shall breach the sanctity of our defense while we live. Go and cleanse this place the lady speaks of."

Rocky nodded and jogged over to the Populace Accessible shop to refill on elixirs, grenades, and other useful items he had been forced to expend during his most recent fighting. Sela and Zippo joined him. After they had refilled, they returned to the tent to wait for Azoth to return. Rocky used the time to scan through his notifications that he had minimized or ignored during combat. He clicked summarize to reduce the number of notifications and began.

For killing 14,023 Undead Creatures: Level Apprentice 12-26: You as part of the army have been awarded 1,323,451 Etherience.

For killing 25 Undead Summoned Creatures: Level Journeyman 25-41: You as part of the army have been awarded 22,200 Etherience.

For killing 24 Necromancers: Level Apprentice 18-22: You have been awarded 13,100,322 Etherience.

For killing 20 Sapients: Level Apprentice 15-20: You have been awarded 10,245,092

For killing 1 Undead Champion: Level Master 65: You have been awarded 31,243,343 Etherience.

Your personal Etherience amounts to: 55,844,270 Etherience

100,936,443 Etherience remaining until level 24.
—
Congratulations! You have completed a Portion of a Chain Quest!

Chain Quest (Change as per AC - 2.2a)
     Red Quest

Party Quest – Druid
Contain the Destruction

You and your party have examined the area of destruction and found that the influence of Apep is trying to destroy life on Gaia. Furthermore, Apep, using his minion Apothis, is attempting to seize control of a contract creature of Gaia, Bathilda. Not only have you extended the time remaining on this endeavor, you have also found out how to put a stop to it.

Rewards:
Your party has been awarded 150,000,0000 Etherience (Each)
Your party has been awarded 1,000 Crystallized Ether (To leader)
Your Greater Territorial Perk has been deferred until the quest chain is complete!

160,651,643 Etherience remaining until level 25.

Atlantian Code Section 2 Subsection 2 (a) – Gaia reserves the right to change quests from single quests to chain quests when the need arises. This allows Gaia, in situations of dire need, to create follow up quests when the outcome of the action may affect the entire planet. Gaia can increase rewards, defer rewards, or change rewards as she deems appropriate.

—

Congratulations! You have reached level 23! You have been awarded 1 Stat point and 1 Skill point.

Congratulations! You have reached level 24! You have been awarded 1 Stat point and 1 Skill point.

—

You have been offered a 2nd part in a chain quest!

Chain Quest
    Red Quest
        Party Quest - Druid
           Free Bathilda
Find a way to obtain Bathilda's contract item, The
Pendant of Smog, before she can no longer resist the
subversion attempt by Apothis' Necromancers.
Remove the Restriction placed on her by Apothis'
command "To not move a claw."
        Rewards:
                Greater Territorial Perk
                Etherience
                Crystallized Ether
                Territorial Growth Boon from Aura List

Since this is a chain quest, it has been accepted on your
behalf by Gaia.
—

Congratulations! Your Soul Blade 'Dark Tidings' has
consumed enough souls to gain a level! Since you have
claimed enough Sapient Souls, a bonus level was
added.
—

Dark Tidings – Soul Blade

    Level 8

    160/160 Ether Pool

    The Strength of Arms VI
+16 Strength as long as the Blade has Ether from its
pool to draw on. Unlock higher levels of your Soul

Blade for more.

The Strength of Body VI
+8 Stamina as long as the Blade has Ether from its pool to draw on. Unlock higher levels of your Soul Blade for more.

* Dark Tidings refuses to absorb any more golem essence. Find it a new source of sustenance. *

* Dark Tidings has found its favorite sustenance. Sapient Essence will count double. *

There was a lot of information in his most recent notifications, and he flipped back to the massive amount of Etherience that was granted when he took out the Abomination Champion. The Atlantean system had clearly deemed the ring's stored attack as his attack and credited him with a solo kill of a Master class opponent. This was made even more obvious by how little he had gotten for the smaller Abominations that he hadn't helped with in the least.

The final notification for his sword increasing in levels also made him scan the Etherience gains more closely. He felt his heart sink when he saw it. The twenty sapient humans the system had credited him with. Those had been his friends. He felt his brain go static and his body go numb, all of his thoughts looping on that moment, staring down, ring extended, closing his eyes against—

He felt a light slap on his cheek; Sela stood in front of him. She grabbed his chin and forced his eyes to meet hers, ensuring they focused, before she enunciated, "They are not your fault! Your actions and quick thinking saved the Territory! Now you have to do it again. We need you to snap out of this!" She tapped his cheek and smiled. "I need you…"

At his blinking shock, she smiled further and let go before she turned and commanded, "Assign your stats and do what needs to be done. We have to get moving as soon as the others join us! It's a long way down."

He blinked but focused his mind back to the next steps with an effort of his will. The quest change to a chain. Right, should he be upset with Gaia changing their initial quest or overjoyed? If the next quest gave similar rewards, the whole party would be leveling up faster and getting more crystals, but the Greater Territorial Perk might have been something they could have used, considering that the Territory was about to be lost!

He Analyzed Sela and Jason to confirm their Etherience gains.

Selaphelia Ardensai
Level 23
Apprentice Dark-Druid
Health Points 190/190

—

Jason
Level 22
Apprentice Fire-Mage
Health Points 180/180

He then took a moment to look over his own Character page and assign some of his current stats, starting by dumping his two new skill points into his Shadow Clone, increasing its stat transfer and thus its effectiveness in combat.

Rockland Barkclay Level 24
      Class: Apprentice-Dark (Azrael) Revenant,
      Level 1 Strategist
Leadership Class:

Class Skills: Dark Blade, Dark Mend, Soul Blade, Dark Cloak, Shadow Clone

> Health Points = 290/290
>
> Dark Ether Pool = 230/230

You have 0 stat points and 0 skill points to distribute. (Assigned and awaiting confirmation.)

> Stamina – 29 (Strength of Body +8)
>
> Strength – 35 (Strength of Arms +5) (Strength of Arms +16)
>
> Agility – 40 (Speed of Arms +5)
>
> Dexterity – 33
>
> Intelligence – 23 (+2)
>
> Wisdom – 30
>
> Charisma – 32
>
> Luck – 10

Weak Skills

> Non-Class Combat Skills: Combatant – 24 (+2), Ether Channels – 18, Ether Cleanse - 5 (+1), Ether Manipulation – 17
>
> Common Skills: Barter – 8, Camouflage – 7, Endurance – 25, Tracker – 16, Trance Meditation – 19
>
> Profession Skills: Actor – 5, Butcher – 23 (+1), Cook – 2, Herbalist – 19, Miner – 1, Skinner – 22, Teacher - 12 (+2), Trader – 5

Moderate Skills

> Non-Class Combat Skills: Stealth – 6 (+5), Swordsmanship – 5 (+4)
>
> Common Skills: Analyze – 12 (+2), Perception – 3 (+2), Sneak – 16(+3)
>
> Profession Skills

Very shortly after assigning his points, Azoth landed with Joe and Smith, filling out their group and making it five. Once Smith found out why they had been summoned, he tried to push for the entire A-Team to join them, but Rocky looked at the countdown timer and shook his head. With only five hours, fifteen minutes, and change remaining, they didn't have time to gather up more people. Sela had just told him that it was a long way down. On the quick visit to the shop, they had purchased glow strips and flashlights for everyone to use if Zippo, for some reason, stopped being able to provide light.

Rocky crossed all of his metaphorical fingers and prayed that Zippo wouldn't get hurt.

They began jogging out of the Grotto as soon as Rocky managed to convince Azoth to keep a watch on the citizens and army from the air. Azoth insisted that he could join them in the tunnels, and Rocky had to flip the narrative on him by assuring him that he was needed more here. He had tried to tell him it was because of his size, but Azoth didn't seem to understand the concept of small spaces that couldn't be made larger using brute force.

With just under five hours remaining on the timer, the group arrived at the entrance to the tunnels Sela had been forced to traverse after her resurrection. Rocky took a deep breath and blew it out. "Not like the fate of everyone is riding on this!"

CHAPTER TWENTY-FOUR

The group had been descending into the darkness of the deep tunnels lit only by a small ball of fire conjured by Zippo for an hour already based off of the countdown clock, and they hadn't seen or heard a thing. Rocky stared at Sela's back. "You sure this is the place of power?"

She turned around and stuck her tongue out at him, then rolled her eyes. "Honestly, if that was the first time you asked, it might be original. What is the count on that question now, Zippo?"

Zippo piped in happily, "Twelve, he has averaged one every five minutes or so." Rocky stuck his tongue out at Zippo in turn, and the kid gave him the finger. Rocky opened his mouth wide in shock and looked around at the other two-party members, Smith, and Joe. Both of them wore serious expressions, and Rocky gave up his fake outrage.

Instead, he turned to face the front again and thought about Sela. Currently, she was using one of her druidic gifts to see the space around them. She claimed she was feeling out the path to the center of the massive complex of tunnels, caverns, and drops. Unfortunately, by the number of turns they had taken and the general slope of all the passages, they were taking it was still below them and still a ways off. Rocky couldn't trust his inner sense of direction right now because it was somewhat convinced, they had been traveling in spiraling circles.

In truth, he knew what he was doing, asking all the questions and trying to manufacture humor. He had seen a lot of needless death over the last few hours, and he was worried that he was in for some more. If he could go back in time, he might have cleared out Chalk River before the trip to Ottawa, like Sela had strongly indicated at the time they received the first part of the quest. That would have stopped there from being as many souls to protect right now, and perhaps the Dungeon would have been far weaker. Perhaps Apep's influence would have been tremulous.

Every time Rocky had felt they were about to win, something had come up. They had stopped the storms, which meant they could attack en masse, but Apothis had created an army of sacrifices to place in their path. Rocky had removed what shielding the weak creatures had by killing their support, and suddenly, they had all morphed into stronger undead minions. Finally, he had made it to the Dragon and here again, they had been missing something crucial to their success. Now, they were spiraling deep underground, and Rocky had to admit that he didn't want to see the people he was with get hurt. The others who had died in the recent battles hurt him, devastated him in ways, but to lose the people around him now? That would break him, and he knew it.

So, comedy becomes the crutch once again!

A few spirals later, Sela froze stock-still, and Rocky held his breath listening. He couldn't hear anything at all, so he, like the others, waited on what she might do with held breath. A moment later, she continued on, and Zippo opened his mouth, "Se–"

She pointed right at him unerringly with her back still turned and hissed as quietly as she could. Then she turned back to them and whispered, "After the next corkscrew, we are going to level out, and it is crawling with creatures of some sort. I would guess that it is human feet on the stones, but this skill only gives me a general size of the contact points."

Her eyes widened for a moment, and she looked back quickly, holding up a hand. A slow count of ten later, she turned back and continued her whisper, "There is no possible way to avoid them. Whatever is down there is going to have to be fought. I think it is going to be best to just fight anything that we find as we move forward. If we avoid any of the groups I am feeling down there, they will likely just attack us from behind later when we can ill afford it."

Everyone looked serious, and Rocky swallowed while looking around at each person individually, measuring their strength. Then he decided to take charge; a little unsure but counting on his gaming experience, he whispered, "Sela, cat form. My clone, and I will be in the lead, forming a wedge. Zippo, you hold the middle as our light source and only cast spells forward if you see an opening where your splash damage won't hurt Sela or me. Joe and Smith, you have the rear. Try to bunch up groups when you can." Rocky made a motion with his hands that was meant to signify overflow. Then he pointed at Zippo. "If something attacks from behind, signal Zippo to light 'em up!"

Everyone nodded, and Rocky summoned his Shadow Clone, who came into existence staring into his face. He quickly held up four fingers, then poked Rocky square in the center of the chest before putting its hands up in surrender. Smith looked uncomfortable with the mime show and whispered to Joe beside him, "Think they need a minute?"

Somewhat disturbed himself by the display of emotion from his clone, Rocky blinked before mentally commanding it to do what he needed. The clone got more serious and pointed to its daggers then held up its hands showing a small space between them. Rocky realized what the clone was trying to say, perhaps because it was a part of him or perhaps because it wasn't a terribly complicated message. Its daggers were short, which wasn't ideal for the current situation.

Rocky looked around and then nodded before changing his own position of the wedge flank to the wedge leader, effectively swapping himself with the clone. The Shadow Clone widened its eyes and then nodded. Rocky had to wonder how people that had this skill remained sane—constantly interacting with a part of yourself that is also not a part of you couldn't be good for future mental health.

Rocky activated his Dark Cloak as the group moved in formation down the last twist. They came out on level, interlocking brick. It was beautifully crafted with onyx stones shining from amidst marble. Rocky only glanced at the white and black chessboard-like pattern for a brief moment before he snapped his head up to look for enemies. His eyes found the same stonework on the walls but placed strategically to look like a dark black cityscape. The buildings it depicted, while clearly structures, were so alien in shape compared to what he was used to that his eyes were unfortunately caught by them for a split second too long.

His Dark Cloak screamed a warning to him as a pale white hand attempted to locate the warm flesh underneath, and he made a quick, compact, vertical slash to remove the offending limb. The creature was getting ready to leap at the swirling shadows when a laser bolt put a hole in its forehead, and it fell dead. Rocky didn't need another reminder of the stakes, and he waded forward in the Seraphin sword forms, keeping his body compact and his movements precise and deadly.

The choice to move himself to the lead turned out to be a prodigious one as his blade carved a space around him that forced enemies to bunch together and impede each other as they tried to circle him. Sela and his clone both hugged a body's width from the wall and struck out at the creatures that flowed off the side of his attacks. The hall was only about ten feet across, and his blade easily reached out three to four feet on each side of himself. This left his two assistants only a one-to-two-foot zone they had to cover; the rest of their energy was spent peeling the extras off of his edges.

As they moved, Joe pumped out a laser bolt at the occasional creature, and Smith would fire some sort of spectral bolt, a new skill, that carried through multiple bodies, killing them and leaving behind a green circle on their skin. The circle would slowly grow moss as Rocky waded by the corpses.

Within moments, Rocky was feeling his legs burn from keeping them bent and fluid. His arms were covered in the Zombies' blood, which was mixing with the few cuts and scrapes that got through his sword forms. Each member was stepping over and, in some cases, on to dead Zombies as they advanced. Rocky tried to glance around to get an idea of how far they had moved forward but felt sharpened fingernails scrape his armor for his distraction. He pumped his blade with two charges of Dark Blade and sent it flying down the hall in front of him, turning the advancing creatures into a bloody, blended liquid. Then they dispatched the few who had been lucky enough to avoid the powerful attack.

As soon as he cleaved the last one from shoulder to pelvis, he felt his entire body go heavy, and his breathing came fast and shallow. Sela, in her cat form, also had her head down and was panting heavily. Even his clone was leaning against the wall looking tired. Rocky forced himself upright and spoke between gasps, "This…. is… going… to take a… while!"

Zippo, who hadn't done anything yet but provide light, asked the obvious, "You sure you can handle this?" In the distance, more Zombies began hobbling into the light of Zippo's hovering Fireball.

Rocky groaned at the sight and checked his Ether and health pools. He had cast a few Dark Mends and the one Dark Blade spell, which left him with one hundred fifty Ether and full health. As the enemies continued to close the gap that his Dark Blade had opened, he finally caught his breath enough to talk normally, "Think you can give us a bit more breathing time Zippo?" he asked as he pointed at the advancing undead.

Zippo smiled and began enlarging his hovering Fireball. Once it was five feet in diameter, he stepped to the front and shot his hands out in front of him. The shadows shifted as the light source began careening away from the group, and the moment it struck the leading edge of the wall of undead flesh, a massive whoosh sounded as much of the air was sucked into the conflagration. It had the desired effect, however, and the moment it hit, Zippo began summoning a new light source to hover above his hand. Rocky kept catching his breath and did a quick inner search for any infected Ether in his system. He found a few and used the smallest amount of his own Ether that he could to dump the infection using Ether-Cleanse. This, unfortunately, took forty more of his dwindling pool, but luckily, the flames still burned in front of them.

Rocky noticed that Zippo held one hand still pointed at the fire and realized he was probably the reason it was still burning and keeping the enemy back. "How much longer can you hold it?" he asked once he noticed.

A bead of sweat fell from the kid's forehead, and he sheepishly responded, "Not much longer if you want me to keep my Ether above half. Maybe another twenty seconds."

Rocky nodded at him and then turned to appraise the group again. Everyone was breathing normally again, which was good, and his own Ether Pool was climbing back up to the one hundred thirty point mark. If they repeated this pattern, they should be able to–

The fires died out suddenly, and Rocky looked to Zippo, who had gone pale.

Not the kid's doing then…

Three Necromancers stepped out from the horde of undead where had been standing still behind the fire. Each one began gathering shadows to them, and Rocky leaped into action, having seen the destructive power of their shadow bolts in action. As he closed, he knew he wasn't going to close the distance in time, but he pushed his legs as hard as he could over the sticky, bloody tiles of the hallway. When he was ten feet away, they all shoved their hands into the ground, sending a pulse of shadow through the walls, ceiling, and floor. Rocky closed the last three steps and cut them in half. Not sure what they had done, he backed away as the horde began slowly plodding forward again.

Zippo gasped, "The corpses are melting again!" Rocky looked down to find that the blood, innards, and skin his Dark Blade had rendered from the closely packed undead was indeed beginning to melt into pools then flow into spheres before finally coalescing together into the forming shapes of Abominations.

As he backpedaled towards the group, he looked back and saw the thousand plus meters they had traversed was pockmarked by a repeating scene, and he swore at himself for not realizing the trap. The only bodies that didn't join the grisly flesh bubbles were the ones that had burnt.

Well, you have certainly stepped in it this time!

As the first Abomination formed up, he used Analyze.

Abomination
Level 20
Apprentice – Necromancer's Pet Horror
Health Points 490/490

Zippo shouted, "They're lower levels than the ones we faced above ground!" Simultaneously with Zippo's revelation, Rocky swung his sword at a still-forming blob, and it passed right through it, trailing liquid skin and muscle. Then the blood and viscera on his body joined the mass as it sloughed off of him, then his sword, and rejoined the forming Abomination. Rocky tilted his head and considered; it would seem that they had to form before he could damage them with a melee weapon. Another quick glance back counted more than twenty behind them, and with the five in front aided by the massing Zombies behind, they were in for some anvil and hammer treatment.

Rocky thought desperately as he stepped back into formation in front. For a quick stop-gap measure, he turned to

Sela. "You and the clone are going to have to hold this side. I am moving to the back!"

Smith chimed in, "For each one we kill, I can raise a spirit of the creature to fight on our side to a maximum of two. They weren't extremely effective against the Journeyman level ones on the surface, but that was because the spirits are maxed to my level. I think they might be more helpful here…"

Smith had faded off, clearly indicating that he was only guessing and praying for what he surmised to be true. Rocky nodded to him as he squeezed by. "When I kill one, give it a try! Let's not count on it until we see it in action."

A moment later, twenty-five bellows of Abominations sounded, reverberating off the walls and making him wince as he stood staring down the nearest creature that began charging from eight feet away. This one and a few others had two hooks for hands, while others had the three skeletal claws. There seemed to be three unique variations of Abominations, in fact, and that made Rocky assume that the shapes depended on the Necromancer.

A massive hook swung a clumsy attack at the shadows that he was enveloped in. He didn't even bother ducking, seeing that the bone hook would miss him high. Instead, he pivoted on his foot and stepped forward using his body to brace the sword as it cut through the thing's stomach. As it howled, he turned the blade and stepped again, striking in the opposite direction and feeling his blade click as it bounced off the creature's spine.

He had almost cut the thing in half with two strikes, but the descending second bone hook told him it didn't mean the creature was dead or even dying. To avoid the pulverizing blow, he let his momentum carry him into a front roll towards the wall and came out of the somersault with a leap at the structure. Planting both feet on the wall's tiles, he bunched his legs and sprang back at the creature just as its hook crashed into the floor. Rocky took a vertical axe-chopping swing himself and cut the creature's skull in two. Its body went limp, and it fell to the floor. Instantly, smoky, white vapors began forming above its body as Smith's spirit pet started to form. Rocky pointed at the corpse. "Can you burn each corpse while being controlled about it?" he shouted a bit too harshly, hoping Zippo wouldn't take offense.

Zippo nodded weakly before realizing that Rocky couldn't see that gesture, so he added, "Yes, Rock. I got this." As soon as the spirit was fully formed, the corpse lit up and began slowly burning.

In the other direction, Rocky's Shadow Clone blinked out of sight as the first creature struck at him. A half breath later, his Shadow Clone was on the Abomination, backstabbing its daggers into the base of the thing's skull. Sela, seeing the distracted opening, slammed her horse-size bulk into the side of the creature while hunching low at the last second. The creature fell, and the Shadow Clone's repeated stabbing finally made the body go limp. Again, a spirit began rising from the fallen Abomination as Smith summoned his second and final spelled pet.

Rocky had continued wading forward to engage the second grotesque creature that had formed in the hallway they had painstakingly traversed. As laser bolts struck and staggered the charging beast, Rocky slid on his knees, leaving his sword out beside him and in line with the creature's stubby legs. His sword failed to sever the limb entirely, but the momentum of its charge and his strength broke the short femur, which caused it to perform an unintentional, headfirst baseball slide as it skidded to a stop in front of the spirit Abomination. Two hooks came down on the creature's skull in unison, and the struggle for another of the undead amalgamations ended. Both of the newly dead corpses lit up, and the fight continued.

Three hours, fourteen minutes, and a handful of seconds remained by the time they had managed to finally fight free and have a moment's respite. The ones in front had died rather quickly with the three melee combatants working together.

Now though, Rocky felt tears running down his blood-stained face as he stood over a nearly cut in half Joe. In the middle of the fight, Rocky had been attacked by three Abominations in unison—one from behind that he had left for Smith's spirits and two that he had been holding back with hit and run maneuver tactics utilizing his speed. A scream from Smith had announced the start of the trouble, as a load of bricks had tumbled from the ceiling right on top of him.

Both of his spirits had rushed to his aid and began clearing the rubble, which admittedly probably saved his life when combined with the Health Potion his freed arms had allowed him to drink. Unfortunately, it had nearly cost Rocky his and had definitely created the disaster for Joe.

Currently, Rocky was regretting his choice of tactics, but the whole reason he had chosen to whittle down their health was that they had been extremely effective roadblocks against their remaining brethren. Whenever the spirit finished off one, he would let it pull one of the two injured meat shields to itself and finish it off. It had worked in clearing over ten of the creatures, but in the freak accident that followed, the tactic had shown its weak point—Smith.

In that instance, he had tried to react in time by sending a Dark Blade at the two he had been holding at bay, hoping to destroy them and the five or so bunched closely behind them with his nearly depleted Ether. Unfortunately, a single charge of the spell only pushed the creatures back and held them at bay while the final one's hook entered the Dark Cloak and careened towards his stomach. He felt his Dark Cloak shift the strike slightly, but even if it didn't instantly kill him, it would injure him severely enough that surrounded by three enemies, as he was, he would inevitably die.

In that moment, when death stared him in the face, Rocky had only hoped that the group would still manage to dislodge Apep's hold on the Territory, but unbeknownst to Rocky, Joe had a skill that he hadn't told the group about.

Suddenly, his view of his own impending death had changed, and he was watching the battle from about twenty feet further down the hallway from right beside Zippo and a recovering Smith. Extremely confused and with his nerves on high alert, he had started charging back before he had even thought about what had happened, charging towards the cloud of darkness that was slowly dissipating as a bloody hook of an Abomination exited the other side of it. He screamed and tried to cast Dark Mend on the body he knew must be in that swirling, dissipating cloud of smoke. It had rebounded and adhered to him instead, and he felt tears begin collecting in his eyes as he cut viciously through the Abomination that had done the deed.

As soon as Smith had gotten control of himself enough, which had taken only a few seconds, he had sent both of the spirits to hold off the Zombie horde relieving Sela and Rocky's clone to rush back to his current fight. As the smoke finally dissipated and his trusted friend came into view, eyes no longer reflecting the light he was used to seeing, he felt his rage stutter his heart and then consume his other emotions in cold strong hands. He drank an Ether Potion, noting the de-buff distantly for overuse, adding itself to his status ailments on his interface. Then his blade began sucking in what little light the tunnel had.

A part of his mind stayed composed and screamed at the part of him now holding the reigns that he couldn't expend another Dark Blade strike at the creatures. They had already proven that the ones struck would die, but their bones would act as a strong shield for the ones behind them. All another strike would do would be to bottom out his Ether pool again.

Surprisingly, he felt the angry, competitive part of himself acknowledge that sane part and begin stepping forward in the Seraphin blade forms. He had used the Dark Blade skill as a close-range melee attack before—one time against a troll, other times more recently against strong enemies and so blinked as he saw his instinctual competitive side hold the skill to do so again. His brain screamed at his anger, telling it to stop acting stupid and retract the spell to return the Ether back to his pool. In the past, each strike against his opponent, he still released the skill held in the blade.

His first strike felt like a knife through butter as the shadows on the sword formed an edge that weighed nothing and cleaved the two Abominations in half. Rocky blinked, and his 'intelligent' side of his brain went catatonic.

By the time Sela and his clone arrived, he had dispatched five more of the creatures, Zippo's flames had already begun licking up their bodies, and as a group they easily waded through the remaining four that were at their rear.

Once the coast was clear, he had made his way back on leaden feet and was now standing over a dead Joe.

In front of them, Smith's summoned creatures easily held the horde of lesser undead at bay, which allowed the four living members of the party to gather over their fallen member. Sela growled deeply, which forced the glance at the clock, which in turn made Rocky snarl. He turned to Zippo and stuttered out with deep emotional turmoil, "Burn the corpse. We have to keep going."

Joe had just saved his life, and all he could do for him was turn away and ensure that these minions of Apep didn't use his corpse. He growled as he stalked towards the two massive Abomination spirits that held back the Zombie horde. That wasn't true; all he could do was save the damn Territory and all the people in it!

That's what Joe would want. He would save the people his friend had protected desperately since the crash!

All he could do was win at any cost!

CHAPTER TWENTY-FIVE

After receiving three more robes and staffs from looting the necromancer corpses, plus some Crystals, the group continued on. They were significantly bolstered by the two Abomination spirits, so the group made much quicker time through the deep tunnels. Every so often, Rocky, his clone, and Sela would take the front spot to allow the spirits a chance to heal some of the minor wounds they had been suffering, but for the most part, the spirit Abominations were in the lead while the others took pot shots of opportunities. Zippo, of course, burned every fallen Zombie corpse to prevent another ambush like the first.

The timer read one hour, seven minutes, and forty-five seconds when suddenly, the two spirits ran out of targets. The group blinked in surprise at the lack of bloody carnage, and all simultaneously looked up at the spirits that were walking away towards a left turn in the tunnel. Smith held a hand up, and they stopped as the group stood stock-still and stunned. All eyes fell on Sela in her cat form who looked back at them and then the corner. Everyone cringed at the sound of nails on a chalkboard, as she drew an 'X' with her sharp claws on an unlucky onyx tile that was nearest her.

Rocky unclenched his tightened jaw and sputtered as she began a circle, "Stop, stop… We get it, Sela, we are near the goal?" She cat-grinned up at him, and he shook his head in exasperation before shaking his whole body to get rid of the skin-crawling feeling the noise had induced. Once he was satisfied, he put on his best announcer's voice and whispered, "Let's see what we have around corner number one." Then he crept to the edge of the wall and looked around the corner.

Around the corner was, simply put, nothing. Two feet from where the corner started, a wall of dirt was blocking the entire passage, and Rocky turned back to look at Sela. "Yeah…

Sela, there is a wall of dirt here. Nothing else. Are you sure we went the right way?" Rocky had seen a few other turns they could have taken, but the massive horde of enemies and Sela's insistence that this was the right way had convinced him this was correct. Until now.

Sela shifted back to her human form and scoffed at Rocky but didn't bother to whisper when she maintained, "You know damn well it is the right way." She walked up and touched the wall. "By the look of this wall, they have a low-level geomancer on the other side of it." She looked at Rocky, intoning emotionlessly, "There was something suspicious about that ceiling falling on Smith, and I think we found the culprit." Rocky snarled at the wall and raised his sword. Sela moved quickly and put a hand on his arm. "No, you idiot. That could bring the whole tunnel down on us. I changed to human form to have better control over the Earth. You all just have to kill whatever I am going to be fighting against."

Suddenly, the wall dropped, and they all jumped and spun to face down the now open hallway. Frankie stood in the middle of a group of five Necromancers, each with a Dragon Heartstring. Behind Frankie, a rodent-looking man sat cross-legged, covered in dirt and tattered clothing, and wearing a Heartstring around his neck like Derik once had.

Frankie walked out from the group, and Rocky immediately noticed his new arm. The fact that it was black and twisted might have been the reason, or the fact that it had a Heartstring wrapped around it that glowed red could have drawn his eye. Regardless, Frankie saw him looking at the arm and sneered, "Do you like my new arm? Apep gifted it to me after I caught the group of hold outs that this Geomancer," he pointed at the cross-legged Geomancer, "was hiding from his rains." Frankie held his arm up, admiring it like it was beautiful instead of grotesque.

Rocky Analyzed him as he continued to ogle his own disgusting arm.

Frankie Cocozza
Level 33
Journeyman ~~Psychologist~~ Apothis' Ether-Manipulator
Health Points 810/810

Rocky's eyebrows rose at the massive increase in terms of levels Frankie had undergone in the few days since he had seen him last. Frankie finally pulled his eyes away from his disgusting arm and saw his face. "Ah, you must have seen my new rank and levels! Yes, well, you see; while the Zombies are just constructs of the Dungeon and thus provide little Etherience when sacrificed, all the citizens who have been caught by the storms and were later converted to Minions do!" Rocky felt his stomach twist at the implication that one cockily spoken statement held.

Every Necromancer he had fought, every Necromancer he had killed was a converted human that had been caught in Apep's rains? Then on top of that corruption, they had sacrificed them to increase the levels of this parasite?! He did a quick scan of the individual behind Frankie.

Devoted of Apothis
Level 22
Journeyman Irradiated Necromancer
Health Points 509/509

"You seem to be missing a member of your party! My old 'commander'," Frankie turned the title into a curse as he spoke it. "Good, old, reliable Joe. I told him all that time ago that his Sacrifice skill was only going to get him killed. Obviously, right!" He broke into maniacal laughter as the stunned group looked on and began growing red in the face.

Rocky, who had not been using his Dark Cloak skill when the wall came down, felt his inner 'beast' bristle, and the skill craved release. He held it in and hissed between his clenched teeth, "You are scum. Even if everyone on the earth is under your command and you somehow live long enough to die of old age, you will just fade into oblivion one day and be forgotten instantly! Joe will be remembered, Jack will be remembered, Alex will be remembered, Oliver will be remembered. The atrocities you committed will be remembered, but your name will not!"

Frankie stopped laughing after the first sentence, and his face grew red shortly after. As his rage became apparent, the four Necromancers stepped forward, but he held up a hand and spat out, "You people and your ideals–" His words sounded like some sort of poison he needed to expel from his body. Then he was cut off as Rocky's Shadow Clone popped into view behind the group of Necromancers, sinking a dagger into the base of two of their skulls and cutting their bodies' communication to the brains.

Rocky sprang forward and let Dark Cloak activate as he did. On his left and right, Smith's spirits surged. Zippo's Fireball flickered as he looked for an opening to unleash hell. It was Sela who acted oddly as she screamed and knelt down, placing a hand on the ground. Rocky swung his sword with a wicked smile, seeing two spectral bone hooks mimicking his attack. Frankie casually lifted his disgusting black arm and caught all three blows on its edge. Sparks flew, and then it was Frankie's turn to smile as he kicked Rocky in the chest, causing him to fly backwards.

Rocky turned the momentum into a roll and watched on in horror-filled fascination as Frankie touched one spirit and then the other. Smith screamed and began to sweat as his constructs began deflating like balloons. After they both were nothing but smoke, only a small blue line was left connecting Frankie to

Smith. Rocky scrambled and used his newest style of Dark Blade to attempt to sever the connection. It did cut off the strange blue connection, but it simultaneously knocked out Smith.

Frankie chuckled and licked his lips. "I wasn't finished with that one yet!" Frankie looked like he would have sprung forward into a charge, but Zippo had finally seen his opportunity; he let fly a string of Fireballs. One after the other, they impacted the man, and flames whooshed out around him. Rocky felt his connection to his clone drop off as the flames intensified, and he put a hand on Zippo's arm to stop the fifth formed Fireball spell.

They both watched on as a mound of earth emerged from the smoke where Frankie should have stood. A heartbeat after that, a charred foot broke the surface of the mound and began pulling a singed looking Frankie clear. Behind the man, the Necromancers turned to join the fight, and Rocky leaped into a forward charge again. Two shadow bolts flew towards him as Frankie dusted himself off. In counter to the spells, he unleashed the double charge of his Dark Blade that he had been holding on his sword and began charging it again.

The spells collided, detonating as the Dark Blade lost power but continued on. Frankie batted the weakened spell aside, but Rocky struck at his front leg as he braced himself for the flashy move. The blade severed the limb like it wasn't even there and continued on, scoring a strike on his back leg as well. Frankie screamed and collapsed forward, his weight no longer held by the limb.

Rocky stomped down hard on Frankie's head as he ran over the man to continue on towards the Necromancers who shot whips down the hall at him. For a second, he thought they had missed; then he screamed as their targets became apparent to him. Zippo managed to deflect the one coming at him with his shield skill, but the one targeting Sela wrapped around her arm.

With a rictus smile, the minion pulled, Sela opened her eyes screaming, and the tunnel began to shake as Rocky decapitated the two defenseless, snarling Necromancers.

When the dust settled again, Rocky was coughing and stumbling around blindly in the extremely dark space he occupied. He thought for a moment that he was covered in rocks, dirt, and the other caved in remains of the tunnel, but when he activated his light strip, he found himself looking down a clear hallway. On the ground ten feet in front of him, the Geomancer was passed out but breathing. Rocky walked over and pulled the Dragon Heartstring from his neck, summoning it into his bag of holding; he knew that wouldn't be the end of the corruption to his Ether if he was anything like the people from his Territory, so he considered killing him.

He glanced down and used Analyze.

Harold Dawmer
Level 13
Apprentice Geomancer
Health Points 70/170

He had already seen enough death for the day, though, so he tried to look back at his party for guidance but found the tunnel completely caved in. He tried his radio and received only static. Then he shouted Sela's name into the dirt.

Zippo's voice answered him, coming muffled and scared. "She is okay, Rock. We managed not to get buried, but that Necromancer did a number on her arm. She is unconscious, and so is Smith." There was a pause, and then he continued, "I poured a healing potion down both of their throats, and they seem to be getting better, but I don't know what to do!"

Rocky took a deep breath to calm down; the last thing Zippo needed was Rocky's added worry on top of his own. "Take the more injured to the surface and come back for the other?" he suggested once he breathed out, hoping that Zippo would be able to handle it. He glanced to his corner and saw the clock counting down from just under thirty minutes and tried to calm his nerves. From the last moments of that fight, it was clear that Sela had been in a struggle with the Geomancer for the earth around the tunnel.

A collapsed tunnel clearly favoured Frankie which was also rather obvious to Rocky. While Sela had people to protect and keep alive and needed to get to the end of this passage, Frankie only cared about himself and wanted to prevent them from going further. It would appear that he had nearly succeeded but had been buried in the cave in for his efforts. Rocky hoped he suffered in his last moments or was still suffering!

Rocky took the moment to loot the corpses of the Necromancers and put their staffs and equipment into his bag of holding. After that was done, he also had four new Dragon Heartstrings in his bag. He looked at the cave in and the fifth Heartstring it held, but now wasn't the time. He would have to clear the cave in eventually anyway or find another way out.

Zippo screamed back after a time, "Sela has lower health. I will carry her out to get help. We will be back!" The fact that Zippo was going to be moving and working towards something was all Rocky cared about. The kid was extremely strong, but Rocky remembered the last time he had lost his two friends. It hadn't been pretty, and he hoped that losing Joe wouldn't cause the young man to slide back into the place he had been before. Unfortunately, Joe had been the person Zippo had spent the most time with out of the entire group, and that meant he was probably the one who knew him best.

Rocky shook his head and mumbled, "Enough worrying about the fire-starter. You should be worrying about yourself!" In answer, he walked over to the still unconscious Geomancer and poured a Potion of Dreamless Sleep that Smith had given him down the man's throat. That should at least keep him knocked out until Rocky had solved the takeover or died trying.

With that grisly thought, he started walking down the eerily quiet hallway. After a short distance, the corridor turned left, and a faint, red glow emanated from whatever lay beyond. Rocky turned off his own light and cast both his Stealth and Shadow Cloak skills. Then he crept forward to find out what awaited him.

CHAPTER TWENTY-SIX

As soon as he turned the corner, Rocky found out what was causing the ominous, red, glowing pulse. A few feet in front of him, a small three-step staircase descended into a massive, open room. The room was stylized in the same pattern as the maze had been but was furnished with strange-looking pieces of equipment. He could only describe the stone benches and seats as equipment, as the room looked like a deck of a massive starship from Hollywood. It even had three massive stone chairs in the near center of the room, with the middle one raised higher than the other two. 'Chairs' was probably even the wrong word for the eloquently carved stone monsters; they more closely resembled a throne with two small thrones surrounding it.

Part of the reason they conjured the image of a throne in Rocky's imaginative mind was that on the highest and largest one sat a dark-robed figure holding a glowing red staff. This staff, unlike some of its lesser copycats, was holding a full nuclear rod as its focus gem; wrapping and securing the pulsing piece of glowing metal were radiant Heartstrings tied in opposite, traversing spirals before being anchored to sharp, wooden, thorny protrusions that jutted from the black staff.

While the color and intensity of the staff drew his eye first, a second glance later, it was what was inside the open robe that he couldn't look away from. The creature inside looked like a half-rotten corpse. Its face was gray and somewhat human-looking, but his chest, hands, and torso had bones poking out of what little gray skin remained. Most of the creature's organs were clearly visible, and Rocky could even see the beating heart in its chest cavity!

His Analyze skill triggered due to his intense scrutiny.

Apothis
Level 75

Master Necromonger of Apep
Health Points 4,500/9,000
Boss

The box finally broke him out of his daze, and Rocky blinked, looked around, and tried to understand why Apothis was missing health points. He saw nothing else in the room but stone equipment tables with spots for legs carved underneath them but no chairs. Then his eyes found the next oddity in the room. It wasn't a person but a massive, black, stone altar that dominated the center of the cavernous space.

Rocky would have dismissed the thing as another table if it wasn't for the 3-D hologram that glared from its surface back at him. He may have further just dismissed it as some sort of spell if it wasn't showing him a near-identical scene to one he had seen nearly five hours before. Tao and Gamma stood sentry around the Guild Tent, striking out at any Abomination that was raised from yet unburnt corpses.

A few of the returned military had started fires, and when the coast was clear, they ran out to place a burning log on to a dead enemy. From that point of view, it looked like they were winning or at least doing an excellent job of weathering the creature's attacks. The military tanks and other equipment, while intimidating, was practically useless at current with no charges, but he could even see through the holographic tent to the tightly-packed citizens within, all safe.

That was why he felt his stomach drop. In the cavern walls around the Grotto, he could see hordes of undead just waiting to be unleashed. They only occupied the south and west walls currently, and Rocky could actually see why that was as he could also see his two Dungeons hard at work destroying any enemies that quested into their cardinal direction of ownership. Rocky smiled as LFD's prized, mutated rabbit Thumper ripped in half a Zombie before throwing it into a pit that LFD had clearly dug.

Maximus had a massive army of creatures in formed ranks waiting for anything stupid enough to try to utilize his portion of the Grotto wall. Rocky hadn't known how much help he had been getting from all his allies in this fight, but he still felt sick seeing the vast numbers that the enemies still had in the wings. There were easily one hundred glyph circles on the cliff tops and fifty Necromancers inside them with staffs planted. Each Necromancer was taking turns raising Abominations from the abundant Zombie corpses.

While his people were surviving, Apothis had turned this into a war of attrition, and soon, if nothing was done, he would own the Territory. Twenty-four minutes and fifteen seconds from now, to be more exact! Rocky began considering his options. In his bag of holding, he had numerous grenades, more MKZ turrets, and a few proximity mines. The big problem was that four thousand five hundred health wasn't going to vanish unless he hit him with everything.

What was the best way to do it? He smiled grimly and instantly knew that a 'part' of him really wasn't going to like this. He ducked back around the corner and summoned his Shadow Clone. It blinked its dark black eyes at him and crossed its arms. Rocky smiled awkwardly at it as he started pulling out all of his explosives and affixing them to it.

He stepped back and looked at his Christmas tree of death. His clone stared back at him with the most unimpressed face he had ever seen. Then, as if inspiration struck, his clone lit up and pointed at its butt before moving a grenade from its chest to clip it there. When it turned back around, it held its arms wide and spun silently, showing off. Then it gave Rocky a very rude gesture before going back to a cross-armed, emotionless stare.

I get it! But you can come back to life. So...

He placed a proximity mine in the spot the Shadow Clone had just moved the grenade from and gave his clone a double thumbs up.

His clone vanished from view as he commanded it to attempt to sneak up on Apothis. He gave it the count of ten to get in position. At ten Rocky, from Stealth, unloaded all ten of the MKZ laser turrets out into the open doorway from his bag of holding and dove back around the corner.

He was jerked to a stop before he hit the ground and hovered in the air. A red glow surrounded him, and he heard, "I see you are done examining the battle for your precious citizens! Don't worry, I will take good care of them once I am done," Apothis crooned into the red, glowing room.

The MKZ turrets started ionizing and shot a single round each before they were dislodged and rushed to meet their neighbors in a hovering circle above the ground. They screeched and groaned as they bent in on themselves, contorting over each other to tangle and form a ball of component parts.

Rocky slowly floated up and into the doorway just in time to see a second spell that Apothis had hidden behind the throne blast a space beside him. It was so fast Rocky almost missed it, but a shadow ball the size of his entire body whistled forward until it thudded into his Shadow Clone. His clone materialized for a moment with a stunned look on his face before the spinning spell removed it and all of his grenades from existence.

In shocked panic, Rocky strained every muscle in his body to the limit, expecting a shadow ball was coming for him, and he felt like he was pushing against a mountain. He couldn't budge the invisible restraints an inch as he slowly floated towards the half-decayed and dark-robed figure. Apothis smiled. "You think I wasn't aware that you were there! Foolish child. I knew you were coming as soon as you dispatched my minions and that fool, Frankie." The contorted ball of what used to be MKZ

Turrets fell to the ground behind Rocky to punctuate Apothis' point.

Apothis walked down from the throne and went to stand behind the altar. Then continued lovingly, "I just wanted you to see your people and what I was going to do next! I do have to thank you for bringing me such powerful creatures to seduce, though." He swept his skeletal fingers through Tao and Gamma. Then he closed his eyes.

The mass of Zombies began exiting the caves in the Grotto walls that they hid in. However, they didn't attack. Instead, they began forming up ominous line after line of undead Zombies. The two golems who were too far away to strike the lines, but they seemed to grow wary as they dropped into deeper ready positions. The military who had been running around burning creatures dropped their torches and retreated to the tent and set up a perimeter at something Gamma shouted but couldn't be heard by Apothis or himself through the image.

"Was it you that destroyed my last Hulking Abomination?" Apothis glanced at Rocky suspiciously. "I have to admit that I didn't expect anyone to be able to stop him, let alone to hold back my perfectly planned ambush." He tipped an imaginary hat towards the frozen Rocky. "I must give you some credit for all you managed, but it ends now!" As he finished the final statement, his body began to glow red, and more of his skin, organs, and blood began to dissolve into the swirling, red mist that flowed through and around him.

Rocky watched in horror as he became even more skeletal and used Analyze again to try to understand what was happening.

Apothis
Level 75
Master Necromonger
Health Points 1,325 / 9,000

The red mist of his spell shot straight up through the rock, and a moment later, the fifty Necromancers with staffs planted in the ground each seemed to shudder as something flowed through them and then back out towards the hordes of the Dungeon-created undead. In the hologram, the hordes of Zombies began melting and reforming into massive balls of cracking bones, liquid flesh, and innards. Rocky felt his eyebrows try to rise, but even these muscles were locked in place.

Apothis gasped when all the red mist left him and then leaned heavily on his own staff before standing up straight for a moment and grinning triumphantly from his now half skeletal face. "For each Hulking Abomination, I create, I must pay half of my current health pool for seven days, but," he pointed to the hologram where the creatures Rocky knew too well began to take the shape, "I don't think your two Knights can hold back my Champions and protect the citizens at—" he cut off and growled as a black blot flew into the image for a split second and left just as quickly.

Both Rocky and Apothis stared at the empty place where one of the fifty Necromancers had stood a moment before. Then something falling from above caught both of their gazes as the same missing Necromancer fell flailing through the hologram to the Grotto floor. The empty glyph spots took on a whole new meaning now, and Azoth's recent timing couldn't have been more perfect. The crestfallen and shaken look of Apothis told just how unexpected the resumed attack was as he shouted, "I thought we had killed that stupid flying Lion!"

Rocky couldn't help the guffaw that escaped his lips when he saw Apothis' reaction. The sound of his chuckle still on the air, he suddenly felt all the wind get blown out of his mouth as his back struck the wall hard. Apothis was snarling in his direction and had raised a hand. It had all happened too quickly. Rocky hadn't even had time to close his mouth, so when he struck the wall ten feet behind him with a booming impact, the taste of iron filled his mouth as he bit his tongue nearly in half. His heart sped up from the show of power and his instant recognition of his mortality sneering at him from behind the altar.

"You think you and your foolish pet have won." Another Necromancer disappeared and appeared a moment later, falling back through the hologram. Apothis' scream of frustration told the story that while they might not have won, they had outplayed him in this one moment. Tao and Gamma engaged the Abominations, and Rocky felt like he could feel the ground shudder with each blow. The skill the Knights showed was amazing, but every blow that they made was stopped before it reached Abomination.

Rocky instantly understood what the Necromancers were doing. He had seen it before when they stopped the laser fire of the army from striking the Zombies outside of Chalk River. He suddenly was flying through the air again, and he bounced off a table, hearing a massive crack as his shin ricocheted off of the obstruction to his path. Then he crashed headfirst into the opposite wall. His world started to go black on the edges as he floated back towards the altar to see the face of his assailant glaring at him.

He focused on the fight to push back unconsciousness and not look at his twisted legs. From the pain signals his brain was shouting, that last flying face plant had broken his nose and both of his legs. Perhaps his collar bone as well if he was reading his debuff bar correctly. There were an additional two empty spots where Necromancers had stood before his trip, though. He smiled, and Apothis snarled, "It does not matter if you win a battle. I have all the time in the world to convert you and destroy everything you hold dear." He pulled a Dragon Heartstring off of his staff and held it up admiringly. "With this around your neck, it will only take a single moment of weakness, and you will be the one destroying your friends down there."

Apothis paused and looked at Rocky, whose smile was now a look of utter horror as he came to terms with just how utterly screwed he was. He glanced at his health and saw that he was less than half full. He glanced at the now smiling Apothis and felt his heart stutter. Was this the end for everyone? Had all the people who had died for him died for nothing?

It's tough to win a game when the other team is–

He cut off his depressing thought as his eyes glinted over something on Apothis' neck. There was a platinum chain dangling from his vertebrae, and the pendant that hung down on to his sternum had a stylized Dragon on it. He thought desperately; there had to be a way to remove that necklace. If he got it off and removed the compulsion for the Dragon before placing the pendant in his bag of holding, he might be able to save his people.

It was probably the biggest Hail Mary he had ever thought of, but a spark of hope kindled in his chest. He knew he wasn't going to survive the ordeal, but like Joe had for him mere hours before, he could give his life for others! The thought almost seemed to trigger the warning that came next.

Warning! Someone has touched a place of power under your Territory. This has contested your leadership for Algonquin Valley. To cancel the contestation, destroy the force holding the Altar of Michabo. If you fail to destroy this force _or offer the altar a worthy sacrifice,_ the Leadership of the Territory will be transferred in ten minutes!

9 minutes and 59 seconds remaining.

Now that your Territory is under contestation, all Territorial buffs, Territorial effects, and Territorial systems are currently unavailable to your population or you. To remedy this, capture the contested place of power before the enemy.

He dismissed the message quickly without reading it with a sense of impending doom. If he could somehow remove the amulet; if he could somehow free the Dragon; if Tao, Gamma, and Azoth could somehow take down the Hulking Abominations; even if all of those events went his way, he would still lose the Territory, and his people would need to flee. Would they be able to survive without its protection?

All you can do is try. Try to give them a chance. One final fight.

He pushed uselessly once more against his invisible bonds. Then the hologram showed Gamma get broadsided by an Abomination and crash to the ground. The golem skidded, leaving a furrow and almost crashing into the massive Guild Tent before he came to a stop. Rocky used it as an excuse to close his eyes.

A loud cackle sounded when he did. "Don't want to watch anymore. Don't want to see the end for your Territory! You will be easier to break then I thought!" Apothis exclaimed.

Rocky clenched his jaw in frustration but entered his meditative state, which seemed to erase the pain in his legs and face. Once he had achieved Trance Meditation, he began checking his Ether Channels. They were clean and normal, but he could feel something oppressive just past his skin—something that was like an itch he couldn't scratch, no matter how hard he strained he couldn't reach it.

"You sure you don't want to see this? They finally found a way to attack your winged friend." Rocky ignored the taunt and kept trying. "Oh, and down goes the swordsman again!" Apothis continued, unknowingly reminding Rocky of a split-second moment during meditation.

Rocky began creating figure eights with his Ether channels, and once he had the flower shape firmly in his mind, he sent a tendril outside of himself. When the overload of information came, he was ready for it this time. He was actually surprised to realize his Dark Cloak was still active but compressed down to a minuscule layer, mere nanometres from his skin. Holding it there was a spell of woven Ether that seemed to be red in his mind's eye. He touched it briefly and knew its name—Binding Chaos, a cast spell. The name didn't help him but knowing it wasn't a channeled spell did. Where his Ether touched the web, he felt it tremble for just a moment, and he prayed he was right.

He flexed his finger nearest to the place of contact and felt it twitch before the web strand that held it broke in two. Rocky stopped what he was doing and waited. Had Apothis noticed the breach?

A snarl and scream from the desiccated skeletal creature nearly made him open his eyes. Then Apothis hissed, "So, the Knights hid a few skills from me! It makes no difference that they have regrouped and hide behind a dome shield! That gives my Abominations time to—" He screamed in outrage again and snapped, "Will someone kill that damn bird!"

Rocky felt his body relax the strain it was holding. Apothis was still commenting on the fight which meant he hadn't felt Rocky's tiny escape attempt. It meant he was right, the Necromonger had no connection to his spell.

Swallowing hard, he began slowly pumping his Ether into the nanometre-thick space around his body. If it wasn't for Apothis' spell, he probably wouldn't have been able to do it. The fact that he just needed to allow Ether to flow into the space and didn't have to control it helped him immensely.

His personal Ether began to combine with his Dark Cloak, and at first, Rocky almost panicked, thinking that it was going to ruin his plans. Then he saw that wherever the Ether was combining with the cloak, the cloak was latching on to the spell around it with tiny spikes of darkness. Where the darkness touched, the spell wobbled but was held whole by his own Dark Cloak skill, just waiting for his signal.

Warning! Someone has touched a place of power under your Territory. This has contested your leadership for Algonquin Valley. To cancel the contestation, destroy the force holding the Altar of Michabo. If you fail to destroy this force _or offer the altar a worthy sacrifice,_ the Leadership of the Territory will be transferred in five minutes!

4 minutes and 59 seconds remaining.

Now that your Territory is under contestation, all Territorial buffs, Territorial effects, and Territorial systems are currently unavailable to your population or you. To remedy this, capture the contested place of power before the enemy.

Rocky dismissed the message and kept filling the space with Ether. He knew he didn't have much time, and while he understood the system and its notifications were just following a protocol, he didn't need the reminder!

With two and a half minutes left, he was ready, and he flashed his eyes open to see Apothis studying the battle intensely. There were thirty-two Necromancers remaining, and Tao sat cross-legged beside the Guild Tent with a dome surrounding himself, the tent, and Gamma.

Thinking fast, he mentally groaned when his brain came up with an insane plan to get close to Apothis. Then he forcefully laughed, which immediately drew Apothis' angry gaze. Once Rocky had it, he put on a smile, "Looks like you are going to have to wait for that self-proclaimed victory, Apothis!" he stated with false bravado.

Apothis' eyes widened, and he held up a fist which triggered the spell to bash Rocky's back into the wall ten feet behind him again. He allowed it to happen, trying to bide his time as he crashed painfully into the wall, biting his almost healed tongue again and coughing up blood. He let the blood dribble out of his mouth, not moving his head, as he floated back and sneered at Apothis, "What, you think because Apep gave you all this power, people are just going to let you win? You didn't earn that power; you are just a dirty, disgusting leech on your master's strength."

What little was left of Apothis' nostrils flared as Rocky's broken legs bumped into the altar and began dragging themselves very painfully across the surface. He felt the sharp pain seize his mind, and he felt vomit threaten in his throat as bile rose, but he forced all of it away to look Apothis in the eyes as they came nose to nose.

Warning! Someone has touched a place of power under your Territory. This has contested your leadership for Algonquin Valley. To cancel the contestation, destroy the force holding the Altar of Michabo. If you fail to destroy this force _or offer the altar a worthy sacrifice,_ the Leadership of the Territory will be transferred in two minutes!

1 minutes and 59 seconds remaining.

I have tried to make it obvious, but you are clearly an imbecile. Place a powerful item on the altar!

Now that your Territory is under contestation, all Territorial buffs, Territorial effects, and Territorial

systems are currently unavailable to your population or
you. To remedy this, capture the contested place of
power before the enemy.

Rocky finally read the notification and blinked in surprise. Apothis took the blink as his dominance and jabbed a bony finger into his chest as he used his other hand to place a Dragon Heartstring around his neck. Then smiling devilishly, he spat, "In two minutes, you will lose this place, and I will become the new leader. Once that happens and I convert you to the dark, we will hunt your allies until the ends of Gaia and beyond if we must. Not a soul will escape me!" Apothis ended by widening his arms in a classic fighter's victory pose.

In that moment of prideful arrogance, Rocky broke the spell on his upper body, and with one hand, he ripped the necklace from Apothis' neck. He mentally screamed, "Be free," hoping it would act as a new order for the Dragon. Then he commanded the item to his bag of holding. In the same instance, he had used his other hand to grab the Heartstring from his own neck. Apothis began chanting something as Rocky brought both hands together, one with Heartstring and one with the scale he had swapped the necklace for, over the altar. Then he dropped both, and time seemed to stutter as they slowly fell to its surface.

Once they struck, the altar lit up, and the light was bright enough to occlude the hologram that was still shadowed against the white background. Apothis finished casting his destruction spell, and Rocky felt it strike his chest. His Dark Cloak lit up with sparks on the edges as Apothis began screaming in dark, hot rage. His cloak was fighting the massive, black, spinning ball of the void?

A familiar dinosaur-like roar could distantly be heard through the multiple layers of earth.

Then the momentum of the spells' fight carried Rocky into his close acquaintance—the wall. He hit the wall hard for the fourth time and felt unconsciousness begin to eclipse his thoughts.

Suck on that! You bleach boned–

CHAPTER TWENTY-SEVEN

Rocky was surprised when he opened his eyes. Well, at least, he thought he opened his eyes as the sensation occurred, but the world was still dark. Panic was avoided because he could clearly see his de-buffs, Health, and Ether bars. He glanced up to read some of the de-buffs that were hovering in the top left of his vision.

Cracked Skull
- **Your protection for your brain is compromised and should be given time to heal before you use your head as a battering ram.**
-25% Intellect and Wisdom
Duration: 11 hours, and 4 minutes.
—

Shattered Femur
- **People say that a broken femur is the worst pain a human can suffer. What do you think?**
- **Set the bones to avoid them healing in improper alignments, or use a spell to straighten them.**
-25% Agility and Dexterity
Duration: 1 day, 11 hours, and 4 minutes.
—

Broken Nose
- **Don't panic. It's just that lump on your face. Use a spell or set it to avoid the risk of having it heal crooked.**
-25% Charisma
Duration: 1 day, 11 hours, and 4 minutes.
—

Major Concussion

- **Your brain has always wanted to meet new people, but the inside of your skull wasn't what it had in mind.**
   -25% to all stats
Duration: 2 days, 4 hours, and 4 minutes.

He grimaced at the major problems and checked his health to find it hovering at sixty points overall. Luckily, he had a full Ether pool, though, so he cast Dark Mend as many times as that allowed him. The pain from his legs, nose, and skull all spiked up simultaneously, as the bones ground against each other because Dark Mend began rearranging them to their proper places. He passed out again.

When he opened his eyes again, he was happy to see at least the Cracked Skull de-buff was gone, and he was sitting closer to half of his full health. He renewed the Dark Mend spells and then chugged a Health Potion from his bag. Another fit of pain struck from his femur, but this time it wasn't enough to put him back out.

The next thing he did was pull his light back out and turn it on, illuminating the space he was in as the de-buffs began blinking at him, letting him know they were about to expire due to Dark Mend speeding up his healing. The room was strangely different than it had been when he last saw it. Instead of black and white tile and stones, the room was now covered in dark black Dragon scale. The crevices between them were patched with a red pattern that pulsed when the light touched it; the effect made Rocky reach out and touch the wall to see if it was breathing. It wasn't.

Once the de-buffs flashed and vanished, he used the wall to climb back to his feet. It was strange to see the room so drastically changed around him, and he marveled at the unique pattern that it now made. In truth, it looked even more like a massive starship with the glowing red lines that appeared to be acting as mortar. He moved slowly through the room and looked at the first table he passed, now that there wasn't a mad Necromonger trying to kill him or his Territory–

His body broke into an instant cold sweat. Wait, where was Apothis?

He ran over to the altar, ignoring the tables for now, and placed his hand on it, hoping to summon back the hologram. The table began to shine on its own, and a moment later, he was looking at his whole Territory. He blinked at the detail and realized that Apothis must have zoomed it in before. He did the same using his hands to help his mind direct the image to the proper place.

The hologram was suddenly viewing the entire Grotto and highlighted in red were row upon orderly row of dead bodies. The one good piece of news was that he instantly saw Sela and Smith highlighted in the blue of the living but laying down and unconscious, still in the Guild Tent. Zippo was at their side which took another large worry off of his chest.

At the bottom of the hologram, there rested a count of Territory citizens and casualties, and Rocky's eyes were drawn to the red number. Two hundred and twelve flashed in red for him to see, and he felt his heart plummet. This probably didn't include the military casualties that had been outside the Territory, either.

He had brought these people here and promised them safety. Now look at them. He thought of all the people he had tried to save and failed: Alex, Oliver, Jack, Phil, Pat, Jeff, and now Joe; all of them dead. Could people have done better without him? Why did he bother trying?

Rocky remembered the creatures he had seen and fought on the trip to the Grotto. He vividly remembered his promise to keep the travelers safe and the massive worm that hadn't even attacked the group but killed thousands with its mere presence in the world. This world had become a meat grinder, and the contraption was designed for human beings. How could he seriously hope his family had survived out there?

A tear formed in his eye. His vision blurry, he caught a glimpse of the living people moving around and collecting bodies into those rows, moving debris and cleaning up after the massive battle that must have taken place. On closer inspection, everyone avoided the group of three titanic figures who stood in the west field, examining the cave entrances in the Grotto walls. First was Tao, who was clear because of his massive longsword strapped to his back, he was kneeling and peering into the caves while Gamma, who had his axe shouldered, spoke to the third member, a Dragon. Bathilda sat crouched on her hind legs and seemed to dwarf the two Knights because of her moving and stretching neck.

If you measured only to the height of her chest, the golems and her were around the same height, at least according to this hologram, but if you added her majestic, curving neck and tail, she should be near double them due to the added length. Right now, she had curved her neck up like that of a swan and was clearly looking over the valley with the two Ottawa Knights. To his surprise, Azoth was pouncing at her tail, which she swung around behind her. A surprised gasp escaped his lips followed by a chuckling, "Azoth, stop that! You are going to get pancaked," he yelled at the screen, but the bird-brain just kept chasing and stomping on the Dragon's tail.

Over his maudlin for the moment, thanks to the strength of his people and the antics of Azoth, Rocky facepalmed and wondered how he would get himself another pet when he got back to the surface. He scanned the people and found that while many were cleaning up, many others were cooking dinner, and others were even trying to get back to construction. He zoomed the image back out and found a few more groups had gone back to hunting, and a few had gone to tend the few fruit and nut trees that they had bought and planted in the space across the river.

Rocky was absolutely floored by the resilience of the people that was on display before him.

It gave him hope and the push he needed to get his mind out of his own dark place.

As he zoomed out, he saw only himself down in the tunnels far below the surface, and he tilted his head as he saw just how large and complex the tunnels actually were. In fact, there were levels far below him, but many of them were caved in or dark on the screen. He zoomed out to see the entirety of the network and almost screamed in frustration when he realized how the attack had gained access to the Territory.

This must be why there wasn't an alarm! Wish I had known it didn't extend below ground…

There on the northeastern edge of his Territory, a tunnel ran out of the screen and borders of his Territory. He estimated the direction and distance and had instantly realized that it was the same exact direction that they had found LFD. They should have gone back and explored all those other floors of LFD's old body! Now he glared at the tunnel, which was shaded in orange, indicating itself in a different color than the blue tunnels and space he stood in.

Vowing he would collapse that tunnel, he got back on track and thought about himself. He had truly been ready to die to buy them more time to live. He glanced around the newly furnished room and wondered what had happened to Apothis after his attack had knocked Rocky out.

He checked his waiting notifications in hopes of answers.

For killing 6,125 Undead Creatures: Level Apprentice 12-24: You as part of the party have been awarded 1,323,451 Etherience.

For killing 34 Undead Summoned Creatures: Level Apprentice 18-22: You as part of the army have been awarded 1,422,200 Etherience.

For killing 7 Necromancers: Level Apprentice / Journeyman 19-34: You have been awarded 4,255,312 Etherience.

Your personal Etherience amounts to: 7,000,963 Etherience

93, 935,480 Etherience remaining until level 24.

—

Congratulations! You have sacrificed two epic level items to the Altar of Michabo.

Due to the two associated Epic level items, the sacrifice has been upgraded to Legendary status. Altar of Michabo will now be considered a Legendary Place of Power.

Legendary Place of Power Benefits:
- Access to Territorial Holographic Overview
- Access to Sacrificial Benefits for all Listed Citizens
- Access to Etherience Modulator Settings
- Access to EtherNet (Currently missing Interaction Module)
- Access to Territorial Growth Boon Options Locked Benefits x 25 (Capture other Territories or gain higher Territory level to unlock more benefits)

—

Reconfiguration of Tunnel Design Notification.

- **Due to a more powerful material being sacrificed, the tunnels of Michabo will be reconfigured. During reconfiguration, everyone other than the leader will be removed from the area. For their own safety, anyone inside the complex will be teleported to a place that they deem safe.**

Number of individuals teleported out of the complex: 6
Number of Dungeon creatures eradicated: 1012

He blinked for a moment, trying to count numbers of living people down here when this must have happened. If he assumed that Sela, Zippo, and Smith were amongst the group down here, that made up three. Clearly, he knew Apothis was one of the numbers as well, but those final two made him a bit sick to his stomach. He walked out into the hallways where he had fought Frankie and found the corpses of the four Necromancers and the newly formed hallway where Frankie had been buried.

Are you serious? It saved him from under a cave in… and it took his pet Geomancer?

Rocky clenched his jaw and walked back to the operations room, as he had aptly named it in his mind. As he walked, he continued scrolling through his notifications.

Congratulations! You have reached level 25! You have been awarded 1 Stat point and 1 Skill point.

Congratulations! You have completed a Portion of a Chain Quest!
Chain Quest
    Red Quest
        Party Quest - Druid

Free Bathilda

You and your party have managed to procure Bathilda's contract item, the Pendant of Smog, and remove the compulsion trapping her in place. This quest was considered far outside of your level to complete. Due to its difficulty, Etherience was increased for you and your party.

Rewards:

> Your party has been awarded 200,000,000 Etherience (Each)
> Your party has been awarded 1,000 Crystallized Ether (To leader)
> Territorial Growth Boon Awarded (See list)
> Your Greater Territorial Perk has been deferred until the quest chain is complete!

0 Etherience remaining until level 25.
106,064,520 Etherience banked.
Stasis entered.

—

You have been offered a 3rd part in a chain quest!
Chain Quest
> Red Quest
> > Party Quest - Druid
> > Cleanse the Land

The land around your Territory has been infected by the Irradiated Ether and needs to be cleansed by fire. To ensure that this infection does not linger, remove its source, Apep's Dungeon and its leader. Failure to completely eradicate this plague will result in future attacks on your Territory and erosion of borders.

Rewards:

Greater Territorial Perk
Etherience
Crystallized Ether

Since this is a chain quest, it has been accepted on your behalf by Gaia.

Rocky was shocked to see the list of rewards he had just received, and furthermore, he was pretty excited to see what sort of growth boons he might have access to. He also found it strange that he had entered Stasis again. He hadn't seen that since his earliest levels. Why was it back this time?

He opened his Character sheet, hoping to get to the bottom of the reappearance of Stasis but placed a point in Intelligence, his emerging dump stat.

Rockland Barkclay Level 25
    Class: Apprentice-Dark (Azrael) Revenant,
    Level 1 Strategist
Leadership Class:
Class Skills: Dark Blade, Dark Mend, Soul Blade, Dark Cloak, Shadow Clone
    Health Points = 290/290
    Dark Ether Pool = 220/240
You have 0 stat points and 0 skill points to distribute.
(Assigned and awaiting confirmation.)
    Stamina – 29 (Strength of Body +8)
    Strength – 35 (Strength of Arms +5) (Strength of Arms +16)
    Agility – 41 (Speed of Arms +5)
    Dexterity – 33
    Intelligence – 24 (+1)
    Wisdom – 31
    Charisma – 33

Luck – 10

Weak Skills

> **Non-Class Combat Skills: Combatant –
> 26 (+2), Ether Channels – 22 (+4),
> Ether Cleanse - 10 (+5), Ether
> Manipulation – 24 (+6)**
> **Common Skills: Barter – 8, Camouflage –
> 7, Endurance – 25, Tracker – 16,
> Trance Meditation – 19**
> **Profession Skills: Actor – 5, Butcher – 23,
> Cook – 2, Herbalist – 19, Miner –
> 1, Skinner – 22, Teacher - 18 (+6),
> Trader – 5**

Moderate Skills

> **Non-Class Combat Skills: Stealth – 13
> (+7), Swordsmanship – 9 (+4)**
> **Common Skills: Analyze – 14 (+2),
> Perception – 4 (+1), Sneak – 18(+2)**
> **Profession Skills**

He clicked first on his skills and placed his final point into Shadow Clone. Then he tried clicking the rank up option for his class.

Warning!
Ranking up to a new level can take seconds or it can take weeks. Ensure you are somewhere safe before you perform this action.
Would you like to continue?

Yes | <No>

Rocky selected no. While he really thought he could use the extra power that it would give him and probably even more so the new skill tree it would unlock, right now, he couldn't afford weeks. They had seven days until Apothis would be back to full health, and Rocky didn't intend to give the undead snake the time he needed.

Be careful. It's not like you beat him this time. A few hours ago, you were his little puppet.

Rocky shook his head to stop that chain of thoughts and then stormed out of the room to begin his trek to the surface. He couldn't sit down in the dark all day. It was time to see the butcher's bill firsthand, and since his walk was already as angry as he could make it, he decided to turn it into a sprint to try to help clear his head.

While the trip was drastically faster without enemies to fight and because of his pace, which he eventually pulled back into a fast jog, it still took close to two hours. When he reached the surface, he mentally asked Azoth for a lift and soon was trying to answer questions that seemed to have no connection to each other. "Azoth meet Dragon. Rocky know Dragon? Azoth kill lots of cloakies, did Rocky hear? Why Zippo, Sela, and Smith pop into Guild Tent? Where Joe?"

The last one seemed to puncture a hole in Rocky's chest, and in answer, he could only pat and pet Azoth, who grew distracted and forgot the question. When they landed in the Grotto, Rocky asked Azoth to fly directly to the shop. A few minutes later, they were flying again, but this time, they were headed to the previous Dungeon LFD occupied. Rocky had debated about waiting for Sela and Smith to wake up, but he truly did worry about how many new enemies could flood their subterranean passages if he did. Instead, it was only Zippo and him who made the trip.

They entered the caverns cautiously but soon found out that as far as enemies went, the halls were nearly entirely empty. With just scattered Zombies throughout the myriad of levels and tunnels, Zippo and Rocky made quick work of each floor, placing plasma mines throughout the entire subterranean complex. It was on the fifth floor that they discovered the tunnel that connected back to Chalk River, and they didn't follow it to its end. Instead, they placed a plethora of mines and kept searching for the tunnel Rocky knew existed.

They did eventually find a tunnel that led to another staircase on the sixth floor. Once they saw how deep it went and how many floors it contained, Rocky chose to just plant mines throughout the connecting tunnel and across its roof. He had only purchased one hundred of the devices, and they had cost him nearly three hundred crystals that he had paid for from the two thousand from the chain quest rewards. He had gained some other Crystals from looting Necromancers as well, but in comparison, that was pocket change.

With no more plasma mines to deploy, Zippo and Rocky returned to the entrance and called Azoth back. He returned with blood coating his mouth and carrying the carcass of what looked to be a mutated cow. "This thing tasty. Rocky want treat? Is Rocky good boy?" Despite the role reversal and hilarity of Azoth's clowning, Rocky did want some beef, but seeing the mutated remains of what used to be a domestic creature, he instead asked Azoth to show him the herd.

Azoth obliged, letting Rocky butcher and store what was left of the cow before they took off. Once in the air, Rocky depressed a switch he had purchased with the mines, and the corrupted, black earth under them rippled like it was water, and they had just dropped a stone into it. A few heartbeats later, they were flying over two depressions in the earth that were hundreds of feet deep.

Let's see you dig that out before we come for you, Apothis!

Approximately five kilometers away, a massive herd of cattle grazed on the edge of the black, corrupted grass. Not a single one crossed into the corrupted zone, but near on two hundred of the creatures grazed peacefully. At first, Rocky couldn't understand how they had survived. However, a challenging half moo, half roar sounded from the herd, and three massive bulls trotted towards the area that Azoth, Zippo, and Rocky hovered.

Rocky Analyzed the creatures and instantly knew how they had survived. While the cows themselves were Apprentice to Journeyman rank with levels near his own, the bulls were quite a different story.

Bull
Level 44
Master-Gorer
Health Points 5,750/5,750

"How did you avoid those, Azoth?" Rocky asked, genuinely curious as to the tactics the Chimera had chosen for his hunting. In answer, Azoth mentally showed him a picture of a creature chowing down on a cow to the east, which had the effect of making Rocky look in that direction. Far off in the distance, a massive cat was head deep in a cow. As if sensing his look, the creature looked up and regarded him with purple eyes.

Purple Princess!

Azoth mentally showed him the marks of combat on the cat's body and finally responded, "They too busy fighting black beauty!" Rocky could hear the tones of admiration and wonder in Azoth's mind voice, and he scratched the Chimera behind the ears. For now, they seemed to be pretty well defended, but Rocky would have to put the question to his people if they could find a way to domesticate this herd. He also was pretty confident that Purple Princess over there was a girl and that Azoth had a bit of a crush.

Maybe someone can tame her? Sela can talk to animals.

Having accomplished what he had set out to do, Rocky stopped trying to distract himself and asked Azoth to return home. It was time to address his people. Time to stop avoiding the responsibility he had as their leader, even if he had never asked for it.

Once he landed for the second time in his Territory, he was bombarded with questions about what happened today. Why were they attacked? Who attacked them? In response, Rocky asked the people who were most avid and intense in their questions to gather everyone together. He stated to the group in a loud voice, "When everyone is here, we will go over what happened." Many didn't leave, but some did, and after a time, the others realized he would not answer until everyone arrived, no matter how insistent they were.

There is no point saying twice what hurts to say once.

Rocky remembered the team manager's words to him when he was let go. He smiled at them, now seeing in them the truth that they held. When his team had let him go, they had insisted on waiting for his agent to arrive before beginning the meeting, and now, from his new perspective, he understood the action on a deeper level. In some ways, it was to protect himself from repeating the news over and over again, but mostly, it was to ensure that it was heard by everyone so miscommunication couldn't occur.

His thoughts were interrupted by the approach of Tao, Gamma, and Bathilda, who all were picking their way very carefully towards him. Rocky chuckled, seeing the two Knights trying to clear a path for the Dragon who checked under her belly and then foreclaws before each step. It was like watching one of those animatronic creatures that moved in jerky bursts. To save her from any more awkwardness, Rocky met them about three-quarters of the way; that was just how slow the behemoths were moving.

"Tao, Gamma, Bathilda, nice to see you all! What happened up here once the party left the Grotto?" Rocky called in greeting, face hard, and his voice emotionless. His tone was unintentional, but being back in the Grotto, seeing the death firsthand was making him feel sick to his stomach. The question was easier explained; while he was aware of a portion of events, he wasn't aware of a rather large chunk at the beginning and another portion in the end.

Tao began with the first moments of the attack, "We heard screaming and rushed back from gathering wood. Only a few holes had opened in the South and West walls at first, which limited the enemies' numbers for a time. Gamma bravely shouted for everyone to get in the tent quickly."

Gamma scoffed, then growled, "Stop making it out like I was a hero. We protected everyone but should have been here when it started. We had pledged to be your defenders!" The group was looking at Rocky at that point, and he nodded, unsure what to say. That seemed to be the signal, though, because Gamma continued to fill him in, telling him of the enemy trying a few different tactics to break through to the people in the tent and of some of the braver individuals in the military and outside of it that saw the Abominations were just reforming over and over again and how they had found out fire worked to end that cycle.

Wish I had put it together sooner. I could have told them!

Tao took over at this point, continuing sedately and haltingly about the Hulking Abominations and his decision to trigger his Sanctuary skill. After this description, Tao pointed to Bathilda and stated with a bow, "Bathilda the Dark Scale will tell her tale of great victory from there."

Bathilda blinked at the golem and then turned her massive head to Rocky, who craned his neck straight up to try to meet her eyes. He felt extremely small and silly in the posture, but he held it all the same, not wanting to disrespect the Dragon. "I used my Fire-Spit to burn the undead creatures from the safety of the sky?" she finally added, sounding like she was questioning how great a victory her arrival had really been.

After a moment, Rocky coughed. "Yes, well, that certainly explains why there are two large, charred patches of earth in the Grotto. Thank you for saving my people, Bathilda…" he finished rather lamely, then realized he had five Heartstrings that belonged to her and an explanation for what happened to another one. He pulled the five strings out of his bag and sheepishly began with a clumsy bow, "Umm… I have five more of your Heartstrings… uh… great Bathilda."

The Dragon tilted her head questioningly at his tone. Then she asked with humor lacing her words, "You do realize you saved my life, right?" She bared her teeth at him and continued, "I am not going to kill or eat you after something like that!"

Tao poked her in the side and pointed to her mouth. "You need to work on your smile more. It is more like this." Tao pulled his lips back from his mouth and made a face that could only be described as constipated. Rocky blinked in reaction, trying to understand what was going on.

Bathilda adjusted her lips and looked at Rocky again, teeth further bared, "Is this better?" This time, her nostrils flared, and she looked like she was ready to strike out like a snake. Tao looked at him as well with his constipated face, and Rocky couldn't help but burst into laughter.

For the next thirty minutes, as people began gathering near the stage, Rocky explained what had been so funny and how Tao and Bathilda should never make those faces again. Tao looked studious as he listened to what Rocky listed as wrong with his 'smile', and Bathilda looked embarrassed like she was not used to failing at something. After the explanation finished, Rocky talked to them about what came next and even managed to find out about a quest Bathilda had for cleansing the blight from the land in the area. Her quest even stretched farther as she was expected to cleanse sites like this one all over the world!

Which unfortunately made it so she couldn't stay and help defend Algonquin Valley.

"Actually, it used to be a quest for destroying and cleansing the site of that initial explosion," Bathilda continued after she told him of her new quest. She paused for a moment and looked around at everyone listening to her. Instead of trying to talk more quietly, she increased her pitch, "I originally landed and began summoning my deepest fire to breath it down the massive, steaming crater I had found and deemed to be the cause of the problem." She took in a deep breath like she was going to breathe fire here, and everyone gasped.

Rocky did along with everyone else, but when she continued, he realized she was just an excellent storyteller, "Suddenly, something below me ordered 'Don't move a claw!' and mid inhale, I felt something take hold of me, a magic I had never felt before." She wrapped one of her foreclaws around her neck dramatically and swung her head around in the air like she was being attacked.

"I couldn't move my feet, no matter how hard I fought. My head and tail, though, were my own…" Bathilda continued to entertain the people present with the story of how Apothis had captured her and how she had thought she was doomed. By the time everyone was present, she had reached the point of the story when Rocky had arrived and given her a chance to fight again. It hadn't lasted long, but she had made the most of it, fighting with tooth, tail, and fire until they had finally set up the spell circle again. The way she told the story, she had killed thousands upon thousands, and Rocky again admired her skill in storytelling.

When she ended the story with finally being set free and her eternal gratitude to whoever had accomplished it, Rocky shook his head as he saw the obvious cue, she had left him. He stepped forward with the pendant and five Heartstrings. He reverently placed both hands on her lowered chest and saw the same glowing magic take over, and the pendant begin growing larger and larger until it fit snugly around her neck.

The crowd erupted in cheers and jubilation, and Rocky turned to them a hero who had bad news and some sad tidings, but thanks to Bathilda's help, the blow was muted.

CHAPTER TWENTY-EIGHT

Once Rocky announced what had happened and why their Territory had been under attack, he was surprised and somehow disappointed to find that no one was upset with him. No one was angry with him. The why was rather simple, though, to the people of the Grotto. Everyone across the entire world was fighting desperately for their lives. They had been fighting for their lives for the last month in two locations, and unfortunately, every one of them had become far too familiar with death. There was anger, though, for sure, but it was directed at the circumstances, inwardly at themselves, and in a rare few survivors, at the golems.

Tao and Gamma surprised Rocky by sitting and taking the verbal abuse. Going so far as to, when Rocky went to intercede on their behalf, silence his interruption and allow the grief-stricken citizens to continue. Rocky swallowed the lump that formed in his throat at the scene, and instead of interceding, as he had planned, he went to sit between the two. He felt constant emotional turmoil as so many problems were laid at the feet of the two honorable Knights, but he tried to offer them his support. Even with him present the people chose to berate the golems and not him. He stayed quiet like the Knights and listened because he knew that they were the outlet, but he was the one at fault.

It grew worse before it got better, as the grief-stricken began pulling out hair and running hands over tired faces. He felt something inside himself shrivel up as another woman cried, "We thought I was pregnant. How can I bring a child into this new world without him?!"

He didn't believe she was looking for an answer, and his soul reached out to her. Luckily, another individual reached out to hug her, and they held each other as their world metaphorically broke around them. Rocky swallowed and continued to listen as a burly man forced out, "I have no one left…" He looked around at the other grief-stricken citizens, "How many people have already died? This place was supposed to be safe…"

His anger had been simmering the entire time, but those words engaged a switch inside him; he felt his emotions begin stirring together, creating a maelstrom of hate. Apothis had attacked his home; he had attacked their new home. The only thing that assuaged the firestorm of hate was when he vowed he would never let someone attack this place again. In that place, listening to the cries of people he had tried to protect, he silently swore he would destroy Apothis and any threat to the Valley, even if it killed him!

The scene continued until everyone had voiced their piece; Rocky stood up to help the broken-souled, cried-out citizens back to the Guild Tent. As he lifted the first individual, he was surprised to find Sela beside him, helping. He didn't know when she arrived, but he was happy to see her. She was looking at him with tears openly running down her face. He brushed a hand across his own face, which came away wet, trying and failing to find a bright side in this situation.

After a moment of their eyes being locked, they carried each person who had just lost a part of their very souls back to the Guild Tent. During the screaming, each one had torn out hair, clenched their fists, and screamed themselves red in the face at the loss of their other half. Some of the group women, some men, every one of them equally broken that day. To help with the self-inflicted injuries, Rocky cast Dark Mend on each soul they carried back, feeling it wasn't close to enough to heal the deep hurt they suffered and vowing he would find a better way to help these people.

When they were done, Sela stood beside him, and together, they looked up at the night sky. She whispered, "The first lesson a commander must learn is that a decision must be made logically and quickly." Rocky glanced at her face reflected by the light of the stars and saw that same strength he had seen in her the first day they met. "The second lesson a commander must learn is that once a decision is made, it must be seen through to the end. The last thing a commander must learn is that there is an acceptable cost in every decision and there is an unacceptable cost." She finally turned to him and reached up to place a hand on his shoulder. "Today, you made many difficult decisions, but they were all right decisions. Today, you followed those decisions through to the very end, even putting your life on the line to complete them. And today, we paid an acceptable cost to save the lives of thousands. Today, I am proud to be your..." she took a deep breath and nodded at him, squeezing his shoulder simultaneously as she finished, "I am proud to be your Guide and to follow you."

They stood there like that for a while, and Rocky reached out and pulled her into an embrace that felt right. He didn't realize he was crying at first, but once he held her body close to his and had her unwavering strength in his arms, his shakes and shudders were obvious. Sela held him back and let it run its course, nodding as he recited names on a list that she knew existed but wished didn't until he finally let go of her with an embarrassed, "Thank you..."

She smiled and changed the topic to something different, "I think we have left Garnell waiting long enough, don't you?" Her voice uncharacteristically wavered slightly, and she gave a small cough at the end to cover it.

Rocky smiled, the expression looking odd when paired with his puffy eyes and nostrils. He nodded, and together, they walked to the shop and put on disguises. Once they were in the bazaar and made their way to Garnell, they were surprised that he paid for a private first-class meeting room but accepted the invitation.

Once they were in the opulent private room again, Garnell immediately started to speak, "I have been made aware of veins of information. I should say I have been made aware of a universe-altering Eternium vein of information!"

Rocky blinked behind his mask and turned to Sela confusedly to find her doing the same to him. Rocky turned back and spoke into the silence, "I think that was cryptic enough to leave us a little out of the loop, Garnell. What exactly have you learned, and why does it affect us? Or I guess how?"

"Sorry about that. I can't speak about the information meself yet. I have signed an NDA that lasts two-weeks." Garnell paused with a shrug and then held out a hand. "I am the middleman here. If ye meet with someone who asked me to make introductions, I will gladly share the benefit she had promised me with ye."

Sela tilted her masked head. "Only meet with this person? No obligations besides that? What has she offered you for this arrangement?"

Garnell sure was leaving them with a lot of questions in this meeting. It was strange because excitement and worry radiated from the Karacy in equal parts, and it was clear for everyone to see. Garnell spoke into the silence, "It's a bit open-ended of an offer. First off, it is a favor in return for the information she shared with me." He looked at them sheepishly. "If after ye meet with her, ye feel the information she has for you isn't enough in trade then I will gladly make a deal through my wares or a favor to be named later."

Sela seemed to shake herself as she declared, "We will meet with this person, but we will do so in our current garments. We may choose not to speak with her after her news. If that is the case, we will leave after the meeting and come back to discuss our repayment at a later date, agreed?"

Garnell nodded eagerly, and then his eyes stopped focussing on them as he looked at something in front of himself but invisible to them. After a long few moments, his gaze changed back to them, and he claimed, "One of the other party's people has gone to inform them that ye are here. I doubt it will take very long based on the last meeting we had."

They stood in place awkwardly for a full five minutes, not sure how to react in the strange situation. Sela seemed to choose to stay silent and stoic, and Rocky attempted to do the same. After the five minutes, though, Rocky whispered, "Can we sit down at least?" Sela jumped at the noise, which could only mean she too was a bit out of her depth here.

The group sat down, and Garnell opened his mouth but shut it with a click a few times before he finally started, "Don't worry. I have shared with her nothing about ye. Just that ye may be the people she was looking for." That statement brought more questions to mind for Rocky and did little to make him feel at ease with the meeting.

A multicolored Kobold popped into existence in the room, and both Sela and his heads shot in its direction. Garnell jumped up from his seat, gushing, "Good, ye are here." Then he pulled a chair out from the other side of the table, looking awkward and excited as he moved.

The Kobold sat down and studied the masks and kimonos they wore. After a time, she impatiently asked, "Are you two from the Etherless Void?" In answer, Rocky looked at Sela, and she looked at him. Then they both looked back to the Kobold, and Rocky knew, under his mask, his face was pure confusion, so he assumed Sela's was the same.

The silence stretched for a time, and the Kobold looked to Garnell, who shrugged sheepishly and nodded in their direction. "They have accepted the meeting under the condition that they don't have to talk with ye if they choose not to. Maybe explain the whole situation to them?"

"Where would I even start, Garnell?" the female-sounding voice of the Kobold spat out, seeming exasperated before she took a deep breath and visibly calmed herself. "Okay, this will make it harder, but let's start at the beginning of my story and the plight of my people."

For the next hour, the little Kobold told a harrowing tale of planetary invasion, systematic genocide, slavery, and oppression. Rocky was riveted by the tale she spun, and his heart went out to her and to the other Kobolds who had been nearly obliterated on their own planet by the Guild Collective. That was when the story finally connected itself to them. "We got lucky and found a Territory deep within the planet that the Guild Collective doesn't know exists. Even the Mechano-Lords and their 'technology' can never sense us so deep beneath them." The instant she added Mechano-Lords, Rocky had jumped slightly. It was accidental, but he saw the Kobold's eyes widen in recognition.

"You have heard of the Mechano-Lords then? Perhaps this is the meeting I desired!" the little Kobold crooned as she stared interestedly at Rocky. A moment later, she continued her story, "The Territory has kept us hidden, and thanks to some special skills of our people, we have managed to infiltrate every guild within the collective. We are aware of the missions they undertake and plans that they have for the future." She waved her hand grandiosely in the air. "For example, they recently tried to acquire a new planet to expand upon. The Mechano-Lords attempted to set up a beacon but failed."

She smiled a toothy, tiny Dragon smile at the masked Rocky and Sela. "I have made an assumption that they bit off more than they can chew and in so doing have met an enemy that I would like to make an ally." She finished the last sentence and began clicking tiny Dragon claws on the table. "You see, they had another project that I have been keeping a watch on as well." She took a pragmatic pause the sighed, since neither he nor Sela responded, and continued, "There has been a known area of space for eons, an area that has been a dead zone to any who enter it. This area was named the Etherless Void, and it was a dead zone. Dead, you see, because all technology was based on Ether, so practically all of it was useless inside."

Suddenly, a map popped into the space of the table between the four. The Kobold pointed to a planet that was rather large on the map, "This is my planet, and this was the line that denoted the borders of Etherless Space." She pointed to a long, red line that exited the map in both directions. Sela and Rocky followed her hand as she started pointing to blinking dots that were scattered throughout the Etherless Void. "These were study drones; they have been releasing them ever since they captured my planet. They hope they can discover something in the Void and utilize it for their rise in power and profit. Well, in some ways they have."

"About a month ago, the previously dead Ether batteries on each research vessel began cycling back on and recharging. A few days ago, they had enough power to begin transmitting again." She pointed at the Etherless Void and stated, "Now, the Ether converters could only work if Ether was restored to the Void. Then some new sub-race of humans who called themselves Floor Idians appeared and have been selling powerful Planetary Essence-based potions they call gasoline."

She clasped her tiny hands together and smiled. "Pair all that with the Mechano-Lords failure, and I believe that some planetary gods inside the Etherless Void are coming back to life as well." The Kobold finished her story with her hands held wide open again over the map as the vessels blinked at them all.

Sela touched Rocky's arm, nodded at Garnell, and then vanished. Rocky looked at the Kobold, then Garnell, and then thought 'exit'. As he made the motion, he heard one final statement from the Kobold, "I can only keep the information about the return from them for another week! At most!" Then he was in the pie-shaped room, blinking in the fluorescent lights.

Once they were outside the shop, Sela began furiously pulling off her mask and kimono as she turned to Rocky, who began doing the same. "That seemed to make far too much sense for what I have seen. I wanted to scream at them both! I wanted to demand answers!" Sela stormed back and forth, kimono and mask in hand. "What caused this?

Rocky, who had his own questions, didn't bother with answering hers. "Did she just essentially say we were going to be invaded?" He looked at Sela and took her mask and kimono to store in his bag of holding as well. "You missed the last thing she claimed, too. Supposedly, the Guild Collective will find out the news in a week!"

Sela blinked at him, mouth forming a sneer. "You don't wonder about the larger picture at all. I mean, one-day, boom— Ether is gone. Then billions of years later," she snapped her fingers, "boom—Ether is back. That doesn't make you the least bit curious?"

Rocky blinked at her words and took a moment to think about an answer; "Sela, I am curious, sure, but one of these two happened a billion years ago, and the other could mean we have ships landing to take over in a week!"

"It wouldn't be a week. What do you think? To travel through space is instant?" She glared at Rocky, her anger at his dismissal of her questions clearly getting to her. "Come on! Depending on how far from that border we are, it could take anything from a full year to multiple years to make the journey!"

Rocky scoffed at her, "Yeah, because I know all about Ether space technology. It's not like I wasn't just thrust violently into this world a month ago!"

They must have raised voices in annoyance with each other because Smith, Zippo, and Amber walked up to them and stood in between the two as they both breathed heavily. Once he had a moment to think, Rocky realized this was obviously a sensitive topic for Sela. The question she had asked was the explanation for what happened to her family. This may even be part of the explanation of what happened to her.

Rocky had thought he was logical during that conversation, but now, he saw that his actions came across as insensitive and childish. He turned to apologize to Sela only to see her storming away towards the Guild Tent. His mouth opened but nothing came out as he watched her stride away.

An hour ago, she was there for you, and now, you just blew her off in a moment she needed you!

His mood fell further as he stood and watched her go. Smith interrupted his downward spiral, "It's not every day that you meet a woman like that, is it?"

Rocky nodded, and Zippo chimed in helpfully, "Ewwww gross! That's Sela... Come on. That's just gross." Then Zippo and Amber walked away, following after Sela. Smith and Rocky almost began crying with laughter behind him.

SELA

Within a few minutes, Sela had calmed down enough to think rationally about what had just happened, and she instantly knew that Rockland hadn't ignored the problem like she thought. He truly was acting in something that she used to term 'war mode', only seeing the next immediate problem and not seeing the looming one. Often, when put in a non-stop, stressful situation, an intelligent person will become reactionary instead of being proactive. Add to that the fact that a problem from a billion years ago is so much further removed than something that could be here in the immediate future, and she understood.

Sela understood the logic Rockland was following, but that didn't mean she agreed that it was the more immediate threat. If a catastrophe had happened that literally could put a planetary god to sleep for a billion years, it was definitely the greater threat. To then find out that it wasn't just Gaia who had been asleep but that an entire section of space had been Etherless, that knowledge had shaken Sela to her core.

When she had lived, there was a contingent of Gaia that studied the Ether and how it acted in space. Millenia of studies showed that Ether slowly expanded, almost seeming to flood into channels, rivers, or lakes that would spawn shipping routes, back channels, and universes of new planetary gods. This process wasn't instant as the Ether would need to grow potent enough to support life as they knew it, but then one day, planets just seemed to begin forming around a central, concentrated point of powerful Ether, and soon, new races would join the ever-expanding Etherverse.

Many of the first conflicts between Gaia and Mars had occurred because of the conquest of these new universes and their ripe resources. Then those conflicts escalated as Mars began committing genocide of the local inhabitants of a new planetary god before colonizing. The culture of Atlantis couldn't stand by and watch this happen to more innocent people, and soon, every new planet was put under the protection of the Atlantian flag. It was then quested out to guilds, the Gaian Military, and mercenary forces to repel Martians and safeguard the new Planets.

So Sela was intimately aware of how new galaxies were treated, which meant while she knew they would lose to an invasion force of greater strength than them. She also knew Gaia was not as defenseless as a newborn hatchling planet, and while the invasion could be partially devastating, Sela could also guarantee that the Guild Collective was about to step into a situation they were ill-prepared for.

Thus, it was only logical to focus on a problem that could destroy everything they would be fighting for.

Sela was even more disturbed because there was something sinister that was starting to form in all of her recent 'discoveries'. The lies she had been told when she lived, the

Dungeons, the places of power, the Tectonic Dungeons and even others about Gaia were beginning to stack higher. Why would her family hide so much from her? She had been a loyal commander in the army of the Cathodiem Guild; she had been in line to inherit one of the Seraphim positions and possibly even one day rule as the head of the Cathodiem Guild.

Zippo jogged up beside her, cutting off her internal musings, and she smiled at him, happy for the distraction. "Good afternoon, Jason. How are you doing?" Sela watched as a myriad of emotions played across Jason's face. Sela knew exactly how he was feeling and hadn't needed to ask. How else does one feel after losing a close friend, a father figure, and fighting nightmarish creatures that used to be legends? Her question had been to allow him to talk about it.

"I am so sick and tired of losing people to this Apothis and other evil people." He paused, closing his fist, then opening it to reveal a small Fireball that grew larger incrementally as he continued, "I want to become strong enough to never let anyone I know die again." His forearm flexed, and his fingers began to curl as Sela watched in amazement as Jason began contracting the Fireball into a small shape. "I want to burn Apothis from this world. I want to dig up Corsair and take him apart, melting every piece to ash." The ball flashed for a moment before it changed color from orange to red and then stabilized.

Sela blinked and tilted her head before using Analyze on Jason and gasping at what she saw.

Jason (Zippo) Jackson
Apprentice Red-Fire Mage
Level 24
Health Points 170/170
Strong-Analyze has failed to provide additional information.

She turned to look into his eyes as they reflected the miniature red sun of fire; a tear leaked out of his eye before it evaporated in a quick puff of steam. She put a hand on his shoulder. "Jason, I am pretty sure you will be strong enough before you know it. You just specialized like Rockland, and I have with the Dark!" Zippo blinked and looked away from the Fireball, simultaneously closing his hand and extinguishing the ball. Then he focused on something in front of him which was probably his notification for the specialization.

After he finished, he searched her eyes to see if she was trying to lie to him, to make him feel better. Seeing nothing to indicate the practical joke of getting stronger he thought was present, he asked, "I don't think you have ever really explained to us what that means…" He let the end of his words fade off as he began focusing on something invisible in front of him again.

Sela blinked and thought back, realizing that Jason was right. She had, like many other things, assumed that the knowledge she had grown up with was still common knowledge now. She laughed in realization, finally fully pulling her mind off of her previous negative thought spiral. Smiling with delight, she assented, "That's pretty simple actually, and I guess I should tell as many people as are willing to listen."

She put her arm around Jason's shoulder, realizing he had grown taller again when his shoulder was only slightly below hers and began steering him towards where she could see the Knights near the center of the Territory. Jason smiled back at her, picking up on her change of mood. "Yeah, it would definitely be good to start spreading knowledge like Rock is trying to do with his Montessori sessions."

Sela's smile widened as she recalled another amazing creation Rockland had put in place. The man was far from perfect, but his openness to the changes that the world was going through combined with his understanding of the world that everyone had come from were creating something that she couldn't even hope to have begun. Instead of yelling at him, she should sit and discuss her worries in a civilized manner. He seemed to respond better when you weren't calling him an idiot, even when he was an idiot.

About fifteen minutes later, Rockland ran up to the meeting area, looking excited by the prospect of something that was clearly on his screens. The fact that he was jogging around with a screen open in front of him made her shake her head. Just when she thought he was amazing, he would do something so stupidly childish that oftentimes it reminded her of some of the first lessons, taught as a faux pas, by her tutors. It was somewhat endearing because of the sheer power the man had combined with some of the innocence this seemed to represent to her.

Jason nudged her with an elbow and shook his head before muttering, "Gross…" Sela straightened her head and looked at the young man, smile fading in confusion.

What?

Rockland seemed to almost bounce on his toes as he proclaimed, "Did you see the options for the boon we received!" Sela shook her head while still feeling confused about what Jason had found gross. Rockland continued again, distracting her, "I think this one will finish construction on any project that has been started and has the resources nearby. What do you think?" He sidled up beside her, and Sela began reading the notification he was talking about.

Boon of the Builder Level 1
- **This boon is primarily for the reconstruction of Territories after suffering an attack. If a building has an intact foundation and the material remains relatively undamaged, this Territorial Spell will finish repairs. In the event that the building material is damaged or inferior, the Territory will convert it to the**

strongest stored pattern of material known. Additionally, a conversion effect of material will remain in effect for one year, and construction speed will be boosted by 25%.

This spell cannot stack with any other Territorial Spells or Personal Spells and is only available to those with a Place of Power.

Sela read it and placed a hand on her chin before asking, "Do you think it will work on buildings that were never constructed in the first place?" In response, Rockland shrugged and showed her the list of other boons available, which dispelled her next question of what other choices they had.

After a few minutes of going through the massive list, it was easy to tell why Rockland had chosen the one he had. There were other options with a variety of effects. However, it became clear quickly that the ones that didn't require a place of power were just weaker versions of the ones that did. In addition, many of the other stronger spells had to do with increases to birth rates, Etherience boosts, or increases to stats while within the Territorial borders for citizens. The one he picked was probably the best for their current position.

Sela nodded at his decision. "I am calling an impromptu meeting to explain specialization. Maybe tell everyone about this decision as well?"

Rockland jerked his head back, confused, "Yeah, you haven't ever explained that." He paused and scratched his head. "Sela, one day, you and I have to sit down and discuss the list I have for things I don't understand."

Sela laughed at his look of confused consternation and reached out to place a hand on his shoulder like she had Jason but hesitated before turning it into a punch. "Once we crush Apothis and have a moment to breathe, let's do that!"

Her dismissal of answering some of the questions now made Rockland grow confused again until she turned and spoke loudly, "Hello, everyone. Thanks for gathering again on such short notice. I know today has been difficult, and we will be putting together a plan tonight to make sure it never happens again, at least not from Apothis and his undead scum!"

A small cheer started but died out quickly as Sela continued, "We have a lesson, some announcements, our plan for revenge, and a couple requests of everyone present. I will start out by teaching everyone something that was somewhat common knowledge when I was alive. After that, Rockland will tell you about the system bonuses we have earned and about the attack we will make on Apothis!" This time, a shocked look passed over a few faces before a cheer attempt began again. However, this time, more and more voices added to it until it came from everyone present.

Sela waited as the cheer, which had a bit of a vindictive and angry lilt to it, subsided before continuing, "Today we will talk about specializations. It was theorized that there are untold numbers of paths to take while specializing, and those paths can combine to create some truly marvelous or truly terrible effects." Sela put a hand up to make sure everyone was listening. "I do not mean terrible in the way I have heard some people use the word 'sick'. I mean bad, contradictory paths that can lead a person to depravity of the mind and soul. It is important that you do not specialize in contradictory paths!" A long pause let her point sink in. "Today, I do not have time to list these out in entirety, but they are sometimes quite obvious. Light and Dark, for example. Red and Green. The list can go on."

Sela looked around, watching some nods as people began to see the more obvious opposites. Some weren't as obvious, like Blood and Stone, but she would write them down and post them for people to see. Regardless, it would likely be a long time before someone got a second specialization. After she was sure everyone present was taking the news seriously, she continued, "As for specializations themselves, they are relatively simple to explain but immensely more complex in reality."

"You have probably seen Rockland's Dark Cloak ability or the fact that my vines are pitch black. This is because both Rockland and I have a Dark specialization. Simply put, this adds the element to our skills, increasing their strength in most cases." She smiled, then put up a single finger. "However, this also makes them weaker against certain other specializations or elements. Dark versus Light is again an easy example, in that neither one is strong against the other. However, if a user of Dark creature attacks a Light specialized individual at night, their attacks will overpower the Light's if the skills are at an equal level. If the Light specialized individual attacks during the day, the reverse will happen."

Looks of confusion passed over people's faces, and a disembodied voice yelled, "How do we acquire specializations, though?" Many noises of agreement sounded out, and Sela smiled as she waited for silence to fall again.

Once silence did descend on the clearing, she pointed at Zippo. "Acquiring a specialization will be easy for some of you. Zippo, for example, just gained the Red specialization, which is a particularly powerful path for fire users." Shocked exclamations rippled through the crowd when she indicated the fifteen-year-old. "In many cases, extremely strong emotions or life and death situations will trigger the event. Yet, it was theorized that the higher your personal level is, the wider you have opened the doors within you to allow your affinity to bleed through. So, it is thought to be a combination of the two. Gaining levels and pushing yourself hard in situations that are challenging for you!"

Silence reigned when she finished, and then Tao spoke primarily to himself, "Knightly Orders believe that once a specialization is achieved, it can be increased through training and self-exploration." Sela glanced at Tao, but he wasn't speaking to her specifically. Instead, he was talking to himself as was his way of sharing his knowledge and wisdom.

Sela nodded her head and pursed her lips. "That is a bit of an unknown. Raising your specialization level or strength is definitely possible. It is thought that each specialization needs different criteria to thrive." Sela pointed at Zippo again. "For Fire Mages, they can raise from Red to White then Blue and possibly others. For Light, someone can go from Light to Beacon to Radiant and possibly higher. For Dark, I know they can become Darkened, but I do not know of a third off the top of my head." At this point, she shrugged and made a motion with her hand that signified she was unsure. "Each one of these has been reached in numerous different ways to my knowledge, but Tao is correct in that many people do increase them through many hours of self-introspection." Everyone's head twisted to look at Tao who nodded while looking away into the distance.

She blinked, trying to think if there was anything else to mention, but instead of obfuscating the issue, it was probably better to write down some of the other specializations she knew and allow others to digest the information when they chose. Sela decided she would post a list in the Guild Tent when she could. Since she was finished, she pointed to a surprised Rockland who seemed to startle for an instant before he walked to the front of the small stage to speak of the rest of the issues.

Sela, who already was aware of his announcements, listened with just half an ear as he went through the request for people to place the materials needed for each building they were constructing beside the building sites. He continued to ask them to lay out the foundation for as many buildings as they had available materials, which was a few additional than they had begun constructing thanks to Tao and Gamma. Rockland added in the reason for the request, and Sela saw even some of the most bereft individuals pay attention as what their acquaintances and loved ones had died for was explained.

Then everyone was intensely focused as he explained the attack. Waves of anger and a deeper tingle of revenge radiated from everyone present.

Chapter Twenty-Nine

With everyone working together, they were able to get the current building sites completely stocked with the materials they would have required to finish, according to the schematics. They also managed to outline and lay down a foundation for three additional buildings. Due to the bonus, they were easily able to convince the populace the need for a Town Hall, a Mess Hall, and a Barracks that could house the military. So, with everyone chipping in, they managed to at least pour the concrete foundation on all the remaining construction sites.

Rocky had been ready to initiate the boon after that, but Sela pointed out they should probably at least wait until the concrete dried. This hopefully would ensure the boon spell would see the buildings with a 'completed' foundation. Rocky was a little disappointed until Sela pointed out that if they used the spell the following morning, they might be able to gather materials for two more Longhouses. This brightened his mood a bit making the wait a bit more bearable. They poured two additional foundations just in case, and with the golems' help, they did manage to convert enough wood and metal.

Currently, the remaining members of the A-Team were gathered around the campfire with Sela, Zippo, and Rocky. Tao, Gamma, and even Bathilda were also present, all here to help discuss a plan. Unfortunately, Tao and Gamma wouldn't be able to join the attack, but Bathilda, who had been out most of the day cleansing a large portion of infected fauna with her Dragon breath, would be able to support the attack from the sky tomorrow.

"We know it's a Dungeon that can produce massive amounts of the mindless Zombies. We also know that the Necromancers can use the bodies to create Abominations. Finally, we know that Apothis is extremely weakened because he raised three Champions. Sela, what is stopping him from raising more, though?" Rocky asked the group but directed it to Sela since she was probably the most knowledgeable.

Surprisingly, it was Bathilda who answered, "Well, you did say he had raised three, and each one took half of his health pool to create?" At Rocky's confirming nod, Bathilda nodded as well. "He can raise at most two more, then. In all cases I have seen similar spells used, the individual cannot cast the spell if his health is below five percent."

Sela nodded along. "I agree with that statement. We had a few guildmates who could summon Harpies, Stags, Earth Elementals, and other creatures as well. The ones that required health points were always stronger minions but had severe limitations cast upon them. What other spells did he use, Rockland?"

Rocky blinked and racked his brain for exactly what Apothis had used against him. "Well, he did manage to encase me in some sort of Ether enclosure called Binding Chaos. He also blasted my clone right out of existence without triggering all the grenades and the mine on him." Sela's eyes opened very wide at that statement, but he continued, "He was able to fling me around pretty good like Professor X, too." She mouthed the word Professor X, and Zippo leaned in to explain so Rocky didn't have to stop. "Otherwise, in that last moment, he did use some sort of shadow ball or that erasing spell on me, and he was a Necromonger, not that it tells us much."

"So, once we enter the Dungeon tomorrow, what's to stop it from spawning Zombies beside us continually? Or collapsing a tunnel on top of us?" Amber interjected.

Sela answered, "Dungeons can't access a space directly around a party and thus can't create creatures right around them. Well, truthfully, they can, but the creatures get mutated and twisted, becoming useless, so most Dungeons don't bother. As for the tunnels, think about the tunnels a Dungeon creates as veins or body parts. Theoretically, a person could cut off their arm if it would win them a fight. However, in practice, it is much harder to do. Not to mention the chance that the Dungeon injures itself far more than it anticipated, and it kills itself in the process. Often, Dungeons won't risk it. However, if it does try to, I will be able to feel it and counteract it enough to protect us."

Rocky looked around and noticed that everyone seemed to be determined, and with no further questions forthcoming, he nodded his head and dismissed everyone to their beds. He sat there in the company of Sela, the golems, Bathilda, and Azoth. Azoth walked over and sat next to him, which allowed Rocky to pet the big fluffball, so he did. The group all sat in quiet contemplation of what tomorrow might bring as the sounds of the sawmill provided background noise.

Tomorrow morning, they would cast the Boon spell, and hopefully, the Territory would gain some levels. Additionally, he may finally get access to the Leadership skill tree for Sela and himself. At this point, he was looking for any edge he could get before going up against Apothis. If he was honest with himself, he was scared of taking on the creature on his home turf.

He knew it needed to happen, but to do so in a Dungeon that spat out hordes of Zombies, with Necromancer support, and bosses they hadn't yet seen? The unknown of the whole situation gave him chills. Not to mention the Master class Necromonger himself, who definitely held a grudge against him.

The group sat there, slowly peeling off as they headed to bed until it was just Sela, Azoth, and Rocky. Rocky actually thought he was alone because he couldn't see the Amazonian beauty on the other side of Azoth's bulk. He jumped slightly when her voice cut through the night, "Tomorrow is going to be about destroying the Dungeon. That is the primary goal. If we ensure its destruction, then the Territory will be safe. While it will be very good to destroy Apothis and Frankie as well, we can't put them before our primary goal."

Rocky nodded along as she repeated his own words to the group back to him. "Yeah, but if Apothis or Frankie get away, all our problems could just start back up again," he whined at her, knowing it was a complaint and nothing more.

If they fled, they would need to rebuild their power. The time that awarded Algonquin Grotto would see it much stronger and much more prepared for future trouble. At least that was the hope.

Azoth eventually fell asleep under the starry skies and the pets of his two favorite people. Rocky, seeing this, curled up beside the big Chimera and was surprised when Sela came and laid down in front of him. He raised his eyebrows and blinked rapidly as she laid down and put her back to him, snuggling up tight. Feeling his tight muscles behind her, Sela laughed. "Relax, it is chilly out tonight. Let's share our warmth." Her voice sounded slightly hurt even with her chuckle, but that might have been wishful thinking from Rocky.

Of course, it's your imagination. It's not like she is the one who forgot that she is your ancestor.

He woke up the next morning and blinked the fuzziness out of his eyes to find a peaceful visage of Sela's face looking at him from a foot away. He smiled and considered kissing the top of her head. He figured that might be crossing a line in their friendship, but she was asleep and looked so calm beside him. He chose to go for it and brushed his lips against her forehead.

As he pulled back, he saw her waking up and smiling at him as she stretched, creating long, graceful shapes as she made small noises of pleasure. "Good morning," she hummed.

Finding himself off the hook for the forehead kiss, Rocky slowly sat up a huge grin on his face. "Good morning!" He got the rest of the way to his feet and again marveled at how he no longer had any pain. It had only been a little over a month, but he was strong, flexible, able to sprint for a prolonged period, and jump higher than he ever thought possible.

He took a deep breath, taking in the fresh air that was laced with smells of fire and ash. Then he held out his hand to help Sela up, just as she finished her stretches and sat up. She took his hand, and he pulled her up. Thanks to his new strength, she ended up cradled up against his chest. "Oops, sorry, Sela. I don't know my own strength yet."

She just made a comically sour face, took a small step back, waved her hand under her nose, and teased, "You also need a bath!" Azoth chose to wake up, and he took a sniff of Rocky and joined in on the moment by feigning falling over dead.

"Rocky smell like dead moo-moos," Azoth added as he got up and played the same prank on Sela. Sela fake snarled at the furball and then jumped on him to give him some very interactive scratches as Rocky watched. It seemed that it was hard not to be in a good mood when they were about to cast a spell that would take away months of work and create so much for their Territory.

Rocky did some stretches and looked up at the rising sun. He and Sela had noticed that the Town Hall would carry with it a massive clock tower. Additionally, the schematic had called for a medium-sized bell, which they had put the metal beside the structure for from the leftovers.

The blacksmiths had also discovered how to smelt bronze on their own, through trial and error, but because of the timeline, they didn't have much of the material. It didn't specifically call for any one metal in the construction, luckily, which allowed them to put smelted bars near the construction sites. Here they were again hoping that the spell description would turn out to push the construction through despite the lack of specific materials.

Sela stood up and took a moment to set herself straight before saying, "What do you suggest? Bath first or do you want to go check on the two additional Longhouses?"

Azoth chimed in, "Bath first!" and began cleaning himself with his tongue and paw in perfect mimicry of a house cat.

Both of them glared at him, and Rocky laughed, "Let's go check on the Longhouses first, then head over to the bathhouses. They are on the way anyway."

Together they walked in silence as the morning grew marginally brighter. They passed people who were running around on errands, setting up for breakfast, or in some cases, putting materials in place for the final two Longhouses. "Were they up all night?" Rocky asked with concern.

"I hope that they woke up this morning and started early, but by the look of that one," she nodded her head in the direction of a man who ran by with deep shadows under his eyes, "I think some of them might have been up all night."

As the man came within arm's reach, Rocky held out a hand in the universal gesture of stop; using Analyze, he got the gentleman's name, "Arthur, please tell me you haven't been up all night?"

The man only smiled with excitement. "Well, I have been up all night, but many of us noticed you drinking that elixir you use to stay up. We asked Smith who told us what it was called, and a large group of us purchased a few Elixirs of Shortened Sleep!" Rocky blinked and tilted his head, not seeing why the man would look so tired if he used the Elixir. "Then we drew straws and are taking shifts of sleep then coming to relieve the others. We planned to all get a full night's sleep before morning training. I drew the short straw and am in the group that will sleep last." He took a short pause and looked at the sun. "That should happen in the next half hour, I think."

The A-Team had chosen not to imbibe the Elixirs of Shortened Sleep last night, as had the military. They all knew they might need to be taking Health or Ether potions today and, in some cases like Sela and Rocky, needed the diminishing returns de-buffs to drop off. Rocky looked at Sela, and seeing her amazement, he made a split-second decision. "How many of you were there, and how much did the Elixirs cost?"

Arthur tilted his head and shrugged. "We each bought our own, and it was decided to only have two hundred people work through the night. Only about one hundred and fifty were needed to cart finished material. Only ten blacksmiths could work in the forge at any one time as well." He made a gesture with his hand meaning he was unsure of something. "As well as a few other limitations that were considered. So, two hundred total with twenty-five sleeping for an hour before coming to relieve the next twenty-five. My elixir cost two gems in the shop!"

Rocky smiled and nodded to Arthur, which seemed to be the signal for the man to take off at a near sprint. Blinking after him, it was Sela who broke the silence, "I am assuming you are going to use some of the Territory funds to pay them back with perhaps a bit of a bonus?"

"Yeah, I think the quest rewards were damn generous, and we should probably add a large amount, if not all of it, to the stores. Then we can use it to pay back a minimum of forty-crystals to this group who took the initiative. What do you think?" Rocky answered as he watched the man shrink into the distance, stop at the lumber mill, and then with his shoulders loaded with wood, start to jog back.

They started walking to the sites of the final two Longhouses, and Sela responded as they got there and saw groups of people running in and out of the last remaining construction site, dropping material. "I truly think recognizing the initiative at the meeting is the right decision. Paying them back what they paid is a must, but I think giving them extra might be a bit of a dangerous move." Rocky turned to her looking confused, and she pointed to people who were sleepily exiting the Guild Tent and getting ready for the day. "It sounds like they had to exclude some people from the group due to numerical restrictions and to save on elixir costs. It also sounds like this was a decision made by the populace as a whole to better the Grotto for everyone. I suggest we create quests for things like this in the future, which will let people know what to expect."

He tilted his head, seeing her points, and then he smiled. "I see your points and wish we had thought of a quest last night."

Sela smiled. "We really need to get some administration set up for the guild so that we don't have to."

They continued walking, both contemplating steps that would need to be taken if they did manage to rid themselves of the danger from Chalk River. In Rocky's case, that brought to mind the danger they would be facing later that day. The fact that he was about to bring others into that danger with him and more. Part of the current problem was that his level one leadership class limited the number of ranks he could bestow under someone.

This brought him back to his intended commander's death. Sorrow filled him again, and he seriously considered pushing back the attack to hold some sort of funeral for the fallen. They had discussed this as well and agreed that it was best to hold one after the danger was truly dealt with to the best of their ability. Rocky shook his head and wished for the millionth time since the Ether had arrived for the return of the relative peace the world had lived with before it had changed.

Of course, that wouldn't happen, and he knew it, but perhaps they could achieve something more passable here. That would require him to create jobs, housing, markets, laws, and many staples that societies needed to function. Even with only four thousand individuals presently in the Grotto, there were small problems currently for sleeping spaces, eating times, bathing, and many other meaningless squabbles. Luckily, it had been dealt with by the military and in large part Joe. Now, though, Rocky needed to find someone else who might be able to fill the role of a man who truly had been the most level-headed and genuinely kind-hearted individual Rocky had ever met.

Joe did so much. Not just for the Territory but for me, personally. I feel like we just lost the heart of the Territory. How do you even fill such a gaping hole?

Luckily, they arrived at the residential complex, which broke him from his internal maudlin. It would seem that twelve Longhouses had their foundations poured and material surrounding them to finish construction. This included the seven that had been underway and the one which was a few planks away from completion. Rocky could see that the twelfth and final poured foundation didn't have as many planks and accompanying metal bars beside it yet, but it was nearing its full schematic criteria.

If the numbers were correct on his Territorial Building page and subsequent schematics, the Longhouses could each accommodate one hundred people, meaning that they would still need housing for a lot of people. However, having the tent accommodate two thousand did significantly lower that, and if it came down to it, the tunnels might be functional as living spaces if he rearranged them properly.

However, it was dark down there, and there was no chance for sunlight hundreds of feet below the Grotto.

As long as the spell does what I hope it will! Abra kadabra… nothing!

Rocky chuckled to himself as he began walking towards the river to take a morning bath. He could just picture it now, standing in front of all the citizens, building up a big scene, and then having nothing happen. The makeshift council had deemed it a worthwhile risk because even if the spell didn't complete the buildings, its boons that would take effect would drastically increase construction afterward anyway.

Sela had been following along in silence, and when Rocky chuckled, she had snapped out of her internal musing to look at the man. "Bathe, training, then announcement, or?" Sela queried, trying to get a feel for the intended schedule.

At the sound of the question, he slowed his walk to turn and look in her direction. "I think that's the best option. See you after your bath?" he answered and rhetorically asked, then turned left to head in the direction of the 'men's' bath curtain, leaving Sela to turn right. Sela took a deep sigh looking after him, then shook her head exasperated before walking in the opposite direction to use what society seemed to expect of her in this new world.

After Tao led martial training and Meditation, Rocky got up on stage, accompanied by the council. He stood and felt everyone's anticipation sharpen as he waited for the murmurs and talking to die down. It didn't take long because once people realized he was waiting for silence, they turned to their neighbors and hushed them to speed up the process. Once silence reigned, Rocky held up his hands and, with a huge smile, shouted, "Hocus Pocus!" with a relatively good mimicry of an aged wizard.

He had simultaneously pressed the accept boon option on his open notification, but only Sela could see that. There was a moment of confusion that was visible as it pulsed through the crowd, neighbors turning to look at each other as Rocky's strange choice of announcement reached people's ears, but it only lasted a moment. A heartbeat for Rocky after he clicked the accept button on the notification, he heard or perhaps felt a rumble begin beneath his feet.

Everyone else's heads shot downwards, and Sela smiled, seeing the varying levels of agility come into play, making it almost look like a ripple shooting across the crowd. She could actually feel what was going on in the earth and knew that the rumble was being caused by spectral vines shooting out from the place of power deep below them. It wasn't really moving the earth so much as vibrating with a frequency that seemed to resonate with the earth. Thus, the shaking.

A moment later, the vines shot from the surface at all fifteen building sites and surrounded them in a brown and foggy white dome of tentacle-like vines. Definite movement occurred under each dome, but Rocky couldn't see through the outer layer and into the internal structures that he hoped were being built. Creaks and cracks could be heard coming from each site, and he saw many citizens tilting heads trying to see what exactly was occurring. After ten minutes, people grew anxious; after twenty, people looked to him for answers, and Rocky shrugged before realizing a shrug seemed insufficient to answer them.

So, he raised his voice and shouted, "It would appear that the spell isn't instantaneous. I was going to tell you all to stay clear of the build sites, but I know that you won't entirely listen to that order. So, instead, I am going to say do not under any circumstances attempt to enter the vines or spell. If it is converting perceived resources into building materials, it could mistake you for the latter and kill you." Some of the giddiness of the crowd subsided and was replaced with shudders, but most of the excitement remained. "Go on, then. I know you won't be listening to me for a bit anyway."

The council, military, and Bathilda took the next hour to stock up on necessities from the shop. Then they went over the tentative plan to have the A-Team, Rocky, Zippo, and Sela enter the Dungeon. In preparation, Rocky had even convinced Bathilda to allow him to keep and refill the spell ring with her breath spell.

The military was to stay and maintain a perimeter in what they hoped would be outside of the Dungeon's influence. In doing this, they hoped that if Apothis or Frankie attempted to flee, they would see them and be capable of messaging Bathilda for her help. Bathilda was wearing a tiny radio communication earpiece for just that eventuality.

Rocky didn't really know what to expect from Apothis. Everything to this point, the degenerate had been working from a position of assumed strength. In fact, he would have succeeded and captured the Territory if not for Tao and Gamma. He would most likely still have the upper hand if it wasn't for Bathilda. Now that he was acting from a position of weakness, Rocky didn't put anything past the creature.

Their discussion was interrupted by a commotion that started near the site of the Longhouse that had been nearly completed before the spell began. Zippo didn't even wait for anyone else and took off running towards the noise, finally acting like the child Rocky expected. Azoth leaped into the air, and soon, the entire group was making their way over to the dark building that they saw in the distance.

At first, Rocky thought it was dark because of a shadow, but as he approached, he began to make out a pattern that he thought he recognized. A few meters later, he was certain as his eyes brought it more into focus that he was looking at Bathilda's Dragon scale with the strange reflective coagulant between the joints. In places, the mortar pulsed as people shone lights on it. He glanced to his left and saw the Dragon approaching and wondered if this was going to be a problem.

Bathilda was still mostly pure white scales other than a single stripe that ran down her back of her original dark black color. This building was made from the scales he had stolen from the ground and, as such, was pitch black. Right now, she looked like she almost had a racing stripe crawling down her back. Hopefully, she wouldn't make a big deal out of the stolen scales that Rocky hadn't asked about taking. She arrived first and began sniffing the structure, looking contemplative as the remainder of the council arrived.

"Are these Dragon scales?" Her head swung around until her eyes alit on Rocky, who nodded. "My scales?" Rocky made a face and shrugged, not sure if they were technically her scales. Bathilda saw his hesitation and looked back at them again. "Based on my scales then?"

"Well, you see…" Rocky told the story of his confrontation of Apothis, fully, for the first time. People around him paid rapt attention to his retelling of the battle that Apothis had dominated from the start. How Rocky had managed to finally 'defeat' him was both spectacular and extremely lucky. As he told his story, he saw a few people attempt to enter the new building, but the doors seemed to be locked. He truly didn't care if they did go in and explore, assuming that the building would be relatively empty on the interior.

Bathilda sat down on her haunches heavily and spoke, "I hadn't quite understood my connection to this place or why I was instantly considered an ally when I crossed the threshold." She looked at Sela and Rocky. "It makes sense in a way, but I have neither seen nor heard of anything like this." She paused and placed her foreclaw on the Dragon scale patterned building. "I fear this might make your Territory more of a target from galactic forces." She sighed deeply and met Rocky's eyes. "Dragons have been hunted for material to make armor sets, weapons, and sometimes ornaments. Obviously, Dragons are not defenseless, and while some items do still exist, often owning one will bring the ire of Dragons down upon you as well." Her foreclaw that was still resting on the building, tensed as she emphasized the last words. "Even now, the only thing keeping me from tearing this apart is because I know that you have not killed any Dragons to obtain it, but my soul screams at the sight."

Rocky gulped as her claws continued to flex on the scaled building. A moment later, her claws began to create a noise that reminded him of nails on a chalkboard. He held up a hand and was getting ready to stop her, but Sela put a hand on his arm and pointed at the places her claws were touching. The building wasn't being damaged at all. Small sparks were flying from the contact points, but the scale and mortar of the building were entirely undamaged. Bathilda stopped her 'attack' a moment later and made a whistling noise from the vocal cords in her throat.

Sela smiled at the Dragon and asked, "Done with your inspection?"

Bathilda nodded and stepped back without another word, but a serious look of concentration set on her draconic face. Rocky looked at her for a moment before he went to the door to see why no one had been able to enter the structure yet. As he began walking, Smith ran into view. "You have got to see this!" Then he looked at the building and amended, "After you see that!"

Smith fell in with the rest of the council, and they walked towards the building. Rocky noticed that the construction looked much larger than he remembered it being when it was nearly complete. "Is it bigger than it was before?" he asked the group. Sela nodded instantly, and he re-examined the exterior as he got closer. It had looked small next to a Dragon, but in truth, it was easily a five-story construction now as opposed to the two-story construction that the plans called for.

Come on Harry Potter tent. Come on spatial distortion making it bigger on the inside! Just this once!

Rocky placed his hand on the door, and at first, nothing happened until a notification window popped up in front of him.

Welcome to the Algonquin Draconic Longhouse I

As a leader, you must decide how you would like to configure this Longhouse.
This Longhouse can be used as a dorm or apartment-style living.

Dorm living spaces: 500
Apartment units: 125

Which style would you like?
Dorm | Apartment

In the future, this decision can be changed at the cost of five thousand Territorial Essence.

He blinked at the notice and looked over at Sela, who shrugged, not sure what the best option was. To Rocky, the math was pretty simple. They could take the twelve Longhouses that were being constructed and create six thousand bedrooms that had no areas to sit and relax, or they could create fifteen hundred collections of rooms that may even include a kitchen. His dilemma was that one would create rooms for his entire population when the twelve Longhouses were finished; the other would only create a little more than half if he assumed people would live together in those apartments.

Before deciding, he minimized the window and looked for what Territorial Essence was. It took him searching through a large number of screens, many of which he didn't have access to, until on a faded-out control screen, he saw it listed. When he tried to click on it to get a bit of a better description, it popped up a different notification.

You will have access to your Territorial Management page once you have completed a Town Hall.

Sela had been looking over his shoulder the whole time, so when he looked at her and she shrugged, he repeated her shrug and went with the dorm option. He would have really liked to do apartments from the start, but very honestly, with the remaining three Golem Knights out rescuing more humans who would hopefully soon be civilians, it was definitely better to have roofs for six thousand people.

Sela did chime in a suggestion when she saw his long face as he chose the dorm option, "We could always do six of them as dorms and leave the next six as something to allocate after, or perhaps create one of the remaining six as apartments right away and have them bolster the economy by renting the apartments or putting them up for sale?"

Rocky nodded along and saw a few members of the A-Team look thoughtful or aghast at the suggestions. Seeing this, Rocky amended, "I like that idea. Keep the dorms free for anyone but have something people can aspire to?" That statement changed the looks of indignation to a somewhat disgruntled agreement.

Another notification had popped up and was waiting minimized for him to acknowledge it. He did so.

Algonquin Draconic Dormitories I
- **The reconfiguration of this building will take sixty minutes.**

59 minutes 15 seconds remaining

Followed by another.

Algonquin Draconic Dormitories I
Tenant Assignment Authority: Territory Leaders
Tenants | Guests
\- \-

By placing an individual in the Tenant column, they will have access to unlock the doors to the building. They will be assigned a unit inside the dormitory and be the only one capable of unlocking the door within.

Any Tenant can offer guest rights to an individual or remove guest rights from an individual. If an

individual is in the building and not a guest, they will be notified about the breach. If the situation is not remedied, a quest will be issued to nearby law enforcement or military personnel to remove the intruder. In case of emergency, Tenants can remove guest rights from a person, and the quest will be issued instantly.

Rocky quickly looked around him and spotted the Bachus jacket of Bart from the A-Team. He was a member of the council and was already in charge of training new hunters, organizing meals, the job categories, construction projects and much more. Right now, most people considered him to be the Territory manager and Rocky appointed him access to assign tenants to buildings. He additionally gave him access to put others in charge, assuming that each building would be best served by someone living there having some sort of access.

Bart's eyebrows shot up, and he looked to Rocky after reading an invisible screen in front of him. The man looked surprised by the assignment. "I am pretty busy already, Rocky, but I will find someone capable of completing this task before we leave for the attack." With that, Bart strode off to find someone who would be able to make those decisions for their first building.

Turning to Smith, Rocky raised an eyebrow. Smith seeing his attention, asked, "What, we can't go inside?"

"Not for an hour. What was your message about?" Rocky returned with a shrug.

"Follow me. I don't think I can explain it. It's easier if I show you," was all Smith cryptically responded.

He led the way over to the north Grotto wall, and there stood some very familiar tentacle-like spectral vines. They were actually in two places. One of which was the sheer face of the Grotto in a large semi-circle. Rocky walked over to a vine-free portion of the wall and placed his hand on the surface. "Maximus, can you hear me?"

"Good afternoon, Champion," the stone under Rocky's hand seemed to say to him.

Smiling, Rocky asked, "What are the vines doing exactly?"

The rock seemed to make a throat-clearing sound before Maximus began, "Quite a few things, actually. With my help, they are creating a sewage system that will bring waste from your buildings and outhouses to the north where I can absorb them, clean the water, and then send it back to the river. LFD is also helping build any sewage systems and water systems needed by connecting it to the river. Those vines are deep underground, and you probably can't see them currently, but you will be able to see two large lavatories and bathhouses being constructed near the river. The vines you can see beside you are helping build my interior and entrance. They are quite spectacular, and I thank you for the use of them, Champion."

Smith, Sela, and Rocky stood looking at each other for a moment before Smith spoke, "I think the Dungeons are creating plumbing? But honestly, that seems too good to be true!"

Rocky chuckled, but Sela just stated sadly, "It actually fits to what used to happen in the Shining Citadel. However, at the time, I thought it was cleverly used engineering keeping the city running." Rocky's chuckle cut off when he heard the tone of her voice. It was the same melancholic and bitter sound he had heard the last time Sela spoke about her past. The whole situation was strange to Rocky; something had changed in the tone she used when speaking about it. She used to be proud of her old city, her old guild, and her family. Now, she was unsure of them, at least if he was reading her tone and body language correctly.

Without really considering, Rocky walked over and placed a hand on her shoulder, hoping to comfort Sela. Then to distract her, he smiled and reminded, "We should have leveled up the Territory, though! Let's take a look."

Opening his notifications, he was delighted to see the first message.

Congratulations!
- **You have reached all the criteria to increase your settlement level. Current level two, Stone Age Settlement.**

To reach level three, create a Town Hall, reach a population of one hundred and ensure there is housing for fifty percent of your citizens.

Upon reaching level two, you have unlocked the Leadership Class Etherience bar and Territory skill tree.

Rocky opened his character sheet to see if his Leadership class could finally be clicked on.

Rockland Barkclay Level 25
    Class: Apprentice-Dark (Azrael) Revenant,
    Level 1 Strategist
Leadership Class:
Class Skills: Dark Blade, Dark Mend, Soul Blade, Dark Cloak, Shadow Clone
    Health Points = 290/290
    Dark Ether Pool = 230/230
You have 0 stat points and 0 skill points to distribute. (Assigned and awaiting confirmation.)
    Stamina – 29 (Strength of Body +8)
    Strength – 35 (Strength of Arms +5) (Strength of Arms +16)
    Agility – 41 (Speed of Arms +5)

Dexterity – 33
Intelligence – 23
Wisdom – 31
Charisma – 33
Luck – 10

Weak Skills

Non-Class Combat Skills: Combatant – 26 (+2), Ether Channels – 24 (+2), Ether Cleanse - 10, Ether Manipulation – 24

Common Skills: Barter – 8, Camouflage – 7, Endurance – 25, Tracker – 16, Trance Meditation – 19

Profession Skills: Actor – 5, Butcher – 23, Cook – 2, Herbalist – 19, Miner – 1, Skinner – 22, Teacher - 19 (+1), Trader – 5

Moderate Skills

Non-Class Combat Skills: Stealth – 13, Swordsmanship – 11 (+2)

Common Skills: Analyze – 14, Perception – 4, Sneak – 18

Profession Skills

To his delight, when he mentally clicked on his leadership class, a new screen, similar to his combat class screen, appeared.

Leadership Class
Strategist Level 1
Skill Tree
Current Skill Points to Assign: 1

Skills

Production

- Production will increase the amount of material dropped by monsters who die inside your Territory Borders. In addition, this will slightly increase the rate that your profession skills increase.

0/5

More skill points increase effects. Five skill points needed to unlock subsequent skills in the tree.

Army

- The army will increase the combat skill gains of individuals when you are leading large raids. This will also slightly increase the speed of your personal combat skill gains.

0/5

More skill points increase effects. Five skill points needed to unlock subsequent skills in the tree.

Enlightened

- Enlightened will increase your popularity amongst the people for the good decisions you make. It will also slightly mitigate the anger towards you when you make bad decisions.

0/5

More skill points increase effects. Five skill points needed to unlock subsequent skills in the tree.

Adventurer

- The adventurer will increase yours and your party's Etherience gains slightly when you are fighting together. Inside Cardinal Dungeons, this effect is doubled. Inside other areas of

**interest or non-Cardinal Dungeons, this effect is
increased by fifty percent.**
0/5
**More skill points increase effects. Five skill points
needed to unlock subsequent skills in the tree.**

Looking at his options, Rocky was stuck with a bit of a conundrum. He couldn't increase his power for the upcoming fight. It seemed all he could do was plan to increase his strength in other categories that might greatly help him in the future.

Enlightened would increase his ability to be a competent leader, which he wasn't sure applied to him if he wanted to hand that duty off to others. Army would increase his strength greatly when leading large groups of people, which could be absolutely necessary for the future, but currently, the group was often small that he led. Production would allow his Profession skills to really soar and could make him stronger because of his own crafting, however, again long term. Adventurer was easily the most versatile because more Etherience was something that was always going to be a huge bonus and could help him right away. Well, after he chose to rank up at least.

This also didn't show him the next tier of skills. Each skill had a link to two additional skills in the fog of war, and he really wished he knew what they were. Sela beside him was studying his screen with hers open beside her. It would seem that they had different skills available because of their different leadership classes. Hers was much more reliant on her champion pet, which was very odd since she was her own champion. In truth, her first tier was all about an aura her champion—or she—would be giving off: Fear, Intimidation, Inspiration, or Calm.

Rocky read hers as she read his, and he considered her best options as well. Inspiration or Calm would have been what he leaned towards because people gaining confidence and working harder for Inspiration was an excellent effect to have on party members. Calm was also fantastic, as it seemed by the description to have an effect that would keep people working hard despite outside stresses and factors. Fear and Intimidation seemed to, unfortunately, be effects that would affect everyone around her, both allies and enemies and made them seem like instant dismissals for Rocky.

My mom always said make a good first impression, and I don't think instantly causing fear or intimidation is going to do that.

Sela interrupted his internal musings by saying, "I think you should go with Enlightened. While your other options are all really good, I think having the people in the Grotto happier will be the fastest way for everyone to grow. You have already seen with Derik how counterproductive different opinions on things can be."

Rocky was less sure about her snap decision. While it was definitely a good option, it implied that he would be making a unilateral decision for everyone in the Grotto, which he did not intend to do. Coming from a democratic world and society, he truly believed that a group making decisions could be used to create a better community where everyone had a chance to be represented. He understood that it could also become corrupt but intended to be the council's power check if it did.

He was leaning towards Adventurer or Production. From his point of view, a society which was rich in resources and produced goods would have more income. More income would lead to better luxuries, which in turn, would lead to better living conditions. As for Adventurer, that would be a much more personal reason for getting stronger faster. Currently, he needed to weigh how important it was to have a powerful group of fighters in the Territory versus a monetarily wealthy citizenry, which hopefully would lead to a happier populace.

Instead of answering, he asked Sela, "What do you think you will go with?"

"I need to find out if these auras can be controlled, turned off or on at will, or perhaps have lists of people exempt from their effects." Sela made a motion at her screen. "They are all really effective but to be able to cause intimidation or fear effects will be very useful if I can turn it off or ensure it only affects people, I wish it too."

Rocky figured that was a part of her past life as a Justicar and a leader of armies. She probably could see many uses for such offensive and powerful abilities. He wondered if that spoke to an upbringing difference between them or just a difference of priorities. He did admit that those two were the more powerful abilities if they could be controlled but was wondering if a future surge of the population would make the inspiration and calm buffs viable.

Everything feels like a bit of a cheat, doesn't it? How exactly do all these effects work on others?

To him, it meant that the system was manipulating people's inner thoughts, just like the swearing that he tried not to think about. The fact that this Atlantean system was able to affect people's moods, thoughts, and even change what they said was very disturbing. Rocky had been coping with that by trying not to think about it. Yet, now deciding on skills that would be doing that in his favor, he couldn't help but have the issue at the forefront of his mind.

Is that why I am leaning towards less intrusive skills?

He put that decision on hold for now because he wanted to look at the Territorial Skill Tree as well. It seemed like it would be best to see if any of the skills could stack with each other. That might make his decision a bit easier. Even if they didn't, he hoped it would take his mind off of the invasion of his personal thoughts.

Territorial Skill Tree
Skill Points available: 10

All skills will affect any and all Territories owned by the same leaders. Skill points are awarded at 5 per level in most cases. To discover more, level up and capture additional Territories.

Skills

Stat Boost
- While individuals reside within the boundary of this Territory, all stats will be increased by x. Where x is the number of skill points in this skill.

  0 / 50

At fifty skill points, the skill will upgrade.

Resource Boost
- Every resource that spawns within your Territory will give x% more when collected. Where x is the number of skill points in this skill.

  0 / 50

At fifty skill points, the skill will upgrade.

Etherience Boost
- All individuals who gain Etherience within your Territory will be awarded x% more. Where x is the number of skill points in this skill.

  0 / 50

At fifty skill points, the skill will upgrade.

Growth Boost
- All women will carry to full term faster by a factor of x%. All children will grow x% faster to

maturity. Where x is the number of skill points in this skill.

0 / 50

At fifty skill points, the skill will upgrade.

Well, there was absolutely no way he was going to put any points in Growth Boost. It seemed like it would be extremely beneficial to him if this weren't other people's lives he was affecting. He couldn't even imagine the uproar if people found out that he was fooling around with pregnancy rates and children's growth. If this was a pure game, he probably would take that option. If you consider that you probably gained skill points for each Territory level and that every level would have a population requirement, then this skill was self-perpetuating.

Yeah, I think one rule carries past the apocalypse, and that's don't mess with a pregnant lady.

Stat Boost he could see being extremely effective currently but more so for fighters and, to a lesser degree, crafters or resource gatherers. Resource Boost was something that would benefit everyone equally and so would Etherience Boost. If he was honest, those two also seemed like they would stack with his leadership skills, more so for Resource Boost though; while Etherience Boost would stack, it would only stack for his party.

He asked a question as it came to him, "Will Resource Boost affect how much meat we get from animals, farmed goods from our orchard, as well as things like ore veins, and system loot?"

Sela put her hand on her chin and puffed out her cheeks as she considered, then responded, "I think so… To be honest, though, I really don't know. While I am sure that these existed in all the Territories owned by Cathodiem, I was never consulted on point allocations. I can guarantee that they had points in all categories though!" She pointed at each one in turn. "New recruits were often power leveled through farming Territories we owned. They were stronger," she pointed to Stat Boost, "they would gain more loot," she pointed at Resource Boost, "and they could level faster." She finished by pointing at Etherience boost.

She took a pause then pointed to the last one. "I have spoken with women of the Grotto who think they might currently be pregnant, and I was shocked to discover that they expected their pregnancy to last nine months." Sela looked at Rocky with wide eyes. "When I was alive, women traditionally gave birth in three months, and children were fully grown and matured by the age of eight."

That news of biological growth increases to maturity made Rocky stagger a bit. Add that to pregnancy term decreased, and he honestly felt dizzy, even a bit lightheaded. He knew that one of the groups most affected by the Apocalypse were children under the age of eight and the parents of those children as well. He had blamed that on the system not granting them access until they were eight years old. When he had first considered that age, he had been sure it was still too young but had thought it was chosen to reduce the mortality rates of young children in this world of monsters. Now, though…

You are telling me that they chose eight years of age because most children were fully grown by that time?

He sat down, blinking rapidly as he spoke in a muted voice, "How many Territories did guilds own, or how many did Cathodiem hold?"

"On Gaia? More than a hundred. Across the entire universe? Thousands, I guess. Again, I wasn't really given exact numbers," Sela responded, giving Rocky a concerned look.

With that final bombshell dropped, Rocky sat in silence, considering just how large this world was and how many guilds and Territories had fought for it in the past. Then the universe…

Shaking his head, he croaked, "It might be best to wait for all the buildings to finish construction before we begin the attack. Let's try to take every advantage we can."

CHAPTER THIRTY

The Territory boost spell worked exactly as they hoped it would. By the time the barracks, Town Hall, and other buildings had all finished, they interviewed a few candidates who had wanted to take over the housing assignments. They had decided on Farrah, an extremely stern lady who had been in charge of dormitory assignments at the University of Ottawa before the collapse. Rocky hadn't really loved how unemotional she was, but Sela had instantly backed the woman when she saw just how little bull crap she was willing to entertain.

Rocky flashed back for a moment to the conversation.

"I really think that having emotion involved in decisions on where people live is kind of important," Rocky had responded to Farrah, thinking about how many times he had lived in bad areas in his life.

"If people are going to pay for premium rooms, I will give it consideration, but considering that everyone pays the same, which is to say they get it for free, I will be assigning based on gender to cut down on shenanigans, then age to cut down on neighbors who aggravate each other." She paused for a moment, and Rocky began to open his mouth, but she cut him off, "If there are any troublemakers, cliques, or conflicting personalities, I plan to have their privileges removed after discovering who the offending party is."

Blinking, Rocky had been about to politely dismiss the woman when Sela had chimed in excitedly, "You're hired!"

Thinking about it now, Rocky could only think that something about the woman must have reminded Sela of someone or something from her past. Farrah's class was an Administrator, and Rocky had to wonder what sort of skill tree that came with. When he had brought up his curiosity about some of the class's skill trees to Sela, she had punched him in the shoulder. "Umm, that's a very private matter. When I lived, asking about skill trees and skill allocation was like asking a person you just met to see them naked."

Then what is it like when you have access to others' interfaces?

Regardless, Rocky had immediately converted eight of the Longhouses to dormitories and two to apartments. The remaining two he was going to keep in reserve until more people arrived and he saw the rate people upgraded to apartments. An issue with the apartments and dormitories became quickly apparent after a tour; they were unfurnished inside. The dormitories had a space for a bed, a chair, and a desk inside every room, but that was all. Whereas the apartment had three rooms that were much more spacious and one small room that was clearly meant to be a bathroom. The three rooms of the apartment were a kitchen, a living area, and a bedroom.

You could tell which room was meant to be the kitchen and bathroom because of the roughed in pipes for water, and the kitchen room had a lot more wall sockets. The fact that the sockets in the wall were shaped entirely differently from anything he had seen before had been rather confusing at first, but once Sela had explained, he had realized another problem that they had. No electricity.

He had a single Ether converter that they had stolen from Corsair during his time in Ottawa, but according to Analyze, it was only good for powering one to two buildings, depending on loading size. Essentially, once they returned back from the invasion of the Dungeon in Chalk River, they would need to price out quite a bit of equipment from the shop. Rocky glanced at his total Crystallized Ether and sighed, knowing that it was going to be wiped out by upcoming purchases or damn near close.

There was one good thing that had come from their meeting with the rainbow Kobold and Garnell, though. They knew other Territories and groups were out there surviving. They needed to meet up with them and start working together if it was possible. Perhaps they could even capture more Territories as well since Sela had explained her guild had thousands.

It sounded like the people in Florida had captured a large refinery or something that still had stores of gasoline. Most gas stations at this point would have been reabsorbed or turned to golems, in his opinion. What made gas so expensive though in a universe that runs on Ether?

Another question for Sela when we have made this place safe!

They had given the current Ether Converter to the Mess Hall, considering that it was the only building that everyone would use. Even then it needed to be stocked with all the equipment, utensils, plates, bowls, and cups. Luckily, the common area had rather beautiful tables and benches in black scales.

Speaking of décor, the floor and interior walls of all the buildings were a beautiful, cream-colored wood that was somehow insulated from the Dragon scale exterior. The contrast this gave the black scale benches and tables made the Mess Hall seem much fancier than it truly was.

As for windows in the buildings, Rocky had first believed that they were all windowless. He had been standing in the Mess Hall and examining one of the many areas that seemed to be intended for a window because the interior creamy wood was cut out perfectly in places with windowsills. However, these cut outs only led to the backs of dark black Dragon scales with its red foreign grout. He had been mentally adding in buying glass windows and some sort of high-powered cutting tool from the shop to his shopping list when he had reached out to touch the interior side of the Dragon scale.

A small menu had popped up on the interior of the dark scales. Since notifications were something he was used to every day, he had stepped back, thinking to read the newest message. To his surprise, the menu stayed glued to the interior surface of the window, so he stepped back in and read the options. It seemed like if the building had power, it would give options for the windows. You could adjust the opaqueness of the scales, allowing in zero to one hundred percent of light from outside. You could also set the windows up on timers, which were something amazing to see because they all came with a clock that needed to be set to the current time and day. In essence, you could have the windows close themselves for your bedtime and be an alarm for when you wanted to wake up.

Finally! This means I can probably figure out what time and day it is, but I don't want to have to walk around and find a window to know.

It also gave him a reminder of what every single day of the week used to be called.

Voskresenie (Sunday)
Mōnandæg (Monday)
Mars (Tuesday)
Woden (Wednesday)
Thorsday (Thursday)
Freyaday (Friday)
Saturnday (Saturday)

He turned to Sela. "How did you guys use to tell the day and time? I have meant to ask you this forever!"

Sela nodded to herself. "Well, the day and time are set in the Town Hall of a Territory. Then as long as that Territory allows you access, you can look up its day and time in your interface."

Rocky instantly saw a problem with that logic, "Doesn't that mean that you could set the day and time to whatever you want and from one Territory to the next, it could be different days entirely, simultaneously?"

She shook her head "Yes, that is something that can be done, but most people choose to use the Atlantian Net to automatically set their time and day based on their current geographical location. A long time ago, before Atlantis existed, a place called Asgard came up with a theory for time and time zones based off of Odin's travel through the sky." She pointed to the sun, and Rocky chuckled to himself, putting up a hand.

This sounded very similar to Greenwich standard time, so he interrupted her, "That's good enough for that particular lesson. Most people will be familiar with the idea because we used a place called Greenwich, England and nearly an identical premise." He paused and added, "And most people call 'Odin' the Sun."

Sela just shrugged, not truly caring what people called Odin. Rocky made it a priority to power the Town Hall so he could begin setting up schedules for himself and perhaps others within the Territory. They had also examined the Town Hall and barracks. The Town Hall was a four-story building that seemed to be a massive audience chamber on the first floor. Rocky considered it to be something like a court of law with pews and a raised platform at the front where someone would listen to issues. The next floor had three smaller rooms that were identical to the first but more private and personal. On the third floor, there was a ton of rooms that Rocky couldn't tell the use for because they were empty of furniture. Finally, on the final floor, two massive suite apartments were only clear to him because of the obviously roughed in washrooms and kitchens.

The barracks was quite literally just a four-story building with a massive washroom roughed in on each floor and then large open rooms that Sela informed Rocky would normally have cots. The interesting part of the barracks was that each room had access to an outside door with stairs to the ground to expedite mobilization in cases of attacks. They had placed the barracks' foundation closest to the entrance to the Grotto specifically because of this fact when planning, but he was still surprised by the ingenuity of the creation. In truth, they wouldn't need anything more than a tiny portion of the first floor right now, but in time, they might use more.

Rocky looked back over his notification, truly disappointed that he hadn't gained a level in his Leadership class. He was extremely unsure how he was supposed to be gaining Etherience for his Leadership class because not a single completed building had increased it.

They had increased the Territory level, though.

Congratulations!
- **You have reached all the criteria to increase your settlement level. Current level three, Quaint Village.**

To reach level four, build a Mess Hall and increase the population to two hundred and fifty.

Level 4 – Community Quaint Village

Congratulations!
- **You have reached all the criteria to increase your settlement level. Current level four, Community Quaint Village.**

To reach level five, build a Crafters' Hall and increase the population to five hundred.

He had lots of new building blueprints that came with the new Territory levels, and he had twenty skill points to assign as well. Together, he and Sela had looked through the interface to discover how to begin accumulating Leadership Etherience, but unfortunately, that tidbit of information was either well-hidden or didn't exist. They would have to discover it in time, it seemed. He didn't feel comfortable asking anyone in the shop either, except for maybe Garnell.

Sela explained her assumption that there would be quests or decisions that, when made or finished, may award Etherience. Rocky had theorized that the Etherience would be awarded as things occurred in the Territory. In short, neither of them knew, but they were going to try a great many things to earn additional leadership skill points.

This also brought them back to the Territorial management page. Now that the Town Hall was constructed, he could see a great many options available there. The one that interested him was how the Territory itself gained Ether in its pool. From initial readings he found, this pool could be used to grant short-term boons in spells, build buildings, expand borders, and many other things that weren't as clear.

He smiled and then read down to the bottom of the screen to find how they were collected. He discovered that for every one hundred people, the Territory would gain one point of Ether per day in the pool. Doing some quick math brought him to one hundred and twenty-five days to change one of the buildings from dorms to apartments. They were definitely going to need to grow the population because the spells were ten times as expensive, starting at fifty thousand Ether.

As for the current skill points from his Leadership class, he placed it in Production. His reasoning was simple when combined with their decision to place the Territory skill points all into Resource Boost. These two, in conjunction, would help the Grotto grow and provide for people as they began rescuing them. Those two skills also had the most overlap of domains for a greater number of people, and so Rocky had made the decision.

Now Amber, Smith, Sela, Zippo, Azoth, and Rocky were walking towards the boundary of the Territory, preparing to invade the Dungeon and minions of Apep. The other three members of the A-Team were staying behind. Mr. Pips because he was claustrophobic. Bart to continue to help train and organize the still relatively new populace, and Derik because of his 'exile'.

Rocky seriously considered having Derik accompany the group. After the man had come to the aid of the military and saved the day, they had quietly gone back into exile, which had surprised Rocky a great deal. He thought Derik would have tried to hold it over them and bargain with it. Instead, the four exiles had traveled back with the military and Derik's group, other than checking on loved ones when they returned, left on their own again to fulfill the exile.

The four returning citizens were actually an excellent help as well and were going to help update hunting maps, guard, and train the other citizens. They were higher leveled then the A-Team even, due to surviving out on their own so long. They had refused to join the mission, though, as they had only just been reunited with families.

The army itself had already left with Bathilda and had begun forming a large perimeter around Chalk River. Bathilda had been out of the Territory, cleansing the land for the entirety of the day again, and when she had returned, she had proclaimed it to finally be corruption free but extremely desolate. Reaching the edge of the trees, Rocky felt his mouth fall open at what almost looked like a sooty dessert.

A brief pause followed where everyone in the group looked around in shock except for Azoth, who had probably already seen this particular view on his hunting flights. Rocky was more stunned by the sheer scope of the area that had clearly been set ablaze. As far as he could see, the land was a smoking carbon mess. To him, it truly looked like an apocalypse… but he had read that forest and prairie fires were a good thing for the ecosystem in a long-term view. So, he had hope this would come back flourishing in the future, especially with the system's aid.

Amber tried to lighten the mood. "Well, talk about an oasis, huh?" she joked while looking back into the lush forest of the Territory.

Amber's voice broke the group from their momentary shock, and they all took their first steps on to the dark earth. To Rocky's keen ears, it sounded like he was crushing plastic under his boots; each step let out a whine as the carbon atoms ground together. The ground he trod on was a sobering reminder for him.

I avoided this quest originally to go to Ottawa, and now, everything for miles is dead.

Not that he would have particularly done anything differently; 'there was only one of him' as people used to be fond of saying. Glancing back, he understood Amber's sense of humor when he could see the lush, humongous trees dominating his vision surrounded on all sides by blackened earth. It sure was a good hyperbole for humans currently.

The group passed by two military guards who stood to attention and saluted them until they walked past. In the distance on both sides of this original group, separated by five hundred meters, were another two pairs of military guards. For this trip, the group had chosen to use different channels on the radios. First off, if the fight was above ground and the radios still reached each other, Rocky's group was going to be engaged in fighting and possibly using their communication devices frequently. This would mean that the military and Bathilda may be drowned out or cut off. The multiple channels had been decided after the last attack when Rocky had constantly been interrupting transmissions to update Sela.

Probably because of my bad radio etiquette. Joe was probably the only one willing to put up with it. I promise I will do better, man.

Once the group passed the guards, they began to sprint towards Chalk River. It would take them some time to reach the Dungeon entrances that the Necromancers had utilized in their previous distraction. On the way, Rocky considered the group's current composition.

Smith was an excellent option for creating minions that could tank a vast majority of the damage, and if they died, they could be summoned again. Amber, the only other member of the A-Team still alive and accompanying them, was a close-range melee class who had skills that increased her speed, targeting, and critical hits. According to Sela and Smith, who had fought with the Fencer, she was quite good against living targets that had weak points, but they were all a little unsure how that would function against the undead. Sela was currently in her human form and was going to use her daggers, earth sense, and vines to try to support the team with a bit of range. Zippo was again the heavy hitter for splash damage and would be an absolute necessity since he was on corpse burning duty. Everyone carried a torch and a flashlight; the torch was a low budget firestarter, primarily meant as a backup if Zippo ran out of Ether but could also act as a source of light if the flashlights were all broken.

Of course, there was still himself and his pet, but Azoth was going to have to remain above ground again. It was unfortunate because he had been such a huge help during their first trip to and back from Ottawa. Now it seemed like almost every fight they undertook was below ground. As for his class and how it fit with the current group, Rocky felt like he was a bit more like Sela in that he was utility. He was the only one with a healing skill, but he could also do some massive damage from range or from the front.

They reached the entrances and decided entirely at random to enter the closest one they had arrived at, which turned out to be the eighth from the left. Azoth left the group in a huff and had every member picking chaff out of their eyes for a few moments after he took off suddenly with no warning in a bit of a childish temper tantrum.

Shaking his head at Azoth's antics, Rocky waited for everyone to get their vision back as he stared down into the dark tunnel of the enemy Dungeon.

Looking down into the dark depths of what Rocky could only imagine was going to be similar to his most recent experience in Algonquin Valley, he shuddered. Surreptitiously, he glanced around, looking at each member of his party again. Every time he made a commitment to keep people alive, it seemed to backfire. First with the children he had saved, then the survivors he led from Ottawa, and finally with Joe. A part of him wanted to go the rest of the way alone to avoid any more needless death, but he knew that they needed every single person present if they were to have a chance. His goal was to mitigate those risks as best he could.

I would have taken more if anyone was strong enough and willing. I wonder if I can buy something to cure Mr. Pips. The Dungeons were going to open tomorrow as well which might have been helpful for power leveling.

Sela had informed him that Dungeons can take days or weeks to clear when he had voiced his thoughts of waiting and running through the Dungeons for a few days. No point letting his enemies regain strength.

Clearing his throat to clear the moment of emotion and the threatening lump in his throat, he turned to face front and took a single step across the threshold. Out of the corner of his eye, he felt something move, and his natural reaction was to blink. A sharp force ripped him backward from behind, and by the time he opened his eyes from a single blink, he was on his rear end in the black soot that surrounded the charred stone of the cave.

Sela was standing over him with a hand out. "I think it's probably best that I lead the way, Rockland. That bone scythe trap nearly cut you in half." She gestured past herself back to the mouth of the cave where Rocky could see two clear slits in the wall. Everyone around him was white in the face and looked extremely uncomfortable with what had just happened. Rocky gulped as he took her hand, and she helped him up. Sela smiled. "I didn't expect a trap right at the entrance. I am very glad I was right behind you."

Then she walked forward and examined the floor and the walls of this entrance. A few heartbeats later, a forty-pound stone fell from the roof of the cave and landed on the place Rocky had stepped. Two massive bone scythes shot from the walls with such speed that they just looked like a white blur. Sela reached out a hand and touched the stone, pressing it down, but with the mechanism not reset, the blades didn't trigger again. She stood up and turned back. "I have some experience with this sort of Dungeon, and I need you all to know it is slow going." Looking each member of the team in the eyes, she enunciated every syllable in what came next, "Do not charge any enemies that appear. If they are range, we do our best to destroy them from range. If they are melee, we are going to have to let them close with us. We fight only in areas that have been cleared already, we mark all traps that can't be disarmed, and we disarm all traps that can."

She paused as everyone took a moment to process her information. Jason and Smith seemed to grow calm at the pronouncement. Amber, on the other hand, went pale, and he could see a small shake in her hand. He guessed the thought of dying by a trap underground was her idea of a nightmare. For Rocky, he was glad that they had Sela who had clear experience with something along these lines. However, he could also feel a cold pit in his stomach; it felt like doom, like this was starting out on a very bad foot. He could just feel something was going to go wrong.

Sela kicked off her leather boots and placed them in his bag of holding, to everyone's raised eyebrows. She then walked forward into the cave with confidence. The rest of the group looked at each other, and Rocky realized they were waiting on him, so he stepped in after her. Sela was moving slowly, taking each step with deliberate care and her head on a swivel. Rocky tried to mimic her, and he activated his Dark Cloak to help with the low light. Sela stopped. She called back over her shoulder, "Going to need some light, Zippo!"

Apologizing profusely, Zippo pushed past everyone, including Rocky, before casting a Fireball and having it hover above his head. Rocky walked up beside him to ensure his safety and instantly felt the waves of warmth coming from the miniaturized red sun. The heat was uncomfortable, and he felt bubbles of sweat surface on his skin, but Zippo didn't seem affected by the conflagration.

Rocky, who had been about to tell the young man to stay close, felt the words catch in his throat. The boy wasn't weak anymore, and just being within ten feet of a stable, small Fireball of his, Rocky could barely stand it. Looking to Sela leading the way alone, he forced himself to remain closer to Zippo.

It's just like a sauna, no need to panic. Wait, can I get a sunburn from that thing? Is that why Zippo is so red?

His thoughts were cut off as Sela bent down and put a hand on the floor. Rocky watched as five bone spears came out of the walls on both sides, puncturing the air in front of her outstretched hand. She held her hand on the mechanism and glanced back, "Rocky, could you please cut the bones spears so they no longer come out of the wall."

He moved forward and viciously sliced Dark Tidings through the bones, cutting them cleanly like a lightsaber cuts through steel. Smiling, he nodded to Sela, who then piled the bone spears on the mechanism and continued. Rocky had been expecting constant fighting, but they were nearly a hundred meters in and hadn't seen a single enemy.

At that thought, he thought he saw movement. In the dark tunnels, the enemies were hard to see because they were literally pitch black, but he caught a glint of light reflect back down the tunnel toward them. "What is that?" he asked, hoping to stop Sela. She backed up and got behind him as the creatures drew closer. Once they were in view, he used Analyze.

Bone Reaper
Level 9
Journeyman–Dark Aberration
Health Points 350/350

The four creatures had no skin, and their bones were a shiny obsidian that reflected Zippo's light. They weren't humanoid-shaped in the least, having canine backward-hinged leg bones that propelled them forward at drastic speeds, and their arms from the elbow joint on were curved blades. Rocky literally felt himself tense in fear at the dangerous look of these creatures. He shook it off just in time and stepped forward to slash at the lead Bone Reaper.

His blade was caught on the creature's two scimitar forearms, and he felt a jolt run up his arm from the force of the creature and its speed. Only his increased strength and two-handed grip allowed him to hold on to his blade as he felt his feet slide back. His strike did stop the charging leader though, which forced the following three to try to flow around it close to the walls. That decision cost them as Amber performed a flunge with her rapier-like sword. The strike rang like a bell as it contacted a sternum, and a pulse ran up the blade into the creature arresting its momentum and even flinging it back.

On the other side, they weren't as lucky, Smith cast a Spirit Ball into the space, and the creature ran through it, causing its legs and arms to lock up. It careened forward into a face-plant body slide as the final member of the pack sliced deeply into Rocky's arm, which forced him to let go of his blade with that arm.

Mentally, he screamed as his skin parted and hung open, showing bone and muscle beneath, but he swallowed back the bile and forced out a scream of rage as he pumped Ether into his sword. The initial creature who'd been pulling back one of its arms to strike at Rocky was flung backwards in a screeching cacophony as the Dark Blade skill clashed with its two forearm swords.

In quick succession, Rocky cast a Dark Mend on the arm and saw tendrils of smoke begin closing the wound as he also cast Dark Cloak and Shadow Clone. It was a huge expenditure of Ether, but these creatures were strong as evidenced by his updated Analyze on Amber's target.

Bone Reaper
Level 10
Journeyman–Dark Aberration
Health Points 300/375

Amber was shaking her arm out like the blow bothered her as well. Rocky shouted out to the group, "Focus fire on the one that got through. Get it down so Smith can raise its spirit. I will hold off the others as best I can."

Recruiting tanks! Looking for tanker classes. I will personally power level any tank we find!

Tilting his head back, he imbibed a Health and Ether Potion simultaneously. The taste of vibrant watermelon ran over his tongue, and he felt his arm mend in super speed, skin folding closed and the puckered, red skin beginning to fade. The electric blue lightning nearly tasted fizzy alongside the Health Potion.

He was going to glance up to check his totals when he saw the fourth and yet unaffected skeleton strike at him again. One of its arms punched forward in a piercing attack while the other slashed diagonally. A quick step right away from the slash put him in front of the recovering Bone Reaper and simultaneously forced the creature to adjust its attacks as its own thrust now hindered its slashing arm.

Not that Rocky was an expert, but a single sword was hard enough. He couldn't imagine the difficulty of dual-wielding long blades like these creatures. The entire left side of the creature was exposed, and Rocky brought his blade down on its shoulder and felt the blade chip out a small piece of bone before rebounding. Cursing internally, he jumped back as the now recovered Reaper swung at him in the gap his overhand strike left in his defense. The blades swished the air, and the creature bunched its legs to lunge.

The one he just struck was pulling back for another strike, and he took a chance sidestepping through the space directly in front of the creature while leaving one foot braced on top of the creature's foot. Then Rocky reached out and grabbed the creature's uninjured shoulder and heaved it into the path of the now jumping Reaper.

The absence of the grating of Dark Blade on forearm swords was his first clue that his skill had run out of juice, and the lead Reaper was now free to attack him again. Rocky quickly stepped diagonally to gain the cover of the two other Reapers who'd just collided and gone down in a crash of onyx bones. The third creature joined the pile up a moment later, and Rocky breathed a sigh, thanking all the gods. He now knew that these creatures were unintelligent.

Zippo, who saw an opportunity, cast a firewall in a tight circle right on top of the creatures, and Rocky jumped back as the heat rose and glanced at the other members of the party who had surrounded and were taking shots of opportunity at the final creature. Seeing their fight under control, he turned back and found that the creatures in their panic were only getting more tangled as they began to gain a red heat that suffused their limbs. When the first creature stood up and stepped out of the wall of fire, Rocky was waiting and slashed at it. The resistance from before was gone, and his blade cut through the creature, cutting it in half.

Smiling, he called, "Turn it off, Zippo I am going to step in and end this." A moment later, the fight was over, the creatures lying on the ground dead and the group breathing heavily. "Well, hopefully, raising a few of those creatures will allow us to have them tank from now on."

Smith frowned and pulled his lips back from his teeth in a recognizable gesture before saying, "I have already tried to raise them, but it doesn't seem possible with these things. Maybe because they were just animated bones?"

Rocky felt a groan escape him.

This is going to suck!

CHAPTER THIRTY-ONE

The Dungeon crawl was literally a crawl, and the group was forced to try multiple different tactics that often left them waiting for Rocky's heals to repair damage done rather than potions. Sela felt that this crawl was going to lag terribly, so she quickly 'suggested', "Save the Alchemy Potions for emergencies. Rocky, you are going to have to play healer unless someone else is hiding a skill or talent?"

Everyone chuckled, but Smith looked at the group seriously before adding, "I have a first aid profession–" Sela cut him off with a wave of her hand and a chuckle. He'd offered the same last night, but it was clear that first aid wasn't as effective as a healing skill.

Even with the tactic change and all the traps, there were only two reasons they were still alive. First, Sela found ways to use her vines to hinder the creatures. In the first fight, Rocky hadn't even realized her attempts because the creatures scythed through the grasping foliage quickly. Now though, she would use a vine to trip a creature, and since these skeletal nightmares had no hands, getting back to their feet was proving difficult. Zippo, in addition, used his force shield to stop charging Reapers, and the remaining members took potshots of opportunity.

The second reason was that the groups of Reapers never numbered larger than four. At first, Rocky thought the Dungeon or Apothis would change tactics soon and felt like they only had a matter of time before a flood swept over them. However, they had turned a corner and found two of the packs of creatures fighting each other, and that's how the mystery got solved as they picked off the survivors of the skirmish.

These packs couldn't work together; it was most likely why Apothis and the Dungeon hadn't used them in the previous attacks. While the Zombies were weaker than the Bone Reapers, they were capable of amassing larger numbers and resurrecting them into Abominations. In this case, none of their slain enemies had been reanimated yet.

Zippo attempted to burn the first group of bones to ash, but the bones just grew red hot and never caught fire. The creature's bones almost seemed to be an alloy, but closer to an alloy mixed with clay because they didn't melt either. Regardless, Rocky had been looting each creature and then sweeping the bones into his bag of holding. Beside the onyx bones, the creatures on occasion dropped:

Bone Charm
- **Crafting material**
  - **This charm is already enchanted with some sort of spell to innervate the undead. This may be useful in crafting or understanding the spell.**

Rocky kept track, and only one in ten seemed to drop the item. Looking through the bones after a particular fight, he discovered all creatures had a charm, it was actually their sternum, but in many cases, killing the creatures destroyed the item. Still, they wiped out twenty of the packs, and he carried eight of the strange drops.

The group continued to follow Sela at a distance of five feet, Zippo still taking up the second position. With his force shields, he could literally stop a pack dead and give Sela a chance to retreat and fight from range as the group got into position. The tactic seemed to have become second nature as the next pack rushed towards Sela.

Zippo flung up a force shield, and the group bounced into it, creating fissure cracks all over what looked like regular air until they made an impact. Sela, by that time, was already behind Rocky and Amber, kneeling and casting a single thick vine that shot out of one wall and embedded in the other at knee height before slumping to the ground limply. She had tried keeping it tight immediately in an earlier fight, but the creatures, as stupid as they were, still noticed it and slashed it apart as they approached.

Zippo would cast and lob in a fresh Fireball, not willing to throw the light source, and simultaneously drop the force shield. The Fireball splashed against the creatures, and they would charge recklessly forward to extricate themselves from the splashing fire. Once the pack was a few inches from the limp vine and moving with speed, Sela tightened the tripwire, and the group sprawled out across the ground in a messy tangle.

Smith surprised the group early with his dual spears, throwing them through the creatures into the ground under two of them. The weapons would suddenly extend four curved metal hooks that surrounded the bones and dug into the earth, holding two of the creatures fast. Sela would use vines to wrap rib cages and legs as Amber and Rocky hacked and slashed the creatures until they went still; simultaneously Zippo would firewall a target if he was above fifty percent Ether, but that was rare as he usually unloaded first into packs of the skeletons.

When the battle ended, they looted and moved on, starting to feel like they were making pretty good progress. Sela ensured that they didn't get cocky though with a few words, "The Dungeon is alive, and while it won't collapse a roof on us, that doesn't mean it doesn't have other tricks. Be alert!"

The words seemed prophetic a short, slow walk later as the floor collapsed into a pit, leaving a small walkway on both edges of the hall they walked. As he crossed over, he looked down into the pit and saw sharp rocks and upward facing stalagmites waiting at the bottom, which was thirty feet away. He blinked and thanked all the gods he could think of for Sela's presence.

After many more successfully avoided traps and fights, the tunnel they followed, which led straight for what seemed like kilometers but was difficult to tell in the confines of the earth, finally came to an end that split in two directions. Sela knelt at the crossroads with her hand on the earth and concentrated. After several long minutes of silence, she explained, "This way," she pointed left, "is another long hallway that only connects to the other tunnels for the entrances that we could have come from. This one," this time, she pointed right, "is the same but has a branch tunnel that leads to a room which seems to have no other exits."

She looked at the group seriously. "It could be a trap or a boss room we have to beat to move on." Her face grew solemn. "If this is a delving Dungeon like LFD, that is a relatively common occurrence." She put up a finger. "Unfortunately, this could also be a puzzle Dungeon due to the number of traps, and in that case, there is something we are missing. The key."

"What is the likelihood of each, Sela?" Rocky queried, trying to discover something logical he could grasp.

"Well, puzzle Dungeons have no boss level monsters, which we can agree Zombies and these Bone Reapers are not. They often have something that leads you to know it is a puzzle Dungeon as well. In this case, the traps are a possibility." Sela shrugged. "We may have to trigger every trap in all tunnels to find the key or to open the path past that room."

She licked her lips and tilted her hand back and forth in a comsi-comsa gesture. "Boss level monsters also rarely leave the room they are created in because if they die outside of a room, then they are unable to be resurrected as they were." She put a finger up and smiled. "Also, if a boss monster leaves its chambers, the rewards increase drastically, and the Dungeon is theorized to have to create a new boss from scratch instead of resurrecting the old boss." She finished with a shrug, telling Rocky that she really didn't know if the last part was true or not.

"How far to the room?" Rocky asked, and Sela informed the group it was very close, maybe five minutes away. So Rocky made the decision, "I say let's try to get a look into the room first then. If it has a boss monster, we can attack. Sela, if we enter the room without the key or the exit open, will it trap us in?"

Nodding, Sela grimaced in what looked like an apology. "Unfortunately, the answer there isn't clear. First, a boss monster sometimes spawns when you enter a room. If it is a puzzle Dungeon though, then it is a very good possibility it will lock us in as punishment, yes." Rocky growled, seeing the problem they now faced.

He was forced to change his mind. "Let's stop by and look in if we can, but I think we have to clear all the tunnels and traps to play this safe." His voice wavered with the frustration he felt at the possible delay.

His frustration grew as the group was looking into the boss room. Sela pointed at a point on the floor and stopped the group cold. "There is a door right there that is triggered once you enter the room." Only a narrow area of the room could be seen from this distance, and even though they had Zippo lob Fireballs in, no monsters came out.

In the end, they'd been forced to backtrack and fight their way through all twenty of the tunnels, disarming every trap and killing hundreds of packs of the Bone Reapers. It was slow going, especially because as the only healer, Rocky had to take extended Ether breaks, which probably helped Zippo as well. In fact, it was probably one of the slowest and most frustrating days Rocky experienced in this new world. They cleared twenty-one-kilometer-long tunnels of packs and traps.

At the last tunnel, he had exited and gotten a final update from Azoth in the dark of night. Azoth had exuberantly told him, "Bathilda and I race. We see who faster to circle Territory, then black sooty land. She won, but she say Azoth is strong flyer!"

It was great to hear that they hadn't seen any sign of movement above ground throughout the day or twilight. They'd set up the circle perimeter specifically for early detection of an invasion when the strongest in the Territory were away trying to clear the Dungeon. Unfortunately, this was the last communiqué they would have, and if Apothis was smart, he would bide his time. That being said, the Golem Knights and Bathilda would hopefully be more than a match for him.

There were a few upsides, though. Rocky's bag of holding was definitely starting to weigh him down with all the bones he stored after the second tunnel, and after a quick discussion, he'd run outside and dropped all the bones in a massive pile. He requested an update from Azoth, who happily flew down, "No hides or eyes of anything, Rocky! You all done now?" Rocky felt his brow furrow at the creature's mixing of common idioms.

"The saying is 'not a hide nor hair', Azoth, and unfortunately not, buddy. We are going to be down there for a few days, but I will come out and say hi every few hours now, okay?" he responded while reaching up and petting the creature's chest. "Do you think you and Bathilda can bring these bones back to the Grotto?"

"Azoth thinks Rocky wrong. Hides have hairs… Scratch higher and bring Azoth treat?" The birdbrain offered his thoughts in such a way to make it an ultimatum for carrying the bones. Rocky laughed and agreed wholeheartedly. After he scratched the creature thoroughly, he'd re-entered the Dungeon and gotten back to work, stopping every two tunnel clears to get updates, unload bones, and pet Azoth.

By the end of that day, the group was exhausted and standing back out in front of the room with all traps now sprung. In the room, no exit opened according to Sela, no key magically made itself known, and the group now stood deliberating in confusion. "If we enter and it traps us, can we tunnel out?" Smith asked.

Sela nodded, but her face scrunched into a grimace, "Yes, but it will take quite a while. Longer than a week, definitely." Everyone groaned and looked confused, knowing she could move earth as a Druid. She saw their confusion and elaborated, "Dungeon's don't like their interiors redesigned. I would be fighting against something to dig through, and this door takes up the entire hallway we just walked down."

Rocky looked back at the five hundred meters of the branch hallway, seeing the problem and trying to get the conversation back on track, "Should we maybe take turns sleeping, then?" Sela started to shake her head, and he cut her off desperately, "We could use the elixirs and sleep in pairs? If it is a boss room, I don't know if we should go in this tired" He looked around at the exhausted faces of the group as he spoke.

Amber and Smith even nodded, but Sela finished shaking her head emphatically. "If we pause for too long here, the Dungeon can start respawning mobs and traps under Atlantean Code. Additionally, every delve or puzzle Dungeon must provide a safe haven in a boss or puzzle room for a full rotation after a group defeats it." She pointed into the room. "So, it is better to defeat whatever is in that room first, then take a break."

Shit.

The group was silent for a long time, no one able to come up with any other questions. Sela nodded once and then held up a hand in invitation. Rocky took it, and he held his up to Zippo. Soon, the whole group was holding hands for support as they stepped across the threshold.

CHAPTER THIRTY-TWO

As they walked over the threshold, ticking clicks sounded, and Rocky felt his hand clench. Beside him, Sela punched him in the arm. "You are stronger than you look. Let go of my hand if you are going to try to break it!" He felt his cheeks flush and looked over to his other side where Zippo was wearing a slightly pained expression. He released his vice grip on his hand as well and apologized to them both.

The group continued to walk forward and entered a large, perfectly circular, cathedral-ceilinged cavern. It would have been beautiful if someone had chosen to give it any semblance of décor. Instead, it only had a raised stage to the left side of the entrance that spanned a quarter of the space. Sitting on a chair on that stage was a black-robed skeleton holding a very familiar staff. Thinking it was Apothis, Rocky used Analyze and wasn't sure whether to be relieved or nervous from what he saw.

Rattleshirt
Level 22
Journeyman–Master of Bones
Health Points 1,250/1,250
Boss

Pretty sure we just wasted that whole day because this is a boss room. Stupid delving Dungeon making traps. Honestly who does that?

He knew he was just tired and complaining about anything at this point; if he was honest, a few people in the group leveled from the grind, and that was a good thing. Rattleshirt planted his staff with a boom and pushed out of his throne. "Finally, Apothis got to have all the fun and leave the Dungeon! But not Rattleshirt!" The skeleton's jaws clacked together as he spoke, making it seem like someone was using him as a puppet.

"No, Rattleshirt, we need you to stay and guard the Dungeon. Apothis is special, Rattleshirt. He is a Dungeon boss, yes, but also a minion of Apep." He accompanied his speech with a raised hand that mimed talking at him.

Zippo beside him looked at Rocky with a raised eyebrow, cocked his head, and pointed at the eccentric creature with one finger, seeming to ask, 'what in the abyss was going on?' Rocky shrugged in answer as the party pulled out weapons and started to get ready for combat.

Rattleshirt finally 'remembered' them and shook himself. "Right! Time for Rattleshirt to shine!" He raised both of his arms and the staff. Four red streaks shot out from its head into the far side of the circular cathedral from the stage.

In along the wall where the red streaks struck, four Bone Reapers began to take shape, coming to life from the stone beneath them. The bones were literally forming from the obsidian stone of the room. With each bone created in their slowly forming bodies, the room gained a bit more size. He shook himself and screamed, "Take them out before they form! Amber and Sela, you are on the boss!"

The group, having fought together the entire day, jumped at the commands. Zippo Firewalled a forming creature in one corner, and Smith threw his two spears at two others, knocking them off the glyph that a charging Rocky could now see under their feet. As soon as the creatures were dislodged from the spell and the formed bones were pinned to the wall, they stopped drawing materials to themselves. Mid-charge, Rocky changed tactics and shouldered his target off the spell. His creature was knocked free and stopped forming but began slowly walking back to the spell circle in nightmarishly uncoordinated steps.

Rocky saw that he wouldn't be as useful as another member of the party and yelled, "Sela, switch! Keep them off the spell circles."

Sela had been trying to stab Rattleshirt when his order came through. The boss skeleton batted away her strikes with his staff and did the same with Amber's thin fencing blade simultaneously. On the run, Rocky summoned his Shadow Clone and saw it blink out of sight as Sela disengaged from the boss monster. Rattleshirt saw an opportunity now that he was only facing one opponent, and he released his staff with one hand and shot that arm forward towards Amber.

Out of the ground at Amber's feet, an obsidian spear shot upwards and nearly skewered her heart. At the last second, Amber jumped up, and then with a screech, the spear shot through her leg, arresting the leap. As Rocky closed, he saw Rattleshirt prepare to strike at her again, this time using his staff to bat at the awkwardly hanging form of a screaming Amber.

Still eight feet away, Rocky cast Dark Blade and used a single Ether-charge, targeting the base of the obsidian spear and Rattleshirt since he was stepping forward to attack. Rattleshirt just managed to change his attack into a horizontal block as Rocky's vertical dark phantasmal strike began screeching against his magical staff. The strike pushed Rattleshirt's feet back and simultaneously broke the obsidian spear, unceremoniously dropping Amber to the ground in a tangle of limbs. He used a quick Dark Mend on her and rushed by.

To buy the A-Team member time to get back into the fight, Rocky went all out as he closed. He struck with his Soul Blade in a diagonal slash, planning to cleave through his own Dark Blade skill. The red staff pulsed, and Rattleshirt tilted his weapon to deflect his original Dark Blade into one of the walls where it dug into the rock and changed tone to an eerie wail. Rocky's diagonal strike made it through, however, and broke the creature's clavicle before rebounding and bouncing the flat of the blade harmlessly off of the head of the creature.

Both combatants staggered from the blow, but Rocky got his guard up first as Rattleshirt shot the butt of his staff at

Rocky's head. Angling the blade, Rocky deflected the strike over his head and riposted towards the boss's ribcage. Since the Dungeon boss never reset himself from his first strike, Rocky's strike hit and broke off a rib bone. This time, though, Rocky pulled back his strike and entered his guard again.

Rattleshirt shot his hand towards Rocky, and seeing the familiar motion, he leaped to his left before setting his feet again and chopping vertically down on the arm. His blow broke the skeletal ulna, and again, Rocky didn't follow the attack up, instead choosing to return himself to center. Out of the corner of his eye, he saw Amber chugging a potion and the others keeping the skeletons off of the glyphs.

The fight continued like that for a few short seconds, with Rocky chipping away at Rattleshirt, keeping the boss distracted. Then a healed Amber and his clone entered the fray simultaneously. Based on the timing, it seemed that the Shadow Clone was waiting for an opportunity to do the most damage. As Rocky jumped backwards to avoid an awkward vertical strike from Rattleshirt, Amber lunged forward, hitting the boss in the sternum, and sending a skill pulse through the creature's bones. With uncanny timing, two black daggers attempted to sever the cervical spine that held the boss's head.

It was a masterfully timed strike by both of the combatants, and Rattleshirt definitely felt something as his body shuddered. Instead of his head popping off, as Rocky kind of hoped for, a pulse of red magic jumped from Rattleshirt's body and flung all three of them away. Rocky and Amber were catapulted off the stage and landed on their backs with a sharp exhale as the breath was forced from their lungs by the hard floor. His Shadow Clone bounced off the wall behind the boss and came down hard but didn't disappear.

On the stage, Rattleshirt lifted his staff, and it began pulsing with a red aura. They were all forced to look away as the brightness overwhelmed them. A moment after he averted his gaze, Rattleshirt cackled and shouted, "Come to me! Transform!"

The red pulse shot out from the staff as it began to crumble into dust, impacting on the wall with a rush of air. The two Dragon Heartstrings that adorned the staff quickly wrapped around Rattleshirt's wrists. Then a few things happened in the comparative dimness that followed. First, the bones that were still attempting to form Bone Reapers and the ones that Zippo heated up until they were blood red and immobile flew towards Rattleshirt as he continued to cackle. Second, a bunch of small holes opened up in the circular cathedral in the direction of the tunnels they just fought through.

Rocky blinked as the bones started to form something that looked like two massive shoes. A moment later, some tiny chips and bone fragments began zooming in through the holes in the domed ceiling. They joined the other few bones and finished forming a pair of massive shoes that seemed welded to both of Rattleshirt's feet. To prove Rocky's thought wrong, both of Rattleshirt's feet slipped out of the encasement as he continued to cackle. His body rose to hover fifteen feet in the air. He held both his arms out in a move that seemed to exult in power and closed his eyes.

Rocky looked around nervous, but nothing else seemed to happen. At least he couldn't see anything else.

A tense minute followed in which Sela, Zippo, Amber, Rocky, and Smith stared at the cackling form of the hovering boss. Everyone took their eyes off Rattleshirt simultaneously and looked at each other. Zippo shrugged and then threw a Fireball at him, testing the situation. On impact, the boss's eyes snapped open, and in screaming agony, he fell the fifteen feet back to the ground with his black robe alight in red flames.

The group approached the smoldering and screaming corpse in confusion. Rocky used Analyze.

Rattlegore
Level 22
Journeyman – Obsidian Bone Apostle
Health Points 110/12,500
Boss
Burning

Not sure what changed but not willing to let the creature back up and into the fight once more, Rocky decapitated the cervical spine of 'Rattlegore'. The screaming cut off and grinding stone could be heard in two directions as an exit and the entrance reopened. "Umm… was he expecting all of the Bone Reapers' bones to join him and create a massive bone suit?" Rocky asked, sounding confused.

Zippo nodded, facepalming a little bit, having his errant thought confirmed by the question. At everyone's nodding head, Rocky reached out and hugged Sela, lifting her off the ground as he laughed. "Thank you, thank you, thank you, oh my god, thank you!" His voice was getting more manic the more he thought about the consequences of the alternative.

Sela swatted his arms away until he put her down. As she dusted herself off, a smiling group of others all patted her back in a much more subdued form of gratitude.

Then Amber interrupted, "So, any good loot?"

Rocky reached down, touched the cooling corpse of Rattlegore, and thought loot. He didn't receive anything, which caused him to blink in surprise. "I don't think there is anything on the corpse other than these two Heartstrings?" he responded and quickly placed the items into his bag of holding.

Sela shook her head and moved over to the boot and touched it. A moment later, she was holding a chest piece that was made of dark black bones and seemed like it would be tremendously strong. "Technically, this was the boss," she stated as she rose to her feet. "You all okay if we hold on to this and tell you what it is after we have a person in the shop unlock it?"

Rocky Analyzed the item as Sela held it.

Rattleshirt's Breastplate of Protection
- **This breastplate is made from a bone so dark it is nearly black, and appears to be unbreakable.**
  Quality: Good
  Stats: Unknown

Amber put a hand up unashamedly. "I think the material that bone is made of will be better protection than my current chest piece. Think I could at least wear it until we are done here?"

Rocky looked at her current armor. His jaw clenched, remembering whose it had been before it was gifted to Amber. Currently, Amber was wearing Oliver's set of gear. It was the same set that Sela wore currently. In fact, Rocky left an additional set of Alex's back in the Territory along with all their current Crystallized Ether.

Sela answered Amber, though, "While the tensile strength of the material may be stronger, currently, it can't draw on Ether to fortify it. So, unlike the Bone Reaper's obsidian bones, this won't turn a blade." She pointed at what Amber wore. "Trust me when I say that is better."

Amber blinked, fingering her leather armor that seemed far too soft to her fingers, brain trying to compute the changes to the world and nodding after a time.

The group took some time and looked around the room. They found it to be entirely empty, despite Rocky's gamer hope for more loot or chests. After that disappointment, he began pulling sleeping bags out of his bag and setting them out as Sela pulled out more premade travel bars that they purchased in the shop and had been eating all day during breaks to regen Ether.

They hadn't expected them to be needed but luckily bought fifty of them, mostly because the merchant's description for the item was, "Total meal replacement, dude!"

Sela put the chest piece in the bag of holding and pulled out a few sleeping bags. Smiling, Rocky took one of the bundled up, deflated items from her. He had been amazed by the item when he purchased it. It was definitely not the sleeping bag he was used to from his childhood. He turned a small knob on the side, and the contraption began to expand with air rapidly.

After approximately thirty seconds, the contraption was set up and ready for someone to sleep within it. It honestly looked like an inflated tent that was made of reflected aluminum. Inside, there was an extremely comfortable pool-shaped air mattress, approximately the size of a queen-size bed. While the roof only allowed him to crawl in, it was the mattress itself that made the contraption expensive. The pool shaped mattress had a jelly-like substance that was filled with nanobots. Once you laid down, it would form perfectly to your body, cover you up like a blanket, maintain your perfect temperature, act as a pillow, and even clean you as you slept. All of that folded down into a square that was about the size of a purse, and Rocky couldn't be more amazed at the contraption.

By the time he broke himself out of the moment of reverie, everyone had a 'sleeping bag' set up, and they were all standing around munching on a meal replacement bar. Sela hadn't started yet and had instead chosen to kneel down to be in contact with the ground. Rocky walked over, unwrapping his bar, and asked, "Can you tell what's down there?"

Sela didn't answer right away. Instead, she took a few more moments kneeling before she stood up and dusted her hands together. Turning around, she firmed her lips. "No idea on what creatures are in the next area, but it is a straight shot tunnel to another room like this one. The tunnel descends slowly another few hundred feet, too."

Rocky, who was just happy to take a break and rest after the long day, responded with a full mouth, "At least we know it's a delving Dungeon, right?"

Sela nodded, and a small smile touched the corners of her lips. "You do have a way of looking on the bright side, at least for a Dark specialized class."

The group surrounded them, and Rocky looked around at everyone. They all survived to this point, and he really wanted to somehow ensure that they all made it through to the very end. He opened his mouth as he pulled out an Elixir of Shortened Sleep, "If we—"

Sela placed a hand on the vial and interrupted him, "I don't know if we should use the vials. While it may speed up this trip, it will also reset the counters on our Toxic Blood de-buffs. I currently don't have any stacks but want the possibility of gaining them to drop off overnight." She paused and looked at the group; everyone but Zippo raised fingers, signifying how many stacks they had.

Only Amber had more than one, and that was due to her most recent brush with death. Amber spoke sheepishly, "My Toxic Blood timer won't drop off for twelve hours, though?"

Sela nodded. "This place, by Atlantian law, is now safe for twenty-four hours." She paused, and her head fell, and voice grew deadly quiet, "I have slain many Dungeons in my time, and I have also made the mistake of pushing forward at speed when this refuge was available." She looked back up, and a sheen of water was covering her startling blue eyes. "It was never the right choice."

In the silence that followed, you could have heard a pin drop. Sela continued after a time, "We still have time currently, and if time becomes an issue later, that is when we should push on." People finally started shifting awkwardly after she broke the awkwardness with her follow up. The group quickly disbanded for a time as everyone went around and took care of their own business.

About thirty minutes later, everyone finished going through their notifications, character sheets, and their skill and stat allocations, so the group met to say goodnight before each member climbed into their 'sleeping bags'.

Let's hope this Dungeon follows the rules.

Chapter Thirty-Three

The group woke up the following morning and ate another meal replacement bar. Following breakfast, they went through a Meditation and group training session as they would have if they were back in the Territory. In truth, they were waiting the last few hours for Amber's Toxic Blood affliction to wear off.

After training, they still had about two hours to kill, so Rocky brought up the little iridescent Kobold and her message. "So, what are we going to do about the Guilds and their possible invasion?"

Sela looked at the group and saw the confusion of the others, and so before answering his question, she rehashed for them their meeting in the shop. Afterward, there were a few people who panicked. Amber must have forgotten, or not listened during the meeting, because she shrieked, "We only have a week! I mean that would have been good information—"

Rocky cut her off by chuckling, "Don't worry; they still have to travel here, so it is going to be longer than a week." Sela gave Rocky a look full of mirth, and he pointed at Amber surreptitiously and shrugged, trying to convey that he wasn't the only one who thought they would just warp in.

Listen, I bet any human who is up to date on sci-fi shows thought the same thing.

Sela did respond after the panic died down, "I truly don't know what the best way to handle it is. We have no military might, and while we may be able to learn some more information from our little friend, I don't know how much help she will be." Sela licked her teeth, and her face grew pensive. "We could always go back and try to destroy the beacon. Now that we have the Ottawa Golem Knights, they might be able to command the other boss golem to drop the beacon?"

Rocky considered this and thought it was probably a pretty good idea but then realized Sela had continued talking, "… the old Gaian Military would have been a huge deterrent for any invading fleets. I think they had five Leviathans and an entire fleet. I mean, if the Kobold tells us a timeline, we might be able to build a few ships but nothing major."

It was Smith who chimed in, "Are there any other weapons that could deter invasions? I mean, we used to have nuclear–" He cut off as he looked around him in a dawning moment of comprehension.

Sela shook her head, "Unfortunately, we don't have any Epic or Legendary ranks to rely on. I mean, in a year, we might barely push someone into the Master rank, but that would be a stretch. Unfortunately, in those guilds there must be some very powerful upper brass, I think."

Rocky tilted his head. "What about Bathilda?" His voice sounded hopeful even to his own ears.

"Not possible. Bathilda is very powerful, but she is under contract with Gaia, who will want more life on her planet. More life for Gaia means more Essence, she doesn't care one-bit what race that life form claims." She paused and then intoned, "My grandfather used to say, the concept of ownership was made by the weak to hold on to what they have. The strong never have to worry about property, for they hold everything if they wish it." She took a significant pause, looking at everyone in turn, then breathed out, "Gaia is very much like that. This whole planet is hers, and we just live on it."

The group all nodded along with her statement, each finding their own meaning in the anecdote. Rocky chose to break the silence, "Well, is there a possibility of something ancient still being on the planet? Something like a military outpost or a defense system that just needs the power turned on?"

Sela chortled, "Well, we would have to find Atlantis before we would know what may or may not have been left behind."

The group all shook their heads, all having heard of the myth of the Lost City of Atlantis, but Rocky had to wonder if it was somehow discoverable now that Ether returned. Perhaps they could find it, but where in the world would they even start?

"My affliction just dropped off," Amber punctuated as she shot back to her feet and dusted herself off. "Are we ready to go?"

The group got to their feet and slowly made their way to the open exit. Sela raised a hand stopping the group. "If we leave this room, it loses its status. Anyone needing to go to the bathroom or collect themselves, now is the time!"

A few members, including Rocky sheepishly, took the opportunity to head to a faraway wall and relieve themselves. After they all returned, Sela nodded and moved forward in the lead, exiting the room into the new hallway. As soon as she crossed the threshold, a roar sounded, and bare feet slapping on stone could be heard echoing down the tunnel.

Oh, great! Here comes the meat wagon.

Surprisingly, what came into Zippo's reddish light wasn't Zombies, or perhaps they were Zombies, but they weren't the Zombies Rocky had been expecting. Instead, these pale-skinned creatures were far larger than the hordes they fought recently. Each creature stood a full shoulders, head, and neck above Rocky, and he was six and a half feet tall. The creatures also moved much faster and had far superior coordination than the creatures they fought through to get to the place of power.

Zippo didn't hesitate, and as Rocky used Analyze, he cast another Fireball and launched it.

Goliath Zombie
Level 33

**Journeyman - Einherjar
Health Points 1,400/1,400**

The Fireball splashed over the creature and crawled over its skin, splashing on to the other five who followed. Those were the ones Rocky could see, and the sounds from the hallway made him think a whole lot more were en route. Each creature did catch fire, but all that seemed to do was enrage them as they picked up speed. Rocky yelled, "Force shield!"

Zippo's hands shot forward, and the lead flaming Zombie hit the solid air a moment after, sending massive, veiny cracks spidering out in all directions. The second one hit the barrier, and it collapsed in a sound like a popping bubble combined with breaking glass. Sela tried her vines, but the creatures were so stable on their feet that the vine pulled taut then rang like a broken string instrument as it snapped apart.

Rocky stepped forward and slashed the air using Dark Blade, trying a single charge of the skill. One of the other Zombies, still on fire, took the horizontal slash to the upper thighs. The blade spell cut flesh and tore into the creature until they could hear it scratching against bones. The creature, however, hadn't remained idle; it reached down and grabbed the blade with both hands, then… turned it, vertically. Suddenly, the creature was holding the dark phantasmal slash in front of it in flaming, skinned, and bleeding hands, as it fought back against the skill.

At first, Rocky couldn't understand why it had done what it had. Then the other Zombies, a few still burning, swept by it on the sides. Breathing out in shock, he cast his Shadow Clone and prepared for a hard fight by dropping into a ready fighting pose, sword above his head. Smith cast a Spirit Ball which hit another creature in the chest and stopped it dead as it slowly sunk into its skin. The one he struck looked down at the smoky white ball in confusion as the others streamed around him, continuing to advance.

In his ready position, Rocky waited and swung as the newest frontrunner came into range. His blade met with an outstretched arm and lopped it off cleanly. He sidestepped and used his lowered hips to knock the massive creature off course. It careened off his hip and into the wall as he swung a return upward stroke at the next approaching Zombie, attempting to break the charge.

He fought desperately from the chaotic center of three Zombies, one so completely ablaze his fat was dripping out of gaping wounds. Amber, his clone, and he were in a rough triangle, and each enemy attempted to wrap deadly, long, pale fingers around any body part they could. His Shadow Clone was on his left, barely holding them off of his rear with his two black daggers. Rocky managed to 'disarm' another one and stab the burning one in the eye before he felt the inevitability of disaster.

Surprisingly, it wasn't him who broke the tide of the battle. It was a screaming Goliath Zombie as it exploded into flying shrapnel that destroyed three of its brethren who were in tight confines. Since those groups were being held back by Amber and Sela, a recent addition to the line in cat form, it, unfortunately, meant that they also felt the sting of bone shrapnel. Luckily, their armor and raised arms, or paws, took the worst of it.

Smith realized at the same time as Rocky that it was the one he had hit with the Spirit Ball. From that point on, the group changed tactics. Smith immediately hit another Zombie with Spirit Ball, and the group slowly retreated, trying to cluster more Zombies around the unlucky undead. This hallway was far wider than the previous entry halls, and they only had about ten feet of the length before it would open back up into the cathedral space.

Rocky tried to estimate the time and guessed it had been about twenty seconds from the time the ball had sunk into the

Goliath until the first explosion. With slow steps backward, the group swiped out, trying to trip up the massive monsters. At the count of seventeen, he turned and yelled, "Run!"

The group took off in the other direction, attempting to cross the cathedral room to the other entry hallway.

Cool kids don't look at explosions. Cool kids don't look at explosions.

A scream sounded behind him, followed by another soundless explosion, which really ruined what he was going for. However, when he made it to the other hallway and turned around, he saw chunks of creatures populating the doorway into the cathedral. Two legs were still upright in the space, and they both slowly tumbled to each side as he watched.

Then a horde of the creatures began streaming out of the doorway. It was shocking to Rocky, but he was glad Smith kept his cool. Smith shot three Spirit Balls into the horde that erupted from the mayhem, all of them fanning out. Rocky resumed his count and shouted to Zippo, "As the lead ones get here, Force Shield!"

"I'm out of Ether!" Smith shouted as soon as he finished. That meant that after this, they would have to try to hold them back and slaughter them some other way. Zippo timed it perfectly, and the group's charge was broken in the doorway. The group started their slow retreat down the skeleton section hallways and at the count of nineteen, Rocky commanded, "Cover!" and put his arm up over his eyes and head. Three screams rose to a crescendo, and then he felt a few bones ping off his Nanoweave covered arm and frontal armor.

In the opening that afforded them, Rocky dropped new MKZ turrets and heard the batteries begin ionizing and firing. The shots hit the lead Goliaths and singed a few holes in them but otherwise did little damage. In moments, the Goliaths knocked over and destroyed any functionality the turrets had and kept charging. In response, he growled and hucked a few grenades with underarm bowling throws at the corner of the hallway where the wall met the floor, hoping that they would make it the full twenty feet to the entrance but at least past the soon to be flattened MKZ turrets.

Smith chugged a second Ether potion, and Rocky declared, "If this works, try to avoid more of those. No need to get or stack the debuff higher." At his mental count of five, he again covered his face with his arm.

This blast was much more powerful than the Spirit Ball assisted explosions. It rocked the group as two miniature suns bloomed, one at the entrance and another fifteen feet away. Rocky felt the blast punch him in the chest and push him back on his behind.

When he stood up, he could still hear the angry slapping of feet, so the group continued this tactic, using Spirit Balls every fourth wave and grenades the rest. It took what felt like an entire day and twenty of their plasma grenades but probably was actually only an hour before they were left with two final creatures to dispatch. A paltry two Journeyman creatures were not as bad, and together, Amber and Rocky tag teamed them with support from his Shadow Clone. Once they swept them up, Rocky breathlessly huffed out, "Mind burning the corpses, Zippo? We don't want them to be raised into super Abominations"

Zippo nodded, finally having something to do. His fire had only seemed to make the creatures more dangerous, and Rocky even heard the kid muttering about making his Fireball explosion as strong or stronger than the fusion grenades.

He began burning the creatures as the group caught their breath and cleaned bits of bone, brain, blood, and viscera off themselves. Rocky felt his gag reflex come to the surface when he discovered a tooth lodged in his beard beside his mouth and further when he found a shard of bone sticking into his butt and skin like a splinter.

Talk about a pain in my ass!

Sela was probably the worst of the entire group, her feline hair liberally coated and tangled in copious amounts of gore, but she seemed to ignore it with ease. Rocky cast Dark Mend on every member of the party, dropping his Ether bar below half again before it started its slow climb back up. He'd been healing and chugging the Ether Draughts that entire time.

The group walked slowly through the cathedral room, ensuring that Sela and Zippo didn't miss any loot or cremating any body. The last thing they wanted was to be caught in the middle of an ambush. For loot, the bodies gave a few pieces of cloth material and some nonenchanted weapons. The occasional corpse contained ruby or other 'valuable' stones, but those seemed uncommon in the sixty-plus bodies they looted.

As they neared the exit door, Smith stepped forward. "Hold up. Now that I have Ether, I should try to raise two spirits if I can."

Smoky mist began rising from the center of the gore until they formed two misty copies of the Goliath Zombies they faced. Rocky felt a smile touch his lips; they had tanks again. With plodding deliberation, Sela and Zippo cleared corpses until they were standing back in the exit hallway.

Sela moved back into the lead at this point and took a few tentative steps forward down the sloping hallway. Another hundred yards in, there hadn't been a single trap, and the group's tension was palpable as they waited for something else to occur. What felt like hours but was definitely only ten minutes later, the group reached the next cathedral chamber. Rocky wiped the sweat from his forehead and realized he was holding his breath.

He shook himself, starting with his head and then moving to his body and finishing with his hands; he saw most others in the group do the same. It turns out that being deep underground, waiting for an attack can be a little disconcerting.

Sela looked back to the group and shifted back to human. "Well, we must have killed all of the creatures at once. Does everyone have full Ether?"

Everyone nodded, so once again, they linked hands and walked forward into the room. As soon as they crossed the threshold, they heard a grinding begin again as the entrance sealed itself behind them. This time, the room didn't have a stage, and the walls were ringed with weapon racks—all of them were empty except for two, which held a massive axe and sword. Leaning against the wall between the two, a truly huge humanoid lounged, arms folded.

A deep, thundering, Nordic voice reverberated from the cross-armed figure, "Finally, a worthy challenge! I have been getting very sick of battling those brainless Goliaths." The figure stepped forward, and Rocky used Analyze.

Ragnar
Level 45
Journeyman – Vanir
Health Points 2,900/2,900
Boss

Rocky couldn't help but step back as he saw the bloodlust and glee in Ragnar's face. It was the first time he'd seen anything like it. He could tell from that one look that it didn't matter how much pain Ragnar was in, he would be having fun. To prepare for the battle, Rocky summoned his Shadow Clone and got into a ready stance.

Ragnar smiled and held up a hand. "Hold! I have a proposal. Would you care to hear it?" Rocky felt his face crinkle, and he sneered accidentally, not trusting the Apep-aligned creature. Ragnar saw this and belted out a laugh before calming and continuing, "I do not like my situation any better than you do, young man, but Apep consumed my world untold millennia ago. And it has been a long time since I have been spat back out of his chaotic darkness. Give me the chance to follow my true path to glory again."

The group looked at each other, not understanding what the boss was getting at. Sela, however, tilted her head and crossed a fist over her heart before bowing her head. Ragnar's eyes opened, and he mimicked the gesture, saying, "Blood and sacrifice teach more thoroughly than time!"

Sela raised her head, eyes resigned. "No fight is inevitable until it begins," she whispered, then turned to Rocky. "May I borrow your sword?"

Unsure what was happening, Rocky tilted his head and looked at the sword he held in his hand. "Sela, what exactly is going on?"

"He is proposing a duel. It is a duel to first blood drawn. The victor can ask a boon from the defeated within reason," Sela calmly explained while pulling one of her daggers and still holding out a hand for the sword. Rocky looked around at the others who all looked as apprehensive as he did about the situation.

"Why don't we just fight him normally?" Rocky asked.

Sela's mouth twitched up on the sides, and she whispered, "We might do that anyway if he wins. I do not follow the path of the warrior. Experience tells me that this may give us a safer and easier option."

Ragnar pulled the massive sword from the weapons rack and was doing some stretches and warm-up exercises while he waited. Rocky swallowed and held out his sword to his Ancestral Guide. Sela took the blade and handed it right back. "Make it lighter and finer, but keep it the same length." He did as she asked until she was satisfied. Then she took the sword back. Once it was to her liking, she performed a few stretches and swings of her own. When she was done with her own warm-up, she smiled broadly at Rocky's sword, and he felt his eyebrows rise.

As Rocky watched, Sela looked to Ragnar and crossed her mithril dagger with the Soul Blade, Dark Tidings. Ragnar touched the flat of his massive, notched sword to his forehead and then sprang forward at Sela with a speed Rocky hadn't expected. He watched as Ragnar chopped down with a vertical swing that Sela sidestepped effortlessly.

To his surprise, Ragnar's blow seemed clumsy and off-balance. However, Ragnar smiled broadly and stopped the wild swing halfway to the ground. His front foot was set at an angle, and he pushed off of it to change the strike to a horizontal blow at the retreating form of Sela. Sela firmed her lips and used a cross guard to catch and then deflect the massive sword.

The power from the strike forced her to step backwards, which made a follow-up strike from her impossible. Ragnar pressed forward, bringing his sword to a vertical position in front of him before stepping towards Sela with his left foot. He turned his wrists as he moved and brought his left elbow in close to his body. The effect was that his blade turned, and his step into Sela's space brought his sword in a fast twist at her right side.

Instead of deflecting as Rocky expected, Sela stepped to her right, Ragnar's left, and the blow missed her by inches. She shot out with Dark Tidings, and Ragnar torqued his waist. The ringing of sword on sword clanged and reverberated through the room. Now though, Ragnar was off balance, and Sela struck out with her dagger in a piercing strike.

Ragnar released the sword with one hand and deflected Sela by striking her forearm with the back of his. Sela grunted but turned the deflection into a roll, coming back to her feet in a ready position and back in balance again. Ragnar didn't put his hand back on his massive sword and, instead, began wielding it as if it was a one-handed sword instead of the two-handed long sword its massive size warranted.

Then the two were moving again in quick questing strikes, each attack seeming to flow into the next. At one point, Sela had literally been forced to leave the ground with her feet, and if Rocky's eyes had been correct, she used Ragnar's front leg as a springboard to disengage from a tangle of limbs. Ragnar, who seemed like a clumsy oaf at first, was something entirely different.

He wasn't fast at all. In fact, Rocky assumed Sela would win numerous times based on her speed alone, but Ragnar would take one purposeful step forward, and his bulk would cut off her swing at her wrist or forearm, forcing her to backpedal. As Rocky began to get used to the speed of the fight, he started seeing that Ragnar was mostly in control of the combat. A half step by the hulking man forced Sela to react in a pattern that Ragnar seemed to control.

Sela was only still in the fight because of her significant skill and speed, but if the copious amounts of sweat were anything to go off of, it wasn't going to last much longer. "Come on, Sela! Don't let him control the pace!" Rocky shouted an encouragement that helped him in basketball. He honestly wasn't sure what else to say. How do you encourage a sword fight?

Since I don't have my sword, maybe a set of pom-poms?

Sela tilted her head and looked down at Ragnar's feet before smiling and nodding. Then she side-stepped left, and Ragnar had to adjust his feet to follow her. She kept strafing left, and Rocky grew confused as to what changed. It was very difficult to see a difference, as she circled her opponent. Then she changed from a strafe to a diagonal lunge again to her left. Ragnar switched the position of his feet and seemed to falter for a split second but deflected her quick questing strikes all the same.

She retreated quickly before he could counterstrike and changed directions going to his right. Her smile grew. "Ragnar, how come you want to move in straight lines?" Sela asked mockingly.

Ragnar growled and jumped forward at her, switching his feet again to try to pin her on his right. Sela, who had clearly been expecting this tactic, flung her body hard to her left, just barely managing to beat his lunging right leg and descending sword. As she moved, she switched sword hands, and suddenly, both combatants were standing stock-still as Sela held her blade to Ragnar's throat.

Ragnar smiled and pointed at her trailing right shoulder that had a small, bleeding cut on it. "It was to first blood…" he mocked, raising an eyebrow.

Sela looked down and nodded. "You are very skilled, Sir Ragnar. However, we both know I chose not to cut your throat."

He bellowed a laugh out and nodded himself. "The competitor in me wishes to call this my win or a draw to save face, but what is left of my honor will not allow that." He flipped his sword, so the point was touching the stone floor and bowed his head, "Well fought, Lady. I concede to your skill and pray we can do it again someday. I have not had a fight like that in millennia."

Sela saluted Ragnar with the flat of the Dark Tidings to her forehead. "For my boon, I would like our party to be allowed to pass."

Ragnar's face hardened, and he grimaced before looking around the room. "I have no love for Apep and would love for you to kill that prissy priest Apothis, however can we chat before I let you through?"

Sela looked confused and glanced back at the group. Rocky nodded warily, expecting a trap and saw Amber, Zippo, and Smith narrow eyes as well. Ragnar also saw their reactions and smiled before holding out his sword to the group. "Do not fear. I will not attack you. Apep forced me into servitude, and I wish only a moment to ask a favor."

He handed his sword to Sela and then motioned with his head at the axe. "That weapon is also supposed to be loot for those who kill me. It is yours; I refuse to use the thing anyway!" Rocky raised his eyebrows and waited as the extremely competent warrior seemed to deliberate and grow embarrassed.

"Spit it out, man," Amber insisted. "It looks like you are about to ask Sela to prom or something." Both Sela and Ragnar tilted their heads, confused by the statement. The others chuckled, and Zippo made a disgusted sound.

"I do wish to have another duel with her in the future. Is this the prom you speak of?" Ragnar asked, confused.

Amber just shook her head and continued, "Never mind that, just get on with your favor, is what I'm saying."

Ragnar nodded, and his face actually reddened before he blurted out, "I would ask for saving! It may be pointless, but I would ask that you take my corpse out of here when you leave." He paused and looked at everyone while taking a deep breath to calm himself. "I have been trapped in servitude to an enemy of mine for far too long and am losing hope for salvation."

You have been offered a quest!
Request
  Party Quest – Request
   Release Ragnar
Ragnar has asked for a chance at salvation. Find a way to rescue his soul from Apep.
  Rewards:
   Unknown

Rocky read the pop-up and blinked in surprise at the vagueness of the quest and its origin. He wasn't sure what he could do for Ragnar, though. "What exactly can we do to save your soul?" he asked hesitantly.

Ragnar shrugged. "I don't know. In the past, people have taken my body out of the Dungeons that Apep controls and given me a proper Viking send-off. That never worked, so I am hoping you will try something else." He looked directly at Rocky. "Maybe this time it will work."

Sela looked at Rocky and shrugged before turning back to Ragnar. "We will try, Ragnar, but we are not sure how much longer this Dungeon will take."

Ragnar made a dismissive gesture with his hand. "Worry not, this is the last boss room before the final floor with Apothis. Be careful with that one, though. He is very devious and will always try to find a way around his Dungeon boss constraints." At the group's surprised exclamations, Ragnar looked around, wondering what he revealed to cause the reaction. Then he simply asked, "Did you not know he was a Dungeon boss?"

Sela shook her head, as did the others a moment after. "That is the only way Apep can give his minions access to new worlds. It causes a relatively large constraint due to the Etherverse laws and additional planetary system laws that are in place, but as you can see, he usually uses the Dungeon to create invading forces and corrupt populaces to his will," Ragnar explained to them all.

A brief pause followed before he resumed, "The laws on most planets will only allow him to take a certain number of Dungeons on a surface before he must conquer new Dungeons or Territories to expand. Here on this planet, it is actually a single Dungeon at a time." His eyebrows rose and he smiled. "I have never seen such well-worded and stringent laws to limit his power before. It is almost like it was written specifically for him… but this planet cannot be too old, so how that is possible, I do not know."

Sela was smiling but kept mum about the details, so Rocky and the others followed her lead. "Alright, Ragnar, does

Apothis have any weaknesses?" Rocky asked with a bit of hope in his voice.

"Well, I saw he was low on health when he popped back into the Dungeon a few days ago. So, I assume he has been using his Champions and sacrificing his health," Ragnar answered quickly while raising a single finger. "That is the only weakness I know of. He is quite a powerful Necromonger with a myriad of spells at his disposal, but he often overuses his Champions for the shock and awe they provide."

Then Ragnar chuckled. "The little slimeball also loves to teach every captured servant to be a shadow of his class. I am sure you have met his little dolls already." The group grew red in the face with anger, realizing he was insulting converted humans. Seeing this, Ragnar laughed harder. "Oh, get off your hill of indignation. They are dead, and their souls belong to Apep. If I can't make fun of them, who can?"

The group wasn't mollified by Ragnar's uncaring attitude, but they also didn't make an issue of it after they saw his pained eyes regarding them. "We will destroy him and try to save you, Ragnar," Sela acknowledged finally, and Ragnar smiled.

He used the same salute again. "May your blood breed true and your line live for generations." Then in a quick motion that made Rocky jerk forward in an attempt to needlessly defend the group, Ragnar picked up his sword, reversed it, and fell on it.

CHAPTER THIRTY-FOUR

The group stood stunned as the grating of the door on the other side of the cathedral reverberated into the silence. Rocky stared at the growing pool of blood that was coming from the body of Ragnar and felt mixed emotions. In some ways, this Dungeon boss was his enemy, but it also seemed like Ragnar was another victim of Apep, like many of the people who lived in this particular geographical area of the world. Long moments passed as everyone stood still to assess the suddenness of the situation.

Sela eventually broke the solemnness, "A true warrior is someone who can give their life for something bigger than themselves." She knelt down and flipped over Ragnar's corpse before closing his eyes. "We will succeed where you have failed, Ragnar."

Then his corpse vanished, and Rocky felt a small weight added to his bag of holding, and just like that, the group began shifting around as if broken from a trance. Sometimes, the saying 'out of sight and out of mind' is so painfully real, it's terrifying. In this situation, as Amber went and picked up the massive axe and brought it back, Rocky could truly see the moment on everyone's faces where they were no longer solemn or affected in any way by the sudden death of a man fighting eternity.

He felt his stomach fall out.

If we die in this world, will we be forgotten as quickly? Joe, Alex, Oliver, Phil, Patrick, Nick, Jeff, Jack… At this moment, I am starkly aware that millions have already been forgotten.

During his contemplation, he heard Smith exclaim to Sela, "You are some sort of sword-wielding badass! That was very impressive!" This was accompanied by a pat on her shoulder.

His dour mood was further cut off when Zippo called back from looking into the new open doorway, "Umm, guys, there is no hallway on the other side of this. It's just a solid wall with a lever." The group all turned and slowly made their way over to Zippo's side, where Amber handed over the massive battle axe. Rocky could tell she was struggling with the weight of the object due to her high agility and dexterity build.

He Analyzed the Sword and the Ax.

Great Ax of the Vanir
- **This Ax is extremely heavy and unwieldy but has an edge that will never dull.**
  Quality: Excellent
  Stats: Unknown

—

Ragnar's Longsword
- **This sword is far too big to be used as a longsword by most living beings. Its craftmanship and history is ancient.**
  Quality: Excellent
  Stats: Unknown

He blinked at the level of the quality of the items—they were higher than anything else he had seen to date, but since they were locked and unwieldy, he tossed them into his bag unceremoniously. Mid-sigh of disappointment he reached the group who were all studying the 'exit'.

A single look at the 'exit' was all it took to see the very obvious lever that was set back in a cubby hole. The bar was ominous only because it was so inviting. After all the traps in the first hallways from the day before, the group just stood there like Zippo, staring at the jutting stone. Rocky cleared his throat and questioned with a slight break in his voice, "So, anyone else for looking around the rest of the room before we pull that thing?"

The group nodded, but before they dispersed, Sela put up her hand. "I will take a look at the lever and see if it is obviously trapped."

For the next forty-five minutes, the group checked the entire room, looking at weapon racks, cracks in the floor, walls, and even examining the ceiling, but they found nothing. Sela spent ten minutes studying the lever before she had joined the group with a shrug to Rocky. "The lever looks trap free, at least in the immediate area around it."

That's how a sweaty, nervous Rocky found himself looking at his clone, who was implying he should kiss his butt while simultaneously holding the lever and glaring at the group. "You sure no one has any rope?" he muttered, thinking about every Dungeons and Dragons campaign he was ever in.

No wonder an adventurer's pack always has rope.

Knowing he had the bag of holding and that if anyone should have brought rope, it was him, Rocky grit his teeth and apologized mentally to his clone. With one last glance at the group, the clone pulled the lever and sprinted out of the alcove. A heavy, grating sound of a gear sliding against an internal mechanism sounded and was followed by an ominous silence.

The heavy breathing of the group could be heard as everyone looked around to try to spot something that changed. A massive crack sounded, and all heads jerked to fix on a spot just outside the alcove. Where the wall met the ground, a split was forming and expanding horizontally, starting out slowly, but then the ground they stood on trembled and jerked down half a foot. Everyone cried out in shock, and Rocky could hear someone screaming very loudly.

The jerking motion changed instantly to a steady descent, accompanied by the grating of stone. Sela punched Rocky in the arm. "Stop screaming and scaring me! Idiot…" she teased, her cheeks flushed red with embarrassment.

That scream definitely sounded feminine. I won't put it past myself to scream that way but…

Rocky laughed, trying to get rid of the nerves from the moment before, as the massive stone elevator lowered them ever deeper into the earth. Zippo, who was very pale, stuttered, "My heart feels like it wants out of my chest."

Smith chimed in, "I knew it was an elevator all along." He was grinning broadly in his best impression of a comedian.

Amber looked around. "I thought we were all going to die a horrible death!" she added with particular emphasis, which killed the mood, and everyone groaned while glaring at the oblivious woman.

"What?" She asked cluelessly

They pulled some trail rations out of the bag of holding as the elevator continued its descent deeper, and the group all ate distractedly as they rode it down.

It continued deeper still as the group handed back the wrappers to Rocky who put them back in the bag. At one point, Zippo left the group to pee on the wall, which left a rather amusing watermark that continued up as they fell away.

Rocky was examining the trail because at about ten feet away from Zippo, the water just seemed to vanish as something absorbed it. It was a good piece of information to know about Dungeons and the distance away from objects, creatures, bodies, or loot that you had to be before it absorbed them. Then he considered if that was true of all Dungeons or was unique to each one.

He stumbled as the elevator slowed down and continued to apply unseen brakes until it jerked to a stop. The group looked around and held their breath. If Rocky was to estimate, they could be a few kilometers under the crust, and the atmosphere both mentally and physically felt heavy.

Once his senses acclimated to the depth, he heard dripping water and could smell the pungent, cloying odor of sulfur heavy on the air. There was a tunnel that exited the room in the same place as the lever had been above. Rocky tilted his head and broke the onerous silence, "Take a look around the room. There should be another lever to go back up."

The group did so, and it was Zippo who again found the lever, which made the group sigh in relief. It appeared that they had an exit if needed. Sela looked at the door and asked, "It looks like there is a fire of some sort burning in there?"

As they exited the elevator room, Rocky immediately found the fire. It appeared that this level had some sort of lighting installment that looked strangely like something out of an Indiana Jones movie. The right turn in the hallway made it impossible to see further into the other rooms, but what Rocky could see of the first room made his stomach do a few somersaults. The 'hallway' wasn't actually a hallway. It was a door that opened up into another room. The room had a pathway that was raised up from the ground, and below the path was murky, bubbling water.

He sucked on his teeth as he looked at the cloudy, steaming water and considered, from his position now on the left side of the doorway, he could see another door that led out of the room to the right. Rocky circled his position and saw another door that led left once he reached the right side of the exit. It would appear it was a maze of some sort with some sort of incentive to not fall off the pathway.

He used Analyze on the water and was surprised when it did return information.

Deuterium Oxide

- **This substance used to be water, but due to its heavy use as a coolant, it is now something different. This substance is highly irradiated and is boiling hot. Its effects are unknown. Further study is needed to gain sufficient information on its full list of properties.**
  Maybe jump in and see what it does?

Rocky raised an eyebrow and shook his head before speaking the obvious, "Let's not fall into the boiling, heavy water." Luckily, Rocky had some idea what the substance was after reading the description. It was the water that had been used in cooling the nuclear power plant, and he felt himself shudder thinking about the radiation they were all standing in.

Luckily, the Atlantian system would have warned him if it was detrimental, and a quick double-check of his de-buff bar showed nothing new. At least it was one less thing to worry about, but he doubted that falling into the substance would be kind to his health and de-buff bar.

Sela nodded and asked her customary, "Is everyone ready?"

At everyone's stiff nods, she began the slow study of the doorway and the floor just inside of it. As she stepped over the threshold, a loud pang reverberated through the air, and she grimaced. It echoed off the walls, and the audible noises of surprise that followed it made the group's eyes widen. It wasn't the harsh, crude noises of aggressive monsters but the sharp intake of breath from human beings that made the group weary.

There wasn't a slapping of feet or any rushing monsters after the shocked noises accompanied the doorbell, so the group, after a thorough once over by Sela, entered the first room. "Left, or right? Rocky asked a kneeling Sela.

She shook her head, "The water is making my earth sense very cloudy. I can only see a few rooms away in either direction." She shrugged and continued, "I can tell you that the left has one path out of the next two rooms, and the right has multiple paths out of each room." She finished by adding her hands to the shoulder motion in the classic scales gesture that signified she didn't know.

Since it had fewer paths, Rocky pointed left and crossed his fingers on his right hand. Sela moved off in that direction and the process repeated for a few rooms before Sela entered a doorway and jumped back, just barely avoiding a shadow ball that dug itself a furrow into the wall in the room the group stood central in.

Sela shouted, "Six of them in the next room." Then she moved back and out of their line of sight. Rocky acted quickly, summoning his Shadow Clone and entering Stealth himself. The clone also entered Stealth, and they rushed through the doorway.

In the next room, Rocky saw six Necromancers on a raised dais hanging from the back wall. There was a gap of about five feet between them and the pathway that the group would be forced to use. It was clearly a well thought out strategic position, and he felt his teeth clench in frustration. As he approached the gap to jump across, a few things happened simultaneously.

One of the Necromancers sent out their red field skill which had detected Rocky in the past. It wrapped around him in mid-air, highlighting his leap at the six grouped up Necromancers. Rocky would have sworn, but he saw another highlighted form behind the group and smiled instead as they all began to charge shadow bolts. Mid-cast, his Shadow Clone spun into the middle of the group and scattered the cronies like bowling pins. A few spells were released, but they were half-formed and aimed very poorly.

One of the two who were still standing screamed, "You beasts attack the sanctum of Apep! We have vast armies and–" Rocky cut him off with a slash across his throat and continued moving to the sounds of gurgling the man's monologue turned into. He pushed his legs for every ounce of strength he had, trying to down another brainwashed cultist before he finished his spell.

Out of the corner of his eye, he saw his clone toss two of the black-robed fanatics over the edge, and moments later, he lucked out. The piercing, blood-curdling screams that sounded from below froze everyone on the platform for a split second. Rocky's muscles flexed at the sound, but he had too much momentum to stop and half ran, half stumbled into his intended target, which bumped the black-robed figure off the edge into the milky, bubbling water.

The combination of the first screams paired with the grisly scene in front of him seized his body. Luckily for him, though, Sela had left the cover of the previous room and also jumped over the gap to finish off the final two members of the cultists; otherwise, Rocky might be in the same position as his last victim. The man he just bumped into added his soul freezing scream to the other two, creating a cacophony of pain and horror.

As he stood on the ledge and watched, the man's skin began to bubble and blister. The cultist was now so delusional with pain he tried to reach a hand up to Rocky requesting help, but his skin seemed to just slough off of the limb, melting like candle wax. A moment passed, and suddenly, he was bleeding from his eyes, ears, nose, and gums as he continued his wail that seemed to never end. Sela grabbed him from behind and forced him to turn from the grizzly sight, but it was a bit too late. Rocky knew he would be having nightmares of this place for a long time to come. The screams took another few long heartbeats to finally cut off in a silence that might have been worse.

Zippo, Smith, and Amber stood at the entrance and stared in horror as Sela and his clone moved around and looted the three dead still on the platform. Rocky felt his legs turn to jelly, and he sat down, swallowing hard against the lump in his throat.

Heavy water can't do that! It's like this Dungeon took the long-term effects of radiation and sped them up... confining it to the water alone?

His legs had gone weak because his body was currently sending him a deluge of information. His stomach was telling him it was time to run, leave this place, and avoid a fate that looked like the worst death imaginable. His heart hammered, telling him that he was somehow excited by the prospect of the challenge that the Dungeon represented. Finally, his brain just kept telling him that they had to keep going, that they were the only chance his people had.

Honestly, 'Jump in and see what it does!' Who writes these notifications!

In the end, the group took a long, unintended rest in the room as everyone, but Sela warred with their nerves and emotions. Rocky finally did get himself under control by entering Meditation, and to his surprise, he was able to see through his clone's eyes. He'd completely forgotten about the skill symbiosis and now used it to send his Dark Clone to scout the room ahead of them while in Stealth. It was by far the safest means to scout the following rooms, and with the group standing watch over him, he didn't need to fear being ambushed.

To his surprise, his clone walked through room after room and met not a single piece of resistance. The creatures he did see were all retreating from the room away from the group. The pattern of only one exit per room continued, and twenty rooms later, his clone arrived at an exit to a raised walkway. Rocky didn't let it leave the area but had it look out into the massive cathedral cavern that presented itself. Over the retreating backs of Zombies and Necromancers he saw a room so vast, he couldn't see the back wall clearly despite the lighted path that still ran the entire room and in a web-like pattern over the domed roof that rose one hundred meters.

Lining the walls on platforms were more Necromancers, and at the ground level stretched an army of Zombies that seemed to have no end. Apothis was nowhere to be seen, though, and that made Rocky nervous. He had his clone search through the Necromancers high up on their perches, one by one and still, no luck. It would seem the final boss, Apothis, wasn't in the room or at least he couldn't see him.

Rocky exited Meditation and mentally commanded his clone to keep an eye out for any changes. Then to the group, he whispered, "If we continue down this path there are no more enemies lying in wait over the platforms, but there is a massive cathedral room overflowing with Zombies and cultists." Sela opened her mouth, and Rocky held up a hand, knowing what she wanted to ask. "Didn't look like Apothis was in there."

Everyone tried to talk at once, some suggesting they check the other path, some suggesting they go clear out the room. Sela finally clapped her hands, which stopped the discussion. "We should at least have your clone check the other pathways thoroughly." A few people opened mouths to argue, but Sela just shook her head. "Remember the first boss?"

CHAPTER THIRTY-FIVE

So, Rocky might have killed his clone several times, but it wasn't his fault—kind of. He did make it to the end of the other pathway successfully, eventually, though.

It turned out the other pathway had multiple traps, but again, all the enemies were in the process of retreating or already retreated.

The group moved back to the elevator room, while Rocky sat for hours attempting to navigate every possible pathway on the maze-like side. However, when he reached the end, he discovered only Apothis sitting in a massive stone throne.

The throne base was a glowing, green stone with red veins pulsating within it. It looked like a Dungeon core that had grown larger while more Heartstrings wrapped around it. The whole contraption was nearly at ground level without touching the ground at all. It was suspended from supports that led to the cathedral roof identical to the one teeming with monsters.

In Rocky's opinion, as soon as they killed the one group of enemies, Apothis ordered the Dungeon to pull all monsters to the one room. Now it looked like the end of their first pathway had clearly been a trap on a grand scale. Another issue came up on a few occasions, and Rocky wasn't sure how to feel about it. His clone definitely was showing that confrontational personality again, and by the ninth time he re-summoned the eerie mirror of himself and gotten his eighth rude gesture, he caved and talked to Sela about it distractedly as he controlled the minion.

"Are skill clones alive?" he asked, his voice feeling separate from himself while secluded inside his meditative state.

Sela laughed and responded, "Not really, Rockland, but yes, in a way. They are a part of your brain that you don't utilize. When they are acting autonomously, they are essentially a part of you and respond as you would in most situations." You could hear the smile in her voice. "When we get out of here, remind me to tell you of Asmodean the Cracked."

Since he couldn't really feel the interest that the statement piqued deep within him, he just nodded and continued his exploration.

Now though, about three hours later, the group was moving through the carefully plotted course and making their careful way around traps that he 'discovered'. Sela found a few more that he hadn't, and by utilizing his knowledge of the rooms, they avoided dead ends.

It seemed like the trap cathedral was overstocked with the monsters from this floor and that normally, each room would have mutated Zombies and Necromancers present. If they'd been forced to fight through each room, Rocky wasn't sure they would have survived. The really terrifying part was that the Ether Mutated Zombies were able to walk through the water, as his clone had seen in a few rooms they were exiting. He assumed they attempted to pull people off the platform and into the stupidly fast-acting, irradiated water, which made him sweat and shiver simultaneously.

It would be a nightmare if Apothis hadn't bet everything on us continuing down the easier course.

As they neared the final room, he stopped and asked again, "Are we sure that this is the room we want to go to. I am pretty sure that was the Dungeon core under him."

Smith responded, looking at everyone, "Remember, our only goal is to kill that core or free it. I think if we can manage that, this whole trip is worth it. Plus, Apothis is crazy weak right now." He paused and looked everyone in the eyes. "We agreed that this is probably the best time to attack him because he will hesitate to raise more of those monstrous Abominations."

There was nothing left to say, so Rocky nodded, acknowledging the point and shrugged sheepishly to say he had to ask. The group walked together into the final room where his clone waited, and after a deep collective exhale, they exited into the boss's cathedral. Rocky's thoughts of success and self-congratulatory attitude was cut short when Apothis laughed uproariously and cackled his next words, "Welcome! After the first boss, I knew you would find your way to me!"

Hell Mode initiated!
- **For entering the final unprotected boss room with the boss below 20% health and no minions, you have initiated hell mode. Defeat the boss for increased rewards.**
This boss has been given the ability to spawn Ether Mutated Zombies for the next 3 hours.
Good luck!

Rocky felt his blood go cold and stutter in his veins as the chair Apothis sat on rose quickly into the air and entered a fortified, small, glass room that overlooked the cathedral. The glass security room hung from the apex of the dome, and a Fireball splashing against and around it notified the group that it wouldn't break when first attacked. He Analyzed it and Apothis inside.

Dungeon Core Protection Unit
- **This glass dome can be purchased by Dungeons at an immense Ether Cost and will protect their core from attacks for a time if under siege. This glass is Ether-infused with huge amounts of personal Ether and Essence by the Dungeon. To destroy the core inside, a group or army must first destroy this near-perfect defense.**
Health Points 999,985/1,000,000

I should have known this was a trap. I felt something was off!

A group of one hundred Ether Mutated Zombies began materializing in swirling, blue, smoky light on the now empty floor of the boss room, and Rocky heard Sela mutter, "This is going to be a war of attrition. We have to outlast three hours. That cage is going to be near impossible to destroy!"

Then her head snapped up, and she shouted to the group, "The Zombies are weak. Try to kill them while conserving Ether. Zippo, you will need to light them on fire as soon as they fall!" The group got into a wedge with the two Goliath Zombie Spirits in the center, Amber and Sela on the left, and Rocky on the right. Zippo and Smith stood behind the group and prepared to support as they could while conserving skills, laser bolt charges, and Ether.

The first group of summoned minions hit the two massive spirits, and a crashing boom sounded through the boss room. Rocky slashed out and cut through two soggy, bleached creatures as the two tank spirits slid back under the combined weight of the charge. The group hacked and slashed at the creatures attempting to push back the mass of rotting undead. They only succeeded in killing small pockets as the numbers slowly began to overwhelm them.

They'd only halved the first group when another group of one hundred crashed into the first from behind, which, of course, slid the tanks and group back a few more feet. In a panic, Rocky glanced behind them and saw they were being forced towards the rooms with the bubbling, fast-acting heavy water. Currently, they were only ten feet from the entrance to the boss room.

"Get ready to rush forward and reset our footing!" Rocky yelled, then unleashed a horizontal double stack of his Dark Blade. It turned the one hundred and fifty strong horde into a meat grinder. It successfully cut through all the way to the back of the group, leaving only twenty of the creatures alive.

In unison, the group led by the Einherjar spirits engaged the twenty Zombies who'd been left alive after his skill use. Just as they engaged, Rocky saw another group charging from the center of the room and shook his head. Heat rose all around him as Zippo lit the bodies on fire in carefully controlled fires. Even with the control, Rocky felt sweat prickle his skin and drench his forehead.

This time, the group of Zombies crashed into the Einherjar, and they slid back a full ten feet on the slick, bloody cave floor. Rocky, Amber, and Sela were left to take the charge and were subsequently pushed back and injured. Rocky received scratches all over his chest, arms, and a few even reached past his sword and scored his face. Sela used entangling vines on the area in front of her, which allowed the group to retreat and reset. The minions still came through the vines but, this time, in smaller groups.

They fought on, killing in massive numbers until the horde held back by the vines numbered near five hundred, and the sheer weight snapped the vines with a large whip-crack-like sound. In response, Rocky released another Dark Blade to break the horde, and the group rushed forward to re-engage the two hundred who survived.

His stomach did a flip when he saw that his Ether was already at three quarters in the first few minutes. This time, when the group of new summons crashed into the back of the horde, Zippo summoned a firewall to allow a retreat and regroup. However, within moments, the dead, burning bodies smothered the skill. With little time to prepare, Rocky's retreating group took a three hundred strong charge head-on and were rocked back, as Smith cast a few of his new spirit blasts into the horde.

A slow count later, and they exploded like the Einherjar on the floors above. This explosion decimated hundreds of the creatures, and again, the group rushed forward. Rocky glanced at his health bar and saw it too was at three-quarters full. He cast Dark Mend and glanced at the others' health in his top right. Then cast another Dark Mend on Sela and Amber, who also were below three quarters.

His Ether dropped to fifty percent, and he felt his heart beating in anxious, desperate thumps. He tried to get a headcount of the enemies in front of him as he chugged an Ether Elixir restoring eighty points to his pool. He saw Zippo and Smith do the same as the heat in the room kept ratcheting up as Zippo burned more and more bodies.

Natural Regeneration Halted
- **Due to extreme conditions, the entirety of your body's natural regeneration has been halted as your body tries to protect itself from the extreme imbalance.**
  - **Natural Health and Ether regeneration stopped**

The message immediately made Rocky aware of how much he was sweating. He literally felt like he'd taken a bloody, sweaty shower. He used Dark Mend on the entirety of the group and fought on as Zippo cast a massive Fireball into the center of the thousand-some Zombies. Rocky simultaneously cast a double Dark Blade after the Fireballs only caused a death toll that seemed to be a drop in the bucket.

Smith shot evenly spread-out Spirit Balls, and Sela rushed over to pull a few grenades out of his bag of holding. She lobbed them over the head of the mass in front of them and far into the back of the mounting enemies. The explosions and deaths were staggering, but still, at least four hundred of the creatures lived as they rushed forward only half the distance that they normally would have. Taking a note out of Sela's book,

Rocky pulled two gravity grenades and lobbed them into the air over the horde as well.

Five seconds later, the group gained a moment's respite as the newly summoned minions were pulled into spiraling circles around the two pinpoints near the center of the cathedral. Rocky fought on and realized he didn't feel the sweat anymore. Instead, his skin felt cracked and dry, and as he gasped in a breath, he instantly felt his breath catch from the sheer heat of air.

Sela shouted, "Zippo, no more fire. This room can't heat up anymore, or we are going to be cooked alive!"

At that moment, Rocky glanced up at Apothis in his clear, safe dome and saw him wearing a look of utter euphoria as he watched the battle. The Zombies in front of them were being pulled back over the two-inch-deep blood and gore, and their group looked down to find themselves sliding slowly forward into the center as well. In a moment of panic, Rocky thought they might get sucked in, but Sela cast a vines spell that she used to wrap each of them and secure them in place for the time being.

They all chugged Health and Ether Draughts simultaneously and took the rest of the thirty-second break to catch their breath. As the floating horde in the center continued to circle the grenades.

Toxic Blood x1
- **You have high PH levels in your blood due to the high use of Alchemy Potions**
  -10% Effectiveness of Future Potions
Lasts 24 hours, will renew and increase every time a potion is used.

As Smith saw the gravity effects weaken, he cast ten spread out Spirit Blasts into the couple thousand strong horde. Smith simultaneously fell to a single knee after the casting and began breathing heavily. A few moments later, as the Zombies stumbled to their feet, some exploded, and the falling group of hovering Zombies was reduced back to a few hundred.

As the remaining Zombies climbed back to their feet and charged, Sela released her vines from the group, and they all took a single step back. Behind the charging boss summons, Abominations began taking shape from the unburnt corpses. Smith, who'd barely been able to keep his feet under him, groaned, "We are losing this war of attrition."

"Any new ideas?" Rocky screamed to everyone and saw shaking heads all around.

"I've got one," Zippo shouted and then put both arms up above his head. "Firestorm!" Rocky was pretty sure the words weren't needed as he didn't have to yell out a skill name when he used one. However, the building smoke that circled above the center of the cavern certainly was a testament to the power that was about to be unleashed.

Sela punched Zippo in the arm, which interrupted his spell, "Do you remember that if it gets any hotter in here, we will all spontaneously combust!" Then she looked at Zippo's surprised and not sweaty face. "Maybe not you…"

Smith cleared his throat. "I can now raise five spirits. So, if we kill three of those Abominations, I should be able to raise them." That would definitely be helpful, and Rocky considered the best way to make that happen before lobbing three plasma grenades into the forming group. Hopefully, that would kill a good portion of the clumped-up Zombies and the forming Abominations.

A few seconds later, three miniature suns bloomed, and fresh carnage was liberally painted on to the chamber. Three spirit Abominations began forming instantly, but so did hundreds of more corporeal Abominations from the flesh and blood that copiously littered the cavern. As he watched, a hundred plus more Zombies formed out of thin air, taking on a blue outline and then just seeming to pop into existence.

Smith's three new spirits wobbled back and formed into the line with the two very wounded and nearly wispy smoke Einherjar. Instead of joining the front line to meet the charge, Rocky placed himself behind a spirit and saw the others do the same. Just as the leading edge of the horde struck the spirit summons, he leaned into the corporeal spirit with all of his considerable strength. It had mixed results; the creature took a great deal more damage, but they only slid back on the slippery floor about five feet instead of the ten plus that had become more commonplace.

Once the first charge was 'withstood', the group took attacks of opportunity reaching around and through the spirit summons, while Sela and Amber ensured that their set edge wasn't overtaken. Sela used her vines on one, which was very useful, while Amber supported the other. The fight was considerably more manageable with the extra summons until the wobbling tail of the Abominations crashed into and through the Zombies to engage the group.

One moment, the prospect of a slow victory was looking possible, and then the next, Zombie bodies were being somehow launched into the air in the back of the lines. Within a few heartbeats, the front line was filled with massive Journeyman Abominations that brought down massive bone scythes on to the summoned spirits. The two Einherjar immediately dissipated, leaving a gap in the center of the formation, which was a significant oversight on Smith's part.

Rocky struck out desperately at the two standing with bone scythes now buried in the rock floor. The remaining three of Smith's summoned spirits began looking like leaky smoke balloons after the first strike by the Abominations, and Rocky felt the weight of the fight fall back on to his shoulders. Without Zippo burning the dead, this fight was going to be over very shortly.

He saw his Shadow Clone pop out of Stealth and sever the spine of one of the massive Abominations, which did seem to turn it into a twitching mound of flesh on the ground. However, after the blink of an eye, his clone was overwhelmed by the others and puffing into black smoke as it too died.

Smith raised two of the dead Abominations back as spirits, and the group stepped back as they continued to fight against the hundred other Apep Abominations and the horde of Zombies that filled in the gaps. They would have already been overwhelmed if the massive Abominations didn't kill the Zombies as well with their awkward, jerky attacks.

Slowly, the group retreated step by step, trying to stay alive and conserve precious Ether. That proved impossible when Smith yelled, "I am stacked to sixty percent of Toxic Blood!" Rocky, who hadn't time to look behind him, couldn't figure out how that happened so quickly but then looked at his debuff bar and saw he was at seventy percent.

Making it to three hours seems impossible. He hasn't even cast his Master class Aboms skill or a spell.

Blinking, he began trying to figure out how long they'd been fighting. It couldn't have been that long, could it? They'd regrouped and set their line how many times? Maybe eight, or was it ten?

Sela growled out a command, "Gravity grenades!" Rocky reached into his bag for three grenades, but a moment later, he found he only held two of the devices. He tossed the two into the center of the chamber and continued his slow retreat as he searched through his bag. Five seconds later, they were being held by vines, and Rocky finally got a chance to look backward. They were about five feet from the entrance to the room, and the bubbling water behind him made him shiver despite the heat.

After the quick search of his bag, he realized that they were nearly out of every supply they brought. There were four more plasma grenades, and they'd run entirely through the gravity grenades, which had been their primary weapon to use when they needed a reset.

In desperation, he turned to Zippo. "Okay, Zippo! Use it!" Zippo smiled tiredly and shot his hands into the air again. Dark black, sooty smoke began to collect over the two spheres of Abomination and Zombie Flesh. Then it started swirling faster and faster before orange sparks began appearing within the dark black clouds.

Rocky looked at his Dark Cloak, which was the only thing darker than the storm. Soon, the wind in the basin was blowing erratically, and with the air moving the heat got warmer through convection. That was when tornadoes of orange fire shot out of the clouds towards the gravity grenades and began lighting the corpses aflame.

The heat continued to climb until Sela stopped Zippo again. The creatures were all ash now anyway, but each lungful of air was painful to Rocky. He and the rest of the group were kneeling and sucking in short, gasping breaths of air. Sela only stopped Zippo by grabbing his robe hem and tugging insistently. The kid looked down at the group with a crazy firelight reflected in his eyes but managed to reign himself in.

Shit, I am going to have to keep an eye on that!

The area in the center of the room was so hot that a portion of the group of Zombies that popped into existence immediately caught fire. The rest quickly moved away and began charging the kneeling group that hadn't managed to reset their position. Rocky forced himself to his feet but almost fell back over on shaky legs.

Extreme Dehydration

- **You are suffering severe dehydration, along with many other injuries. Drink lots of water and get out of the heat to begin remedying the situation.**

Lasts until proper levels of hydration are reached.

Well, this wasn't good. Rocky glanced up through hazy eyes to see Apothis smiling wickedly. The horde was halfway to them when the demented boss raised a hand to stop them. Rocky fell on to his behind again and squinted, trying to understand what was happening. The group of Zombies began melding into Hulking Abominations in front of his eyes, and he shook his head. It would seem that Apothis wasn't going to be taking any chances of letting them live.

A small click and whoosh sounded, and Rocky felt his cracked lips part in a groan.

I have a feeling the windbag wants to gloat.

"Have you finally witnessed the power of Apep?" Rocky shook his head as his suspicions were confirmed. "We both attacked each other on home turf, but you were always destined to lose! Apep can resurrect his minions as many times as needed, whereas you will remain beyond the vale."

Rocky looked up to see that Apothis was standing in front of his throne with a massive, skeletal grin plastered on his inhuman face, which continued to have his flesh peeled off of it as he fed the two Goliath Abominations that were now forming from his health pool. Rocky felt his teeth clench in anger as he used Analyze to see his extremely low health.

Apothis
Level 75
Master Necromonger
Health Points 334/9,000
Boss

If only he could hit him once, but Apothis had chosen to only lower the glass sphere enough that his demented voice could be heard. Rocky tuned back in to what the Necromonger was saying, "… you can join us and live forever. Once we have Gaia, we will one day own the entire universe. It is inevitable. Nothing can hold out against us forever."

That's funny because it seems like a few billion years is a convincing statistic to the contrary.

There was no way in hell he was going to join Apep. The only question that seemed to remain was how the group was going to die. Without the ability to use Zippo's firepower to prevent the rise of elite undead and even the two Champion level undead in front of them, the group stood absolutely no chance. Rocky's head fell in defeat as he felt the soul-crushing weight of the defeat fall on to him. They should have found another way; with his group's death, the only thing between the Territory and Apothis was Azoth and Bathilda.

His head chanced on the ring on his finger that Bathilda refilled with her most powerful skill, and he blinked. Having already accepted his death, the ring gave him an option. The room was already sure to increase in temperature even more if he used it, perhaps even enough that Zippo would feel it, but that wouldn't be what killed him and the group. In this enclosed space and the sheer power of the Dragon breath skill in the ring, the group would be charbroiled in the backlash of the flames. The only question remaining was would it be enough to destroy the protection dome?

In the background, Apothis still gloated, and the Champion level Abominations finished forming. Rocky forced himself to stand and lamented, "I am sorry everyone." The look of shock and anger on everyone's faces made him squint. They must be thinking he intended to join Apothis, and the utter earnestness of their reactions gave him an opportunity.

He stepped forward to get closer to Apothis and farther away from his companions. "Apothis, you have truly beaten us, and I am not ready to die." To Rocky's ears, his words sounded so contrived, and he felt sick just uttering them, but he continued forward towards the Hulking Abominations that moved together to block his approach. "I have only just begun to grow and understand this new world of Ether, and Apep is probably the best teacher I could ask for–"

Behind Rocky, he heard angry 'curses' from his group and the heat of a Fireball forming from Zippo. In desperation, he placed his hand without the ring behind his back and crossed his fingers, praying that Zippo would understand what the childish gesture signified. As always, the reference was missed by Zippo or it went over his head. However, Smith understood and with sheer will, tackled Zippo before he released the ball of fire.

Apothis wasn't stupid, though, and he saw the byplay for what it was. He screamed, "Kill him!" as the dome began to close.

Rocky sneered as he knelt down and held his hand with the ring above his head, pointing it through the massive Abominations at the protective dome encasing the Necromonger. The hooks of the Abominations were poised above their heads and had begun their descent. Rocky screamed, "Run!" and released the spell, hoping he may have given his group the head start it needed with his theatrics and the fifteen feet he walked forward.

He saw the initial blue burst of the skill, and then the sheer wattage of the light blinded him and forced him to close his eyes. The heat made him nearly pass out, and he bit his lip, drawing a great deal of blood to remain conscious. He brought his other arm up to support the first, hoping he hadn't wavered from his target as the spell continued to pump out of the ring.

Talk about giving someone the finger!

Thanks to Rocky's warning and shout, Sela, Zippo, Smith, and Amber barely managed to get around a wall in the maze before the backlashing blue fire rushed into the first room they'd just managed to vacate. Luckily, the walls mostly trapped the attack, but even so the heat and tumbling rocks that accompanied it were the last things the group heard as they passed out. Sela's last thought was of how proud she was to have been selected to guide Rocky, who undoubtedly just sacrificed himself to save them and possibly the world. Too bad the fire sucked all remaining oxygen into its devouring depth, and they were all going to die regardless.

Chapter Thirty-Six

Sela

Sela was looking at Algonquin Valley from high up in the blue skies, surrounded by white, floating clouds. She frowned for the thousandth time, trying to understand why she was trapped in some sort of alternate space devoid of time. She looked over at the rabbit-furred man who stood behind her with his arms crossed and rolled her eyes for what felt like the thousandth time.

The man was attempting to intimidate her with his icy glare, but she wasn't willing to play his games. It was clear that she was in this place thanks to him, and at first, she tried to talk with him, but he only looked at her angrily in response. She had attempted to walk away, only to find that she was in a circular space about thirty meters in diameter. Since that rather frustrating discovery, they had both remained silent. For how long this particular stalemate lasted, Sela wasn't sure, but she was sure she was going to win.

It was Michabo who cracked first and startled a contemplative Selaphelia with an aggressive question, "Why exactly do you think you were chosen to be resurrected?"

Sela narrowed her eyes and returned the rude question with her own question, "Where exactly are we?"

"No, Pakak, you fail to grasp your current situation. I ask the questions here. The first time I'd no choice since Gaia requested I resurrect you, but this time, I saved you of my own accord. That means we can keep you here as long as we wish." He paused for a moment, and his face darkened like a thundercloud as he sneered, "Perhaps you would prefer this?" The scene she had been observing blinked out and was replaced by utter darkness.

Her heart began hammering against her ribs as her body reacted to the loss of her vision. However, the fact that she could feel the desperate rhythmic staccato meant she had some of her senses. She clenched her jaw and glared in the direction that she thought the man might have resided in before. In answer, she received a deep, dark chuckle. "You think because you still have a body, it will be better. Think again!"

Her body was suddenly gone, and instead, she was only aware of the deep silence of the void around her. Without her heartbeat to ground her, she felt her brain begin to crack. Instantly, her mind—or was it her soul—was spinning in place, looking for any sign of a lifeline, any variance in her surroundings. She found nothing.

Selaphelia screamed in terror but found she could hear the noise of her panicked shouts and felt herself calm slightly. This wasn't so bad; she still had her sense of hearing. She began to hum a song from her childhood, a song her grandfather used to sing to her as they trained—a soldier's dirge to the fallen. She felt her racing thoughts come fully back under her control.

As if in answer to her refrains, a drumbeat began to sound, adding to her melody, somehow turning it more animalistic and tribal. She continued to hum as a haunted, deep voice sang a song in a language she didn't understand. Despite not knowing the language of origin, she felt the artistry and beauty of the twining melody. She felt her soul weep for the tragedy it conveyed, for the loss it heralded and delivered with haunting notes of profound beauty.

When the song continued, it grew darker and more painful until finally, it ended in a beautiful crescendo of something that spoke of rebirth and a spark. A chance. Selaphelia felt her body return when she finished humming with the end of the beat. Then she saw the scene she had been observing come back into focus. Once again, she was high above Algonquin Valley, amongst the white clouds in a blue sky.

The man still looked at her with hostility, his rabbit ears twitching, and his dark skin flushed, but this time, when he asked his question, he was calmer. "Do you know why you were chosen for the resurrection?"

After the loss and pain of the recent song, Selaphelia sighed and responded quietly, "I am assuming because I am Rockland's guide?"

In response, the rabbit ears and head of the man shook back and forth. "This has very little to do with the child. It is impossible for him to know anything about the crimes of his oppressing ancestors." He took a brief pause and spat to the side. "I want to know why Gaia would choose to resurrect you!" He pointed angrily at Sela and added, "You, who are one of them. One of the beings who deigned to call themselves gods! One of the very people who plotted against her!"

Selaphelia stepped back at the tirade from the man and looked around, thinking he must have meant someone else but knowing he had indicated her. She met his eyes and saw the anger and betrayal there. This powerful person believed every word he uttered, but Selaphelia was absolutely certain she hadn't oppressed anyone in her life, and she definitely never called herself a god.

She opened her mouth and confusedly stated, "I think you are—"

"You think I don't know the enemy when they are standing right in front of me!" He pointed at her again, and his voice grew in octaves as he continued, "I know you were part of the Cathodiem guild! I know you were high ranking! I know you were part of the war with Mars, and I will not reveal the plans—"

He cut off as his eyes snapped to a place in front of him. His jaw clenched, and he swiped his hand through the space his eyes had been riveted to. Clearly, he just got a notification. Selaphelia, who had tried to Analyze the man as soon as she arrived and also tried to access her interface frowned. She tried again and still couldn't access anything.

"Choose a class and be reborn," he spat out like it was some sort of poison in his mouth. Then he turned and began walking away from her before he added over his shoulder, "One of you will not be reborn unless you choose to donate your Stasis bank and your whole party does the same—not that I expect you to think of anyone but yourself!"

He vanished a half step later, and in front of her finally popped a notification screen.

ROCKY

His eyes opened into darkness lit by a recognizable, pulsing, red grout, and he turned his head from side to side, trying to remember how he'd gotten here. Between the red lines, black Dragon scales adorned the walls, and again, he wondered what brought him back here. Hadn't he been somewhere else?

He sat up and rubbed the sleep out of his eyes but found that there wasn't any. Instead, his face felt entirely smooth and unblemished. His beard that he'd grown accustomed to since the fateful crash of energy was missing. He took in a deep lungful of breath and felt his lungs and body react as it should. Had he been shaved by a nurse or something?

"You think that is air you are breathing?" an amused voice parroted from behind him. Rocky jumped to his feet and spun. What he saw made him tilt his head questioningly. He definitely didn't know this strange creature.

Standing there was a strange-looking man wearing what could only be described as a giant rabbit fur draped over his entire body. He wore the head of the creature like a hat, and the long ears were sticking straight up, making it appear to almost be alive. The front paws of the rabbit skin were draped over each shoulder and hung loosely in front of his tanned and muscled chest. A massive braid also hung over one shoulder and was plaited and tied with a leather cord. His bottom half was covered by brown leather trousers, and out of his mouth, he blew smoke rings from a hand-carved tobacco pipe.

"Not even going to comment on my perfectly chosen movie quote?" The man chuckled, and this time, since he wasn't imitating Morpheus from the Matrix, Rocky could hear his Native American lilt. The way he phrased the second question made him look around himself again.

"Are you saying this place is virtual reality?" Rocky asked as he looked for some glitch or seam that might not load properly to tell him his last few weeks had been some sort of crazy government experiment or something.

"Ahhh, the old trapped in a game plot. I can see how that might be an easier explanation for recent events." He took a deep drag off his pipe, which lit itself and made Rocky even more sure he was in a video game. "I'm afraid that this dance of life is truly taking place, Rockstar."

Rocky's brow furrowed at what appeared to be his new nickname. The man's choice of wording and his clear humor at the whole situation made a few things come together in Rocky's head. "Wait, you are the person adding the little notes on to my notifications, aren't you?"

The man smiled and removed the pipe from between his teeth with a flourish, "My name is Michabo, and yes, I have been helping to guide—"

Rocky sputtered in shock at Michabo's choice of words, which cut him off. Michabo's smile widened, as Rocky indignantly spat, "You have been making fun of me since the first day, you mean!"

"The path we chose to walk all those millennia ago has been very lonely, and you happened to be one of the first people I found interesting upon waking up." Michabo changed demeanor and almost seemed to gain massive puppy eyes, making Rocky feel sorry for him momentarily.

Then he shook himself and commanded, "What the Atlantean hells, stop that!" Michabo winked at him, and his smile and normal demeanor returned, showing that he'd been play-acting. As Rocky watched, he saw one of the ears twitch and move, showing that the rabbit pelt was actually alive. Rocky pointed at it and sputtered anew, "Okay—Michabo—I think you should explain."

"Ahh, I shall start near the beginning, then?" he responded quickly and took a quick puff of his pipe before tapping the mouthpiece on his temple. "This all started due to the disparity that grew from Gaia's champions' strength. You see, Gaia is the mother of all things, and all things should have equal rights upon her." Rocky squinted, not understanding where the story was going.

Michabo saw his look and shrugged. "Perhaps an abridged version as bringing you and the others out of that destroyed Dungeon took almost everything we'd stored so many millennia ago." He ran his tongue over his teeth and continued, "To put it simply, this path you have set moccasin upon was put in motion more than a billion years ago. The guilds had grown too powerful and even managed to begin to hinder the all-powerful Gaia."

Michabo pointed his stem at Rockland, and his face grew stern, "In fact, your ancestors were some of the most powerful." Rocky blinked in the long pause that followed, unsure how to feel. Eventually, Michabo continued, "We're still not sure which guild reached and cleared the Tectonic Dungeons first, but we are relatively sure that the first individual to arrive was male…" He faded off, looking into the bowl on his pipe. Then he took a deep drag and began to blow out the smoke into a beautiful artistic scene of pale white fog.

In the smoke tapestry, there appeared to be a woman bound in seven chains and a lone man standing before her, looking at the restraints. The smoke shifted, and it almost seemed like the man was rebounded as he approached and attempted to break the massive chains that held the damsel captive. Michabo smiled at the picture and then blew a few more wisps of smoke that added ears to the man and a small group of faceless people who crowded in the entrance to the cavern that held the captive.

"I did one day arrive at the prophesized end of the labyrinth and believed myself to be the first to have found her. However…" A few tears rolled down his cheeks as he took another drag on his pipe and blew out to adjust the fading scene. In the reconstructed scene, a small girl with baby rabbit ears ran past, touched the chains, and then attempted to wake the captive woman. However, all of her frantic motions seemed to do nothing. Michabo, who seemed to not be able to approach any farther, offered her all manner of weapons to help her break the chains, but nothing seemed to work.

The scene seemed to almost be stagnant as Michabo continued to breathe out smoke until Rocky realized that what was changing was the size of the little girl or the girl who was attempting to break out the female captive. Rocky smiled, seeing the detail and pride that Michabo wove into the image, showing his love of all the women who attempted the feat and even more so for the young woman with the rabbit ears.

Then the scene shifted, and a large group of heavily armored and deadly looking people stood in the entrance to the chamber. Who they were was unclear, but they radiated power and death. Michabo was on his knees before them, seeming to beg for something. His daughter was being held by one of the figures, his knife at her throat, and behind the group lay many butchered corpses of some of the other women who'd attempted to liberate the trapped woman.

Before the scene could go any farther, Michabo swept his hand angrily through the smoke. "They said they were merciful that day, letting me keep my life! That the power in that room was only meant for the first person who'd arrived there!" he snarled.

Rocky gulped, understanding that those faceless figures had not given his daughter back to him. He felt himself shudder in revulsion. Somehow, he knew that the women were killed needlessly but for a nefarious purpose he couldn't understand. So, he asked, "Why did they kill the women?"

In response, Michabo smiled sickly and shook his head. "That is the very center of this little web. I have already risked quite a bit considering my suspicions. Ask your Guide if she ever met an Epic ranked woman, and then ask her how many Epic ranked men lived on Gaia. We were hoping for Gaia to choose someone else, but…" He shook his head and then shrugged as he faded off on that line of thought.

Both of Rocky's arms raised on each side of him, palms up, asking for more information. He flicked his fingers wordlessly, saying tell me more, but Michabo shook his head sadly before stating firmly, "That is enough to get you asking the right questions. You will get more when we know you are on the right side."

Blinking, Rocky tried to think of something that might get more information from the very old Native American man in front of him. Unfortunately, the only thing he could think to ask next gave Michabo the ability to completely change the topic. He opened and closed his mouth as he continued to think of something subtle that might get an answer.

However, he was cut off as Michabo insisted, "I will answer the question you were going to ask. You are currently in the spirit world. Since you and your party were all able to rank up your classes, I was able to pull you into the Earth as the

Dungeon died. You might remember your 'spirit' companion, Sela, having a similar experience."

Michabo placed a lot of vehemence in his voice on Sela's name during the statement, and Rocky glared at him. The glare didn't do anything as Michabo continued in a more neutral tone, "Regardless, once Apep's influence was wiped out from that place, I regained access. Luckily, your little stunt killed the Dungeon and Apothis. Plus, we had enough power stored to pull you and your companions out of there. Unfortunately, since this is a form of body reconstruction, it has severely limited your rank up class choices." He shrugged, grew more serious, and a hint of sadness crept into his eyes. "A point that I regret is that we only had enough Ether banked to speed the path of rebirth through the seven spirit realms for four of you." He puffed on his pipe and cringed slightly before adding with a mouth full of smoke, "One of you will have to be left in the spirit realm–"

Rockland stopped listening as his eyes went wide in shock, and he felt his whole body tense up in outrage.

EPILOGUE

Deep Under Chalk River – Frankie

Frankie felt the Dungeon die as he ran through the tunnel his Geomancer dug for him. Only an idiot would stay and fight with that cocksure of a priest, Apothis. Planning elaborate traps, gloating at every opportunity. That was not the way you won, and Frankie learned two costly lessons to that effect.

He glanced down at his black leg and then looked at his black hand. He smiled; Rocky should have killed him when he'd the chance! Now, he was going to get to Toronto and convert everyone!

Algonquin Valley and the Grotto would suffer!

It was only a matter of time and strategy…

Somewhere in the Orion Arm

An entity woke up slowly and incredibly disoriented. What was he? Why did he feel so necrotic, so dusty and unused?

Automatically, his mind flitted over the dry and arid surface of his body in a way he was familiar with but unsure why it felt so natural. His entire surface was devoid of nearly all life. The life that did live seemed to be contained in small, pressurized domes. The surface roiled and bucked with a familiar energy that tickled his memory.

The life forms in these tiny, glass domes seemed familiar too, and his heart lurched to a start because of the feelings. A feeling akin to taking the first breath of air after an extended submersion underwater jolted through the planet before his heart lurched a few times, nearly coming to a stop. With a bit of coaxing, the planet managed to begin spinning his core more naturally, and with it came the blessed heat of life.

What had happened to stop his heart? While it continued to turn and beat, it had been doing it at the most glacial of paces. When the planet quested out to find heat, it found almost none. All of his water was frozen and withdrawn below the surface.

Again, without knowing why, he began pushing his new magmatic blood through long-unused veins. In some cases, he was spilling the scalding, creeping liquid on to the surface, but in others, it was pressurizing before reaching equilibrium. All over the surface, steam began to rise from cracks as the deep-water began to melt, then evaporate and expand.

Within moments, the sky was filled with dark clouds and not long after, the heavens opened and began to rain, snow, hail, and monsoon over the entire planet.

What to do next? The planetary god didn't know, but for some reason, he was leaning towards helping life on his surface and creating more. Something told him he needed to have life to use this energy effectively or to gain power himself. Something deep and forgotten told him the only way to advance himself was to gather more Etherience.

In the back of his mind, an image of green, long-limbed humanoids came to the forefront, despite the few strange, multi-colored creatures that inhabited his surface currently.

AFTERWORD

We hope you enjoyed Excise! Since reviews are the lifeblood of indie publishing, we'd love it if you could leave a positive review on Amazon! Please use this link to go to the Ether Collapse: Excise Amazon product page to leave your review: geni.us/Excise.

As always, thank you for your support! You are the reason we're able to bring these stories to life.

ABOUT RYAN DEBRUYN

Ryan has always been a dream chaser. His first career was as a professional athlete, which taught him the dedication and perseverance needed to chase fantastic goals. A devastating injury removed Ryan from this world before his prime, and taught him the value of an education.

His first book began as a hobby project while he attended Georgian College. Using his hard fought lessons, in motivation, discipline and hard work Ryan published his first book in February 2019.

He is a recent graduate in the field of Electrical Engineering and a full-time author.

Here's hoping you enjoy the worlds he creates as much as he does!

Connect with Ryan:
Facebook.com/RyanDeBruyn
Facebook.com/Groups/RyanDeBruyn
RyanDeBruyn.com
Instagram.com/RyRyDubs
Patreon.com/RyanDeBruyn

ABOUT MOUNTAINDALE PRESS

Dakota and Danielle Krout, a husband and wife team, strive to create as well as publish excellent fantasy and science fiction novels. Self-publishing *The Divine Dungeon: Dungeon Born* in 2016 transformed their careers from Dakota's military and programming background and Danielle's Ph.D. in pharmacology to President and CEO, respectively, of a small press. Their goal is to share their success with other authors and provide captivating fiction to readers with the purpose of solidifying Mountaindale Press as the place 'Where Fantasy Transforms Reality.'

Connect with Mountaindale Press:
MountaindalePress.com
Facebook.com/MountaindalePress
Twitter.com/_Mountaindale
Krout@MountaindalePress.com

MOUNTAINDALE PRESS TITLES

GAMELIT AND LITRPG

The Completionist Chronicles Series
The Divine Dungeon Series
Full Murderhobo Series
Year of the Sword Series
By: DAKOTA KROUT

Arcana Unlocked Series
By: GREGORY BLACKBURN

A Touch of Power Series
By: JAY BOYCE

Farming Livia Series
Red Mage Series
By: XANDER BOYCE

Space Seasons Series
By: DAWN CHAPMAN

Ether Collapse Series
Ether Flows Series
By: RYAN DEBRUYN

Dr. Druid Series
By: MAXWELL FARMER

Bloodgames Series
By: CHRISTIAN J. GILLILAND

Threads of Fate Series
By: MICHAEL HEAD

Lion's Lineage Series
By: ROHAN HUBLIKAR AND DAKOTA KROUT

Wolfman Warlock Series
By: JAMES HUNTER AND DAKOTA KROUT

Axe Druid Series
High Table Hijinks Series
Mephisto's Magic Online Series
By: CHRISTOPHER JOHNS

Skeleton in Space Series
By: ANDRIES LOUWS

Dragon Core Chronicles

By: LARS MACHMÜLLER

Chronicles of Ethan Series
By: JOHN L. MONK

Necrotic Apocalypse Series
Pixel Dust Series
By: DAVID PETRIE

Viceroy's Pride Series
By: CALE PLAMANN

Henchman Series
By: CARL STUBBLEFIELD

Artorian's Archives Series
By: DENNIS VANDERKERKEN AND DAKOTA KROUT

APPENDIX

Alchemy is the Basis of All – Alchemy guild located on Helion Prime. Is studying gasoline which was traded to him by someone in Florida.

Alex Watt – 11-year-old young man that Rocky discovered while entering Ottawa. Family was massacred by Corsair's goons. **Died during the Ottawa Exodus Struggle.**

Algonquin Grotto – This is where Selaphelia Ardensai chose to start the settlement of survivors. It was chosen because of its natural defenses in the mountains and cliff faces that surround it on three sides. On the fourth side is a large river that runs through Algonquin Park.

Algonquin Park – Is the full Park of Algonquin as seen in our current world.

Algonquin Valley – Is the Territory of Rockland Barkclay, and it sits within Algonquin Park. It is quite large but does not encompass the entirety of the current Algonquin Park from present day Earth.

Amber Dell – A member of the A-Team. A muscular native American woman who is extremely pretty when she smiles. She also seems to take things a little too literally often forgetting or not understanding the whole meaning of things. **Apprentice-Fencer.**

Apep – Essentially a black hole, another form of godly being similar to Gaia but more on par with a Star God. Instead of bringing light to worlds a Void god attempts to subvert worlds away from the light to gain power.

Apothis – One of the countless souls that Apep has at his command. Apep continually spins out his head priest Apothis to try to conquer worlds. **Master-Necromonger**

Arena Dungeon – Controlled by the dungeon core Maximus this dungeon becomes the first cardinal dungeon of the Territory, Algonquin Valley.

Azoth – Rockland's pet Chimera. Is able to speak and communicate first with Selaphelia and later with Rockland. Through them both is gaining Sapience. **Dread-Chimera**

Bart – A member of the A-Team. Bart looks like a hell's angel with tattoos long hair and a biker jacket. From everything he has done, to help people survive and organize the territory there is a deep well of kindness in the man.

Bullet – Mutated peregrine falcon that had strong, wind-based skills that nearly killed Rocky and the group.

Cathodiem Guild – Guild that was situated on Gaia over a billion years ago. Guild was very powerful and had great influence with a seat on the Atlantian Council.

Chalk River – Is a town in Ontario that is near a nuclear research laboratory. A few days after the Ether crash, the converted golem from the plant melts down which prompts a red quest.

Corsair (Jack Jameson) – Sociopathic leader of the Ottawa Militia. Created an inner group of psychopaths who followed his orders to kill survivors instead of allowing monsters to gain more Etherience. **Died during the Ottawa Exodus Struggle.**

Dahrix – Leader of the Mechano-Lords guild. All black metal with Damascus steel filigree. Despite his mechanical body he is a hot head.

Dario – The current Guild Prime, who runs the guild collective. It is an elected position and he seems to be a bit wild to be behind a desk.

Delta – A sapient golem who is a member of the Ottawa Knights. He was created from a historical building known as the parliament buildings in Ottawa. An intellectual who prefers logic and his deductive reasoning to solve problems. **Master-Knight of Gaia**

Derik – Derik is a devious human who was a member of the initial group that is saved from the Onikuma by Rocky.

Draksus – Leader of the Ottawa territory. Albino in colour and devastatingly large and strong.

Epsilon – A sapient golem who appears to be the leader of the Ottawa Knights. He was created from a historical building known as the parliament buildings in Ottawa. Extremely devoted to his group of golems and wishes to unite all sapient golems creating a community for them. **Master-Knight of Gaia**

Essence – Essence is the primary resource of a planetary god. It is filtered from Ether through living being but can also be recovered from dead organisms. Gaia wakes to find almost all of her vast stores pillaged (oil).

Ether – Cosmic energy of the universe. It is the primary unfiltered raw power that allows life and planetary gods to form.

Flunge – A term used in fencing for a flying lunge.

Frankie Cocozza – Psychologist to the Militiamen on the trip to Algonquin Valley and continues his duties in the Grotto. Turns out he was also the Psychologist for Corsair and his cronies… **Apprentice-Psychologist**

Gaia – Gaia is a planetary god, specifically the Earth. Each planet is alive and in constant battle with other planets to acquire Essence. What they win if they have the most is still a mystery.

Gamma – A sapient golem who is a member of the Ottawa Knights. He was created from a historical building known as the parliament buildings in Ottawa. Hot headed and rash, but also surprisingly good at building. Works hard to help the survivors in the Grotto despite his early complaints to the contrary. **Master-Knight of Gaia**

Geb – Leader of Bio-Cult and one of the youngest members to a leadership role of a guild on Helion Prime. Likes to call people young man despite her younger age.

Golems – A clever way Gaia has orchestrated to recover a higher percentage of her pillaged Essence. Golems are created from any structure that has no ownership claimed upon it twenty-four hours after the first Ether wave.

Grotto – Referring to Algonquin Grotto

Guild of Mechano-Lords – Patron of Corsair. Headquarters on Guild Collaborative controlled world of Helion Prime. The leader of the guild is Dahrix.

Hectar – Lieutenant Captain – 'Alchemy is the Basis of All'. Has been running tests on gasoline and his discoveries lead to him being forced to report an emergency finding to the Guild Collaborative prime.

Jack Wareham – A member of the A-Team. A rotund man who is constantly jolly and supportive. He unfortunately dies at the hands of Rockland, when no other options are left to him. **Apprentice-Trapper**

Jason Jackson – 15-year-old young man that Rocky discovered while entering Ottawa. Family was massacred by Corsair's goons. Has become a member of the party and is fixated on getting stronger. Changes his name to Zippo to distance himself from the tragedy. **Red-Fire Mage**

Joe Flacca – Member of the Ottawa Militia. Becomes its General after the fall of Corsair. Quickly becomes the best friend of Zippo but dies sacrificing himself for Rocky. **Special-Trooper. Died during the Place of Power Contestation.**

Joaquim Smith – Joaquim Smith is an initial survivor that was in Algonquin Park during the crash. His group of fifteen is lucky enough to be saved by Rocky from a giant Onikuma. **Apprentice-Medicine Man**

Long Forgotten Dungeon (LFD) – Dungeon Rocky and the gang hides in on the way to Ottawa. Rocky makes a deal with LFD, which he terms Little Friendly Dungeon. LFD will help keep at bay the devastation caused by a nuclear meltdown and, in time, help Rocky's settlement level.

Mages Guild – Guild located on Helion Prime. A guild that is entirely comprised of Mage classes.

Mr. Pips – A member of the A-Team. Tall wiry man with very blonde hair, and needs food immediately... according to Rocky.

NPCs – Non-Power Classes

Oliver Grees – 13-year-old young man that Rocky discovered while entering Ottawa. Family was massacred by Corsair's goons. **Died during the Ottawa Exodus Struggle.**

Other planetary gods (spoken of) – Mars, Gelth, Krond, Sinfath, Helion Prime (Planet)

Omega – A sapient golem who is a member of the Ottawa Knights. He was created from a historical building known as the parliament buildings in Ottawa. A California beach bum personality that wants to try all the comforts of the old world. **Master-Knight of Gaia**

Ottawa Knights – See Tao, Epsilon, Gamma, Delta and Omega.

Parliament Knight Golems – The parliament golems are five knight brothers that are sapient. They wish to make a place for golems in this new world.

Quests – Can be issued by Gaia directly (Red) or can be issued by Atlantian Net which is the system that was put in place by ancient Gaians to improve leveling and compatibility with Gaia and Ether.

Ragnar – Another soul who has been devoured by Apep, and is continually spun out to do his bidding. This individual is far less willing than Apothis and Rattlegore and resists the power of the Void god however. His corpse is currently stored in Rocky's bag of holding. **Journeyman-Vanir**

Rattleshirt - Slightly manic soul that has been devoured by Apep. Rattlegore can create a type of skeletal creature that is extremely powerful but territorial. The bones of the creatures he creates are extremely strong and don't burn. **Journeyman–Master of Bones**

Rattlegore – Rattlegore is a transformation of Rattleshirt using a special Skill and consuming all of Rattleshirt's summoned creatures, however, Rocky and company mostly prevented this. **Journeyman – Obsidian Bone Apostle &**

Rockland Barclay – Distant relative of Azrael, General of the Darkest Night, General of Cathodiem Guild. The main character of the story. If you don't know that, you haven't been paying attention. **Dark-Revenant**

Selaphia Ardensai – Granddaughter of Selaphiel. Captain of Cathodiem Guild. Captain of a Century during the War on Mars. Ancestral Guide to Rockland Barclay but not blood related. **Dark-Druid**

Skandranon – Summoned Chimera to serve as Leader of Chimera Roost, which has now become Algonquin Valley. Progenitor of Azoth.

Steel – Leader of the Steel Wolfpack. Extremely large boss monster who evolved beside an iron mine, which led to him having fur with the tensile strength of steel.

Tao – A sapient golem who is a member of the Ottawa Knights. He was created from a historical building known as the parliament buildings in Ottawa. Extremely wise and well versed in some of the mysteries of the Etherverse. Where he gets his knowledge is a mystery but he is soft spoken and takes over morning training for combat and meditation. **Master-Knight of Gaia**

Territory – A Territory is a piece of land that will level along with the leader who owns it. The Territory will convey many bonuses to the inhabitants and stabilize Ether flow, making the immediate area more structured for monster growth.

Yin-Yang Golem – First sapient golem Rocky runs into. This golem is a little bit insane due to its nature.

Zippo – Nickname for Jason Jackson.

www.ingramcontent.com/pod-product-compliance
Lightning Source LLC
Chambersburg PA
CBHW051931020726
47501CB00001B/81